THE SUN AND MOON

PHILIP BALL is a physicist, ch
He lives in London with his wife and daughter.

From the reviews of *The Sun and Moon Corrupted*:

'Ball's tale of a mad communist physicist deftly draws on a long and ignoble tradition of pseudo-science. Intriguing.' *Guardian*

'A fine novel which achieves a kind of well-wrought luminescence and purity of its own: much like the glowing result of an alchemical experiment.' *New Humanist*

'Combining fictional narrative with science is not easy… [but] Ball definitely hits the mark when it comes to maverick scientists… and he succeeds in giving the reader an idea of how science works and what makes scientists tick, while wrapping it all up in an engaging story. A rich and entertaining novel.' *Physics World*

'Philip Ball is one of the smartest science writers working in Britain and there is nothing he seems not to know: physics and chemistry are his specialities, but he's no slouch at biology. Now he has written a novel, set in the 1980s, in which several quests intertwine. Dr Karl Neder is a maverick Hungarian physicist who believes that Einstein's theory of relativity is wrong and that the dream of the perpetuum mobile – motion and energy for nothing – is possible. Lena, a waif of a journalist, is trying to get the story on this elusive man. This is played out against the backdrop of the Cold War and its nuclear driving force. The portrayal of science and science journalism will tickle insiders.' *Independent*

By the same author:

Designing the Molecular World
Made to Measure
The Self-Made Tapestry
H_2O: A Biography of Water
Stories of the Invisible
Bright Earth
The Ingredients
Critical Mass
Elegant Solutions
The Devil's Doctor

THE **SUN** AND **MOON** CORRUPTED

Philip Ball

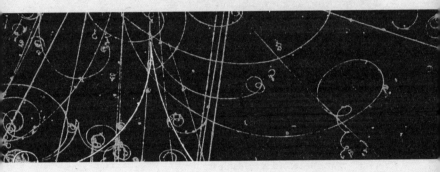

Portobello
BOOKS

First published by Portobello Books Ltd 2008
This paperback edition published 2009

Portobello Books Ltd
Twelve Addison Avenue
London
W11 4QR, UK

A CIP catalogue record is available from
the British Library

9 8 7 6 5 4 3 2 1

ISBN 978 1 84627 109 0

www.portobellobooks.com

Designed and typeset in
Stempel Garamond by Lindsay Nash

Printed in Great Britain by CPI Bookmarque, Croydon

Mixed Sources
Product group from well-managed
forests and other controlled sources
www.fsc.org Cert no. TT-COC-002227
© 1996 Forest Stewardship Council

FSC

Man tries to make for himself in the fashion that suits him best a simplified and intelligible picture of the world; then he tries to some extent to substitute this cosmos of his for the world of experience, and thus to overcome it.

Albert Einstein, 1918

THE CITY

And the city had no need of the sun,
neither of the moon, to shine in it.

Revelation 21:23

1

MANY PEOPLE HAD OPENED THEIR WINDOWS BEFORE THEY left the city, because the days had become rather warm and they had wanted to let in some air. They had laid out laundry on the balconies of high-rise blocks, and the bright colours gave the streets below a carnival appearance, as though bedecked for a celebration of spring. But already the dyes were burning, breaking up, and fading, the brightest and cheapest first, in the sun's strong glare. No one had intended to leave their washing out for so long.

The arrival of spring was indeed a cause for celebration here. It was the most congenial time of year, a brief respite between harsh extremes. And so there was always a parade on Labour Day, and the post office had been decorated in anticipation; on its glass front was taped a big yellow sun. In the backs of shops and offices banners had been prepared, and flags and drapery to hang from the cars and trucks.

In a blockhouse kindergarten, Lena found a neat row of little shoes on the window ledge, each pair with a name painted or embroidered on the inside. They looked as though they belonged in a fairy tale, all awaiting the enchanted feet of elves. Or maybe this was the lair of a witch who had baked the children in an oven and eaten them with plums and almonds.

The city was not as quiet as a city should be when all its inhabitants have gone away. There was always a helicopter droning above with insectoid persistence. The coughs of distant engines starting up were a substitute for the barking of dogs. Occasionally a siren came whining down the wide streets in imitation of marsh birds. Human noises, already turning into the sounds of the wild. Lena sensed green shoots flexing under the concrete, anticipating new opportunities in the world above. Don't get your hopes up, she advised them.

This place has a fever, she thought, without quite understanding what she meant by it. The buildings were streaked with sweat. Pipes oozed dark and viscid substances. House plants hung limp and feeble. But the fever reached further than any of this. It was in the world. It was in the sun, swollen to an unnatural size, like a moon as it rises low on the horizon.

In one of the stark, unkempt squares she found a naked man on his knees, grappling with iron flames that writhed and roared between his hands. It was easy enough to guess who this was, even before she deciphered the plaque: Prometheus, with living fire in his grasp. Of course, she nodded – this is where you live.

It seemed obvious now to Lena that the empty city had always been her destination. A long road between grim tenements and craggy mountains, across plains and forests and rivers, and all the while this bleached and silent place waited at the end.

It was here that she believed she would at last find Karl Neder.

THE CONFERENCE

2

HERE WAS THE HOTEL ERD WITH A LOBBY FULL OF ANGRY men. They radiated irritation in a palpable haze that dissipated in the room's stale air, and it seemed to Lena as though some natural process was at work, a discharge generated spontaneously when enough of these agitated bodies came together. There seemed to be no real intent to the anger, any more than there can be said to be a meaning behind the heat of a fire. It will simply continue until the fuel is consumed.

The reception desk gave a little focus to this stridency. It was under siege from men waving papers and passports as if they were affidavits and appeals awaiting the attention of a court of justice – documents that would establish beyond doubt the legitimacy of their petitions. One figure had struggled to the front of the mass, creased all over as though he had just been unfolded from his own battered suitcase, and he was explaining in jagged splinters of English and German that his reservation had been paid in advance by his university in Belgrade. The receptionist was hunched with his face inches from the desk, scanning the papers before him so thoroughly that he might have been committing them to memory. It was a battle of wills, and all the other staff had gathered to watch, hovering in a manner that implied their assistance might be required at any moment, and thereby making the most of this excuse to ignore the entreaties of the other plaintiffs.

Iain Aitchison was right, Lena thought. Their little pension overlooking Neuer Markt was going to be a haven.

Ψ

The Hotel Erd, then: flaunting its angular body on prestigious Makartgasse, seducing you with a promise of Old Empire decadence. Like a faded Viennese whore, adept through years of practice at shifting all the shame onto its clients. Its plinths and scrolls, its twisting torsos and helmeted maidens and stone garlands screamed Mozart at you, and there was *The Magic Flute* playing in the lobby in case you missed the point.

The hotel preened itself opposite the Neo-Renaissance Academy of Fine Arts where, in 1907, the eighteen-year-old Adolf Hitler failed his entry exam. The guidebooks advertised this as though it was a matter of national pride, implying that the Austrian empire had discerned the Führer's essential vulgarity long before he returned to smash shop windows and eat *Sachertorte* in the Hotel Imperial.

But you did not need to penetrate far into the Hotel Erd to see that this was baroque on a budget. The lobby was etiolated and careworn, and so were the staff, each of them barely restraining a sneer. One of the lozenge-barred elevators bore a sign that read 'Defunkt', and the 'International Konferenze on Space-Time Absolutness' was announced by a handwritten notice propped up on a chair.

And what was space-time absoluteness? Lena had no idea. But as she watched the mêlée thicken and congeal, she realized that these people had come with the intention of expending similar sound and fury on whatever it was they thought was absolute about space-time, and she felt the familiar queasiness, the rising panic in her gut. Out of my depth again. I said I wouldn't let it happen, but it has.

This had never used to matter. For several years, being

out of her depth was almost the only dependable circumstance of her life, and she had never truly feared that bad things would follow, because who would know and who would care? She was just a junior reporter at a trade union meeting or a court hearing or whatever insignificant subplot in the grand narrative of power and policy her editor or her treacherous instincts had propelled her towards. She usually worked for publications so desperate to fill their pages that the most banal copy from a freelance writer was accepted without comment or correction. You could compound clichés and slaughter syntax; the text was only there to fill the space between advertisements.

But that was before what she now felt obliged to regard as her big break. After her exclusive story had spawned copycat headlines in the serious dailies, Lena had resolved to take on no more commissions about which she knew nothing. 'The stakes are too high now,' she told herself, 'for me to go about making a fool of myself. It's time to get things right, to sound authoritative. After all, what I write can make a difference.'

Oh, *right*. Weeks after the celebrated story, she'd not written a single new piece. The South London local papers had clearly decided that Lena Romanowicz was too much of a rising star to turn copy for them now, while the glossies and broadsheets seemed quickly to forget her scoop, never mind that *The Times* and the *Guardian* had both followed it up within days. Commissions did not rain down; nobody, in fact, called at all. (Sobering up the answerphone message had been a needless precaution.) Even *Cosmopolitan*, which had basked in an unaccustomed aura of investigative credibility when it published Lena's article, seemed to have concluded that it was a fluke she was unlikely to repeat.

Finally, she'd resorted to freelance proofreading and subediting, the old standbys of the struggling hack. There were bills to pay, her rent was in arrears. She watched herself reverting to her former life as a shuffler of meaningless words.

And then she saw the article about Karl Neder.

Ψ

'You were reading a science journal? Has he got to you at last, then?'

'I'm being foolish, Davey, aren't I? Well, it never stopped me before. I'm sure there's a story here, but I should know better than to be thinking of writing it. After all, this is the theory of relativity. What do I know about the theory of relativity?'

'Your starter for ten: who invented it?'

'Who –?' She advanced gingerly: 'Einstein, I suppose.'

'There you go. You're way ahead of the layman already.' Davey had a clutch of science A levels, and his physics teacher had entreated him to take the subject further. But his heart had never been in it. Try as he might, he'd not been able to locate the poetry of physics.

'Hoorah for me. I guess some stuff gets in by osmosis. But how does that help me? I don't even know what's relative about it. No, don't try, Davey, it'll depress me. And you know what depresses me most, don't you?'

'You're worried you'll resort to asking your dad.'

'Well, I won't ask him. But then I'll end up looking stupid.'

'I don't think so. You'll end up worrying that *he* thinks that.'

Lena sighed. 'How are you doing, Davey?'

'Better. Yes, quite a bit. Really I am. They – you know, the company – they wanted to give me some money.'

'And you said no, didn't you?'

'Well, I thought about it. I pictured it in terms of a 1959 sunburst Les Paul, or a first edition of Crowley's *Book of the Law* I saw in Hebden Bridge. It was horribly seductive.'

'And then you said no.'

'I'm happy up here, Layn. On my own term[...]
Happy enough not to take public relations b[...]
going to sell my soul, it won't be to an industria[...]
ate, you know that.'

'They couldn't afford your soul, Davey.' Her lip trembling against the mouthpiece, and here now, a single tear that he'd not see up there on the Yorkshire coast, though he'd hear the trace of it in her voice.

'Listen, you don't really need to understand relativity to do this. You just need to understand this man, this – who? Vader?'

'Neder. You're going to sound like Professor Romanowicz if you're not careful. He said that to me, you know, after he read my article. "Lena,"' – she turned out a good impression of her father, and why not, after all? – '"you're a people person. I understand physics, but you understand people."' Davey sniggered, as he always did.

Ah yes, *people*. She envied her father his ability to regard people as a kind of category, a species or genus or whatever it was, or better still, a peculiarly complicated class of fundamental particles. That's presumably what he'd call taking the broad view. To Lena, people occurred one at a time, and that was the problem with them. She wondered whether, to be labelled as someone who 'understood people', you needed in fact to be confounded by them, deeply and perplexingly.

But with Karl Neder she was avoiding that issue, studiously and with considerable effort. She sensed that he would perplex her to a dizzying degree. Maybe that was why it frightened her, yes, it frightened her that her heart had leapt when she read the story in her father's study. She could discern no reason why that should have happened, and it was precisely in this that her misgivings were rooted.

o, I don't read *Natural Science*. Of course I don't. It was ing around.'

'Ah. At the dentist's. Or, let me think, on a desk in Canterbury.'

'Yeah, funny. Well, it's how he relaxes, isn't it? The Goldberg Variations and a copy of *Natural Science*. Or Nabokov coupling with Newton. Ugh, imagine.'

'Well, give me a reference. I want to read it – I'm sure they stock *Natural Science* in the reference library in York. I get the feeling you've been hooked by this Karl Vader.'

'I don't know about that.' It sounded alarming, put that way. 'I'm looking for something to write about.'

'Funny place to look, isn't it, Layn?'

'We have to take stories where we find them. Oh no, I wish I hadn't said that –'

'Don't be daft, I know what you mean. So, where am I going to end up seeing this one?'

'Ani put me in touch with a man at the *Observer*. The editor of their colour supplement, some bloke called Tim Evers. He's asked me to lunch.'

'Blimey. That won't be pie and mash then, will it?'

'I expect it will be dreadful. I've no idea what I'm going to tell him.'

'Just tell him about Karth Vader. Sorry, I'm regressing. Tell him what this man is like. He sounds just the right shade of bonkers.'

'I haven't a clue what he's like. All I have is this clipping. I'll send you a copy.'

'I'll look it up. I like a day in the library.'

DISSIDENT MAINTAINS VIGIL IN SOFIA
Margaret Strong, Sofia – *The Hungarian physicist and political dissident Karl Neder is still sitting on the steps*

of the Soviet Embassy in Sofia, Bulgaria. He has threatened to set fire to himself if the Soviet President Mikhail Gorbachev does not consent to release physicist Andrei Sakharov from surveillance and virtual house arrest by the KGB.

Neder is no stranger to controversy. He has repeatedly claimed to have invented a perpetual motion machine, which he has demonstrated in his private laboratory in Linz, Austria. He has published several papers claiming to show that both the general theory of relativity and the theory of quantum mechanics are incorrect. Neder believes that physics can be described by a classical model, retaining the idea of an electromagnetic ether.

But while his scientific heresies have earned him no more than derision from the physics community, his political activities have been more fraught. He is banned from entering his native country, and also barred from several states in the Warsaw Pact. In 1977 he was detained for some months in a psychiatric institution in Bulgaria.

Now he has returned there to engage in a battle of nerves with the Soviet government. His statement to the press says: 'If Comrade Sakharov is not granted full political freedom, including the freedom to travel abroad, and his wife is not permitted to leave the USSR for medical treatment, I shall immolate myself on the steps of the Soviet Embassy in Sofia.'

Neder has received no response to his ultimatum, but he has reiterated his determination to carry out his threat if necessary. 'Perhaps that is the only way the world will awake to this monstrous oppressor,' he says. 'The time for timid gestures is over.'

'The one thing I've never understood about you,' her father
had confessed some years back, 'is your affinity for oddness.'
She had thought she detected a hint of approval, even admiration, in his voice. Yet as Lena watched the horde crowding out
this forlorn Viennese hotel she wondered if he had a point.
She had assumed that this meeting of scientists, no matter how
nonconformist, would resemble the many other gatherings of
academics or officials she had attended with pen and spiral
notebook, at which maladroit formality or comradely
cliquishness were no more than self-conscious veneers that
cloaked a fundamentally unremarkable wish to belong. She
had not expected the turbulent confusion of the crimson-and-
gilt lobby of the Hotel Erd, where everyone seemed to be
nursing a grudge, a sociopathic disorder or a severe lack of
sleep. Apparently they did not come from the same stable as
the physicists she'd met on the Canterbury campus, who were
either jovial types with a tendency to depreciate their own
research in voices a little too loud, or else owlish academics
speaking a foreign language of particles and partials with what
seemed like infinite patience and precision and sincerity.
Physics departments, she'd decided, were just another professional club, unified by forces that she sensed but could not
quite grasp.

At the Hotel Erd there seemed to be little sign of that sort
of thing. It was more like a railway terminal. Some figures sat
alone in the threadbare lobby armchairs or on makeshift seats
fashioned from their baggage, reading books or notes as
though they were in a library and thus released from the duty
to acknowledge the society of others. Some formed cabals that
might have been plotting coups to take over the whole ram-
shackle affair. Here they were engaged in headlong and

vigorous disputes over past injustices. There they wandered in a daze, as though they had been expecting to find themselves in entirely different company. One or two stood apart and gazed on the proceedings with disdain, implying that the whole event was a tiresome necessity they would be glad to have done with.

But what would I know, Lena thought. What does this *people* thing come down to anyway? She guessed she might have some skill at listening to them and writing down what they said, but that did not in itself make them any less mystifying. Perhaps, she thought, that is how I am going to be filed now, after *Cosmo*. 'Lena Romanowicz, yes, she's a people person. She really got those people to open up. She really got at their pain.'

No I didn't. That pain wasn't theirs.

Ψ

At least she did not have to face the horde alone. Iain Aitchison came recommended by Roy Battle, the jaunty editor of *Natural Science*, who had set her on her course with what seemed like glee. Aitchison was a Scottish physicist who worked at CERN, the European laboratory for particle physics in Geneva, where Lena went in January to meet him.

'He reads around the extremities, you might say,' Battle explained. 'And he goes to the meetings this crowd organizes. His colleagues think it's most peculiar, what with him being a pukka particle physicist – top quark and so on.' (Lena wondering whether 'top quark' was a compliment that physicists bestowed on one another, and knowing better than to ask.)

'Then why does he dabble in the weird stuff?'

'It's not dabbling exactly. He takes an interest. He seems to have set himself up as a sort of unofficial observer of the fringe.'

As she spoke with Aitchison in his severe little office, Lena found it difficult to penetrate any more deeply into the nature of that 'interest'. But there was something else that disconcerted her about his conversation, and it took her half an hour to see what it was. He explained to her his role at CERN; he talked about his work (the top quark, it seemed, was a piece of an atom), his duties, his research group, his views on the state of physics. But not once had he used the personal pronoun. It was as if he wished the central figure of his tales to remain ghostly, a mysterious presence barely glimpsed, certainly nothing to do with this small, aquiline man with unruly eyebrows and a slight squint who was narrating the tale.

'These little beasties called quarks are hiding in the tunnels out there,' he said, gesturing vaguely out of his window at the gelid Swiss drizzle. 'Frankly, Fermilab is likely to snare one of them first, but one can hardly let on about that, eh?'

When Lena asked how big a quark was and Aitchison began to explain that this depended on what one meant by size, she was reminded of something her father had once said about how everyday words corrupt science. ('What is life? A bloody silly question, that's what.')

She glanced around this functional cubicle and wondered if its neutrality of hue and geometry were deployed as a defence against such messy quotidian concepts. Certainly there were no everyday words on the whiteboard, a palimpsest on which eviscerated theories spilled their entrails. How do you search for things that have no 'size as such'?

'Dr Aitchison, I'm told you know about Karl Neder.'

His response was at first disappointing. 'Haven't met the man.'

'But you know of his work.'

Aitchison did not answer at once; but then he made a small sound in his throat that might have denoted either distress or distraction, before rising to pull a box file from a cupboard neatly packed with others of its ilk.

'Oh, so you've got a Neder file too? That's the second one I've seen.'

'This? It isn't all about Neder. You see, Karl Neder is part of a community. You shall have to meet them. Now then, here is what one might suggest to you.'

He extracted a pamphlet, glossily but cheaply bound, which announced The Third International Conference on Space-Time Absoluteness: ICSTA '86: Hotel Erd, Vienna, 15 March 1986.

'Neder will be there, it appears. He is one of the organizers, you see, one of their so-called international committee. You want to go?'

Ψ

They followed a trail of scratchy arrows to a trestle table in a back room, where the participants collected their badges beneath a painted canvas banner confirming that this was indeed ICSTA '86 (the current date inscribed on a paper square, taped over the ghosts of meetings past). Aitchison pinned his name with a flourish onto his corduroy lapel – it identified his affiliation as 'Cern', making it sound like a small town in Romania. Lena had no badge, for she had not registered in advance. Announcing herself as a journalist, she threw the administrator into confusion until Professor Tomas Neumann was summoned to adjudicate.

Neumann was on the editorial board of *Foundations of Physics*. She knew this because it said so on his badge, adding for completeness that he worked in the School of Physics and Astronomy at the University of Trieste and that he was Conference Chair. (Neumann's badge in truth provided a dense paragraph, a miniature CV, and he seemed accustomed to standing stock still, gazing into the space above people's heads while they stooped to read it.) Without Neumann, there would be no Conference on Space-Time Absoluteness, Lena subsequently discovered, because he had persuaded his university to help fund it, to offer bursaries, to print leaflets and place advertisements in *Physics Today* and *Naturwissen-schaften*. Neumann was fifty-five, his hair was exquisitely sculpted and the colour of zinc, his spectacles were precise rectangular prisms; he was a dignified presence. 'We admit the press only by prior appointment,' he said.

'Balls. These people would kill for a bit of publicity,' Aitchison told Lena later. 'Go to most conferences and they welcome the press like the Second Coming. Here they'd normally be lucky to get a trainee scribbler from the local paper. That was all a power thing, as you so cleverly discerned. You followed the ritual of obeisance splendidly.'

In fact she had been about to confess to Neumann that she wasn't exactly there to report on anything, that she just wanted to meet Karl Neder; but instinct had guided her instead to apologize for the oversight in the arrangements, and to explain that she was a writer for the *Observer* in London (which was true after a fashion) and that she would of course be very happy to show the organizers anything she wrote about the conference (without specifying when that might happen). She began to wish she'd thought more carefully about her outfit. Black drainpipe jeans, a man's red shirt, and worst of all, motivated by vague images of Tyrolean snow-fields but perhaps primarily by an unacknowledged impulse for body armour, the heavy black cuirass of her motorcycle jacket. It added up to a student-style confusion that spoke of anything but journalistic authority. Which was perhaps irrele-vant next to Aitchison in corduroys and tank top – no point asking *him* how one dressed at an ICSTA gathering, she'd seen that at once – but it made a poor showing before Neumann's crisp suit and cravat.

Yet in the end he had relented magisterially, and now she had a badge too, and it was blue and handwritten and said 'Press: London'.

But then there came some bad news. No, said the woman behind the trestle table, once Lena was properly labelled and Neumann had stalked off. No, Dr Neder had not yet registered. There had been no word from him, her colleague admitted. They had no idea if he was going to come or not.

That was when a tall, lean man, clothed in black from head to toe like Stoker's vampiric count, sidled up to her and murmured, 'You are looking for Karl Neder?' Lena suppressed a giggle at the comic theatricality of it. She wondered whether she was about to be slipped a piece of paper with a scrawled address: directions to an alleyway where a gimlet-eyed stranger would usher her swiftly into a secret cellar.

'I don't think he will come,' said Dracula. But the Transylvanian effect was undermined by the accent, in which the Slavic corners were rubbed smooth by more than a hint of the Athenæum Club. The man could almost pass for Basil Rathbone. Rathbone pretending to be Dracula.

He wore no badge, which seemed akin to casting no shadow.

'That would be a shame. I was hoping to meet him here.'

'I am sorry to tell you that he does not always keep to his arrangements.'

'Oh, there was no arrangement. I just knew he was on the programme.'

This was the point where one held out one's hand and gave one's name, but Count Basil did not. He made a slight nod and stood waiting with eyes of treacle.

'I am interested in his work.' She pushed on, blindly. 'That is, I don't understand it, but I wanted to discuss it.'

'Do you believe it?'

'I don't understand it.'

'Is it wrong to believe in things you don't understand?'

'On the contrary, you could say that's a precondition of belief, surely.' Oh, you could indeed, if you were Professor George Romanowicz FRS. That's where I get all my epigrams, didn't you know?

Lena could see she would have to take the matter into her own hands, or the Black Count might start quoting Hegel at her.

'So you know Karl Neder then?'

'I have known him for a long time. Yes – a long time.'

'Then what makes you think he won't show up?'

'He knows that I am here, for one thing.'

You can stop trying so hard, Lena wanted to say to him. I'm not your type – it doesn't work for me, this cultivated mystery, this Mitteleuropean urbanity, this elegant and terribly sexy Habsburg accent. It would probably work on any other woman in the room, probably on most of the female population of Vienna, but I'm from the wrong place and the wrong time. She had an impulse to confide in him that her tastes ran more towards thin boys with obsidian hair and bad skin, nursing self-doubt and hidden bruises. Davey, she suddenly thought – oh Davey, you should be here to see this! Imagine if we'd run into this ghoul on the steps in Whitby. We'd have become slavish acolytes for the price of a fish-and-chip supper, we'd do his every bidding, rob graves at midnight and bring him the crumbling, oozing trophies. But that time was past.

All of which did not prevent her, however, from starting to rather enjoy herself.

'In that case,' the words were spontaneously generated on her tongue, she just let them fall out, 'you must be the next best thing. You can tell me all about your friend Dr Neder.'

'I could indeed. But should I?'

'Why should you not?'

'What would you do with that information?'

'I would subject it to proper journalistic scrutiny.'

'Ah. Very good. You're not a scientist then?'

'Oh, please. They've taken the trouble to colour-code me, look.'

'I see. London, yes. Now I start to hear it in your voice.'

'Kent, but close. You do regions, then?'

'I have spent a lot of time in England.'

'That's plain enough. You could pass as a native in Pall Mall.'

He inclined his head at the compliment. 'We spoke English from an early age in my family.'

'And where did your family call home?'

'Let's say, from Hungary. Like Karl Neder.'

'Don't you have a badge?'

'I don't like badges. Look at yours. "Press: London". How unkind that is. You have been transformed into the London press. Not only is that a rather awesome responsibility – one might even regard it as a stigma – but it is so dreadfully impersonal. Besides, it conceals your name.'

'Yes, well, there can be a value in concealing one's name, can't there?'

'Sometimes so. However, I am Kam.'

She wondered what that could possibly mean.

'I am Jaroslav Kam.'

'Oh, I see. Don't any of you Hungarians have Hungarian names?'

'It's Slavic, true, no Magyar there. As for Kam... well, not now. Let me say merely that there are ancestral reasons for this idiosyncrasy, of some, ah, importance to my family. But it has caused problems, of course, you are right to see that.'

'Well it would, of course.' She had no idea what he was alluding to. 'Listen, Dr Kam. Let me get you a coffee, somewhere that isn't here. I'd really like to hear more about Karl Neder. You could tell me about your work too, if you like. I don't know any physics, but people tell me I'm a good listener.'

3

LUNCH WITH TIM EVERS WAS LONG, AND SEEMED LONGER. Two bottles of a fruity white on top of a small charred fillet of something marine, decorated with bitter leaves. Tim had the expense account, but in one way or another it was costing them both dear.

He was blond and fleshy, he lisped theatrically and acted unashamedly like a roué twice his age. He did not lack for wit. There was even a kind of charm in his amorous buffoonery. But not three hours' worth.

('Remember this,' her flatmate Ani had told her. Ani, with half of Fleet Street in her address book and a thick portfolio of clippings with bylines, the trophies of her transatlantic gusto. 'Remember that Tim is basically harmless. And that he's cleverer than he seems, though he knows even less science than you. And don't forget that the *Observer* is a step up from *Cosmo*, if it's gravitas you're after. Worth whatever it takes. So if there's no such thing as a free lunch, you might as well order the lobster and Romanee Conti.')

'What attracts you, Lena? To Neder, I mean. Isn't this all a bit ripe, this storming the barricades of orthodoxy?'

'He unsettles people. I don't think that's supposed to happen.' She was extrapolating, with only a little licence, from her meeting with Roy Battle. 'Cranks get ridiculed or ignored, but he gets under the skin.'

'I think he's got under yours. But that's a good sign, Lena, you need to be involved to make this thing work.'

'I'm involved as a writer, Tim. That's what we do, isn't it? Put ourselves into the story.'

'I can see it's what *you* do.' He looked at her with provocative relish, head cocked to one side. She regretted the lipstick, borrowed from Ani and now smeared ineptly on her wine glass: a glossy carmine paste with some overheated label like Scarlet Letter. But it had seemed rude to go unadorned into a restaurant so select that it didn't have a name. Even when the host was a man like Tim Evers.

'I'm not going to pretend that when I saw your article I had the faintest idea who you were. But you know what? It got me very interested. It was committed. I could see you were someone who can consummate a story, as it were.'

Flirtation and innuendo she could deal with. True, they awakened the old hollowness, the if-only-you-knew feeling, as though she were a crone clothed in illusory youth. But she knew that game well enough. What she felt she could not bear was the way Evers wanted her to collude with him in casting her as a real writer, a journalist with vision and fortitude, nobody's fool. Rather than an insipid wraith who'd once written a story in a blind fury, shoving tears out of the way with her fists, which brought her acclaim that for once she'd not cared for in the slightest.

'There is a potential snag, of course. Our science editor tells me that this man Neder is not taken seriously by any scientist he knows.'

'And yet his situation gets covered in the most prestigious science journal in the world.'

'Yes, isn't that interesting? Now, the reason I wouldn't dream of setting our science bod onto this is that he would simply debunk it. I don't think our readers would care to hear that the foundations of modern physics are after all as rock-solid as the textbooks say.'

'Ah. Whereas I have no credibility to lose.'

'I wouldn't put it like that. I can see you have an open mind. I'm very attracted to that.' He was happy to let that remark sit between them for a while. 'Actually,' he continued in a conspiratorial tone, 'our resident boff tells me the man is a total nutcase. That made it all sound *much* more appealing.'

'It sounds as if your resident boff doesn't go in for fine distinctions.'

'Oh, absolutely not! I like that: fine distinctions. Grades of nut. Do you think Neder is a nutcase?'

'I don't really care about that, Tim. If he is mad, that's fine with me.' The surge of boldness almost shocked her as she said it. But the sentence, when it ended, seemed only halfway through. As if to emphasize that, Evers poured more wine.

'And it's fine with me too,' he said at last, 'so long as it's a good story. Do you know what would make it a good story?'

Lena found a little smile, and let him have it. 'Go on then.'

'Why do people always like to read about monsters who dismember their victims' bodies and put them under the floorboards? Or cult leaders who inspire mass suicides? Or mothers who smother their babies and leave them in bin bags? Not in the *Observer*, I mean, and probably not over chargrilled monkfish on rocket either, so pardon me, but nevertheless? Do we just have a lust for Grand Guignol? Is it a there-but-for-the-grace-of-God thing? I'm not just talking about the gruesome stuff. We love obsessives, mad Blakean visionaries, idiots savants, sexual deviants, the whole caboodle. At face value, we make sure our crazies are emphatically Other, they are what we are not. But what makes them come alive – look at the loons in Shakespeare, Dostoevsky, Conrad – is when we can sense that inside us is a seed of the same stock. That's what creates the delicious frisson.' He winked, though the effect was diminished because his glasses had become slightly steamy. 'Don't breathe a word of that at the *Daily Mail*. And I should know – I used to work there.' No point asking if he was serious or not.

'Now – how does three thousand words sound? With pictures, so take a camera with you. I assume you'll need to do some travelling – just keep the receipts, and if it goes over three hundred then let me know. I'm going to be upfront, because that's the sort of fellow I am, and tell you that I'm sticking my neck out here. You've obviously enchanted me, shame on you. Publication's not guaranteed until I've seen a draft, though you'd get a kill fee in any event. But I've got this sense that you'll come up with the goods. Because, whether you admit it or not, I would say that Karl Neder means something to you.'

Lena flushed, and Tim Evers grinned.

Ψ

Lena's career was not a vibrant one. Frankly, it was not really a career at all. She left her journalism course at City University without a job, with nothing in fact except a book of phone numbers of editors she'd spoken to once on some student assignment, or who other students had recommended, or who she'd simply looked up in the *Writer's Handbook*. She did some proofreading for the *Ham & High*, then at the *Express* and one or two of the women's magazines at Emap. Until the *Cosmo* piece, her only claim to success was a story in *Woman's Realm* about a man in Hackney who collected cast-iron baths. His wife had moved out of the house when it was so full of baths that there was no room for any other furniture. He slept in one; another became a table, and so on. Not only did Lena's name appear at the top of the piece (almost spelt correctly) but there was even a small black-and-white photo of her, three years out of date and clipped from her student railcard.

Mostly she'd supported herself by hunting down other people's typos and grammatical solecisms on the proof pages of deathly books and dreary magazines. The journalism she'd trained for was a venerable profession, governed by codes and unions; competitive and demanding, maybe, but protective of its apprentices. By the time she finished her course, that tradition was unravelling fast in the new political climate. Her father's forecasts when the country changed hands were all proving to be spot on target.

Lena had been twenty years old then. She'd known exactly what would happen if she visited her father before the general election, but she did it all the same. She was angry with herself for weeks afterwards, but she caught the train to Canterbury like a gull obeying the magnetic summons of Dr Mesmer. She'd promised to see him before her Easter holiday spree in Morocco, and she could never bear to break a promise, however rashly made.

Ψ

'This is a dangerous time,' said George Romanowicz in the conservatory of his house on Whitstable Road. 'I don't think many people appreciate quite how dangerous it is. We've lived through the last decade on the dregs of a revolution, and now it's all used up. All that energy, all that hope. Where has it got us?'

'You're giving these plants too much water. They're not all identical, you know. Some like lots of moisture, some can't handle it. You think they're all just *plant-matter*, don't you?'

Lena was surprised that her father continued to tend the potted plants at all, and to replace them when they succumbed to his maltreatment. It was the one aspect of the gardening he did himself, though he showed no inclination to find out how to do it properly. It kept the conservatory looking as she remembered it, which was either reassuring or disconcerting, she wasn't sure which.

Water splashed onto ochre tiles as she carried a brimming saucer to the sink. 'At least when I murder mine, it's premeditated. And you a scientist.'

'A physicist,' said George, 'is closer to an artist than to a botanist. As Rutherford once said, "All of science is either physics or –"'

'Who's this "us", anyway? Not me. What revolution? Johnny Rotten's? Or Che bloody Guevara's? Anyway, I didn't notice one.'

'I wouldn't expect you to. You're the product of it all. Oh, I don't mean that to sound as... harsh as it does, Lena. I don't mean you personally, or rather, not you specifically. I mean the *languid* generation. Who are the radicals now?'

'God, wake up, Dad. Take a look in Leicester Square. The ones with the zips and the green hair.'

'The identikit rebels.'

'Yes, all right, they're the sheep. But things are happening, you know. Who *are* the radicals? Ever heard of Joe Strummer?'

'This isn't radical, Lena. I know who you mean. Defecating on the table isn't radical. Oh, I don't say it's worthless, I can see the point in kicking against all the... the languor, the bloody torpor. But is that really going to change things? Anarchy isn't a philosophy; they knew that a hundred years ago. What these punk people don't see is that power isn't about the Queen any more. It isn't even about the government, not exactly. Power is what you see out there, right outside, on those billboards. That's what's coming, Lena. Stalin thought he could control people with fear and propaganda, but that only sharpens the intelligence. To make it dull, you have to give them pleasure.'

'I like pleasure. What else do I have?'

Lena was pleased to see that she could still provoke her father, although it took all her years of teenage experience to accurately interpret the subtle rise in the tone and volume of his voice.

'There are times,' he said, 'when I wish you would do a little more reading. *Brave New World*, for example. That might make you think rather carefully about the bovine pursuit of pure pleasure.'

Then normal service resumed, as George liked what he suddenly found in his head. 'I always thought it a more powerful vision than Orwell's. Fascism dated fast. But mindless consumption – it took real genius to see that coming. Listen, how long do you think it will be before your Joe Strummer is on those billboards?'

'He already is.'

'So it comes to pass, poor lad. And meanwhile, what's happening?' Lena knew when her father was being rhetorical, and she gulped her sweet, tepid tea, looking out at the riotous foliage. A bee was dashing itself frantically at the windowpane, but these iron-framed windows hadn't been opened for years. In a week's time it would be dead and desiccating on the sill. She wondered whether, with each assault on the glass, it had forgotten the last.

'How much do we hear on the bloody box about America's plans for Latin America? Do you have any idea what this Hollywood cowboy has in store, once he's in the White House? Bellow was right to have seen it coming thirty years ago, with his political intellectuals whirling lost in the arms of industrial chiefs and billionaire brass. But what a match they have over there now: the industrial-military junta wedded to the TV evangelists and celluloid celebrities. Oh, it's not any better here. We're being softened up for a right-wing government the like of which we've never seen before. It's not the fascism of the blackshirts or the boot boys any more, but the fascism of the marketplace, where anything can be sold to anyone in the name of economic growth. Even the military is going to start flogging its wares to all comers, you'll see. And this is dangerous – no, it's terrifying – precisely because we've lost the will to fight it. Because our new leader will preside over the languid generation, and turn them into her own creatures, and no one will stop it.'

'You sound just like the Trots at uni. A Commie in Kent, who'd have thought it? Aren't you banned from the Royal Society yet?'

'You'd be surprised what gets said at the Royal Society. We don't just sit around reading the bloody papers, you know.'

Ψ

What dismayed Lena was that she found all of this admirable. She wanted to see her father as a faintly absurd anachronism, a leftover from the socialist cabal of Huxleys and Haldanes and Bernals, blustering in a comfortable armchair in cosy Canterbury, bantering in the departmental coffee room about Suez and Franco. But she could not shake off a sneaking respect for these convictions she didn't share, for the moral fibre and the mental discipline of it. Her father had publicly declared that he would never accept funding from the Ministry of Defence. It was not clear that he was ever likely to be offered any, but all the same it was a courageous statement when so many others were working on ballistics and submarine hydrodynamics and nuclear shielding. He knew where he stood. Lena had no idea where she stood.

She suspected it was somewhere near her father. But was

that just because he'd put her there? And if she stood any-where near him, she was unlikely to get a word in edgeways.

It made her callow. She sensed that much, dimly. It made her opt out. When the election came, she didn't vote. She despised herself for it, but she sat determinedly all day watching television and drinking coffee. It wouldn't have made any difference anyway, she told herself, as the Conservatives' landslide victory began to rumble in from the polls. This is what people want. But she knew that the reason she could not drag herself to the polling booth was that she would feel she was being a good girl. Sod that. She would be a languid girl.

4

It might have been simple tact that prevented Jaroslav Kam from mentioning Lena's father, but she doubted it. When he told her he had presented a talk last summer at the University of Kent, she cursed herself for having scribbled her name onto her badge earlier, spurred by his remarks at the Hotel Erd. It was all she could do now to restrain herself from plucking the damned thing off her breast, where she felt it broadcasting to Kam a constant invitation to make the connection. But no, she thought, he's made it already, and understands that there's some reason why I didn't mention it myself. He can see it's something I don't want to admit to. And even if he has no idea what the reason is, this gives him a little power over me, though he's too bloody smooth to show it.

His hair was dyed, Lena decided – she knew from experience that colour this uniform didn't come naturally. But she had to admit that the result was effective: it made Kam ageless, and somehow immune to worldly influence. He did not quite belong here – or rather, he could belong equally to any place and time.

Yes, he'd surely have known the name of the head of department at Kent. Professor Romanowicz had probably even introduced the seminar in person. And that's just made him all the more curious about what I'm doing here. Maybe he thinks I'm on a spying mission for the physics police.

Yet Kam had made only the briefest of allusions to his visit to Canterbury – he commented on how his work shed some light on the research of Frank Symons, who, Lena had noted with some astonishment and dismay, was also speaking at ICSTA '86. Symons was a member of her father's department, and Kam said casually that his seminar in Kent had been given at Symons's invitation.

All the same, she was intrigued. Was this really such a fringe event, if it included people like Symons? Would Kam have got anywhere near the physics department of the University of Kent if he was nothing but a crank, as Aitchison seemed to consider them all?

Lena could follow nothing of Kam's work except that it was concerned with water, and also with quantum mechanics. For all his fluency in English, he did not have her father's gift of communicating difficult ideas, and Lena was lost long before he began to expound on coherent proton wavefunctions. 'Well,' he concluded with a laugh, 'it is a long way from what I did with Karl all those years ago.'

'Was that in Hungary?'

Kam was silent for some moments, as though thinking carefully about how to respond, although when he finally said, 'Yes, out to the east,' it was in an offhand manner that implied this was not the subject of his distraction.

'There was a time,' he went on, 'just before war broke out, when the Hungarian intellectuals were keen to assert their nationality. This was the era of Horthy, you see, who called himself regent and acted like a king and outlawed the Communists. There was a lot of fascist talk. Many people spoke favourably of Hitler.'

Lena could not see where this was going. It felt as though Kam were now telling her a legend, something that happened before human remembering, when ancient forces shaped the fate of the world.

'All the old nobility, they were idolizing that petit-bourgeois despot and calling for the expulsion of the Jews. And so they were all taking on these Germanized names, it was absurd – all of a sudden, the counts became Hermanns and Gottfrieds and Werners. So I, a young boy, I could see what was going on around me, and so I wanted to do the opposite, to show I was a proper Székely. I told my father that henceforth I was to be called Károly. He ignored my wish, of course. After the war, when I got to know Karl, I found out that he had done the same. Karl, you see, it also becomes Károly.' He added, as if by way of explanation, 'You asked earlier about my name.'

Friends from boyhood. The man was worth the price of a coffee, then. Even at Viennese rates.

'Both Kam and Neder, incidentally, can be linked to Jewish roots, so ironically we might have been better off changing our family names instead. But that is another story.'

'Why does Karl Neder avoid you?'

'Forgive me, Lena, but I'd like to ask you a question instead. It is not unrelated, perhaps. What is your interest in Karl Neder? I don't think you have come to Vienna to research the science of space-time absoluteness.'

'Bloody right.' Said, to her surprise, like a teenager. 'I haven't got a clue what space-time absoluteness is, and please don't try to tell me. I'm… to be honest, Dr Kam, I'm a little confused.' She looked around the coffee house, more in search of some relief from his dark eyes than to take in the surroundings. But the walls were covered with speckled silver mirrors edged in curlicued gilt, which directed her back to the two of them huddled at their table. As though they were sitting in a vast room full of Lenas and Kams, or rather, surrounded by alternative versions of the same scene. At least I can see his reflection, she thought.

'You see, I could just tell you that I've been assigned to the story by a British newspaper. But I have the feeling that it might not be the story I thought it was. I don't think I'll know if that's the case or not until I meet Neder. But it seems that might not happen now – or not here, at any rate.'

She was regretting having asked Kam about his relations with Neder. Not because she didn't want or need to know the answer, but because she'd begun to suspect that she had better be prepared, had better have a stronger sense of the ground beneath her, before hearing it.

'Oh, don't give up yet. I may not have quite the power to repel him that I attribute to myself. Do call me Jaroslav, by the way.'

Yes, Lena thought, I'm out of my depth. 'Look, I'm very grateful for what you've told me, and I hope we can talk some more about this. But I'm probably a bit tired. We barely stopped to leave our bags at the guest house before we came over. And I should take a look at all this reading material they've given us.'

'We?'

'I came with Iain Aitchison. The Scot.' She felt she was confessing to treason. 'He told me about the conference, you see. Look, I'll see you later.'

Ψ

Talking to Jaroslav Kam only deepened her misgivings about the whole affair. Had she colluded with him in somehow skirting around the matter of Karl Neder? Was the discomfort she had felt really hers, or had Kam deftly given it to her?

What disturbed her most was a sense that her disappointment at Neder's absence was tempered with relief. That was an unpalatable thought: was she reluctant to let him become too concrete? All at once she felt tawdry and futile; she longed to confront Neder and berate him for his slipperiness.

It was absurd, really. After all, she knew almost nothing about Neder that was not contained in the bundle of letters that Roy Battle had allowed her to copy in the offices of *Natural Science*. ('Strictly confidential of course, ha ha!') She had brought them with her to Vienna, and took them out now in her room on Neuer Markt in the hope that they might make her subject less elusive. The documents were hardly reassuring, but she brushed their words with her fingers as though searching for a code hidden in their texture.

Dear Dr Battle,

To my last letter of 27 May 1980 I have not received an answer. With your silence you demonstrated that you do not esteem me, as my letter ended with the words: If you will not answer my letter in 10 days after its reception, you do not esteem me, and maybe, it will be better to break our relations.

But I am sorry to say that such a break is not possible, not on account of my personal dignity, but because the stakes here are the interests of the whole of humanity. However your silence shows an uncolleagial face, and I must say also with sorrow that it is lacking in ethics. Until now I have thought our correspondence was based on the commonly accepted gentlemanhood, but I see now I must take a different attitude.

I send you now for publication the following three papers:

NEW MEASUREMENT OF THE EARTH'S ABSOLUTE VELOCITY WITH THE HELP OF

'ROTATING MIRRORS' EXPERIMENT. (The paper is sent exactly in the same form as it was submitted to you on the 13 Feb. 1980 and rejected by you during a phone conversation on the 23 Mar. 1980. You must look at it again and with new eyes, in light of the following.)

ON THE ACTION AND INTERACTION OF STATIONARY CURRENTS. (This is a slightly revised version of the paper 'Mathematical nonsenses...' submitted to you on the 6 Jan. 1980 and rejected also during a phone conversation on the 23 Mar. 1980. Revisions are as per your criticisms then expressed, which as I tell you, are not serious.)

COUP DE GRACE TO RELATIVITY AND TO SOMETHING ELSE. (This is a slight variation with SUBSTANTIAL EXTENSION of the paper 'Coup de grace to relativity' submitted on the 24 Nov. 1979, rejected by you on the 14 Dec. 1979, resubmitted on the 29 Dec. 1979 and rejected by you during the phone conversation on the 23 Mar. 1980.)

I pose to you (and to the editorial staff of NATURAL SCIENCE) the following ULTIMATUM:

You have to send ALL THREE PAPERS for composition at the same day of receiving this letter. You shall make better drawings of the figures which are not well drawn by me. You have the right to introduce only LINGUISTIC CORRECTIONS in the papers but no changes in the sense. In the most speedy way you have to send me by express the proofs of the papers which at the same day will be returned to you and all papers are to be published in the same issue of NATURAL SCIENCE. I beg you to inform me by phone call or by telegram whether you will fulfil this ultimatum or not. If you will reject it, I shall go immediately to the English Embassy in Prague and after making a one-day warning strike, **I shall commit myself to the flames in front of the Embassy.**

If you will again play the non-gentleman and you will not phone (or cable) me your decision, please, say this decision to your secretary, so that she can communicate it to me when I phone.

I have discovered a perpetuum mobile. Any day of delaying its announcement costs milliards of dollars and poisoning of air, water and soil. I cannot permit you to make this crime against humanity, because you are unable to understand a couple of childishly simple formulas.

Dear Dr Battle, I know how to wring the neck of a totalitarian power! The Internal Minister of Bulgaria (who killed George Markov in London) fulfilled both my ultimatums (of May 1977 and August 1977) in the given 48-hours time-limit. Do you think you are a harder nut for me than the Internal Minister of Bulgaria? I beg you – at the last moment become aware of the seriousness of the situation and do not provoke a scandal which will end with your complete scientific and moral bankruptcy. I send you now the book THE BITTER ROAD IV. Look at least to the pictures to understand who I am.

Hoping even now in your good heart,

Sincerely yours,
Karl Neder

P.S. You may mention this ultimatum in the press and print excerpts of it in NATURAL SCIENCE. You can make **any** comments.

Lena knew about *The Bitter Road*. She had gone to the British Library, where she discovered that, against all expectation, Karl Neder's five-volume work was indeed held in the vaults. Each book was a slim affair, cheaply printed by the Freie Presse der Leute, a firm in Vienna that Lena suspected was basically a vanity publisher. How on earth had they got here? Perhaps (it did not seem unlikely) Karl Neder had deposited them in person.

She collected the neat pile of books and carried them to her desk, clicked on the adjustable lamp and, as the cold London light died in the high windows, made the first ridge down the spine of *The Bitter Road*, Volume I.

It was evident that no one had read these books before her. Their pages were not marked by thumbprints or marginal notes. They were not furred and softened at the corners, but were still stuck together from the downward pressure of the cutting blade.

She could see at least that they were books about science, because nearly every page held an equation. Some contained little else. Brief words of explanation or punctuation were stepping stones through the dense algebraic exposition: *Thus*, and *So*, and *We can write*. Lena had stared for a long time at a dozen or so of the fresh-smelling pages before dejectedly giving up. She could not possibly formulate the slightest opinion on whether Karl Neder's theories were right or wrong. She did not even know what the theories were about.

In Volume I there was a dedication: *To Dora, who put me on the Bitter Road*.

Lena had opened Volume II and quickly learned what she needed to know: it was like Volume I, a maze of algebraic calculus. She had looked at the final pages of both volumes and had found that they each ended with an equation. In neither case did this appear to be a conclusion, rather just a break in the flow of symbols. A marker denoting where, in the middle of Neder's logical flow, his money had run out. Volume II had a short and impenetrable preamble, then took up from where Volume I had left off.

Lena had not opened Volumes III, IV or V.

His papers, a bundle of which was enthusiastically proffered by Roy Battle, were no better, and she'd accepted them only to avoid seeming indifferent to her subject. Now in her Viennese pension she pulled one dejectedly from her folder. It began with the assertion that

$$\nabla \times B = \frac{4\pi k}{c^2} J + \frac{1}{c^2} \frac{\partial E}{\partial T}$$

As a statement of physics this was quite correct, Lena had discovered when, to illustrate her perplexity, she showed the manuscript to Iain Aitchison in Geneva. But he explained that it was not an equation of Karl Neder's devising. It was written by James Clerk Maxwell over a hundred years ago, and it was apparently one of the hieroglyphic poems that scientists like Aitchison knew by heart.

'Have you read Neder's books?' Lena asked him.

'No one has read them. They're unreadable.'

'But you said they're wrong.'

'It would be nice to be able to express the issue that simply. What is in these books is not exactly science.'

'Science doesn't have to be correct in order to be science, surely? Plenty of good scientists have got things wrong.'

'Yes indeed. Even Einstein, as a matter of fact. By and large, however, science needs to be correct if people are going to bother to read it. If Karl Neder's books were correct, they would be revolutionary. Textbooks would have to be pulped, syllabuses rearranged, research laboratories would bear his name. But it is not remotely likely that they are correct, and so it is not worth the extraordinary effort that would be involved in demonstrating why that is so.'

Was that what Roy Battle had been driving at too? She had telephoned *Natural Science*, but when she asked to speak to Margaret Strong, the receptionist told her that there was no one listed under that name. So she asked instead for the news editor, who came to the phone to explain that Margaret Strong did not generally work in the office, although she was indeed on the staff. She was the news correspondent for Eastern and South-eastern Europe, and spent most of her time travelling in those parts. 'She could be anywhere between Poland and Armenia,' he told Lena. 'She pops up here from time to time, but we never know when that'll be. She boots out whichever poor blighter is sitting at her desk, and then before you know it she's off again.'

'Then perhaps I might speak with the editor,' said Lena. 'It's about the article on Karl Neder.'

'Ah,' said the news editor. 'Ah, yes. Then it would be best to speak with Roy. He's really your man on that score.' He put her through to Battle's secretary, who asked if she had a prior arrangement for the call.

'No, but your news editor suggested…'

'You will need an arrangement.'

'Then may I make one?'

'Yes, you may.'

Lena made an arrangement.

She called Battle as agreed on the following day. His was a voice she could imagine narrating a commercial on television. Orotund, confident, well educated but not what you'd call posh. No, not a commercial – it would be presenting a current affairs programme on BBC2. The sales voices were different these days: younger, brasher, smarter, identifiably regional.

The Roy Battle voice, she mused, the calm, sensible, measured voice, was in decline. These were no longer calm, sensible, measured times. Those qualities no longer had any cachet. Lena realized she was thinking like a middle-aged man, and she knew precisely which middle-aged man she was thinking like. Or rather, it was not Lena who was doing the thinking at all; her father's thoughts were accustomed to stroll casually into her mind and make themselves at home.

'I – that is, the *Observer* colour supplement – think this will make an interesting story. So you see, I need to know more about Karl Neder.'

Roy Battle's chuckle turned into a sigh as it ended.

'You'd better come over.'

Ψ

The place was not what she'd expected. Davey had told her that *Natural Science* was where all the top science stories were broken. Thanks to George Romanowicz FRS (who she did not thank), she wasn't exactly *afraid* of science, as most humanities graduates were – she knew it was as routine, as much of a career, as accounting or engineering. Oh dear, that was her father again: 'Science is really just accounting mixed with engineering. You can get a long way in understanding the world with that combination.'

In fact, she'd even done a spot of science reporting during her journalism training: an internship at *Physics Bulletin* on pay no union would have countenanced, excavating facts on the microelectronics industry. And she had coped rather well, which had only dismayed her – for when it came to science, Lena was determined to insist on an ignorance she did not possess. It was her defence against the humiliation she felt at not knowing more. The magazine told her to stay in touch, but she had no intention of doing that. In any case, she had said to herself, reporting on science must be a pretty meagre existence. It was dry as old leaves. It was written for the boys who built home-made rockets, not for her. It said 'Keep Out'. Oh, but that's going to change, her science-minded colleagues at City told her. They considered themselves part of an emerging new breed of science writers, who were writing not like technicians but like journalists. They wrote about sex and evolution, string theory and quantum paradoxes. They weren't interested in proselytizing for the vanished imperial fantasies of ICI, but wanted to talk about why we can't resist ice cream and chocolate, about clothes that change colour and superbikes that can reach 200 miles per hour.

Yet Davey, when she told him of her Neder-plan, found a characteristically different attraction in *Natural Science*. He'd looked up the story as promised, and then with his beach-comber's impulse had become immersed in the rest of the journal.

'Listen to this, Layn: there's a paper called "Why the Rising Moon Looks Big". What a title, eh? Haven't you ever wondered that? I've *always* wondered that. You know what most people think, if they think about it at all? They'll say it's because you see the moon against a reference frame, trees and buildings on earth, and you think, my God, it must be immense. That is, your brain thinks that. I mean, unconsciously. Then it rises, and there's no reference, so it looks its proper size. OK, so that's what they think. Well, it's wrong. Your brain doesn't say that the moon looks big relative to the trees and stuff. It says, *It looks a long, long way away*. We can judge distances, right? That's why we have two eyes, right, to get the parallax. But with the moon there's no parallax. It's too far away. And so the brain says, well, if it's that far away and still looks so big, it must be *really huge*. Our minds blow up what we see like it's a balloon, they make wrong assumptions

45

about scale because we can't judge distance. And then it rises, and it doesn't look so grand at all. It all depends on our being fooled by the wrong frame of reference.'

'So we're just fooling ourselves, then?'

'Well, I suppose that's an old story. "It is the very error of the moon; she comes more near the earth than she was wont, and makes men mad."'

Lena laughed delightedly. 'I've no idea where that comes from, Davey Flint. But you were never going to be a physicist, that's for sure.'

Ψ

She had imagined *Natural Science* to be a grand institution, somewhat like the Royal Society on Carlton House Terrace where her father took her for lunch from time to time. This was the journal (according to her 1981 copy of *The Writer's Guide to British Periodicals*) that reported the discovery of the mu meson in 1936 ('Uh, most of us have yet to discover that one,' Lena murmured to herself), that had carried dispatches from Victorian geologists in Hawaii and analyses of lunar rocks returned by the Apollo missions. Countless new species of insect had been announced in its pages. Einstein himself published a short general introduction to relativity there in 1925.

So Lena was almost shocked to find that the offices of this illustrious periodical were housed in a drab building in Fetter Lane, marooned off Fleet Street while the exodus of the publishing trade gathered pace. And *Natural Science* was merely one title among many published by the Hamilton Group, whose list of journals included *The Journal of Orthopaedics*, *Advances in Brain Diseases* and (she could not resist browsing through a copy in the reception foyer) *Concrete Review*.

But clearly it had pride of place. *Natural Science* was the

Hamilton flagship. That was evident from the Perspex-framed copies of recent covers on the walls of the elevator, which showed lasers shafting from domed observatories and slides of stained cells like bunches of glowing grapes. Yet the offices on the second floor were a far cry from that kind of high-tech universe. They contained mostly paper. Every desk was covered in it; some seemed to be supported by it, stacked high on the worn carpet. Filing trays were full of it. Every inch of wall space was shelved, and the shelves sagged under rows of journals, shoulder to shoulder, bound into rust-red covers labelled on their three-inch spines in plain gold lettering: *Physical Review Letters*, *Proceedings of the National Academy of Sciences*, *Philosophical Magazine*. A few people sat in front of bulky typewriters, but most were scribbling away pen in hand. They looked like science graduates rather than journalists, which is to say, they looked clever and earnest and were dressed like schoolteachers on holiday.

Roy Battle's office was worse. The paper there was bulked into formless, interleaved mountains, the remnants of collisions between tectonic stacks aeons ago. There was an old leather sofa covered in loose sheets, which Battle swept aside to make room for Lena to sit.

It wasn't really an office, more of a partition, a hastily erected box of thin plywood walls to contain the odours of his habits: chiefly port and tobacco, it seemed.

'I'd offer you coffee,' he said, 'but it's from a machine, and only fit for the staff.'

Battle loved his job. Anyone could see that. He was short, pear-shaped, and smiled a lot. His thick spectacles sent Lena searching later through her picture books of Hieronymus Bosch, the sacred texts of a Gothic adolescence, until she found the jovial red-faced demon in *The Last Judgement*. That was it – the most genial hint of brimstone, a Dickensian

Faustus. His suit did not fit, or rather, his shape was not one that suits are made to hang from.

He asked his secretary to fetch what he ominously called 'the Neder files'.

'Every week,' said Battle, 'we receive letters and papers from four or five cranks. These people tend to define themselves by what they don't like, which is usually much the same: relativity, the Big Bang, Einstein. Especially Einstein, poor fellow. Look here, this is the kind of thing.' He pulled a wad of documents straight off his desk, as though he had been studying them just before Lena arrived.

There was a pamphlet that looked like the newsletter of a local society but which turned out to be 'Antigravity Volume XI', written by one Richard Ahlens of Ainsworth, Nebraska. 'Professor Einstein tells us that space is curved,' it announced. 'But space can be flattened too. WHAT DOES THIS MEAN?' Richard Ahlens answered that himself, with ample use of diagrams that reminded Lena of geometrical constructions endured in baffled tedium years ago: 'Bisect the angle ABC...'

'Dear Natural-Science-friends,' Dr Rüdiger Vogt of Hamburg began. 'I was a *Computer-Man* in lots of stations. I am in the Possibility to resolv every Computer-Problem. Nobody knows – *but you*.' Dr Vogt added in brackets, '(I have to go in a Hotel in Munich, where the Conditions for Analysis are better for me, concerning Problems of *Atom* and *Relativity*.).' There followed three sections, titled 'Astrophysics', 'Atomphysics' and 'Space Fligt'. It was all handwritten on the back of old flyers for a piano recital at the Hamburg Konzertsaal.

K.S. Venkatasubramanan from Jodhpur had his mind on another matter:

Introduce Alphabets A to Z and then give the numbers one, two, three and so on from A to Z. By adding 1 + 2 = 3, 2 + 3 = 5, 3 + 5 = 8 and likewise up to Z then we will get 294. Then multiply the Number that is 1 × 2 = 2, 2 × 3 = 6, 6 × 4 = 24 likewise up to Z. Then we will have 929011026060707467800000. By adding both we will have 929011026060707467800294. Introduce πr^2. Then $\pi = 22/7 \times r^2$ then we have

$$\frac{22}{7} \times (929011026060707467800294)^2$$

By concluding it we will get the figure. It is the length in Kilometers of the sky.

But things got even stranger. The delicate hand of M. Sato of Hokkaido Medical University told the tale of 'Alice-God in Wonder-universe'. It was like a poem, beautiful and airy as Oriental silk, filled with a sense of yearning:

We see the Alice God in Wonder-universe. The Universe is very strange, I hear the Universe is opened or sometimes closed, and has a great wall. Also I know the human resembling the god of the universe, and there is a god of anger written in the Bible.

According to the Buddhism, the big Buddha statues exist. So I imagine our earth plancton may be the body of a large person and the human may resemble a bacteria.

I will describe such an idea about the modern universe.

After several pages of this fable, M. Sato's conclusion was a cry of defiance:

In the future 21st century we may go to the outer of the universe and the inner of the universe by the vehicle with very high speed. The inner of the universe is not so pleasant because we humane are closed. We may be like bacterias in the Alice God! We should not be an Alice God's slaves. We should be free!

He had illustrated this manifesto with a diagram of the Alice God:

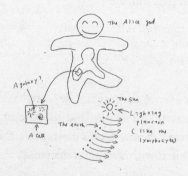

But even M. Sato seemed a model of lucidity next to Dong-yul Jeng, whose 'Comentary' plunged headlong into Joycean stanzas:

NUTRINO AND ANTI SPACE QUORK
SUPER RELATIVE THEORY

photon is 4ev=29.9782km580/s

nutorino energy is littl of photon it isover

photon speed with in the water.

anti space quork is 0energy.speed=∞ km/s

nutorino is 300000 km/s

energy=0.time isstop

nutorino is 4 electric mu tau heavy

heavy nutorino is moment 17 kev.

electric nutorino is less 0.000005 Mev

mu nutorino is 0.51 Mev

time is back or time is stop with anti space

quork and electric nutorino

electric nutorino and anti anti space quork

is back and stop going time for super relative theory.

'What do you do with these things?'

'We have a standard letter,' Battle explained. 'It doesn't necessarily prevent them from sending along their next effort, but on the whole they're simply happy to hear from us. Not all of them are so accommodating, of course.'

'Doesn't that worry you?'

'Well, one wonders. We had a letter a few weeks ago from a prison psychiatrist, imploring us to look at the mathematical theories of one of his patients. The psychiatrist had got the idea that if there was anything in these ideas, his patient's mental complication would be greatly eased by hearing that was so. He never mentioned what the man had done, but frankly, the pages crackled with violence. That is the only way I can describe it. Pages and pages of closely written calculations, long algebraic expressions. Very precise. And quite impenetrable. Do you know about Fermat's Last Theorem?'

'I didn't study maths.'

'It's a famous unsolved puzzle, a conjecture made by the French mathematician Pierre de Fermat in the seventeenth

century, and it's about the relationship between natural numbers – that's the integers, 1, 2, 3 and so on. It's infuriatingly
easy to pose, and a devil to prove.'

Lena saw sparks flash behind Battle's astronomy-grade
lenses. She wondered whether she should have that cup of coffee after all.

'You *do* know Pythagoras' theorem?'

'Um… sides of triangles…'

'Exactly. For any right-angled triangle, the sum of the
squares of the two shorter sides equals the sum of the square of
the hypotenuse. You can put that into algebra: x squared plus y
squared equals z squared. Now, there are some triangles for
which this formula works with exact integers. Three, four and
five, for example: three squared and four squared is nine and
sixteen, which is twenty-five, which is five squared. So, Fermat
wonders whether this formula will work for any integers not
raised to the power two – that is, squared – but to the power
three, or four, or higher. That's to say, whether there are
integers that satisfy x cubed plus y cubed equals z cubed.
This occurred to him while he was reading Diophantus'
Arithmetica, and he scribbled in the margin that he had a proof
that no integers satisfy this relationship for powers of three
and above, but that the margin was too small for him to write it
down there. Ever since, people have been trying to reconstruct
this proof, but no one has succeeded.'

The door opened suddenly, and Battle's secretary entered
with 'the Neder files'. She put them on the floor (there was
nowhere else they could go) with a hint of disapproval. There
were a lot of them.

Lena wasn't sure whether she should be taking notes. Was
any of this relevant to Neder's case? Battle was acting as
though he had all the time in the world, never mind the paper
strata that were presumably awaiting his attention.

'We get, I'd say, maybe three or four proofs of Fermat's Last Theorem every month. Never from professional mathematicians – there are a few who work on it, but most avoid it. They know it's too hard. The trouble is, you can start thinking about it with nothing more than high-school algebra. So that's what people do. And they think they've cracked the problem that has baffled the greatest mathematicians of the past three centuries. No sense of proportion, these people, let alone modesty... but look, here's the Neder correspondence.'

'How do you know,' asked Lena, 'that one of these proofs is not correct?'

'We don't!' said Battle, and guffawed. 'We're not proper mathematicians. And we can't send every one of them out to referees – no one wants to touch the stuff. It's a totally thankless job. Even if, as happens sometimes, we do think a so-called proof looks serious enough to warrant peer review – that is, to be assessed by experts – and our referees come back pointing out the error, well, it gets them nowhere. We send back the criticisms, and the next week, back comes the corrected version of the paper. And the poor referee has to do it all again. So most of them won't go near it.'

'Then maybe someone has already solved Fermat's Last Theorem, but no one will take it seriously?'

'That's possible,' Battle admitted, beaming. 'I don't think it's at all likely, but it's possible. You know about Ramanujan?'

Lena glanced at Neder, waiting patiently in bundles on the floor. But Battle was oblivious.

Srinivasa Ramanujan, he explained, was an Indian clerk who in the 1910s sent pages of theorems to George Hardy, a Cambridge professor and one of the finest mathematicians in the world. 'There is no doubt that Ramanujan's package would have looked exactly like the work of a crank, for there were cranks even then,' said Battle. But Hardy glanced at the pages and saw at once that the work was extraordinary. Ramanujan seemed to have an almost supernatural talent for numbers. 'Hardy admitted that he couldn't tell if Ramanujan's proofs were right or not, but he said that only a genius could have proposed the theorems in the first place.' He invited Ramanujan to come to England, where the young Indian promptly caught tuberculosis from the chilly Cambridge gales, and died.

'If we received a letter from a Ramanujan,' said Battle, 'we would be extremely likely to return it with our standard letter of rejection.'

'Surely *that* worries you?'

'I couldn't do my job if I allowed myself to be unduly *worried* by it. I'm not here to discover neglected geniuses, you know. I'm here to bring out this journal every week, and to fill it with things that other people want to read.'

'That sounds callous, doesn't it?' he added. 'No need to reply. I'd consider it callous myself. But you see, it's all very well to have ideals. In a perfect world, every lunatic who sent us a manuscript would have it scrutinized by a reviewer and returned with the errors pointed out to him. Or her, but usually him, to be honest. That would be nice. It would also thoroughly disrupt scientific research and make it impossible for *Natural Science* to function without a staff three times the present size. We operate in an imperfect world. Science itself operates in an imperfect world. That's what people don't understand. They think every answer is precise – yes or no – and that if there's a precise yes or no to be given, one is obliged to give it. But is it fair to ask that we give a "no" to those people who won't accept no as an answer?'

Lena realized that they were discussing the Neder case after all.

She reached over and tapped the files that lay at her bursting with paperclips and bulldog clips and multi-coloured marker sheets.

'I don't think,' she said, 'that you've quite applied that philosophy to Karl Neder.'

Battle released his curiously high-pitched gurgle of a laugh. 'No,' he said. 'Karl Neder is different.'

5

LENA HAD ENVISAGED RÜDIGER VOGT AND DONG-YUL JENG as solitary figures scribbling obsessively in Hamburg coffee shops and Seoul noodle bars. But what if there was a community of these doodlers and dabblers, and what if that community linked Jeng to Frank Symons, and Symons to her father? She felt she ought to be amused by the thought, but in fact it unnerved her. Was there a map, a geography of this reinvented science? Did Vogt World border Neder-land, and where did they stand in relation to the Kingdom of Kam, whose dark monarch had been admitted to the hallowed halls of Canterbury?

There was a time, long ago, when Rüdiger Vogt and M. Sato would have been monks and priests, and their treatises would have concerned not space-time and neutrinos but the Trinity and the Sacraments. They would have claimed that Jesus was an ordinary man, that Satan inhabited pumpkins, that God's reflection could be seen in a certain pond under a full moon. They would interpret the Book of Revelation in a way that left their readers trembling over the centuries. Wise men would mock them with erasmic wit; ordinary men would laugh and fling dung; holy men would send them to hell. They would have spent their days wandering as ragged penitents or languishing in fetid dungeons, and would have been excommunicated, flayed, burned, and thrown into the pit. Now they received rejection slips. Surely that was some kind of progress? But what if it was the pit that they really craved?

All it would take, Lena realized, was a quick call back to London. 'Sorry, Tim, it just wasn't my scene after all. Don't worry about the expenses.' But you don't have a scene, she told herself. What good is it scooping *The Times* and the *Guardian* if you don't have a scene? She'd suspected all along that that story of hers would cause more problems than it solved.

'I FELT THEY WERE CUTTING AWAY MY LIFE'

*Lena Romanowicz exposes a tale of
grief and greed in a seaside village*

Sally Harvey has a drawer filled with children's clothes that she will never need. 'It used to be a little indulgence, if I needed cheering up,' she says. 'I'd pop into the town and get a pretty skirt or a pair of shoes. Now I just don't know what to do with them. But I couldn't bear to chuck them out.'

Sally won't ever have a baby of her own to put into these pretty skirts. Because she has had a total abdominal hysterectomy, which removed her ovaries and her womb. Sally is one of the six thousand women diagnosed with ovarian cancer every year. Usually that's just a matter of very bad luck. But in Sally's case, it seems highly likely that she has been left unable to bear a child because she lived in the wrong place.

It's looking increasingly like a story of corporate greed and negligence. Sally isn't by any means the only cancer patient in the little coastal village of Westfold. Several of her neighbours have been treated for lung, throat and colorectal cancers over the past ten years.

*'There's a definite cluster here,' says Anthony
Dewdney, an epidemiologist at the University of
London. And Dewdney thinks it may be no coincidence
that there happens to be a waste incineration plant just
two miles away. 'It's always really hard to show cause
and effect in these cases,' he says. 'But if you look at the
statistics, there doesn't seem to be any sign of a problem
until the incinerator came along.'*

Ψ

She had called Aitchison in early March.

'What do you know about this Hotel Erd? It says that special conference rates are available.'

'Don't do it,' Aitchison advised. 'It will be bedlam there.' He offered to find another place, which she gratefully accepted. She had a fleeting notion that he was planning to book them a double room, but she didn't think he was that sort of man. She could not imagine he was married, even. He seemed to her more like a monk, under holy vows to labour underground in the toroidal vaults of a Swiss cathedral where quantum scriptures were picked over in fanatical detail. She thought the image would amuse him no end.

And now they sat perched on his bed, because there was not even a lounge in this precise little *gasthaus* on Neuer Markt, all double glazing and moulded shower units and watercolour irises. 'You didn't seem the aesthetic type,' Aitchison told her, and she realized he meant it as a compliment. Anyhow, he was probably right.

Scattered over the coverlet were the copies she had made of the papers and letters of Karl Neder given to her by Roy Battle.

Dear Dr Battle,

My letter to you of the 20th September has surely already reached you. But no answer comes from you. You boldly go to a scandal and a ruination of your scientific career and moral reputation. I cannot comprehend it. Have you not understood that I have constructed a PERPETUUM MOBILE? It is a machine that will run without input of power. You know this, and you know what it will mean.

Tell me at least a single word. Now in Linz the story will not be as in Genoa where I have escaped from the police. Here I have no fear of the police. I give you a friendly and human advice: read my papers attentively, ruminate a little bit, put aside any other activity for a WHOLE DAY. Until that moment when the situation is in your hands I will do all possible to save your name and reputation. However, when the press will bite, the whole story will go out of my control. Be wise, Dr Battle, be wise!

Now I send you a corrected copy of my paper

ENERGETICS OF CEMENTED FARADAY DISK DEVICE

You have to print THIS COPY. The texts for the other two papers are as sent to you on the 29th June 1982, and as they are published in THE BITTER ROAD OF TRUTH, Vol 4.

With this paper I am aiming only 1% to show the bankruptcy of relativity. My 99% aim is to show the scientific community the difference between motional and motional-transformer inductions, because only after understanding this difference can one understand the

*functioning of my perpetua mobilia. I explain all with
such a simple language as having to speak to children.
I beg you: do not make the fool that you do not
understand what I am saying.*

*Send me the proofs as soon as possible, Dr Battle. I
still hope to win the Nobel prize for this year. Oh, if I
had in my hands 3,000 dollars. And I can exclaim as
Richard III in the Shakespeare drama:*

*THREE THOUSAND DOLLARS FOR THIS
YEAR NOBEL PRIZE!*

*Nobody will give them to me. NOBODY. I am more
sure in this than in the inevitability of nuclear war. I
have only twenty days (the decision for this-year Nobel
prizes are taken at the end of October). Only twenty
days. Nevermind!*

*Awaiting for your call with the consent of
publication,*

*Sincerely yours,
Karl Neder*

Lena had taken away a copy of Battle's characteristically con-
cise response to this one, because it seemed to her to capture
the essence of their interactions:

Dear Dr Neder,

*With very great regret I have to say that I cannot
publish the note that you ask should be published in
Natural Science, but I do, as ever, send you my very
best wishes.*

*Yours sincerely,
Roy Battle*

'Energetics of cemented Faraday disk device' was a paper that had particularly appealed to Lena, and she had Xeroxed the entire thing. Naturally, she could make nothing of the science. Phrases such as 'the Biot-Savart effect' and 'Lebedev light pressure' were underlined, but she could find no reference to such things in any scientific encyclopaedia. 'This effect,' the manuscript exclaimed ('What effect?' thought Lena), 'has remained unnoticed until now. This may seem incredible, but after having established that so many fundamental effects in electromagnetism have remained unnoticed, I do not become more amazed and shocked when I reveal a new huge lack in human knowledge.'

She wondered whether Neder ever imagined anyone reading this stuff. It did not seem written with a reader in mind. Mimicking the formal language of scientific discourse, it seemed in fact more of an internal dialogue. At times even that formality broke down, and then suddenly the author was telling a story:

The history of this effect represents a curiosity. In 1977 I was imprisoned in a psychiatry hospital in Sofia and cured by horse doses of neuroleptics (Mageptil) because of my unorthodox political thinking. In the hospital was imprisoned and forcedly cured another, obviously absolutely normal (like myself), man. He was a very able mechanician who, refusing to work for a salary in a state plant, executed special refined works on his own lathes and milling tools installed in his living room and the apartments of his relatives. He has earned good money and, evidently, the envy of his neighbours has brought him to the loony bin to be liberated of his vicious individualistic behaviour. This man asked me once in the toilet: 'Well, Karl, if you are a physicist, explain why axle

on ball-bearings rotates when current flows through it.' I
could not give an answer, and the mechanician shook his
head: 'What are they saying to the professors in the
universities if they cannot explain to you such a simple
thing?' At that time I did not know that this simple
experiment was unknown to the professors, as the first
publication on this effect appeared a year later. Thus
when this extremely important effect was discussed by the
idiots in a Bulgarian psychiatric hospital, it was still not
registered in the scientific annals of the physical world.

There was a detailed account of Neder's cemented Faraday disk machine, and even a photograph.

The exploded diagram showed a steel casing, and inside that a tight coil of copper wire, and within that a magnet, then bearings housed in a steel jacket, then an axle. The assembly was mounted on blocks of wood and held together with robust screws and bolts, all looking as if it was scavenged from a breaker's yard.

Wires trailed from it, a drip-feed tangle of lifelines. But which way, really, did the essence flow: to or from this squat, shiny device? That, Lena suspected, was quite important.

The machine was called EDEN: Energizer Discovered in

Europe by Neder. He had built it, he said, at the Laboratory for Fundamental Problems in Wipplingerstrasse, Linz. And it ran forever.

At least, it *would* do, as Neder explained.

The measurements show clearly that the machine creates energy from nothing. But as at the reachable rate of rotation the tension produced by the generator minus the back tension of the motor is still less than the driving tension which has to maintain the rotation, the machine could not be run eternally. To run it eternally I need only some $5,000.

No one had yet given him $5,000, so it appeared that EDEN remained sub-eternal, flawed, a prisoner of unrelenting friction.

Before EDEN, Neder explained, he had experimented with over a dozen different designs for a perpetuum mobile. Some had shown promise; he admitted that others had failed entirely, while some were apparently lost during precipitate departures from precarious premises. A few were confiscated by ill-defined authorities, or, he suspected, stolen by 'Relativists'. But there were pictures of these, too, and all seemed to be made of metal disks and cylinders, copper wire, magnets, wood and screws. They were of a kind – a species. Random mutation and natural selection, carrying them always closer to the pinnacle of evolutionary development towards EDEN:

The crucial idea was not Neder's, he admitted that. It was in 1980, he said, that he came across the American journal *Energy Unlimited*, in which a man named Bruce DePalma described experiments with a device that he called a cemented Faraday disk.

Beyond that, things got hazy, and it was not until Iain Aitchison scanned the pages, his grin gradually broadening, that Lena was given a sense of what Neder was up to. 'One glues a copper disk to a cylindrical magnet and drives it into rotation with a motor. Electrical current begins to flow from the centre to the periphery of the copper disk, and the power in this flux of electrons is greater than that needed to keep the disk spinning. More energy comes out of the device, in other words, than is fed into it.'

'I have the impression that's a bad thing.'

'It is quite appalling. One could then use a tiny motor to run a cemented Faraday disk, and out would come enough power to drive a bigger version of the same apparatus. That would then power another, and eventually a humble car motor is driving a hierarchy of spinning machines that produce enough power to sustain the whole of Austria. Oh, quite terrible.' His grin was now at full stretch.

This, he explained, was in effect perpetual motion, and his tone implied that he equated it with something like original sin. Energy unlimited, perpetual motion: it was all the same, apparently. Energy from nothing. If a machine creates more energy than it consumes, you can use it to drive itself, and it will go on spinning forever, a self-contained little universe of motion.

'Well, here's what I don't get,' said Lena. 'Didn't Galileo say that things will move forever anyway, if there's nothing to stop them?' A piece of high-school physics that had always puzzled her, and she had refused to ask her father for an explanation.

'Yes, but that isn't perpetual motion,' said Aitchison. 'What it all comes down to is the conservation of energy. The total energy of the universe is finite.'

'Hang on. Who says so?'

'It's the First Law of Thermodynamics,' the capitals audible.

'OK, but that's just a name. How do we know it's true?'

'Oh, such a good question. Are you sure you're not just playing the ingénue, Lena? If only one's students had the gumption to ask these things once in a while. The whole of thermodynamics – you could say the whole of physics – is predicated on this law, so if it's wrong, the fabric of physics crumbles. But you're right, in a sense, to say "So what?" There's no proof – in a way it's experimentally unprovable. All our theories demand the First Law, and it has never been seen to be violated, but that's not the same as a proof. It's an article of faith.'

He was still beaming. Lena suspected that nothing would delight Aitchison more than the demolition of some fundamental principle of science. She began to think that the reason he went to fringe conferences was partly in the hope of finding a genuine challenge to well-established physical law.

'Do you want to know a secret?' he asked.

Again this suggestive intimacy, this monkish flirtation. She couldn't resist colluding. 'Ooh, yes!'

'The universe does give us something for nothing. All the time. Then it takes it back again at once!'

Lena waited.

'Quantum uncertainty, you see. It allows – you might say it compels – particles to pop into existence, out of nothing, out of sheer vacuum. As long as they live no longer than the limits of quantum uncertainty, which is a shorter time than a man can have any conception of. Or a young woman, presumably. Not just next to nothing, but as close to it as you can imagine getting. And not just one particle, but two – they're always paired. A particle and its mirror image, its anti-particle. They appear out of the quantum vacuum, and in an instant they see each other and embrace' (Why that metaphor? Did Aitchison know his own mind? she wondered) '– and *fzzzz!*, they disappear again. But their mutual destruction produces energy, a photon, a particle of light. So the vacuum is filled with this energy, this fizzing. And here's the best part – in theory, this energy should overwhelm everything else in the universe! It should tear it all apart! Ha ha ha!'

'So the theory is wrong, then?'

'Incomplete, one might say. A little reminder that one doesn't know everything. But the splendid irony is that this vacuum energy is not available to Karl Neder, because he denies the veracity of quantum physics. How wonderful! The man who wants infinite energy, and he refuses to take it where physics is at its most vulnerable.' Aitchison was red with mirth, but Lena could detect no trace of malice in it.

'But look, look, a man can get carried away. Your original question, then. Yes, Galileo said that a body in motion would move forever if no forces acted on it. But you see, that's not the same as perpetual motion, except, ah, semantically, because it doesn't violate the First Law. Energy is neither created nor destroyed. The energy of motion, that is, the kinetic energy of the body, stays always the same. Now, in reality this is never seen. Even a body moving through interstellar space feels distant gravitational forces, it collides with atoms and molecules in the tenuous gas between the stars, and each collision imparts a little drag, a little friction. All the time, energy is being dissipated, in however small an amount. That's the thing, you see. No change happens without energy being dissipated, converted to heat. That, by the way, is the Second Law of Thermodynamics, in a manner of speaking. And these two laws together point to one thing, as the physicist Clausius recognized last century, and that is the heat death of the universe. So you see, some of these perpetual motion chaps have a notion that they are going to save not only the world, but the universe.'

By my half-a-century experimental and theoretical work I showed the following (see references in my twelve books, 60 refereed papers, eight paid advertisements, and numerous papers and editor's comments in the journal NEUE PHYSIK edited by me):

1. The principle of relativity is wrong. *Indeed, I measured three times optico-mechanically and once electromagnetically the Earth's absolute velocity. Its magnitude is 350 km sec^{-1} with equatorial coordinates of its apex δ = -20°, α=12^h (approx.).*

2. The principle of equivalence is wrong. *Indeed, my interferometric 'coupled mirrors' experiment which was carried out during a year showed that when the laboratory's acceleration was kinematic, the laboratory's velocity changed, while when it was dynamic there was no change.*

3. The energy conservation law is wrong. *My machines COL-BAR, MOMOT and EDEN violated this law. Only because of lack of money I could not close the energetic circle in the first two, but the third one was less expensive and I shall run it soon as a perpetuum mobile. The day when I shall present this machine at a press conference will be the start-day for an earthquake in conventional physics, when many centuries-old dogmas shall be renounced and many saints de-sainted.*

4. Displacement current does not exist. *At the age of 19 I understood that displacement current is a phantasmagoria and presented to my teacher in Budapest the following objection: 'If the displacement current between the plates of a condenser acts with magnetic forces on the other currents, then according to Newton's third law the other currents must act with magnetic forces on the displacement current and set it in motion. But how, comrade teacher, can vacuum be set in motion?' Teacher's answer was: 'Shut up boy!'*

Perhaps, Lena thought, the problem here was something to do with the nature of abstraction. Explanations are fine – we can cope with why this leads to that. Cause and effect, that's all very well. But the abstraction of experience just never seems very... convincing. Perhaps we are all Aristotelians at heart, looking for comfortable tautologies about tangible events. Things fall because it is in their nature to fall. A force has nothing to do with it. Forces are hidden – they are occult. And so it all gets a little mystical, and actually one has to work rather hard to be a mystic, at least if it is to be done with conviction. If the world must be divided up that way, into so many invisible forces doing their counter-intuitive work, why does it seem that things happen so much to the contrary? Why should the levers be so obscure and hard to get at? We want Cartesian particles-touching, not action-at-a-distance. The pressure of surfaces rubbing against one another, *that* we understand. But the emptiness of space is inhuman.

It was not that she distrusted science – oh, she'd have been happy to, but that avenue had been closed off years ago by a domestic mixture of shepherding and hectoring. It was just that she appreciated why one might. But the rebellions that

Aitchison dissected, the challenges being mounted at ICSTA '86, were all the more anguished because they could only speak in the language of that against which they rebelled.

Yet she wondered if Karl Neder was going beyond this. He seemed to be trying to turn the uncompromising language inside out, to push abstraction so far that it would start to solidify into new forms. She knew that she hadn't any clues yet about the source of his discontent, which was after all (she told herself) where her story surely lay. He had covered his tracks with a confusion of signs and symbols.

'I'll tell you what worries me,' said Lena. 'I have to write this article, but I take one look at Neder's papers and books, and I don't understand a word. He says he's made a perpetual motion machine, and then he starts to explain it, and I can't get past the first sentence. I don't know what he's saying.'

'That's a deeply sane response.'

'You think Neder is mad?'

'Hmm. Ask a doctor. He's certainly obsessed. The point is that you realize it's right to give up trying to extract any sense from this material.'

'I don't have any choice. And anyway, that doesn't help me. The thing is, he's published these sixty or so papers, and they must have something to say, but I don't know what it is.'

'It's very hard to tell, even for a physicist. This isn't ignorance on your part, or not simply that, if you'll excuse that way of putting it. The general propositions contained in these texts are clear enough: energy conservation can be violated, and relativity and quantum mechanics are wrong. But when you start to look at the arguments, frankly they're more than a person can follow. That isn't a matter of insufficient scientific expertise, you understand – there's no possibility that one is being outpaced by genius, you mustn't imagine anything of that sort. The physicist can pick out any equation from these papers and books' – he reached for the manuscript – 'and see what it means. Look here, for instance.'

Under Aitchison's finger was a cluster of symbols:

$$B_{\omega rad} = \frac{k^2}{r}\, e^{ikr}\, n \times d_\omega$$

'Now, this is disheartening, isn't it? But you see, all he wants to express is that there is a way of calculating the strength and direction of a magnetic field a certain distance away from a particle that has an electrical charge. Good. There's no problem with that. But then this formula leads to another, and then another, and you have to keep your wits about you to recall what "d" is, and "k", and you have to remember to keep asking, "Is this equation right?" and "Does this follow?" and so on. And then you come to a page like this one:

the intensity of radiation reaction calculated with the equations of motion:

$$\overline{\overline{E}}_{rea} = \frac{1}{N}\sum_{i=1}^{N}\overline{\overline{E}}_{rea_i} = \frac{1}{N}\sum_{i=1}^{N} q\,\frac{\overrightarrow{n}_i x(\overrightarrow{n}_i x \overrightarrow{w})}{c^3}. \qquad (21.46)$$

Multiplying both sides of this equation by 4π, we get

$$4\pi\overline{\overline{E}}_{rea} = \sum_{i=1}^{N}\overline{\overline{E}}_{rea_i}\frac{4\pi}{N} \qquad (21.47)$$

and taking the limit $N \to \infty$, we can write

$$\overline{\overline{E}}_{rea} = \frac{1}{4\pi}\int_{4\pi}\overline{\overline{E}}_{rea}d\Omega = \frac{1}{4\pi}\int_{0}^{2\pi}\int_{0}^{\pi} q\,\frac{\overrightarrow{n} x(\overrightarrow{n} x \overrightarrow{w})}{c^3}\,\sin\theta\,d\theta\,d\phi$$

$$= \frac{q}{4\pi c^3}\int_{0}^{2\pi}\int_{0}^{\pi}[(\overrightarrow{n}.\overrightarrow{w})\overrightarrow{n} - \overrightarrow{w}]\sin\theta\,d\theta\,d\phi \qquad (21.48)$$

where (see (1.14.3))

$$n_x = \sin\theta\cos\phi, \qquad n_y = \sin\theta\sin\phi, \qquad n_z = \cos\theta. \qquad (21.49)$$

θ and ϕ being the zenith and azimuthal angles respectively of the spherical frame of reference corresponding to the as used here Cartesian frame.

Formula (21.48) can be written as

$$\overline{\overline{E}}_{rea} = \frac{q}{4\pi c^3}\int_{0}^{2\pi}\int_{0}^{\pi}[(w_x \sin\theta\cos\phi + w_y\sin\theta\sin\phi + w_z\cos\theta)(\sin\theta\cos\phi\overrightarrow{x} +$$

$$\sin\theta\sin\phi\overrightarrow{y} + \cos\theta\overrightarrow{z}) - \overrightarrow{w}]\sin\theta\,d\theta\,d\phi \qquad (21.50)$$

Remembering the formulas from section IV, p. 95, and taking into account that $\overline{w}$ is a constant vector of magnitude $|w| = 2\pi\pi$, we arrive at

$$\overline{\overline{E}}_{rea} = \frac{q}{4\pi c^3}\{w_x\overrightarrow{x}\int_{0}^{2\pi}\int_{0}^{\pi}\sin^3\theta\cos^2\phi\,d\theta\,d\phi + w_y\overrightarrow{y}\int_{0}^{2\pi}\int_{0}^{\pi}\sin^3\theta\sin^2\phi\,d\theta\,d\phi +$$

$$w_z\overrightarrow{z}\int_{0}^{2\pi}\int_{0}^{\pi}\cos^2\theta\sin\theta\,d\theta\,d\phi - \overline{w}\int_{0}^{2\pi}\int_{0}^{\pi}\sin\theta\,d\theta\,d\phi\} =$$

$$\frac{q}{4c^3}\{w_x\overrightarrow{x}\int_{0}^{\pi}\sin^3\theta\,d\theta\,d\phi + w_y\overrightarrow{y}\int_{0}^{\pi}\sin^3\theta\,d\theta +$$

$$w_z\overrightarrow{z}\int_{0}^{\pi}2\cos^2\theta\sin\theta\,d\theta\cdot\overline{w}\int_{0}^{\pi}2\sin\theta\,d\theta\} =$$

$$\frac{q}{4c^3}(\frac{4}{3}w_x\overrightarrow{x} + \frac{4}{3}w_y\overrightarrow{y} + \frac{4}{3}w_z\overrightarrow{z} - 4\overrightarrow{w}) = \frac{q}{4c^3}(\frac{4}{3}\overrightarrow{w} - 4\overrightarrow{w}) = -\frac{2q}{3c^3}\overrightarrow{w} \qquad (21.51)$$

where by analogy with formula (IV, 15.6), we have used the formulas and the only way you can make sense of it is to plod through all the maths, which would take you an hour or more. Just for this page alone. So Neder ends up with a big claim – for example, that the Lorentz equation is wrong...'

'Stop. I've no idea what the Lorentz equation is, so I don't know if that's a big claim or not.'

'Of course you don't. The Lorentz equation tells you the magnitude of the force that one charged particle exerts on another when both are moving. Hendrik Lorentz was a Dutch physicist, and he realized that it was no easy thing to understand electricity and magnetism once you start moving things about. That's to say, there was a theory that accounted for electromagnetism, and it was devised by Michael Faraday and James Clerk Maxwell in the nineteenth century. But once you start to think about electromagnetic forces between bodies in motion, the theory runs into problems. The trouble was that it assumed that there was an ether, a substance like a gas that filled all of space. Just as sound waves are vibrations in the air, light waves were, in Maxwell's view, vibrations in the ether. Light waves, you see, being waves of electricity and magnetism – electromagnetic waves. Do you want to know all this?'

'No. It's horrible. But I suspect I must. Put it this way: you keep talking, and I'll keep supposing.'

'Supposing? Ah, that's excellent. One must always keep supposing in science. Sometimes one feels there's too much theorizing and not enough supposing. Well then, the ether –'

The ether. No wonder the Victorian scientists fell prey to spiritualism, Lena thought. Why call it the ether, if you don't secretly suspect it's something heavenly? Those bewhiskered gentlemen laboured mightily to understand it; they imagined space as a kind of cosmic lattice of bedsprings humming to an infinite spectrum of vibrations. And then, Aitchison explained, came Drs Michelson and Morley, to detect the ether by the breath of cosmic wind as the earth rushes through it. Light heading into the wind should be slowed down compared with light moving sideways. But that isn't what Michelson and Morley found. They found no difference in the speed of light in either direction.

'So there is no ether?'

'Indeed, there is no ether. But it wasn't obvious even then. Hendrik Lorentz explained the Michelson and Morley result without abandoning the ether. His answer was ingenious. He suggested that light *does* travel more slowly when moving against this ether wind, but that we don't notice, because things get shorter too. Running into the wind, light has a shorter track. The effect is tiny, but it compensates exactly, and so the light seems to take the same time to traverse an apparently equal path in both directions. Now, you see, what Lorentz was really trying to do was to preserve absolute space and time –'

'Space-Time Absoluteness!'

'Absolutely – oh, beg pardon.'

'But I still don't understand what that means. I'm just latching onto the word.'

'OK. Think of it like this. According to Newton's laws of motion – Isaac Newton, yes? Good. So, these laws assume you can draw a grid in space, like on a map, and then give everything a grid reference. And an object is motionless when it doesn't move relative to this grid. And the clock ticks identically everywhere – ten past seven on Earth is, so to speak, also ten past seven on Mars, and in a distant galaxy. This is absolute space and time. What Lorentz was saying was that absolute stillness was defined relative to the ether: things are perfectly at rest when they don't move with respect to the ether. And that's where Einstein comes in.'

Lena was now scribbling a little desperately in bad short-hand. The assignment felt impossible, yet Aitchison seemed to regard her story as a fait accompli to which he need only add the finishing touches. She began to feel she was being handed an obligation.

'Einstein continued in the direction Lorentz had started, but with one important difference. He did away with the ether. He used Lorentz's maths, but instead of absolute space and time, he proposed a new absolute: the speed of light. That, he said, was the one thing that never changes, whether the light is launched from a streetlamp or a rocket travelling at thousands of miles per hour. You can't add anything to the speed of light simply by sending it from a moving body. It is always the same. Now there's supposing for you! And that was special relativity.'

'What was special about it?'

'It was special because it was only about relative motion, about uniformly moving bodies. Later he saw what it implied about the structure of space itself, and that was general relativity, which was all about bodies accelerating and moving under gravity. But, you see, the point is that Einstein was inspired to develop relativity by the theory of electromagnetism. That's where it starts. He even called his key paper "On the electrodynamics of moving bodies", and he started it by talking about the difficulties with Maxwell's theory. He wasn't thinking then about cosmic space and time – he just begins talking about magnets and wires.'

From these materials, EDEN was made.

'So that,' said Aitchison with the air of one concluding a good yarn, 'is why, for Karl Neder, electromagnetism is the thing. That's where he thinks he can show Einstein is wrong. He believes that he'll winkle out relativistic effects from classical – that's to say, Maxwellian – electrodynamics. But, you see, *that* is a terribly complicated theory. It isn't properly understood, even now. It's plagued by strange forces and effects that Maxwell and others had to invent in order to make the whole thing work. Neder refuses to acknowledge some of these forces; out of others he tries to conjure up his perpetual motion. But that's the point – ach, was that what we were saying? Shall we see if there's any room service in this place? A cup of tea would be splendid.'

'You make it sound like chasing a creature through a maze.'

'A super analogy. Neder makes these grand claims, but to understand his proof you have to follow the arguments step by step, for pages and pages of all this algebra. You're sure there must be a mistake, but finding it is a lifetime's work.'

'Does he hide it?'

'It's not necessarily a conscious thing. But in effect, yes. The maths are a representation of the state of his mind – it seems rational and transparent enough, and then suddenly you realize that you're a long way from where you started, and the path has been obscured, and you've forgotten the question in any case. To be honest, one might find these books rather frightening – to realize that a man might think in that way. To the physicist they make for uncomfortable reading, which is another reason one hesitates to analyse them too deeply. It's as though he's drawing you deeper and deeper into his neurosis. Surely they could rustle up a pot of tea, though no doubt the milk will be that fake stuff in plastic pots.'

'Perhaps that's what's happened to Roy Battle.'

'Perhaps it is. Battle is a clever man, but maybe he goes too far sometimes. You've read the letters, you can judge that.'

Yes, she'd read the letters. Battle was playing a peculiar game, although it wasn't clear that he recognized it himself.

Dear Dr Neder,

I have reviewed your paper myself, and enclose a list of my specific questions and concerns. Please do understand that there are no circumstances in which I could ask one of our small army of dedicated but unpaid referees to take on this task, because your manuscript begins (deliberately I'm sure) with the inflammatory statement of your theory of absolute space-time.

Let me say that I have great sympathy with your frustration, even despair; but I must tell you frankly how your intellectual position must seem to the outside world. You are persuaded that special relativity is wrong, but your conviction is based on a single experiment carried out in Austria and not afterwards repeated (for financial reasons which I understand). In your 'Coup de Grace' paper, you also outline a number of theoretical formulations which, to be honest, I do not understand.

Nowhere in the huge correspondence between us have I detected a trace of awareness on your part of the enormity of the point you wish to establish. Special relativity sprang from contradictions of electro-magnetism at the end of the nineteenth century, was recognized in 1905 as a valid amendment to Newton's mechanics and has since been shown to be (1) consistent with general relativity, a local approximation if you like, and (2) amply confirmed by, for example, the accelerator experiments which show that the energy of a particle increases with its velocity as $1/\sqrt{(1-v^2/c^2)}$. Relativity has been used to open unexpected avenues of enquiry, such as Dirac's relativistic quantum mechanics (and the existence of the positron).

You ask the world to give up all this on the strength of a single experiment, and because you say so! But unlike Jesus Christ and others successful at changing the way the world thinks, you offer nothing in exchange. If special relativity is flawed, as you insist, what then is the valid amendment to Newton's mechanics that you would put in its place? (You will say that the first part of your 'Coup de Grace' paper contains the answer, but I cannot follow it.)

What is more, I am honestly disappointed by the quality of the experiments that you describe in your manuscript. You claim that your equipment is sufficiently sensitive to detect the effects you report, but you give absolutely no assistance to the reader who might wish to check that point. Here is the sort of thing I mean.

Obviously the sensitivity of your experiment will to a large extent be determined by the dependence of total light transmission on the rotational speed of the disks, the shape of the beam, and the shape and size of the holes in the disks. Unfortunately you do not even tell the reader how many holes there are in each disk, nor even the range of rotational speeds over which you have run the experiment. But from your photograph, I guess there may be about 40 holes per disk.

Moreover, as far as I can see, you quote only one set of results (at 200 revolutions/minute), but do not do what professional physicists would instinctively do – plot, say, I as a function of N and estimate the slope of the line to infer the supposed velocity component along the axis.

Naturally I am disappointed and even slightly shocked that, in a matter that is of such great importance to you, no mention is made of what I would have thought must be a crucial set of considerations.

Please do not reply with another version of your manuscript. Try instead to understand that people like me are not acting (or failing to act as you would wish) out of disregard for you, but because we think your argument, honestly put though it is, is unconvincing.

Yours sincerely,
Roy Battle

*

Dear Dr Battle,

Thank you very much for your comments. You have made some remarks about my rotating-disk experiment, in which I measure the earth's absolute motion. I can refute and address your criticisms ENTIRELY. You state that the number of holes in the disk is important and must be quoted (although you could count the holes from the photograph, which you then did indeed). You counted 40 holes. The holes are 41. Are you now satisfied? Dear Dr Battle, how could you pose this **stupid** question about the number of the holes? This number is of NO importance. Maybe I knew this number when making the disks, but then I forget it. To count the holes, I must lose precious time and go where the apparatus is kept, which is in Salzburg though I am in Linz. I cannot, indeed, even say exactly where the apparatus is now, because the person who gave me possibility to use the equipment of his laboratory took from me the promise that I shall say to NOBODY where the experiment was done. This person is afraid that if his name will be known, one day the Jews may poison him. You *know that the German speaking people have a special attitude to the 'Jewish problem', but do you not find it funny to hear this story 40 years after the death of Hitler? Of course, I do not tell this person of my own Jewish blood.*

Dr Battle, I am not obliged to answer any stupid referee's question. If I shall tell you how many holes are in the disks, then you will ask how many screws are in my apparatus or which is the distance from the room where the experiment was done to the toilet etc etc. You claim that my experiment has not been reported in 'professional' manner. What did you wish to say with the adjective 'professional'? Obviously, because now I am a groom and sleep in a stall (you know perfectly well why: you are one of the persons responsible for the fact that any morning I go not to the laboratory but to clean the excrement of horses), I am not, according to you, a 'professional' physicist. And you with your stupid questions about the number of holes and the slope of a line which one can never use for calculation of v, you are a 'professional' physicist. more modest, Dr Battle, be more modest. 'Скромность украшает большевика /Йосиф Сталин/' – Ask Margaret Strong to translate you this sentence.

Dr Battle, I do experiments to measure the earth's absolute velocity for 10 years. And in 10 minutes you intend to find flaws in my experiments. You are an unbelievable grandoman!

Dr Battle, do not lose your time and do not lose my time. Satisfy the requirements of my ultimatum. I shall be in Graz until the end of this month. Then I go to Como (Italy) where I shall present my perpetuum mobile at the Second Workshop on Hadronic Mechanics.

Before the end of July I must have here, in Linz, the proofs of all three of my papers (with all figures printed, so that I can check whether my drawings are redone well in London and the reproductions of the photographs are satisfying). If you will decline the papers before the end of the month, I shall immolate myself in front of the English Embassy in Vienna. If you will not decline the papers, but proofs will not reach me before the end of the month, I shall immolate myself after the conference in Como (where this immolation will be announced), i.e. after the 3 of August, in front of the English General Consulate in Genoa. I have a whole army of journalists, friends of me in Genoa. I shall organize such a theatre!!!

Dr Battle, do not play with fire. Send me the acknowledgement for acceptance and send me the proofs before the end of the month (please, not in the last one or two days, be once a gentleman!).

Perpetuum mobile, Dr Battle, PERPETUUM MOBILE IS CONSTRUCTED BY ME!!!!!!!!! How can you not understand this?! My apparatus rotated 5 seconds more when the current generated by the Faraday disk was sent to the Barlow disk. THE ENERGY FOR THIS ROTATION CAME FROM NOWHERE, FROM NOWHERE, Dr Battle, understand this!!!!

Important information: *If you reject the papers, I shall edit in the near future the following book:*

THE BITTER ROAD TO TRUTH, VOLUME VI: Documentation on the creation of the perpetuum mobile, on the centurial blindness of mankind and on its frantic perseverance in.

You will be one of the principal performers in this book with your question about the number of holes etc. I can edit this book before going to Italy (you know well that I have better possibilities for a speedy publication of a book than has Natural Science).

Dr Battle, let us be honest scientists, good colleagues, and gentlemen. All depends on your attitude. During a dozen of years you have seen that I am a real gentleman and a noble spirit.

Sincerely yours,
Karl Neder

*

Dear Dr Neder,

Honestly, I am disappointed by the tone of your letter. I am afraid there is still no question of our publishing your paper, for the reasons that I gave earlier. Please do not immolate yourself outside the British Embassy – the people there would be deeply embarrassed.

Yours sincerely,
Roy Battle

6

THE ACT OF ENROLMENT FOR ICSTA '86 ENTITLED LENA TO A plastic bag filled with fuzzy Xeroxes. The bag was printed with the slogan 'Foundations of Physics: Showing the Way to Tomorrow', and inside it were the abstracts of talks and posters being presented at the conference. Everyone here had a story to tell, and fuzzy Xeroxes were apparently the normal medium for communicating such tales. Nominally these stories were in English; but the unofficial language of the conference was mathematics, which Lena neither spoke nor read. She took the grainy texts to the Stadtpark, where the trees were still skeletal and the grass was meagre and dispirited at the end of an Austrian winter. She hoped the cold would keep her awake.

Tourists filed past the gilded statue of Strauss, and among the ornamental shrubs furtive dealers sold dope to backpackers. The city tried to offer something for everyone.

One of the things they hadn't taught her at college was that a journalist enters a life of voluntary exclusion. A life on the outside, a life spent decoding the customs of others, protected by the notepad, stigmatized by the press pass. It wasn't healthy, but she had never supposed that it would be. There was, of course, the myth that journalists have a culture of their own, but that Evelyn Waugh world was dead on its feet, mumbling red-nosed in loam-scented pubs on an otherwise sanitized Fleet Street overrun by coffee bars and greetings-card shops. Young writers like Lena embraced the bright lie of journalism training, enduring months of formica tables and flip charts and shorthand races against the clock, only to discover that what they should have been doing instead was shoring up their self-belief against the pain of being rebuffed and ignored.

But at least she was now accustomed to the pattern. This park bench could as easily be in Bonn or in Birmingham, and instead of scientists her morning might have been spent among local government officers or teachers or industrial architects. She'd experience an initial surge of irritation and scorn at the stupid insularity and arrogance of these groups, which seemed to believe that they alone had all the jobs worth having. Their in-jokes, their over-hearty greetings, their coteries and back-stabbing – Lena knew that at first she resented all of these things merely because she was not a part of them. Time would pass, she would chat to this person and that, most of them would turn out to be friendly, decent people, generous with their time and advice, and she would go home with her half-legible notes and another little world would vanish from her life forever.

It was like joining a new class at school, over and over again. Everyone knew each other, and they regarded the new-comer with a mixture of amusement and suspicion and, more than anything else, indifference. What kind of person would choose that?

It was not even as though the effort was well rewarded. Lena knew she was not particularly good at picking up the scent of a promising story. Whatever instinct impelled her, it was not a journalistic one. Once, she'd driven from London to Aberdeen to hear three days of talks about noise reduction schemes for urban motorways. It was November, and delegates came from all over Britain. These civil engineers and acoustic technicians had decided that Aberdeen in November would be a good place for a conference. It never stopped raining, and the food was unspeakable. After the first day, she bought a flask and took her own coffee. She'd had some half-formed theory that noise was socially defined, that attitudes to motor-vehicle noise were linked to notions of class and social mobility. She thought that the Second World War had reoriented the British response to noise. She spoke about this to delegates in the pitiless bar of the conference hotel. Some talked about the sound of doodlebugs, and the heart-stopping fear of the silence that came after. One of them appeared to know all there was to know about the Italian Futurists and their worship of the machine, their religion of speed. But they confessed that, to be honest, their regular work was just about measuring sound intensity across various types of metal barrier. After three days she drove back through the sleet in a strangely buoyant mood, with nothing even vaguely resembling a pitch for a story.

Ψ

'I suppose you like being on the edge,' her father had told her once. Probably more than once. 'No harm in it. Boundaries are fertile places –' Even he'd been embarrassed by that blunder.

It was true, though, that edges were where she often found herself. Not a loner; more of a hoverer. An observer. The only person who had ever seemed comfortable joining her there was Davey Flint; but they were both seventeen when he did that, and therefore misunderstood by definition.

At the end of the summer that separated school from the rest of their lives, she and Davey went to Whitby in search of vampires. The two of them with their bags of chips were like sad sea creatures on the wharf, sucked pale by the salt water and wrapped in black kelp. People kept asking Davey where the Dracula tour started, which seemed to evoke mixed emotions in him: he was glad that they got the idea, but annoyed that they missed the point. His theatrical plausibility, however, protected him from the abusive jeers and hard stares he got in Scarborough, although in truth there was nothing feminizing about his mascara, which turned him instead into a cartoon.

'Vampires exist,' he said. 'Historically. It's well documented. It's a medical condition, the craving for blood. Clinical vampirism.'

They were very black, where they were not bone white. Lena shielded her skin from the sun all summer. That was why vampires rose at night, she proclaimed – for the sake of their complexion. The undead were unconvincing when tanned.

How wonderful she had found it to be of an age that permitted deep seriousness about absurdity, while at the same time to be able to recognize it as such. Children are as serious and solemn as the world; they reflect only the fact that nature has no frivolity or irony or insight or self-awareness. Their laughter is unalloyed. But young adulthood introduced a parallel world that forced her to juggle with contradictions. Two things simultaneously true: the watcher and the watched, seeing each other and having to accept one another's inconsistent points of view. The confusion pleased her, back then.

Except that, winnowing its way in there almost from the start was an acknowledgement of the fragility, the tragic impermanence of this impossible state. The watcher knows it will win. With every year it gets stronger, and with it the grief at its certain victory. That was why, on holiday with Davey, Lena loved their play-acting, was proud of it and passionate in her pride, because she knew this time would pass, was already passing, and would be lost to them forever. This is pure, she said with her eyes to disdainful onlookers. Me and Davey, we still have some purity in us.

She loved Davey in the same way: passionately, proudly, because he would pass, was passing, would be lost forever. They were munching hungrily at their apple in Eden, sensing what was in store for them and deciding that, in that case, they might as well savour the sweet flesh of it.

She thrilled in her blue-black hair: black of such depth that it had nowhere else to go but back into the rainbow. She was wearing a silver ring inlaid with Whitby jet, but geology could not compete with the blackness of modern petrochemical dyes.

On the cliffs they were stick-like, awkward cut-outs of insect life.

'It would be excellent to have a black dog,' said Davey. 'Just to see it run up the steps.'

'You're allergic to dogs.'

He was pained, because she didn't understand. But he covered it up; that was the essential goodness of his nature.

'I mean right now. A black dog right now. Just here. Like in the book.'

He might as well know. 'I haven't read the book, Davey.'

'No?'

He looked so forlorn, great dark kohl-daubed eyes like a lemur. How he coped with disappointment, she felt, was one of his most attractive features. However baffled or wounded, he remained unguarded and always optimistic. She fought against an impulse to stop loving the idea of him and to start liking the ungainly flesh and blood, profoundly. She wanted to resist, or at least to postpone, that aspect of maturity.

'He comes ashore as a big black dog, see. The ship is wrecked, and all they see is a black dog run into the night.'

'Mephistopheles is a black dog sometimes.' That cheered him.

'I've got it with me,' he smiled slyly. 'The book. We can read it tonight. Right through the night. We can sit under the graves with a candle. That'll be... *unholy*.'

'You're such a Catholic.'

'It's good for you, that stuff. You need more ritual. Atheists live in the shadow of piety, but I intend to rescue you.' There was a bad accent coming on. '*I promise you grand impiety*.'

But later, he found grand impiety heavy going. It was almost more than he could manage. Autumn had begun, and there was a chill sea breeze that his calf-length greatcoat could not exclude. The town suddenly seemed worryingly close and active, even at ten past midnight, crawling with ruddy-faced vampire-haters, full of flat beer and sickly wine. So Lena could tell, up there on the church hill with cold grave-slabs beneath them, that his heart wasn't in it. But even then it was not, bless him, male pride that kept him intent on the task at hand, but an earnest determination to fulfil some personal commitment. He had been much the same way about his O-levels.

So had she, come to think of it: feeling kind of guilty about her indifference, adapting without rancour to the demands being put on her. And as she recalled, her exams too had been rather uncomfortable and had left her buttocks numbed.

'I can't get used to it, Layn,' he admitted afterwards. 'You know, having no – protection. Even Catholic boys are taught to fear *that* more than anything. Maybe especially Catholic boys.'

'Don't worry,' she said. 'There's nothing there. It's stony ground. The doctors say so. Although I suppose that might make your seed wasted, which on a full moon in a graveyard at midnight is a bit dodgy. It might get taken up by an incubus and gestated into a monster that will hunt you down and eat your soul.'

'You really are strange. But that's good: an incubus. There you are pretending this is all make-believe, all just dressing up, that you haven't read the book... but then you come up with incubuses. Incubae, I suppose. Where'd you get it from?'

'*The Displaying of Supposed Witchcraft* by John Webster. Sixteen hundred and somety something. I haven't really read it – it was on my dad's desk, so I flicked through it.'

'Your *dad* was reading it? Mine thinks Dracula is a character played by Christopher Lee.'

'He is, Davey.'

Davey's father was an electrician, and gently bemused by his son. He made quiet, wry banter with Lena in the spotless, cramped terrace house where Davey lived. 'You look like death warmed up, love.' 'I'll have none of your flattery, Mr Flint.'

They shared a cigarette, partly to conserve funds, partly because they liked the mingling of wetnesses and lip-warmth.

'I don't think my dad knows anything about witches. Webster is a sceptic's book – it's about debunking superstition.'

'And that's your dad's duty, as a scientist.'

'Yes, but –' The smoke tasted bitter, and she blew it out as though spewing ectoplasm. 'It's like a vicar reading porn. Webster comes to all the right conclusions, but only after giving a full frontal of the forbidden things. That way, it's OK to look.'

Davey was silent, admiring and slightly awed at how Lena could talk about her father. To him, Professor Romanowicz was too old and eminent to have qualities and characteristics; he was simply a deity who had to be propitiated.

'Did you mind doing this?' he asked Lena. 'You know,

this.' Feeling foolish, but what was feeling foolish to Davey Flint? If there was one trait that marked him as being ahead of his years, it was his appreciation of the comic potential of foolishness.

'I don't mind, Davey,' she said. 'The thing is, you mustn't expect too much from me, as far as *this* goes. I don't mean you shouldn't demand too much; I mean you shouldn't bank on my response. Because I'm a bit – compromised, you know. I'm sort of stuck. But I like it, Davey, I do, because I like you.'

There – she'd said it. But there was nothing to be done. And he, benign spirit, was happy enough with her words, seeing them from only one direction.

Ψ

Most of the other benches in the Stadtpark were occupied by elderly people. They tended to sit without speaking; talk was not their reason for coming here. They looked on with the endless patience of trees. In comparison, the clandestine manoeuvres of the drug sellers and the gesticulations of the tourists took on the aspect of a frantic dance of flies, the futile buzzing of another species, living lives at a faster rate which were over in an instant. These old and breathless observers held the twentieth century in their eyes.

Good God, Vienna. All the talk of the city's 'charm' in Lena's guidebook had not been able to exorcise the despairing ghosts that lived here, and now Jaroslav Kam's words seemed to have summoned them forth. Freud, Mahler, Schoenberg, Musil, Wittgenstein, the tragic Jewish spirits of Central Europe. There was death in these gorgeous stones, death as an escape from lives of agony and humiliation. Three of Wittgenstein's brothers killed themselves; so did Mahler's brother. Freud had an accomplice – a lethal shot of morphine from his doctor – but his pain in North London was not caused by cancer alone. It started in the ravages of the Anschluss, it deepened with the deaths of his four sisters at the hands of the Nazis, and he did not leave Vienna behind him when he fled. And look now, here comes Ludwig van Beethoven, stumbling soiled and swearing through the streets, syphilitic and soundless, after his adopted son has just attempted suicide. Even the Crown Prince Rudolf shot himself in 1887 (the guidebook seemed to relish Vienna's catalogue of personal calamities). It appeared to be the only way to escape that tight-lipped society, in which no one at the Imperial court could continue to eat after the emperor had laid down his knife. Vienna had lived then in brittle opulence, its plate filled and untouchable, waiting for another war.

But wars had shifted elsewhere now, and it seemed to Lena that Vienna no longer knew what to do with itself.

These papers, though. The titles of them. Lena wrote some of them down – there was no way she was going to lug the whole pack back to London in all its cryptic petulance.

```
A discussion of the coupled mirrors experiment.

Hydrinos as relic particles of a hyperinflated universe.

A singularity-free model of the classical ether.

Non-relativistic gravitational lensing.
```

Karl Neder was scheduled to give the first talk of the day on Friday morning, an invited presentation. It did not sound terribly exciting: 'Ampère's floating bridge experiment and electromagnetic anomalies'.

She looked up Kam and Symons, and there they were, back to back in Session V, the topic of which was something called Quantum Coherence:

Quintessence? Wasn't that Aristotle's fifth element, from which the eternal and unchanging heavens were made? The stuff known also as the aether? Was Symons planning to resurrect the ether?

Ψ

After lunch, Tomas Neumann opened ICSTA '86 with a short address. He spoke about two kinds of scepticism.

'We see today,' he said, 'the emergence of a philosophy of negation. It claims that there is nothing to know except language. Maybe in Wittgenstein's city that sounds attractive, but I do not think he would have approved. This is, if you will, the scepticism born of relativity, which says that we cannot compare the truth of your idea against the truth of my idea except in terms of the manner in which we choose to express them. So far, this relativistic scepticism is confined largely to the literary academies, but I do not think it will be content to stay there. In science, the purpose of scepticism is not to induce this kind of stagnation, this defeatism. It is rather the scepticism that prompted Galileo to say, "So this is the way you think the world is? Well, I shall not take your word for it, but shall instead ask the world itself." That is what we are all doing – we are asking the world itself to tell us how it is. It is such Galilean scepticism that motivates *Foundations in Physics* to support this conference. I do not mind telling you, and I do not think you will mind being told it, that I do not expect to agree with all that I shall hear in the next few days.

But I applaud you for daring to ask the questions you do. It will be no secret to you that I have been criticized by colleagues for offering my support to this event. I simply ask them in response: have we then abandoned scepticism in science, and replaced it with dogma? Have we decided that, in the face of centuries of evidence to the contrary, we have the final answers to the deep questions of science? Are you prepared to say so, when even Albert Einstein did not believe it was the case? If even just a handful of the many ideas that will be presented here were to prove correct, the consequences would be extraordinary. I am proud to be a part of this exploration.'

Lena glanced at Aitchison, who was grinning quite as broadly as she had ever seen him. A neutral observer would have taken it for an expression of delight. Lena was not sure what it meant, but she was feeling a little warmer towards Neumann than she had on her arrival. Surely his words were evidence of an open mind?

'Some of this programme,' Neumann went on, 'has been labelled fringe science. What does that mean? It is intended, of course, as a pejorative term, but it seems to me that a fringe lies on the edge, on the boundary. Can there be any shame in probing the boundaries of science? A theory can only be right or wrong, it cannot be "orthodox" or "fringe". Is space-time absolute? Do you know what? I have absolutely no idea, and the fact is that no one else has any idea either.'

('One wonders how many here would agree with that,' whispered Aitchison. Lena, for the first time, felt a twinge of impatience at his facetiousness.)

'So let us lead the way in attempting to find out.'

The hall filled with assertive applause, and the first session began. It was called 'Revisiting the Lorentz transformation', and the first speaker wasted no time in doing that. He wrote the Lorentz transformation on the blackboard with short, stabbing movements. Well, I suppose I'm going to have to get to know you, Lena said to the jumble of symbols.

This man was Georgiu Constantin, a Bulgarian from Sofia. He did not exactly supply a gripping overture. His English was fair enough, but so heavily accented that at times it became a dialect of Bulgarian. While he spoke he walked up and down, seeming to be searching for an exit, so his face was largely presented in profile. When he turned it to the audience, it was as though some internal pulley mechanism yanked his eyelids closed – a reflex, perhaps, to shelter him from the awful truth that there was a roomful of people watching him. He made frequent use of the blackboard, which not only slowed him down but also meant that his words were often carried to his listeners by muffled reflection. Having written out an equation, he would stand staring at it fretfully, as though it might trick him by spawning some unexpected solution.

No one seemed particularly discomforted by any of this, but that was because, as Lena would soon discover, Constantin's tics and quirks were generic, and rendered invisible by familiarity. Many attendees were not watching him at all, they were more intent on scribbling down his equations before he scrubbed them away in a cloud of white dust and began afresh. When a longer-than-normal pause supplied the clue that the talk was over, the listeners tapped their little flip-up chair-tables with appreciation, in the German style. Then came questions, the first of which was delivered by Jaroslav Kam. Even from several rows back, he seemed to loom over Constantin as he stood up.

Just as a film watched in a foreign language opens up a world of non-verbal speech, so Lena began to see how she could observe this conference as physical theatre, every gesture an eloquent statement of status and intent. She had not a clue what Kam asked, nor how Constantin replied, except to say that the real exchange went like this:

> Kam: *You have delivered a talk that has reminded us of some fairly obvious points, and that is all we expected of it, but I don't think you truly appreciate the profound implications of the issues you raise.*
> Constantin: *I am worried that I have neglected to stress some important aspects, but I hope you will forgive me for that.*
> Kam: *We will forgive you, of course we will, since we are all comrades here, but I am slightly disappointed in you.*
> Constantin: *Thank you.*

But later, Georgiu Constantin showed Lena another side.

She had never heard a voice like his. It was three in the morning in the Roter Engel on Rabensteig, in the district the Viennese rather melodramatically call the Bermuda Dreieck, because (they say) you could enter this tangle of cobbled streets and spend the rest of your days wandering in search of the way out. Revellers stumbled from one dim beer cellar to the next, the object of their blurry quest long forgotten. There was Constantin, an American with a Cajun drawl called Jim Crowther, from Louisiana, two voluble Spaniards called José and Juan, and a Greek whose name Lena had missed until it was too late to ask. The Roter Engel was Jim Crowther's choice, and like him it was just the other side of louche. His ox-like figure seemed to be expanding steadily through the night, and quite possibly it was.

At three o'clock the only tourists left were those whose libidos were no longer worth stoking with kitsch cabaret glitter and bowler hats, so there was an open microphone. Lena, doggedly drinking the coarse wine that the waiters served with contempt, felt a surge of panic when Constantin rose unsteadily and mounted the stage.

Then he began to sing, with a lurching Bulgarian rhythm that swept away the bar lines so that the tune became a continuous story, a prose poem with leaping ornaments like sobs and exclamations. He sang in a timeless, genderless alto, a voice intent on singing not for others to hear and praise, but because singing was a part of living. After four hours of knowing come-ons, it seemed to Lena like an act of indescribable generosity. He still had his eyes closed, but now it was for another reason.

'We all learn those songs at school,' he laughed afterwards. 'Our leaders say it is good to know of Bulgarian folk culture. You must be careful about that kind of thing – we know where national pride can lead us.'

Thus he carefully evaded any effusive compliments, although all Jim Crowther could muster was a barrage of bellowed bravos. The Spaniards had started to quarrel like lovers, sulking and pouting. It was probably time to go to bed.

'I'm an inventor,' Jim Crowther began to explain to her earlier in the evening. 'An engineer. It ain't that engineers don't know science – we maybe don't know all the equations, but we know what it's *for*. See, most of the fellows here, they think there's some kind of *deep* secret to it all. I don't know about that, and I don't much care. It's a tool, that's the way I see it. That's how it's always been. You know why people read Copernicus, all them years ago? Not to find out where the earth was and where the sun was, but so they could make better astry-logical forecasts. All them tables of numbers, they were dead handy for that. Do I care if space is absolute? Only if that helps me build a better machine.'

'What kind of machine?' Lena asked.

'You heard of Barry Vender?'

Constantin was smiling and nodding.

'No,' said Lena.

'Vender is gonna do it. He is gonna give us all the energy we want, all for free. I'm building his machines.'

'Vender was big inspiration to me,' said Constantin. 'I am engineer too, but also physicist. In Bulgaria we are too poor to choose, we have to be both. Ha ha! I am making implosion machine.'

Lena rather wished Constantin had spent the morning telling them about his implosion machine. It sounded more interesting than the Lorentz equation.

'Yeah,' drawled Crowther. 'Barry Vender don't do that no more. He's got other ideas now.'

'Is Vender coming to the conference?'

'Nope. I'm his representative on earth – Hotel Earth, that is, huh huh. Thursday afternoon, I'm gonna tell you about the Paragenerator. This thing is gonna be huge.'

'The last machine of Vender does not work,' sniffed the Greek.

'The last machine was sabotaged by the CIA. We've got this one well protected. In a few months we'll have a patent, and then they can't touch us.'

'Do you have it here?' the Greek asked.

'Nope. I'd never get it across the pond – they'd impound it in customs, and the next thing you know, it's being developed by NASA.' He pronounced it 'nay-sir'.

'Why does Vender not come here?'

'He's got a lawsuit to fight. The Patent Office is trying to dodge us. But I reckon we'll get them fixed soon enough.'

A shriek from the stage distracted him. A couple had taken the floor, and rather too literally. Crowther gave the impression of a man who considered sex a spectator sport, which was more or less how it was presented at the Roter Engel. That way, it was like television: you could dip in and out of it, and it carried on regardless.

'Whoo!' he cried. 'Thar she blows! A man could get to love this city.'

Ψ

The next morning Lena timed her arrival at the Hotel Erd to coincide with the coffee break. She hadn't shaken the headache that ambushed her as she awoke; this would have to be a coffee-fuelled day. She detected at once that something was happening at the conference – there was an urgency, a frenetic aspect to the conversations. She hoped for a moment that perhaps the stir was triggered by an announcement of Karl Neder's arrival; but that wasn't it.

'There's going to be a demonstration,' Aitchison told her.

'A protest?'

'Goodness no, not that kind. An experimental demonstration. Some chap called Pindar. Claims to have a contract with NASA. He's going to show us his anti-gravity device. Can't wait.'

'Is it possible?'

'No, it is not possible. It violates the laws of thermodynamics. It violates general relativity too, although one supposes that that's the point. It violates common sense. None of that, of course, would prevent the Americans from funding it. Ah, this is why it's good to come to these things.'

'To ridicule them, you mean?'

'Oh no. They parody themselves already. No, you see, so much of this is just talk. Words, words, words. Miraculous claims and nothing to back it up. You say to yourself, "Well, show us, then. If it's all so easy, show us." It seems that's what Mr Pindar is going to do.'

'Why *do* you come to these things? Really, I mean. I don't think it can be on the off-chance of a spectacle.'

There was a forced quality to Aitchison's smile, Lena thought.

'The curiosity is genuine,' he insisted. 'But one also likes to think of oneself as a delegate, an ambassador. Reporting back to the generals. Someone has to do it, after all.'

'Don't tell me you're just being dutiful.'

'It's quite possible to have fun with one's duty, you know.'

'*Do* you have fun? You're an outsider – everyone is wary of you, no one wants to talk to you. What did you do last night?'

He looked uneasy. 'Ha ha! Well, the Roter Engel didn't exactly appeal. Much better to have a decent meal, read a book and go to bed. But now, look, one could ask you the same question – not about last night, that's entirely your own business, but about your motivations. You might say that you want to see Karl Neder, to write your story. But Karl Neder isn't here, and it seems he isn't likely to turn up. And besides, that still wouldn't answer the question. You've asked for an opinion, and the advice you've received is that this is all utter tosh, and yet you persist with it. Why is that, one wonders?'

'That's what everyone wants to know, it seems.' And she suspected she had the first intimations of an answer. Maybe what she wanted was to be woken up. Yes – the truth was that she longed for it, but her sleep was too deathly, her carapace too thick, to be penetrated by ordinary behaviour. Discovering what had happened to Davey Flint had stirred her from her slumbers; now she was fighting towards wakefulness, and only something extreme could get her there.

But all she said to Aitchison was, 'When I find out, I'll let you know.'

Ψ

Deepak Pindar was speaking after lunch tomorrow. In the morning, Frank Symons would tell the conference about quintessence and the force of life. She realized she had been avoiding Symons. She recognized him, but doubted that he would remember her. It was possible that he had literally never seen her – he had been merely a head and shoulders at the other end of a long table during the departmental dinner two years ago, and it wasn't clear how far his vision reached. But she didn't wish to take the chance. She knew what her father would have said about her being here: some pithy dismissal of the whole enterprise. So she kept one eye all the time on the nervous, sweating figure of Frank Symons, dancing with him around the room like two particles that repelled one another.

Aware that she might snooze, she sat at the back of the lecture hall. She began to see that her suspicion was correct: fringe science conducted itself with more or less the same rituals and habits as normal science. That is to say, some of its proponents fizzed with vigour, while others droned as though being forced into a routine whose meaning had long since been forgotten. Some showed slides packed top to bottom with algebra; some showed endearing photos of their collaborators, standing in the grounds of a concrete institution or wearing woolly hats and squinting into an alpine sun. It became no clearer at all what space-time absoluteness was, or why it mattered. Breaking the fundamental laws of nature started to seem a rather wearisome business. She rose and walked the streets of Vienna, hoping to rinse her mind, but the sky had slumped down from the mountains and the air was heavy and tense.

This was more than sleep deprivation – she was coming down with something. Lena knew that she ought to seek out Jaroslav Kam and get him to feed more of his story into her notebook while she had the chance, but suddenly that seemed like an unimaginably arduous task.

By the evening she was bright with fever, her aching limbs squirming on damp sheets. She was developing the familiar obsessive mental gyrations of bodily illness; incoherent thoughts washed again and again through her listless mind like dreary surf. She began to imagine that the draining away of her energy was linked to some cosmological process, some thermodynamic exigency, which made it desperately important that she be able to understand these talks on hidden forces and secret powers. As she slumbered fitfully, she dreamed that she was being laid into Jim Crowther's machine and hooked up to wires, Frankenstein's bride waiting for the jolt that would bring her back to life.

Ψ

Someone was knocking at her door. Blearily, she groped for her watch and saw that it was only 10.15 in the evening.

'Who is it?'

'Aitchison. Missed you at dinner and wanted to see that you were OK.'

'Yes. Fine. A cold, but I'll sleep it off.'

'Aspirin?'

'No, it's past that. Just need to sleep.'

'Righty-ho.'

He was not so bad. She had been a little short with him earlier. He was just like everyone else, she thought – following his nose and rationalizing it later. Why shouldn't he escape from the tunnels of Geneva now and again? She set her alarm, with reckless optimism, for eight-thirty.

7

FRANK SYMONS WAS A PROBLEM. THERE WAS NO AVOIDING IT, George Romanowicz conceded to himself. He was going to have to do something about Symons. Before Symons became an embarrassment.

Romanowicz liked Symons. Everyone did. Symons was all shyness and stuttering and too-short trousers, but if he felt relaxed, then a sly wit began to emerge. He would choose his Greek symbols with apparent arbitrariness, until you noticed that when combined in equations they spelt out funny definitions (if you knew how to convert the Greek, which the students rarely did): $\phi^i sh.\pi$, $\gamma\Omega\delta=\infty$, and so on. He would turn the wiggles of a Feynman diagram into a lugubrious crab. He would slip into his lectures a remark from Flann O'Brien: 'This conclusion is fallacious, being based upon licensed premises.'

There was no malice in Symons. He attended parties and dinners, where like a contented mouse he nibbled at things that were put before him and asked how you were getting along, and he commiserated when your paper got rejected and admired the photos of your children. If the conversation lapsed, he would never be the one to start it again, but he seemed so happy with the silence that you didn't feel any urgency to fill it. He organized the coffee rota. He participated.

But rumours were circulating about Symons's lab. He

worked alone, and seldom had graduate students, because none of the students could figure out exactly what he did. It was low-temperature stuff – there were always empty cylinders of nitrogen and helium outside his door. Something about superfluids. Even Romanowicz, who as department head was supposed to know all that went on in the building, was unclear about this. He'd seen one or two of Symons's theory papers about Bose-Einstein condensation, and grant proposals that spoke of searching for quantum excitations, but it wasn't exactly his field.

No one expected big things from Frank. When he attended conferences, it was always by application rather than invitation. He was a footsoldier. But science needs footsoldiers as much as it needs generals. People had assumed that Symons would beaver away, freezing things colder than the cosmos and measuring their quantum spasms, until the time came for a celebratory dinner and perhaps an emeritus professorship so that he could potter around the department when the fancy took him, a mildly eccentric presence at the Friday seminar. But that was years away; Symons's age was indeterminate, but surely he was not yet in his seventh decade.

Now they were less sure. Something was up. Symons burbled and grinned and sweated as much as ever he had, but his fish-eyes seemed to lack focus. His jacket was a touch greasier. He would get up and walk out in the middle of a visiting speaker's talk, not rudely but as though he imagined it had finished. Little things, almost imperceptible – until people started talking about what he was building in his lab.

David Riess had glimpsed it one day as Symons came out of the door.

'I was just passing,' Riess told Romanowicz. 'He shut it quickly behind him, I wouldn't say furtively, exactly, but a little... deliberately. It was just a fleeting view that I had. But

George, this is the thing.' Riess seemed embarrassed. 'Inside, it seemed… it looked… like a, well, I'd have to say it looked like a church.'

'Now that is odd,' said Romanowicz urbanely. 'That is an odd way for it to strike you. I can't imagine what you mean by it.'

'No, of course not. Now that I try to reconstruct it, I'm not sure myself what I mean. For one thing, there was the light. It was dim – he is in the basement, after all. There are no windows, as you know. But this wasn't strip lighting. I can only think of one way to describe it, but it sounds absurd.'

Romanowicz waited, then realized that Riess would need a bit of encouragement before he would voice the absurd. Riess was a semiconductors man – he wasn't used to the absurd.

'I'm sure there's an explanation.'

'Yes, yes… Have you been to the abbey of St Denis in Paris?'

'Tell me about it, David.'

'It has a twelfth-century apse with the most extraordinary stained glass. Like jewellery, lots of blue. The effect is sort of gloomy, but – I'm no expert in these things, but I would have to say there is an *atmosphere* about the place. A feeling of reverence. You know me, George, I'm as much of an atheist as the next man, but if I were a medieval French peasant, I do believe I would sense the presence of God in that place.'

'And Frank's lab reminded you of that?'

'It did, yes. I feel uncomfortable even saying it, but yes, it did. The light, you see – it was like daylight coming through those windows and falling down into the chancel. The light was *coloured*, George, I'm sure it was.'

'Perhaps Frank is using lasers?'

'It wasn't like that. I use them myself from time to time. This was… it wasn't like that at all.'

'I see.'

'But there was more, George.'

Faltering, apologetic, Riess explained that he had heard noises. They were very faint, and he wouldn't like to vouch for anything, but he thought it was a kind of singing. Like a sung chant.

'Like monks at Vespers?'

'Goodness, I wouldn't know about that. I was brought up in a Quaker family. At first,' he went on, 'I thought it was a machine noise, a hum. I say "at first" – the whole thing took about three seconds, but when I think back, it all unfolds in slow motion.' Romanowicz could see that Riess was genuinely shaken, although their conversation was taking place a full week after the event. One had to remember that Riess was Anglo-Swiss, that he measured vacancy migration in germanium alloys, that he had contracts with Marconi. No wonder he wasn't used to this kind of thing.

'Perhaps that's precisely what it was – a machine.' Romanowicz briefly considered humming out loud, to see if he could make a noise halfway between a cryogenic refrigerator unit and a chanting monk, but he thought it would alarm Riess too much.

'Maybe. I wish I could believe that. But I don't think so.'

'Well,' said Romanowicz, 'we can hardly hold it against Frank that he uses strange lighting and likes listening to Benedictine chant while he works. But I suspect if that's all it was, you might not have asked to see me, David.'

'No, you're right. Those things weren't what struck me most.'

Riess was silent for some time, but Romanowicz could see frantic mental activity going on in his thinly covered cranium. He knew that when he spoke to Riess, a kind of condescension came over him. That wasn't unusual; Romanowicz was aware that he was condescending towards many people, including his ex-wife. He knew it wasn't a particularly appealing trait, but neither did he deplore it too deeply. It stemmed from the burden of insight. Romanowicz saw things more clearly than most people. It wasn't just that he understood more; that was true of most of the members of the physics department. They knew why the sky was blue, why glass was transparent, why metals gleamed, how televisions worked, what the constellations were and how far away they were, how (more or less) the universe began. But for Romanowicz – and it was not true of all his colleagues – this insight went beyond dry knowledge. Romanowicz knew that he was blessed with an artistic sensibility. He understood quality as well as quantity. His was a somewhat traditional aesthetic, he admitted that. He did not go far beyond Stravinsky, and Mondrian perplexed and irritated him. But he worked at being a cultured man, and it was not just a pose. Of course it was useful, in the circles in which he moved these days, to broaden oneself – he was keen, when at the BBC, to be perceived as more than the starchy boffin who explained the technical stuff. Yet the fact was, he was genuinely *interested*. If he thought that Boulez's atonalism was nonsense, he wanted to be able to say why. Not just to express a dislike, but to justify it. He did not like to have opinions he couldn't justify.

Riess wasn't like that. He wore a tie (Romanowicz left his collar open; occasionally his shirts were daringly collarless). He was one of those people who considered it essential to 'show the equations'. Contentment meant a life filled with careful, sober physics. And like most experimentalists, he imagined that a theorist like Romanowicz knew much, much more than him. With determined humility he'd insist that his equations were 'only a first-order approximation', even that they were 'simple-minded'. 'Marconi only wants the devices to work,' he would say.

'Has Frank been ordering equipment?' Riess had found a way in.

'I don't know about that, David. I'd have to check. His overheads are always modest.'

'Ah. I wondered if he's been having glassware made.'

'You know, that's one of the striking things about Frank. He's always blown a lot of his glass himself. I think he enjoys it.'

'Ah. There was this equipment, you see.'

'That you saw. In his lab.'

'Yes. No. I didn't exactly see it. It was only for an instant.'

'There was something strange about it, I assume.'

For a moment, Riess lapsed into silence again.

'It was towards the back, in the gloom. Made of glass. Oh, I don't know. The fact is, George, the fact is that it damn well looked to me as though it was an angel.'

Ψ

Romanowicz was well aware that his media profile was a mixed blessing. He knew that while an interview on Radio 4 might bring an invitation to give a keynote talk at the Institute of Physics Congress or the British Association Festival of Science, it would also give the heads of certain other physics departments occasion to sneer at his 'stardom'. His forte was 'the physics of everyday life'. Why bicycles don't fall over. Why fridges consume power but get colder. Why clouds form patterns. The mechanics of trees and bridges, of insect flight. The optics of rainbows.

His kind of physics used to be seen as terribly old-fashioned. It was the sort of thing Kelvin and Rayleigh did in the nineteenth century – taking a schoolboy question and developing from it an elegant train of reasoning that took all the right short cuts and ended up with a compact algebraic expression encapsulating everything important. In the 1960s and '70s that kind of thing had become passé; high-energy physics, astrophysics and cosmology had come to dominate the scene, everyone was studying quantum chromodynamics and talking about building new accelerators and X-ray telescopes. This seemed to Romanowicz to be a flight from reality, a fear of the mundane, born of a sudden misconceived optimism that we could comprehend everything.

Yet it was understandable, really. The afterglow of creation had been heard buzzing around a giant radio funnel in New Jersey, vindicating the hubris of the cosmologists. They were right about how things began, with all space and time the size of a marble. And then the question became what happened before the marble, and the only way to explore the inhuman energies of a marble-sized universe was to smash one particle into another at ever higher speeds. And everyone saw that this would eventually compel quantum mechanics to make its peace with relativity, which even Einstein couldn't arrange. The indecently small meeting the indecently large. What a marriage.

But Romanowicz was trained by James Lighthill, the Cambridge mathematician and fluid dynamicist, and his physics didn't demand any Big Bang. It was human-sized physics. Lighthill, a fanatical swimmer and intellectual omnivore, investigated how fish move, he speculated about earthquakes, he looked at the circulation of the oceans and the motion of traffic. In the year of Yuri Gagarin's flight, he talked about manoeuvrable spacecraft, and the Soviets gave him samples of lunar soil in recognition of his achievements. To Lighthill, space was not the quantum vacuum; space was another sea in which to swim.

Romanowicz began his post-doctoral work with Lighthill when he moved to Imperial College in 1964. They collaborated for five years until Lighthill returned to Cambridge to take Isaac Newton's seat at Trinity as Lucasian Professor of Mathematics. Romanowicz had thought it a sign of the times when Lighthill's successor in 1979 was a cosmologist, a young, frail and brilliant theorist named Stephen Hawking.

How Lighthill had loved the moon landings! He'd invited Romanowicz and several other of his former students up to Cambridge, where the physics department was holding a special screening in the Trinity senior common room. Lighthill opened the gathering with a word or two on the American rocket program, allowing himself a little boasting about the space science department he'd helped to create at the Royal Aircraft Establishment at Farnborough. Of course the Brits were going to come a poor third into space, he laughed, but they still had a thing or two to teach the Yanks about supersonics. He offered a bottle of wine to the first person who could make old Isaac happy by calculating the moon's gravity from the movements of the astronauts. In the end the pictures were too blurry to permit of any such analysis, and everyone forgot anyway in the euphoria of the moment.

But Romanowicz's elation at the occasion was severely tempered, because Barbara had just told him that she was leaving him.

He wasn't surprised. He didn't blame her, either. It was all his fault, anyway. His indiscretion the previous year was the most ridiculous thing, but the consequences had been shocking, and still made him wince with shame. He knew how badly he had wounded Barbara, and he had no doubt that he was getting what he deserved.

The pitiful thing was that it was precisely Barbara's resolve that made her decision harder to bear. He had always had a deep affection for her, he imagined you could call it love, but until she announced her intention he had been unable to shake off a sense of disappointment at her weaknesses.

Perhaps it was the infatuation of the first-generation immigrant with an idea of England that had brought them together in that strangest of times, with teeth still missing from the terraced gums of London and everyone not quite sure if the world was opening up or shutting down. In 1958 there was jazz in Soho, and sex and drugs too, if you knew where to go. But homes had Hoovers, and televisions, and ready-mix cakes for tea, and the schoolchildren in their caps and ties had never known war.

It was war that brought Pyotr ('Pete') and Marya ('Mary') Romanowicz to London. They fled Cracow in 1939, with the city in flames behind them. They had money when they set out, but not much remained by the time they arrived in Dover, shocked to blankness by a journey across a Europe that was holding its breath. Pyotr suspected that they might have to board ship for America before long, if they did not wish to see the swastika flying over London just as they had in Cracow. But he had no idea where they would find the resources for that.

They lived in Whitechapel, because although they were not Jewish they were used to living among Jews. And because it was cheap. Pyotr was a lawyer, but wartime Britain did not need Polish lawyers. It needed factory workers, so Pyotr worked in a munitions plant, and so, before long, did his wife. He learnt quickly, and when the war ended he joined an engineering firm, and soon he was chief engineer of microwave and radar technologies. He took immense delight in exclaiming to his son, after the Big Bang's cosmic background radiation had been reported worldwide, 'So microwave engineers have decoded the secret of the universe!'

George Romanowicz was three when his parents made their frantic dash to escape the Nazis. Since as long as he could remember he'd dreamt of sitting in a railway coach. There was no one in it but him and his parents, although they always insisted when they told their tale that it had been packed with refugees. They were speaking to one another, quietly and urgently, but in a language George did not understand (he spoke Polish fluently). He knew that it was Russian. 'Speak in Polish,' he begged them, but they simply glanced at him and continued their incomprehensible conversation. ('You'd be speaking Russian too, if we'd stayed,' his father would tell him when he related this dream. 'Stalin was not far behind Hitler. They had a tidy arrangement over Poland.')

In the 1960s, Romanowicz took to learning Russian. Like most bilinguals, he had an aptitude for languages. He already spoke German and French too, and passable Italian, and was debating whether to explore the Slavic tongues. But he figured that Russian would be useful because there was some important primary literature in fluid dynamics written in that language which would never be translated. Yet even though he advanced well in his lessons, it did not help him to understand what his parents were saying in that railway carriage as the train swept through the fathomless night.

George cultivated an accent. He sensed that the cut-glass voices on the radio set in the post-war years were going the way of the Empire, and that since he wanted mobility he would be better served by the crisp, sinewy vowels of Olivier and Guinness. It was not *upward* mobility that Romanowicz desired, or not specifically that. He was comfortable enough where he was, for his father was well paid now and they lived in smart Chislehurst and his school was a good one. It was latitude he wanted. To be able to chat easily to cabbies and executives, publicans and judges.

He idolized Olivier. He saw him on stage as often as he could, and studied the posture, the timing, the movements of the eyes. He did not for a moment seriously contemplate becoming an actor; he did not like the affectation that clung to the world of the stage, and besides, he was a little too short and a little too square for anything but character roles. But he tried to live as though rehearsing for the lead, even though so often the dialogue was utterly drab and the plotline banal. Olivier showed him that words were tools with which you could build anything; they took the ordinary and made it remarkable.

That was how Romanowicz became adept at making people feel as though something significant was happening in his vicinity. No wonder he was popular. When you spoke with him, you always knew you were getting somewhere. It was a satisfying sensation, and it meant that others sought his opinions. Where's the best club, George? Do you think Eden will go, George? Will the Russkies bomb us? What'll they do to Hungary? What did you make of *The Quiet American*?

That was the talk at Imperial in the mid-fifties: music and politics. When George met Barbara, he didn't notice at first that she said rather little about either subject. He noticed instead that she didn't smoke (he did), that her skirts were the modest side of fashionable, that she smiled often and laughed rarely. He realized, years later, that there was a strong element of narcissism in his attraction to her. She reflected him like a placid pool. She did this with subtlety; she was not a passive admirer. When they talked, she did not offer meek agreement (he would soon have gone off her if she had), but she found ways to substantiate what he said while decorating it elegantly. She took his brash arguments, spruced them up and handed them back gift-wrapped. That was how she used her intelligence. It was not, Romanowicz supposed even in the early days of their relationship, a particularly questing intelligence. He fancied to himself that English intelligence seldom was. It was the Europeans, and especially those east of Germany, who plunged in and thrashed about and pulled up pearls coated in benthic slime. They left things open-ended, untidy, half-formed. That was his inheritance, and he was pleased enough with it. But Barbara had style, calm and cultivated, a little detached. She could finish things. She had a good eye. In galleries, George would dash around pointing at this painting and that, making up theories on the spot, trying to remember dates. Barbara would find a single picture and gaze at it for ages, saying nothing either then or after.

Her surname was Babbage, and she was distantly related to Charles, the Victorian who imagined computers made from cogs and levers. She was pretty enough, and Romanowicz married her without delay, and the following year – it was 1959 by then – they had a daughter and called her Lena.

Yes, it was narcissism, Romanowicz concluded. He liked to be brutally honest with himself. He prided himself on it.

Ψ

As Neil Armstrong fluffed his inaudible lines two hundred thousand miles away, George admitted to himself that he and Barbara really couldn't have carried on. The relationship had become untenable. All those dull, clichéd phrases had sapped his energy; it was almost a relief when they'd occasionally raised their voices in anger, each building on the other's crescendo, though neither of them really knew how to do that kind of thing. 'How could you?' and so on. How could he? What nonsense we put together in the name of rhetoric. He half wished Barbara had been able to ask the right question, which was not how could, but why did. But the answer to that was more shameful than anything, he suspected, and probably she knew it already.

It was Lena, though, who had disturbed him the most. She

had overheard them arguing, and she knew more or less what the words meant. So she should do – he'd once explained them to her himself, proud that (unlike many fathers) he was able to do so, though he'd taken some respite in medical textbooks.

'This lady you loved –'

'I didn't love her, Lena. That's only for your mother.'

'I heard Mummy say you loved her.'

'No, I expect she said we *made* love. Which is different. I can see it's confusing.'

They made this love, and more than that, in Varenna on Lake Como, in the former monastery where Enrico Fermi once worked. A fool's paradise, almost comically romantic. She, however, was no raven-haired Loren, but a postdoc from Nottingham.

'Yes, well she had a baby, didn't she?'

'Oh, God. No, Lena, she didn't. That is, a baby started to grow in her, but she couldn't keep it.'

Lena gave him a hot little glare across a pile of burnt toast. He was going to have to walk her to school today, since Barbara had gone to her mother's late last night, taking the car, and George could see that the stroll would be an uncomfortable experience. He had hoped to use honesty as a shield, but she had a child's way of seeing through ingenuousness.

'I know what you thought.'

'Lena, I never wanted to hurt your mother…'

'I know, I know,' she snapped irritably, in the way she did when she felt she was being given irrelevancies. '*You thought*,' as though announcing an answer confidently in the classroom, one being recited from memory, 'that I wouldn't love the baby because it wasn't from Mummy. But I would.'

And now she was, at last, silenced by childish confusion, because she had not anticipated the tears that ran down her father's red face.

It was Frank Symons who had recommended that they ask Jaroslav Kam to Canterbury, wasn't it? Romanowicz still did not know what to make of that. Kam worked at Perugia – not the most prestigious of institutions – and he had just published a paper in *Physics Letters* that many of Romanowicz's colleagues considered to be unmitigated nonsense. Kam believed that the structure of water was dictated by quantum mechanics. The hydrogen atoms in water molecules are so small, he said, that they follow quantum rules, and there is no getting away from it. This means they are not little billiard balls, but waves, and they can all come into step and behave coherently. Water, according to Kam, is racked with the quantum shudders of hydrogen atoms moving in step, so that one part of the liquid becomes sensitive to what is happening somewhere else, *millimetres* away – which, on the scale of molecules, is like saying on the other side of the world.

To prove all of this, Kam apparently spent a lot of time at the Institut Laue-Langevin in Grenoble, firing beams of neutrons at heavy water and measuring their energy as they bounced off. He claimed to see spikes of energy that were the fingerprint of the 'quantum coherent fluctuations' of water.

It was arcane stuff, and only those like Symons, who looked at the quantum behaviour of ultra-cold fluids, really understood it. But what made people shudder was the implications Kam claimed for his findings. Water, he said, has a kind of life. In nineteenth-century terminology, it has a vital force. The coherence of the hydrogens makes water responsive to the things dissolved in it. Put in a protein molecule, and it is like sticking your finger into an anthill. The hydrogens scuttle around to accommodate this disturbance, a collective entity making itself comfortable. Pull the protein out again, and the water *remembers* what it has done. Water can be trained. It can be trained to hold onto life.

None of this appeared in Kam's paper, but it sneaked out at the end of his departmental seminar, and it shocked the sleepy audience into audible disarray. Kam mentioned homeopathy. He mentioned the origin of life. He spoke about strange magnetic effects that changed water's properties. He imagined water 'conditioned' to act as a medicine, or to repel pollution, or to store energy.

Romanowicz wondered how much of this Symons knew about when he proposed Kam as a speaker. Maybe Frank had only seen the paper in *Physics Letters*, and was as alarmed by the wild speculations as everyone else. But after speaking with Symons he was not so sure. 'The theory seemed sound,' said Frank. He could not vouch for the experiments, but Kam's collaborators at Grenoble had an excellent reputation in the neutron-scattering community. Life force? Wasn't that just a manner of speaking? Wasn't it said that Crick and Watson had found the secret of life in 1953, when all they'd actually done was deduce the corkscrew structure of a molecule? And there was surely more to life than DNA. 'Do you know,' Symons asked, 'what DNA looks like as a gas? It's as though a child has pulled and stamped on the famous double helix, you can barely recognize it. What gives this molecule its order and lets it encode life itself? Water.'

And all of this with Frank sweating and grinning and nodding his head from side to side. 'It's just a hypothesis,' he added. 'And it woke them up, didn't it? Not a bad achievement on a Friday afternoon.'

Romanowicz was not at all sure what manner of problem he was facing here. He always advocated scientific solutions to scientific problems, but when the problem clearly did not involve science, he was prepared to be eclectic. He browsed through his shelves somewhat at random, and on a whim he began to read Gombrich and Panofsky on the abbey church of St Denis. Its construction – in fact a reconstruction – was supervised by Abbé Suger in the 1140s. The abbot was an ambitious, creative man who (Panofsky insisted) almost single-handedly invented the lambent, vertical style of the Gothic tradition. He wrote that he wanted the church to 'shine with the wonderful and uninterrupted light of most luminous windows, pervading the interior beauty'.

Suger was seemingly influenced by the writings attributed to one Dionysius the Areopagite, a mysterious figure who was allegedly converted to Christianity by St Paul at Athens. This Dionysius wrote of a 'divine darkness', which he called 'that unapproachable light where God is said to live'. That, then, was what Suger was trying to emulate: a dark light, a luminous darkness that, so to speak, conjured the divine presence into the church. Through such light, men would know God.

Romanowicz suspected that he was going to have to take a walk down to the basement of his department. But that would have to wait, since Symons was going off to some conference or other.

8

LENA WAS GROGGY IN THE MORNING, BUT HER TEMPERATURE had dropped. Kam had already begun his presentation when she slipped into the hall, but even she could see that the slide now projected onto the screen was filled with old knowledge and generalities – the obligatory *bona fides*. She felt hollowed out, pithed, and her nose was streaming, but that was probably a good sign. In this weightless state, she was content to be carried along on the surface of Kam's quantum water. He showed them all a phrase from the *Tao Te Ching*: 'The highest good is like water. Water gives life to the ten thousand things.'

It was not the first time Lena had heard a scientist make an appeal to mysticism, and she suspected this was tolerated even in the most reductionist circles as a decorative flourish, a token nod to wider vistas of human understanding. But with Kam she couldn't be sure that was all he intended; he had a way of speaking that masked his destination, which had the effect of making you listen closely to everything he said, in case it turned out to be the punchline. Dimly, Lena wondered what any of this could have to do with space and time and relativity, but she had also started to see that what mattered far more was Kam's participation in what was, after all, a sort of fellowship. That was what secured his place at ICSTA '86. Despite what had seemed at first to be haughty aloofness, he spent a lot of time in a huddle with Neumann, scribbling earnestly in a little book, with Symons hovering like a gleeful amphibian at their backs. Her initial impression of hopeless disparity among the attendees was giving way to a realization that the conference was as much a celebration of a subculture as an assault on relativity.

But when Frank Symons came to the podium, Lena could see that something was happening to him. It took her several moments before she identified the nature of the change. He had become *dangerous*. When she'd seen this aura before, it was at the theatre. A character might be going about some business that seemed unremarkable, even prosaic, yet with a sense of such unpredictability that you were on the edge of your seat. There was a feral quality to it. The performer might be washing his hands after a meal, and all you could think of was the blood of a mutilated corpse running into the sink. The actor was applying a second layer of artifice, as though attempting to give a mundane meaning to actions loaded with menace. Like Richard III impersonating a shopkeeper.

What made it all the more disturbing, that March morning in the Hotel Erd, was that the other Frank Symons was still visible too – the bewildered, genial man with his brow wrinkled in eager deference. His body was twice inhabited, and the two spirits seemed to flow in and out of one another continually. Superficially there was nothing amiss: Symons's words were delivered in his habitual, slightly strangulated tone, filtered through the hint of a panicky smile. But it looked to Lena as if he was on the point of fission.

Was she still delirious? Symons appeared to be dispensing wild energy with his words, emitting it into the hall, where it created little ripples and flurries. Here there was a sudden grunt, quite outside the volition of the grunter. Somewhere in the back rows there were voices jabbering in a low mumble, excitedly yet incomprehensibly, and Lena could not make out who was talking. It sounded like an incantation. With slow and ostentatious precision, a gaunt woman whose features were concealed behind crimson-tinted spectacles cracked her fingers one by one. Symons became the conductor of an occult symphony of gestures.

'Quintessence' was, as far as Lena could make out, indeed his alternative to the ether. It was another apparition conjured from quantum theory, and Symons believed that Kam's neutron beams were detecting it at play in water. But it was not just in water; it was everywhere. Like all phantoms, it revealed itself only under conditions of extreme cold. That was when classical randomness gave way to quantum purpose. Symons described the formation of quantum fluids: liquid helium, as frigid as infinite space, suddenly started to flow with determination, refusing to be checked. It crawled up the walls of tall vessels and seeped over the rim: protoplasm infused with vital spirit. All its atoms moved together, all united, all with identical intent. This superflow, this purpose, said Symons, is mediated by the quintessence. Ours is a world of noise, of senseless trembling that obscures this single-minded beauty in the quantum world. To restore this original state requires cold – profound, primal cold.

Lena was shivering now, and it seemed to her that the temperature in the room was genuinely plummeting as Symons spoke. She glimpsed Kam, rubbing his palms together as though to cleanse them of some tenacious, contaminating film. She gripped the seat of her chair, for she had become as light as air and thought she might float away.

The tapping of desktops as Symons concluded seemed to awaken odd echoes in the upper galleries of the ballroom, setting the chandeliers chattering like leaves of ice. Then, as if by pre-arrangement, everyone stood up, not waiting for questions. Every sound seemed disjointed, each one distinct and rough-edged. Aitchison was nowhere around. 'Come to lunch,' said José, or was it Juan? The two of them seemed to have exchanged several features, creating hybrid faces that eliminated any distinctions Lena could recall from the Roter Engel. 'I'm not too well,' she replied. 'I don't think I'll eat.' 'Ah well, still you can join us.' And somehow she did, swept along in a crowd that appeared to move in a single stream to the Alten Fuchs Café on Schillerplatz, which had become the unofficial conference canteen. They were all infected with Symons's fervour, their teeth flashed and they seized on phrases from the morning's proceedings and passed them from table to table like talismans. Deepak Pindar's name was a rumour of miracles, and with it the runic whisper of a 'Novikov effect'. Still Lena had no idea what Pindar looked like, or whether he was among them already.

There was no end of wine. It splashed into Lena's glass over the barrier of her protestations, but when she sipped it she felt none the worse, so she sipped again. Someone was singing, not Constantin but a sonorous bass intoning what sounded like an Orthodox hymn. A glass was toppled, and it tinkled merrily into a thousand pieces, scattering shards of Vienna over the cobbles. A toast was raised to Sir Isaac Newton, another to René Descartes. 'Long live the coordinates!' A wiry man was demonstrating magic tricks with cards; it was not clear if he was a street performer or a scientist.

'Now let us see,' cried Neumann at last, 'if gravity can be conquered!' and with yelps and guffaws they poured back across the square and through the doors of the bewildered Hotel Erd.

Ψ

Deepak Pindar was beautiful, Lena thought sleepily.

The best thing she could do now would be to walk back to

the Neuer Markt and go to bed. After the dilations of fever, her veins felt shrivelled and empty; she was a dried-up husk, the last of her fluids draining out through her nose. It was not altogether an unpleasant sensation, and the wine had cheered her. But she was heading for collapse if this went on much longer.

Deepak Pindar was the colour of honey, and he wore an immaculate short-sleeved white shirt and a golden earring. He was a Keralan-Californian, a prize-winning surfer and a Buddhist. On the table before him was a machine that looked like an electric hotplate. The audience he faced had as many currents as the ocean; but he knew how to ride those.

It was as if he had simply materialized in their midst, an avatar of anti-gravity.

Deepak Pindar learnt physics from Richard Feynman at Caltech. He had been courted by IBM, had made millions in Silicon Valley before he was twenty-five. He set up Pindar Quantum Consultants, specializing in semiconductor electronic engineering. The company worked on components for the Venus Pioneer space programme, and then the US military started to knock on his door. Edward Teller got in touch, and he and Pindar were now looking into X-ray laser technology for Ronald Reagan's Strategic Defense Initiative. It was in the early 1980s that Pindar had come across the Novikov effect. Vladimir Novikov was a Soviet physicist who claimed that superconductors could shield objects from gravity. When the news filtered west, a small team of researchers at NASA's Marshall Space Flight Center in Huntsville, Alabama, was detailed to find out if there was anything in it. The Soviets had already stolen a march, it seemed, and NASA was panicked – which is why word soon leaked to NASA Ames at Moffett Field and then to the Jet Propulsion Laboratory, the central processing unit of the US space missions, from where it diffused into all of West Coast aeronautics.

This much was related in Pindar's opening remarks; but the room seemed on the point of being overwhelmed by other forces. People were bustling back and forth to gather drinks, but few came from the jugs of iced water. Several bottles of wine had been carried back from the Alten Fuchs and were now being passed freely along the rows. A low mutter pervaded the hall, which, formerly chilly, was getting warmer by the minute. Ties were loosened, jackets removed. Thermal fluctuations of a universe approaching its critical point.

Pindar beamed benignly on this gathering chaos as if blessing it.

'Do you remember the first men in the moon?' he asked, and his slide made it plain that he was not speaking of Armstrong and Aldrin. The engraving showed Edwardian gentlemen gazing in wonder at a large spherical contraption.

'Do you remember Cavorite?', for that was how Wells's heroes had fled the earth. Pindar then summoned up a photo of Apollo 11, a giant canister of explosive with men in its nose. 'No wonder we gave up on long-distance space flight, because our rockets have spent themselves by the time they've broken the planet's skin.' Titters around the room. More buttons popped open.

Lena dimly remembered something else from *The First Men in the Moon*. When Cavorite was unmasked from its lead casing, the air above it became weightless and immediately ascended into the sky: the disk was like an air cannon, creating an updraft that threatened to unleash a maelstrom. She looked at the electric hob. Were they all about to be sucked into a vortex and flung into orbit? She sniggered, and the man next to her, a portly Belgian, awoke to snigger in sympathy.

She lost track of Pindar, whose slides were apparently

depicting the theoretical mechanics of his device. The muttering was like a low moan, some elemental resonance from the bowels of the Hotel Earth. And above it, another sound, higher in pitch. Like a choir.

People seemed to be clambering over seats; a few missiles were hurled. She remembered nights when she was young in which she would wake up to a portentous silence and her bed was swimming, the bedroom walls streaming with retinal flashes, everything in motion, and she would lie there for a long time, thinking, 'Is this real? Is this real?'

There were José and Juan, faces now fully interchanged, shirts open to the waist like tattered toreadors. Jaroslav Kam was a shadow stalking the aisles, counting heads as if patrolling his flock, or assessing the toll for the slaughterer's axe. Nearby there was a sound like a woman weeping. It really was a choir, for God's sake! A heavenly host.

A cry that made even Pindar stop, poised as he was over the dials of his machine. The hall, as laboriously baroque as everything else in this building, was overlooked by a series of small galleries, no bigger than theatre boxes. Pindar was looking over the heads of everyone to the gallery at the back of the hall. Eyes swung round in unison, and standing on the railing was Frank Symons, and behind him, an angel.

An angel made of glass, a vitreous Epstein, wings sparkling with glass bars, rubber tubing twisting like aviator's webbing around its frame. And Symons, looking without his spectacles like a naked, vulnerable thing, a mole-like creature crawled out from under the ground and blinking in the sunlight, his eyes unused to seeing and focused on the vanishing point.

'Gravity will be overcome!' he cried. 'The world of noise will be overcome! We will return to the quintessence!'

And he jumped.

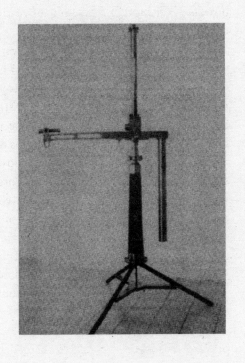

EXPERIMENTS

9

With my mother, Dora, and my brother, István, in the street of the house of my father in Győr, Western Transdanubia. When I tell people I am from Hungary, they always think I say I am from Budapest! Győr is the halfway point on the road from Budapest to Vienna, so it is the fulcrum of the link of East to West in Europe.

The father of Dora was a rich man who owned much land in the Carpathian Basin. His name was András Kovacsy, and I remember him as the 'old aristocracy' of Austro-Hungaria. Once he took me as a small boy for a ride around his estates, and the decrepitude of the peasant farmers struck me deeply. It is hard now for us to think that these were nearly feudal times for my country.

Only on very few occasions I saw my grandfather András, for my mother broke from her family when she married my father Gábor. It was bad enough that his family name sounded German – like all good Hungarian nobles, Kovacsy was anti-Habsburg. But my father was also from Jewish parentage and he fell in with the Communists. András, of course, supported Horthy's rightists. I had also two uncles on my father's side, whose names were Lukacs and Kristof, and an aunt, Bertuska. They were taken to Stalin's gulags under Rakosi in the 1950s, and perished there.

My mother has studied the history of art in Munich during and after the First World War. It is why she chose for me a German name; but maybe also to spite her father, who did no longer speak with her. I think my father agreed to this name because of being a good Communist with a copy of Das Kapital on his shelf, though I never saw him read it. Dora spoke not only German fluently, but Russian and French, and she had a beautiful voice and sang on the piano the Lieder of Schubert and Schumann, and also Russian romances and Transylvanian airs. She did not care for Bartók or Kodaly, but was a passionate Wagnerian. Her greatest delight was to hear classical music. I do not remember my mother ailing, and she never in her life visited a dentist.

*

My native house in Győr, on Kun Béla Street. Béla Kun was one of the great heroes of the 1919 Commune, a revolutionary, a Communist, a disciple of Lenin, a Carpathian Jew. This picture is from around 1952, when my mother was still alive. She lived here with István, but then I was studying in Budapest.

This is in the old style of Győr. Before the Second World War parts of the town were very beautiful, even though much industry moved there in the nineteenth century. It was because of the factories that the town was bombarded heavily by the Allies – and not only them – and barracks and workshops were destroyed but also many parts of the inner town were ruined. My mother and father would once go for coffee into many cafés and restaurants, and Győr was like a small Budapest, which was itself called the Paris of the East. But all this was wrecked by the bombs, and the historic place became very grey and cold, and full of cars and lorries.

Now there is much rebuilding and restoration, and there are again courtyards and squares and markets. The family house escaped destruction and demolition, and it is still there. For many years my father's nephew Tamás Neder lived there, but he died in 1979. I would

have inherited the place, but already I was deprived of
Hungarian citizenship and accused of being anti-
Communist, and the family house was confiscated by
the government.

The Bitter Road to Truth, Volume IV

Dora Kovacsy did not flourish by choosing Gábor Neder over her father. Gábor drank heavily, and when things went badly for him, as they often did, Dora would suffer for it. István and Karl would hear the noises and they would weep, resolutely playing their boys' games all the while. This went on until István reached ten years of age, and decided it was no longer proper that he should cry. Karl, who was two years younger, was determined that he should follow István's example, and when his eyes began to prick he would launch himself at his brother and they would roll around on the boards, pulling and punching and neither of them sure whether this was just play-fighting or something else.

Gábor's furies would sometimes incite him to strike his sons, but on the whole they knew well enough when to steer clear of him. Yet if he was in good spirits, he was then so heroic that this too would bring tears to Karl's eyes, and he would cheer spontaneously. Gábor made his boys feel that they were distinguished colleagues; he would bring them all tea and say, 'It is time for a talk.'

'Well, my men,' he would say, 'we are heading for a battle. Are you with me?' And they yelled that they were.

'Who are we fighting?' István asked.

'We may have to fight the regent,' said Gábor.

'But the regent is the king!' Karl exclaimed, and was at once plunged into confusion.

'No, Horthy is not king, not yet,' Gábor laughed. 'And he will only be a puppet king. You see him among the brown shirts, but all he has is a brown nose. He applauds what the barbarians did in Vienna, and would like to see the same thing happen here.'

The boys did not know what the barbarians had done in Vienna, or who the barbarians were, but they sounded very bad.

'Listen, men,' said Gábor. 'One day people may ask you if you are Jewish. And you are to say that you are not. This is not a lie. I have never brought you up to be Jewish, and I know myself that there is no God. So there is no point in your suffering for the sake of something that is not true. Some of us, whether we like it or not, may have to fight for the Jews, and I'm ready for that. But that is for me to do, not you. I am closer to the past, you see.'

'Some boys beat up a Jew at school,' said István. 'They said he was stealing from them.'

'That is what they will always say,' Gábor growled. 'You know, my men, I am not an educated person, my father was a farmer, but I have heard a thing or two. There was once a very famous painter of Italy called Leonardo, and he was painting a great picture of Jesus and his disciples taking their last supper together. Now, I won't have you believing any of that claptrap about Jesus being the son of God, but never mind about that. So Leonardo wanted a man to sit for him and pretend to be Jesus so that he could paint him, and he found just the man in the city where he worked, which was a place called Florence. And then he went on and painted the other disciples, and finally he came to the last of them, who was Judas.'

'Judas betrayed Jesus for thirty pieces of silver,' Karl said involuntarily, as if a button had been pushed. He blushed.

'That's right. And people say that Judas was the typical Jew, treacherous and always out for money. So, Leonardo searches all of Florence for a man who looks like this Judas to serve as his model, and finally he finds one and he paints him. And then the man tells Leonardo that he is happy to be his model again, and Leonardo sees that he has used the same man as he did for Jesus.'

Karl thought furiously about that, trying to root out the wisdom of this tale. He formulated several theories about it, but was not confident of any of them, and did not wish to risk seeming foolish.

'Are the Germans our enemies?' István asked.

Gábor frowned. 'Well, Hitler is not Germany. It was not Hitler's country that your mother went to, or that Karl's name comes from. But if Horthy invites the Germans to Hungary, then yes, I suppose they will be our enemies. Them and Horthy and Bethlen, and most of all, the Arrow Cross' – now names, just names to the boys.

'Do we have any friends?'

'Allies, you mean? Maybe we do. Maybe the Russians will come to our aid. Or maybe Great Britain.'

'I would like to go to America,' said Karl. 'Will America fight?'

'Who knows? Perhaps the whole world will join in.'

And so when the German army entered Hungary on its way to attack Yugoslavia, István and Karl joined the other local boys who went out to harass the convoys of soldiers. They absorbed, without understanding, the outrage of the grown-ups, who felt that by granting Hitler passage and reneging on the pact of friendship with Yugoslavia, Horthy and the Prime Minister Pál Teleki had allowed their country to be exploited disgracefully. But that was never what Teleki had planned, and in despair he shot himself.

As the German trucks moved across the marshy plain west of Győr, they found the roads blocked by fallen trees or scattered with broken bottles. Their windscreens were struck by stones that arced out of nowhere, shattering them into hails of cubed light. Tyres would mysteriously deflate overnight. One of the boys' favourite tricks was to unscrew the petrol caps of the trucks and pour in a bag of sugar, and then return in the early morning before school to watch the fun as the Germans tried to start the vehicles up. The Hungarian Communists did not dare mount any armed resistance to the might of the Nazi troops, but they turned a blind eye to the pranks of their sons, who could pass through the country at night like earth sprits. The Germans, meanwhile, would not consider these tricks serious enough to warrant reprisals that might risk radicalising the otherwise compliant locals; but still they seethed as their carefully mounted night watches and advance scouts were powerless to prevent the damage.

Some soldiers took the view that their best option was to befriend the Hungarians, many of whom were positively eager to welcome these smart and disciplined troops. The Hungarian fascists took pride in hanging the red, white and black emblem of Hitler's Thousand Year Reich from the windows of their houses and town halls – they quickly discovered that if the flags were draped from tree branches out of town they would be stolen, or defaced, or replaced with the Hungarian national flag or even the hammer and sickle.

István and Karl were not on any sabotage errand when a tank convoy rumbled past the village of Szabadhegy on the outskirts of Győr. The boys were playing football with an old tennis ball as the motorcycles and sidecars coughed their way over the hill. They stood by the side of the road while a column of tanks shook the countryside. How invincible they looked, Karl thought, and he began to understand why the boys' night-time raids were tolerated – they were merely an itch on the gargantuan rump of the Nazi leviathan. It was April 1941.

After the tanks came a gaggle of grey cars in the blocky,

sheet-metal style that looked at the same time both flimsy and ruthlessly efficient. One of them stopped, and the driver threw down an oilskin so that he could lie on his back and stick his head under the chassis. The two passengers climbed out and stood to one side, lighting cigarettes. They looked up at the boys and smiled.

Karl smiled back without thinking, then stole a glance at István and found he could not read his brother's face. A soldier strode towards them and spoke in German. The sounds were familiar – Karl had heard enough Schubert to recognize the broad vowels and clipped consonants, and the language was not uncommon in the coffee houses of Győr. But he didn't understand a word. The soldier gestured at the convoy disappearing up the road, and laughed.

Then he looked back at the car, stepped forward in a more conspiratorial manner and uttered a word whose meaning could not have been more clear: 'Schokolade.' The soldier took out a foil-wrapped packet from the leather case on his belt. He broke off a piece of the crumbly bar and munched on it, then snapped off another two lumps.

István's expression had not changed; it was as though he was trying to work something out. As the German held out his chocolate, Karl's brother stepped back, and it all became a slow, choreographed movement, with the soldier coming forward at exactly the same pace as István sought to retreat, until at precisely the same instant both of them quickened their motions, and as István bent his legs to spring, he was grabbed by the collar.

He was eleven then, and a tall boy, but never an especially strong one: his lanky frame promised endurance, not power. So he was captured rather easily, though he swung his arms frantically to break the grip that held him. All the while Karl looked on as horror flooded through his limbs and turned them stiff. István spat and cursed in ways that Karl had never heard before – not, at any rate, from his brother.

The driver pulled out his head from under the vehicle, and he and his other passenger looked on with mild interest. The driver accepted a cigarette from his companion.

Now the soldier had got István in a grip from behind, so that he could pin back both of the boy's arms with just one of his. He was dragging István to the side of the road.

I could run, Karl thought. I could run into the village and tell the people that my brother is about to be shot, and they would come with rifles and axes and scare these men away. Or I could help István, because this German couldn't cope with two of us. And then his friends would shoot us both.

But Karl didn't move. He stood and watched as the soldier grabbed István's scarf with his free hand and pulled it into a knot. He is going to strangle my brother, thought Karl.

That wasn't quite it, however. The soldier called out something to his colleagues, and the other passenger called back languidly. Another shout, which even Karl understood: 'Kommen sie!' And the other man slowly rose and sauntered over.

At last Karl's voice came, and he yelled, 'Let him go!' He was dismayed to hear it emerge as a sob, and to feel his eyes all swollen and blurred. The two men looked at him with curiosity, as though they hadn't known he was there, and their faces were suddenly featureless, just pale ovals beneath their helmets. Then they turned away and continued with their work. The first soldier kept István's arms pinned to his sides, although the boy was trying to kick and squirm. He hoisted István into the air, and his colleague grabbed the free end of the scarf and passed it over a low branch, just high enough to reach. He knotted the scarf around the branch, and then they let István go.

They have hung him, Karl thought. They have hung my brother.

But his brother was still kicking. He clawed at the scarf, which had been firmly tied around his neck. It would not have been hard to undo it, for someone who was not panicked and choking. The soldiers stood there for a moment, watching the boy writhe, and the first soldier said something to him. Now they will shoot me, Karl decided, but they did not even look his way. They walked back to the car, climbed in, and drove off, having seemingly lost all interest in this little scene.

A sound like a gunshot ripped through the retreating growl of the Volkswagen engine, and Karl waited for a bullet to tear into the back of his head. But the crack was the noise of the branch breaking, and István plunged to the ground. He did not move, but Karl could see he was far from dead. His back was heaving. Still rooted to where he stood, Karl began to weep.

They walked back into town, and István's eyes too were reddened by tears, unseen by Karl.

'It's nothing.'

'I thought they would kill you.'

'Well, they didn't.'

'Papa will kill them now.'

'No, he won't. Because we aren't going to tell him about it.'

Karl pondered this. Dimly he sensed that already his brother was entering that adult realm where things were said and done for reasons beyond his grasp.

'I didn't help you,' he said.

'Of course not. What could you do? They were soldiers, and they had guns. We're only Hungarian boys.'

'That doesn't matter. I should have done something.'

'Not much point. Forget it.'

But Karl knew what his brother's eyes were saying: that he,

Karl, could not be relied on, that he had no power to make a difference.

When Germany occupied Hungary in March 1944, the Hungarian fascists seized the opportunity. As the Russians advanced on Budapest, Horthy bungled his attempts to make peace with the Communists and withdraw from his alliance with Hitler. In October the Germans deported him and put in his place Ferenc Szalasi, leader of the Arrow Cross. Now there was no more of Horthy's half-hearted anti-Semitism; Szalasi introduced a reign of terror. Jewish families were loaded onto trains bound for Auschwitz and Birkenau, or simply hanged from lamp posts or gunned into the Danube. Communists too were murdered without restraint. Gábor became a leader of the left-wing resistance, and at night he and his fellows fought battles with the Nazis among the ruins of their city.

But Gábor was wrong about the Russians. They did not rescue Hungary, because Hungary had become the enemy. The Red Army besieged Budapest, shooting at anyone unwise enough to be out in the streets looking for food. The 'liberators' shelled houses without asking who was inside, and they robbed and raped without restraint.

In Győr such depredations were rare, but the city itself was broken. Once again it warranted the name the Turks had given it in the sixteenth century, after its leaders had set fire to it rather than yield it to the eastern invaders: Janik Kala, 'burnt city'. Allied aircraft thrummed overhead almost daily as the war dragged on wearily towards the final curtain, a bloody play in which everyone had lost interest. There was no one in the city who did not know a family of the dead. Karl, István and their friends learned to speak of the casualties as though they had simply moved away.

'Albert Esterházy went last Tuesday, when they hit Bécsi kapu Square.'

'Albert? The redhead?'

'That's him. His mother's still here. She was out at the time.'

'Posh Mrs Esterházy! That's too bad.'

Food became hard to find. Karl would cycle out of town to buy bread and milk in the villages, but often the soldiers had taken it all. That, now, was the main point of being a soldier: it made it slightly easier to eat if you had a gun. The military attire no longer seemed to be linked to the war, although sometimes the troops fired at one another. But even a uniform carried ever less authority. German and Hungarian soldiers were sometimes shot dead by villagers protecting their fields, their livestock, their families. No one dared shoot the Soviets, however, so they ate best, if not exactly well. People laid out salt and bread for them on their kitchen tables, believing that the Russians understood this as a sign of peace.

It was not uncommon for Karl to pass dead bodies on his excursions. They looked like old men asleep in the hedgerows. Mostly, they'd been stripped of anything valuable, including belts and boots. But if they looked fresh enough he might risk a quick search himself, and once or twice he salvaged chocolate rations. He never ate them, but he gave them to his family. István devoured German chocolate with a passion.

10

Then one day the war ended and the bombs stopped falling. Nothing else changed. The Russian soldiers were still there. Food was still scarce. But the Neder family did not fare so badly, because Gábor was now a hero. He was a member of the Communist Party, and he was put in charge of rebuilding the heavy engineering factories, although he was not an engineer. All the time people would visit the Neders at Kun Béla Street, and they would bring gifts of a loaf or some eggs. At first Gábor seemed mildly embarrassed by this, but then he got used to it. He would entertain his guests with brandy and Russian vodka, and now the boys would be given a small glass of the stinging liquid to drink with the visitors. On such nights, they would all implore Gábor to tell tales of his exploits with the Resistance; hard-fought skirmishes and breathtaking escapes were re-enacted in the kitchen.

On other days a black mood settled on Gábor, and the house was tense and muted, as though it harboured some awful secret. Karl's mother would scold him and his brother abruptly, and tell them to go and visit their uncles. Karl did not understand why his father, a minor local celebrity after all, seemed so troubled.

He went to school for the first time in his life, and there was nothing he was taught that he did not simply absorb as though the information was filling spaces that had been long waiting for it. Within weeks, he could locate any country on the globe. He seemed already to have a thorough grasp of basic arithmetic, although he could not recall ever having been told about it before. Logarithms and cosines lodged in his memory, four significant digits within easy reach. The children studied Russian, and they'd heard enough of it all around them to be conversing tentatively within a few months, to the delight of their teacher, who had been forced to abandon his beloved Latin and retrain in the language of the future.

But nothing took hold of Karl the way his science classes did. Miklós Halász had a lot to do with that, because he was not like any other teacher at the István Szechenyi high school. He came to his classes wearing a flying jacket, and said he had been a pilot for the Allies. He walked with a limp, because (he explained) he had been shot down over Italy, where he was rescued by goatherds in the foothills of the Apennines.

Halász asked his boys if steel could float, and then proved them all wrong by placing a needle carefully on the surface of a bowl of water, dimpling the clear skin. He scattered iron filings to show them the occult patterns of magnets, and let them feel the thrilling shock of electricity from the plastic comb he pulled through his long hair. He mixed ammonia and iodine, detonating at a light touch the filter paper he soaked in the purple-brown residue. His intentional sloppiness with the mixture made the floor crackle underfoot for days. The fact was, he was a magician who had penetrated to the secrets of the world. The boys worshipped him.

There was not much for a child to study in post-war Győr, but Karl learned whatever he could. In the library there was little that could be called 'science' beyond a few old Russian books on electronics, yet he read them, although they were never intended as textbooks, less still for schoolboys. He rummaged among the ruins of offices and workshops, despite the shouted warnings of the Soviet soldiers and the local police-men, and sometimes he would find the smashed remains of old wireless sets, which he would dissect hungrily for their components. His father agreed to find him a soldering iron, and he began to construct circuits from the Russian diagrams, often with no real idea of what he was making. Perhaps a machine that could establish contact with America?

Karl Neder was proud of his scholarly prowess. In secret, he drew up ranking tables of his classmates in each subject, and frequently he'd feel warranted in placing himself at the top – but never without careful justification. It troubled him slightly to find that he was often unable to place István any-where near the top; indeed, his brother, who was in the same class as him (the school made only crude age distinctions), sometimes came distressingly low in an honest ranking. But István did not seem very concerned about his studies; he'd often go along with their father on factory business, and from time to time accompanied him to Party meetings in the evenings. The two of them would sit and talk about local political matters over vodka, an activity from which they seemed to derive little pleasure.

That was how it came to be, in the years after the war, that Karl found himself more and more in the company of his mother. She would sing songs to him, especially when his brother and father were out in the evenings, and those would be the best of times. Karl himself never learned to sing, nor to play the piano; in fact, music confused him. He would get snagged on the melodic intervals, one after the other in rapid succession. He'd rather have heard these pitch-steps in isol-ation, one by one, like so many distinct objects that could then be compared and contrasted. As music, they became like a stream of numbers passing too quickly to be deciphered.

It was not that he lacked an aesthetic sensibility. He shared his mother's passion for German poetry, for Rilke and Schiller and Goethe. He could be moved to tears by the lyrics of a Schubert song. But when his mother sang, it was not the sad melodies that sent him into a rapturous daze, but the sound of her voice. He'd listen as if trying to strip the music out of it, to hear it as mellifluously spoken verse, its rising and falling tones simply a variety of emotional expression.

His father and mother were both somewhat short and stout, and Karl could see that his own limbs were growing into the same proportions. Stocky, with a certain power. His thick fingers struggled to handle delicate resistors and embed them in tiny blobs of solder. But they learned to manage that.

In 1949, Gábor Neder was arrested. It happened just like that. One day he was superintendent of the Kardosz Generator Factory, the next he was gone. Dora Neder received a note from the police saying that he had been taken in for questioning. There was no indication of the nature of the questions, and when Dora went to the police station they were polite but implacable in their determination to reveal nothing more.

'It is a routine matter. We expect your husband will be free to return home in a day or so.'

But a day passed, and then a week, and there was no word.

It was February, grey as ashes in cold Győr. Hungarian politics now had just a single party, the Communists, who called themselves the Hungarian Workers' Party, led by the legendary Matyas Rakosi. All the other leftist parties, the people were informed, had not been disbanded, but had merged with the Communists. So the impending elections could have only a single outcome. Yet Rakosi was taking no chances. Anyone suspected of fomenting opposition to the forthcoming People's Republic was rounded up and imprisoned. Of course, one did not actually have to be an enemy of Rakosi; rather, this was an opportunity for local score-settling and for ambitious persons to prove their worth to the Party by denouncing 'traitors'. Gábor Neder had been a Party member since the early days, when the Communists were illegal; but that was no defence. In fact, it made him all the more suspect, since old members had old ideas, and things had changed. The old Communists were nationalistic and socialist, but what mattered now was how closely one's ideas and priorities matched those in Moscow. The country was about to join the economy of the Soviet bloc, and from his villa on Svabhegy, the now ironically named Liberty Hill in old Buda, the Stalinist General Bielkin looked out over the city like the governor of a foreign outpost.

There was a 'cadre file' on every citizen, filled with personal details and appraisals of character. And apparently, something in Gábor's file was unsettling to the new Party rulers. They did not like war heroes. That is to say, they did not like war heroes who were not Matyas Rakosi, and who thereby suggested that there might be others as heroic as him. Besides, heroes tended to be inflexible, unmalleable; useful in wartime, they were seldom good citizens.

Hadn't Gábor spoken at one Party meeting in favour of political opposition? That's what it said in his file. Was that why he had been arrested? In truth, the police in Győr were not sure what the reasons were. The ignorance they professed at the questions of Gábor's wife was not entirely feigned.

When he had still not returned home after ten days, Dora decided that she would have to step up her campaign. She pestered the police every day for a week. Sometimes Karl went with her after school. He was not sure whether his mother brought him along in order to look after him, or whether he was there to offer support to her. In the evenings she cried, but only briefly and without fuss. István did not come on these expeditions – he stayed at home and looked sullen.

On each occasion, the duty officer told her, 'I'm afraid there is no more we can tell you yet; you will have to try tomorrow.' But on their seventh visit, Dora and Karl did not receive this standard response. Instead, they were told to wait, and fifteen minutes later a man came out who was not one of the regular police staff. He was short, with a long, sloping forehead, laid bare of the hair clustering around his temples which, though meagre, was still black. He had a professorial appearance, one might even say intellectual. He asked them to come through to a cubicle.

'The question is,' he began, 'are you prepared to denounce your husband?'

'And why should I do that? Has he committed some crime?'

'We have good reason to believe that he was plotting against the best interests of the Party. This makes him a destabilizing element and an enemy of the people.' The little man said these things entirely without heat, in fact without even a hint of disapproval. The phrases seemed almost to bore him.

'What is your evidence for that, Mr –?

'Mr Mólnar. Actually, Dr Mólnar, but there is no need for that. I represent Deputy Premier Rakosi here. Mrs Neder, the fact is that the charges against your husband are really quite serious. It will not help you at all to be associated with them. It is possible, of course, that you were unaware of your husband's activities. If that is so, there is surely no shame in denouncing him and clearing the name of your family, since you would obviously have condemned these things had you known about them. All you need do is sign a declaration confirming his guilt.'

Karl's mother seemed to him to expand in all directions.

'Mr Mólnar, my husband risked his life in the war as a member of the Communist resistance. This is known to you. That is all I have to say.' She stood up to leave.

'And you?' Mólnar said unexpectedly. He was looking at Karl. 'What do you say about your father's criminal activities? Are you ready to denounce him?'

Karl had imagined himself to be invisible, and now finding that he was very much a part of the scene filled him with confusion.

This is what he thought of. About six months before, his father and István had returned late from a meeting, and he had been playing chess with his mother. But his father had not entered the room where they sat. He stood in the doorway, and István stopped at his side, slightly unsure where to put himself.

'That's a good game,' said Gábor, and instantly his voice told Karl two things: that he'd been drinking heavily, and that he was dangerous that night.

'Karl plays well,' his mother replied, weighing each word before she voiced it. 'He usually beats me now.'

'*He* beats you? Well, well. He's a clever boy. You're a clever boy, Karl.'

Karl did not want to look at his father. He kept staring at the board.

'You know the moves, don't you, Karl? I could never learn them all. Too many things to think about at once. I was always too impatient.'

'You often beat me –' Dora began.

'Yes, I did, didn't I? So I did. But that didn't prove anything. It didn't prove I was any good. I was just stronger and more stubborn. All those careful moves of yours, all those strategies...'

'Time to put it away,' Karl's mother said softly to him.

'Don't put it away,' Gábor said. 'Let's see if, with Karl's help, I can beat you now.'

'He should go to bed,' Dora said. 'He has school in the morning.'

Gábor walked slowly across the kitchen. No one said anything. He reached the table, and stood staring at the pieces. Karl could hear his father's breathing, an unsteady bellows.

'You'd better go to bed,' he whispered to his son.

There was more to the exchange between Gábor and Dora, half-heard from the boys' attic bedroom, but that much is what Karl now recalled.

'Do you denounce him?'

'Come with me.' His mother took his hand, as though he were a much younger child, and led him from Dr Mólnar's cubicle.

She wrote letters, and got no reply. She made further visits to the police station, but Mólnar was never there. She wrote to the mayor of Győr, who sent an unctuous reply. She even wrote to Deputy Premier Rakosi. But Gábor Neder did not come home for four years.

Ψ

In 1950 Karl went to study at the University of Budapest. This should never have been possible for the son of a convict, but Miklós Halász had made some wise friendships in the academies, he knew how to use his charisma and reputation, and so it happened that certain facts were not disclosed to the university authorities.

Yet Karl found no replacements for his schoolteacher in Budapest, no wizards in flying costume. He sat through dry lectures on advanced calculus and circuit theory and nuclear science. He discovered things that Halász had never mentioned, and chief among them were relativity and quantum mechanics.

Karl could not remember any moment when he had felt devastated about his father's disappearance. At first, it had been merely baffling, as well as forcing him to worry about his mother. Then by degrees it had come to seem like the normal state of affairs, and any disquiet it might have awakened was in any case set aside while he and Dora struggled to cope with István's increasing taciturnity and waywardness. Karl's older brother continued to work at the generator factory as a shop foreman, even though he was only seventeen years old when he started. But he would often go drinking after work, and roll in so late that his mother and brother were already in their beds. In the morning István would do little more than mumble and grunt his way through a glass of coffee before leaving again for work.

No, Karl had not felt any pain at losing his father that compared with the pain he experienced when he first attended lectures on quantum theory. They followed the standard pattern, beginning with the difficulties that physicists encountered when trying to use Maxwell's electromagnetic theory to explain thermal radiation. The result was a catastrophe: the ultraviolet catastrophe, the prediction of an insane explosion of energy that should have made even tepid bodies more incandescent than the sun.

Then there was the photoelectric effect: electrons being knocked out of metals by a ray of light. If the light's wavelength were short enough, these subatomic particles were ejected like spray from the fall of a pebble into water. Above that threshold wavelength, where the rays carried less energy, there was nothing. This didn't make sense, until Albert Einstein showed what was going on. He seized on the mathematical trick devised by Max Planck to fox the ultraviolet catastrophe, and asked everyone to take it literally. Planck's quantized energy steps were not, in Einstein's view, a convenient fiction but a part of the real world. Energy really did come in packets.

Neder was dismayed most of all by what this did to light. It was shattered. Light was no longer a beautiful beam, a wave stretching from here to infinity. Light was quanta. Light was discrete. Light was particles. Call them photons. These photons won Einstein a Nobel Prize.

But Neder could no longer sit in the sun without feeling he was being showered with fine grains. The sun was a sand-blaster. The stars were tiny pea-shooters. The moon was a springboard for little shards that stung his eyes. The cosmos had come apart.

What was most distressing of all was that the world of Miklós Halász was not like this. It did not contain this awful fragmentation. Halász had simply not spoken about it; apparently he had felt no need for quanta. Neder could not understand how a man like Halász could co-exist with a quant-ized universe.

At first he dismissed his university lecturer as a fool, a dupe taken in by some fancy new idea that would not stand the test of time. But all of his fellow students bought it at once. Worse, they embraced it. Quanta left them buzzing with excitement, they could barely talk about anything else. Neder slunk away to the library, where he felt sure he would discover some robust arguments to counter the absurdity. But with mount-ing shock, he found nothing but blithe acceptance. Before the twentieth century, the textbooks persisted with the solid con-tinuity of Maxwell's theory, with its smooth curves and unbroken differentials. Then suddenly, about fifty years ago, they began to reformulate everything in quantum terms, never so much as demurring at that insidious $E = h\upsilon$. All of a sudden

Planck's infernal constant was everywhere, and the mysteries of matter were written in the prevaricating probabilities of Schrödinger's wave mechanics. And there seemed to be nothing to herald the change – no debate, no discussion, just a party line like the one he had been given in the lecture hall. Einstein had pronounced, and everyone had acquiesced.

Of course, Neder knew what Einstein looked like. He'd seen the famous physicist's unkempt whiskers in the newspapers in the month the war ended, and the headlines had spoken of an unimaginable weapon that could wipe cities from the globe in a flash, just as the German professor would wipe his unintelligible equations from the blackboard.

These stories, Neder recalled, had come with another algebraic talisman, echoing the fateful $E = h\upsilon$. He looked in the library archives back to 1946, and was astonished to find a dog-eared copy of *Time* magazine that the Party librarians had somehow overlooked. There was Einstein on the cover, his sad clown's face presiding over a mushroom cloud. And here was his slogan, imprinted on the blast: $E = mc^2$.

With the help of a dictionary, he decoded the cover's caption: 'All matter is speed and flame'.

Yes, Neder had some inkling of the claim: energy is mass, the proportions governed by the awesome square of light's speed. This c^2, Neder came to understand, was the ubiquitous trope of relativity. The equations of Einstein's theory were full of c^2. They were scattered with the ratio v^2/c^2, which insisted that speeds were irrelevant unless they could almost match the pace of photons.

Unnerved, Neder asked his tutors about Einstein's relativity, and, smiling at what they took to be his earnest enthusiam, they directed him back to the university library, where there was a shelf sagging under the weight of heavily bound copies of the German journal *Annalen der Physik*. He pulled out issue 17, from 1905, and found the page: 'Zur Elektrodynamik bewegter Körper'. On the electrodynamics of moving bodies, by A. Einstein. Karl knew a little German by then, but there were many unfamiliar words that sent him often to the dictionary, and it was slow work.

'It is known,' Einstein said,

> that Maxwell's electrodynamics – as usually understood at the present time – when applied to moving bodies, leads to asymmetries which do not appear to be inherent in the phenomena. Take, for example, the reciprocal electrodynamic action of a magnet and a conductor. The observable phenomenon here depends only on the relative motion of the conductor and the magnet, whereas the customary view draws a sharp distinction between the two cases in which either the one or the other of these bodies is in motion. For if the magnet is in motion and the conductor at rest, there arises in the neighbourhood of the magnet an electric field with a certain definite energy, producing a current at the places where parts of the conductor are situated. But if the magnet is stationary and the conductor is in motion, no electric field arises in the neighbourhood of the magnet. In the conductor, however, we find an electromotive force, to which in itself there is no corresponding energy, but which gives rise – assuming equality of relative motion in the two cases discussed – to electric currents of the same path and intensity as those produced by the electric forces in the former case.

As he plodded on laboriously, Karl's heart sank. He understood what Einstein was saying, and it seemed obviously true. Yet it was a problem he had never noticed. Like any student of physics, he had studied Faraday's electromagnetic induction, the principle of the dynamo and the electric motor. Move a wire through a magnetic field and you generate a current; send a current through the wire and you generate motion. It was like some form of occult magic, conjuring forces out of space. Magnetism was in itself straightforward enough, with its tightly wound bundle of field lines. Electricity too was a simple concept: electrons sloshing through a metal like water down a hillside. But it seemed miraculous that these things could conspire in such a manner with the movement of tangible objects. You wave a wand, and energy appears. Motion, he'd assumed, was just something that *happened*, it was not a phenomenon pregnant with generative potential. Yet there it was, in the hydroelectric turbine, and there too in the wires that the boys jerked through the field of a magnet, watching their ampere meters leap in response. The world was full of forces.

All this wonder, it seemed, had blinded him to something that Einstein had noticed at what appeared to be a casual glance: moving the magnet was not the same as moving the wire. There was a peculiar lack of symmetry to the situation. Neder began to sense a gulf separating him, a clever boy who could learn and remember the principles of science, from the kind of mind that discovered new things.

He read on:

Examples of this sort, together with the unsuccessful attempts to discover any motion of the earth relative to the 'light medium', suggest that the phenomena of electrodynamics as well as of mechanics possess no properties corresponding to the idea of absolute rest. They suggest rather that, as has already been shown to the first order of small quantities, the same laws of

electrodynamics and optics will be valid for all frames
of reference for which the equations of mechanics
hold good.

He did not understand this. That is to say, he did not follow the leap of reasoning. Why did the asymmetry of electromagnetic induction imply that there was no such thing as 'absolute rest'? To Einstein, the one seemed naturally to follow from the other; but to Neder, that was not clear at all.

The 'light medium', he gathered, was the ether, the substance once thought to convey light waves just as water bears waves on the sea. He had heard it said that two scientists in America at the end of the last century had set out to detect the ether, and had failed.

We will raise this conjecture (the purport of which will
hereafter be called the 'Principle of Relativity') to the
status of a postulate, and also introduce another
postulate, which is only apparently irreconcilable with
the former, namely, that light is always propagated in
empty space with a definite velocity c which is
independent of the state of motion of the emitting body.

Neder's eyes were watering. He had never seen anything like this before. With such serene confidence, this young man – Einstein had been just twenty-six in 1905 – proposed postulates that were inconceivably bold, even reckless. 'Light is always propagated in empty space with a definite velocity c.' Moving objects go faster if dispatched from a platform that is already in motion. Stroll along the carriage of a speeding train and you could be travelling at ninety, a hundred kilometres an hour. But not with light, Einstein was saying: it would not be hurried, come what may.

He read on, while dusk fell over Budapest and the other students returned to their dormitories for a meagre supper. Neder began scribbling in his notebook: little diagrams of squares and stick men and clocks, arrows directing them here and there on the page. He wrote down equations, in several of which the quantity $\sqrt{(1 - v^2/c^2)}$ began to recur. His journey into the *Annalen der Physik* became ever stranger:

From this point there ensues the following peculiar consequence. If at the points A and B of K there are stationary clocks which, viewed in the stationary system, are synchronous; and if the clock at A is moved with the velocity v along the line AB to B, then on its arrival at B the two clocks no longer synchronize, but the clock moved from A to B lags behind the other which has remained at B by $\frac{1}{2}tv^2/c^2$ (up to magnitudes of fourth and higher order), t being the time occupied in the journey from A to B.

Time itself was unstrung by Einstein's words. Explosive infinities loomed: moving objects gained mass and energy without limit. Einstein was describing a fantastic world, and claiming that it was our own. And everyone, it seemed, was listening to him. They all believed it.

'These cannot be the rules,' Neder muttered. 'They can't be.'

When the librarian came to lock up, Neder switched off the reading lamp and stayed silently at his desk. Not imagining that any student would remain there voluntarily in the late evening, the librarian never bothered to check the building thoroughly, and he did not see the boy bent over a book in the gallery. When he left, Neder's lamp blinked back to life and he read on.

At around 2 a.m., he was overwhelmed suddenly with a strange passion. It was a kind of outrage, which made his hands shake uncontrollably. Without any of the usual inner precursory signals, he found himself weeping. He wept for a long time, and then with equal abruptness an utter exhaustion came over him and he fell soundly asleep, slumped over the journal on the desk.

The next morning, Neder bought his first magnet, a great heavy thing from a car scrapyard, which he strapped to the back of his bicycle and carried to his barrack-style accommodation. He had some experiments to do.

11

THERE IS A BROAD, FLAT PLAIN, A PLACE OF MARSHLAND AND scrub that stews in a mosquito-haunted haze in the summer and is rimed with dark ice in the winter. On this plain stands a castle, and there is no other dwelling place for miles around. To reach the castle you need to know the paths, for otherwise you will find yourself sinking, and not so slowly, into a bog. Trucks have often been trapped in this wasteland, and their abandoned and rusting skeletons now punctuate the plain. Some of them were left by Soviet troops at the end of the Second World War. A few are older yet, the fossils of Romanian incursions. Those who now live in Lázár Castle still make most journeys on horseback, because horses know how to find a safe track through the treacherous Hortobágy, the Hungarian steppe.

Once this place was a sea, surrounded by volcanoes. Now they are quiet mountains that lie on the horizon: the Carpathians, Hungary's lost peaks.

The place is not a true castle at all, but an old inn with walled grounds and outbuildings. It is mostly silent. An old man lives here, supported by a household whittled down by time. The butlers and cooks and gardeners (for there is a garden in the grounds, feebly defying the natural order with its scant crop of potatoes and radishes) cannot imagine leaving the place, but they are not sure what will happen when the old man dies and there is no one left to continue the family line. The old man's son left home many years ago, and he has never returned. He will not forgive what his father did, but at the same time he refuses to censure the old man for it. He stays away, so that they can both leave the matter undisturbed.

Many changes have passed over the lands of the Hortobágy, but they have not reached the walls of Lázár Castle. Most folk do not even remember that the castle is here, and if they do, they would be hard pressed to find it. It is not on any map, and no one is interested in it. It belongs to another era, and it is floating adrift in time.

The old man who lives here is called Arkády Kam.

Kam discovered Lázár Castle in 1921, when he arrived from the east in a gypsy caravan. He was no gypsy, however; he was a Transylvanian count, and he considered himself Hungarian. His bedraggled convoy, two covered wagons and two wooden caravans, was crammed full of gold and silver, jewellery, fine silks and paintings: a small fortune borne on complaining wheels. When Transylvania was awarded to Romania in the Treaty of Trianon at the end of the Great War, Arkády Kam ransacked his own château in the mountains of Székely, bought the horse-drawn vehicles from the local Roma tribe, and set out towards the vast Hungarian plain. He knew what was about to happen.

Under Romanian rule, the lands and property of Hungarians living in Transylvania were confiscated and redistributed to Romanians. Hungarian newspapers were censored, and Hungarian place names were changed to Romanian. It became an offence to sing the Hungarian national anthem or to display the Hungarian flag. In the rest of Europe, this erasure of Hungary from the Carpathians went unnoticed.

Arkády Kam originally intended to head for the town of Nyíregyháza, but there had been no time to plan the journey, and he found himself wandering from village to village in the northern Hortobágy, receiving conflicting directions about which route to take. The region was flooded with refugees from the annexed lands, which was probably why Kam and his hidden cargo aroused so little curiosity. Many of those who fled from the Carpathians were penniless, and occasionally Kam would invite a tattered family to share an evening meal with his entourage. Despite his concealing any show of wealth, it would soon become plain that he was an aristocrat, and any camaraderie or show of empathy was quickly submerged beneath habitual feudal conventions, so that Kam's guests would fall silent and defer to their host. They thanked him with the utmost humility, yet Kam could sense the resentment that these homeless farmers and labourers felt before a lord who, while seemingly reduced to a status no higher than their own, nonetheless continued to adopt the role of a benevolent master. Kam knew that if any of them realized what the wagons contained, they would gladly cut his throat for it. He pitied them, but he did not really feel they were his compatriots, and eventually he took to ignoring them altogether.

Lázár Castle appeared before them in a rainstorm. The water was falling so heavily that one could see nothing beyond a few yards, and so they were virtually at the gated entrance porch before they knew the place was there. Arkády Kam had no idea where he was – even the sun was lost in the sky. The drivers brought the caravans into a courtyard surrounded by stone so resolute that it looked like a geological formation, scoured out of the bog by the blinding rain.

All the doors were locked, and no amount of banging drew any response from within. Eventually the group, soaked and cold and desperate, decided that the place was empty, and they found tools in the wagons to wrench the doors open. Wood splintered, and the harsh sound sent ravens thrashing out of the desolate barns, shrieking curses.

The rooms were bare except for a few tables and benches, so massive that it was not clear how they had ever been introduced. Kam's entourage set about these with axes, and at length and after much exertion they produced enough wood to light a fire in the great hearth of the high-beamed tavern.

Here and there the roof had started to give way, and the paving stones of the floors were clammy with the sweat of the earth. But otherwise the inn was more or less intact.

'Perhaps,' Kam said to his group, 'this place was cleared out when the Romanians came two years ago.' In April 1919 they had briefly invaded Debrecen and Nyíregyháza, only to withdraw before the Allied army. But none of the group really believed that the inn had been inhabited that recently. These rooms, they suspected, had been sealed for many years. What had driven their former occupants out of the swamplands?

The rain kept up for three days, and eventually Kam was forced to send a small party out on horses to look for a settlement and to buy food. They did not return that day, but appeared the next morning from out of a land steaming under a bright sun, announcing that there were several villages a couple of hours' ride to the west. It had taken all of the previous day to find them, and they had not dared set back after darkness.

Arkády Kam knew that, even with a king's ransom in his wagons, he would be unlikely to be able to buy so extensive a residence as this at Nyíregyháza, and the knowledge that here they were not impractically isolated fixed his decision. He told everyone that this place was now called Castle Lázár, which would remind them of the Renaissance palace near their homeland in Székelyföld, and that this was where they would stay.

Kam brought in craftsmen and builders from the surrounding towns, and some even from Nyíregyháza, which turned out to be just twenty-five miles to the north-east. Without exception, these local people were astonished to find that the tavern existed, and none of them knew anything about its history. As they patched walls and replaced glass and tiled roofs, they spoke in lowered voices, as though unsure who might overhear. Those who worked for longer periods sometimes brought tents with them, preferring to sleep outside the walls even in the dank autumn. It became rumoured in the nearby villages that the inn was in fact an ancient manor house, and Arkády Kam its ancestral lord returned after a long and mysterious absence. That he was barely thirty years old did not trouble those who whispered this story.

Seven years later Kam married a girl from Nyíregyháza, the daughter of a banker who took care of some portion of the count's great fortune. She was pale as mist, her hair was velvet black and she looked straight ahead of her as a carriage bore her through the castle gates. A year later she gave birth to a child, and the exertion killed her. Arkády Kam buried her in the secluded garden. He made the coffin with his own hands, he dug the hole, and he insisted that no priest should attend.

When in 1940 Hitler bribed Horthy by returning Székelyföld to Hungary, Arkády Kam made no mention of it to his retinue. He had no intention of going back to the mountains. Perhaps he simply did not trust the politics of Transylvania any longer, and if so, he was right, for under Stalin the region came again under Romanian rule. Stalin could see that Romania was more likely to accept Communism than Hungary, in which case Romania should be as big as possible. The anti-Hungarian tendencies of Communist Romania were even harsher than they had been before: the use of the Hungarian language was forbidden, and teachers who tried to instruct their pupils in their original tongue were arrested and tortured; some did not emerge again from the police cells.

Arkády Kam was a tall man, and so was Jaroslav, his son. Jaroslav stood out among the students in Budapest, and Karl Neder secretly admired his saturnine good looks. But while the other students, and the tutors too, showered him with praise and lavish compliments, Neder affected indifference to Kam's abilities. Jaroslav seemed to take even the knottiest concepts in his stride; he coped effortlessly with differential geometry, with fluid mechanics and thermodynamics. He was able to see the hidden structure of abstractions. He ran study groups, which other students attended just to have the benefit of his explanations of the latest lecture, which he appeared to recall with photographic precision. Neder knew that his own grades were as good as Kam's, but they came at the cost of late nights in the library frowning over difficult textbooks, while Kam was directing student plays or orchestrating debates in Budapest's cafés. Kam always had a packet of cigarettes to share.

Not everyone liked Jaroslav Kam, however. The Budapest police did not like him. Radosz, the police chief in charge of surveillance at the university, was quite sure that Kam was a radical element, a bourgeois intellectual. This was not so bad in itself – the university was full of those, and Radosz did not consider them to be worth much attention. He would arrest one of them every now and then, and bring them in for questioning, and he would make those soft, nervy boys sweat for a few hours behind their clumsy spectacles before releasing them without charge. None of them had the power or the charisma to create any serious trouble, and these little reminders were enough to ensure that no one tried anything stupid. Such people were ridiculous, Radosz thought, but hardly dangerous.

Kam was different. It was precisely because he never put a foot wrong that Radosz knew he had to be watched very carefully. Without fail Kam attended the student meetings organized by the Party, and he would clap with precisely the right degree of enthusiasm – robust but unforced – when Stalin or Rakosi was mentioned. He would shout the correct slogans, and afterwards he would discuss the officials' speeches with his colleagues. In the café groups (Radosz's informers told him) Kam would remain impassive when other students volunteered dissenting opinions, or would murmur some comment about how they should all remember their duties to the class struggle. He would never order luxuries like good wine or cream cakes, even though it was rumoured that his father was fantastically wealthy (Radosz had never been able to discover anything concrete about Kam's father – his one or two desultory enquiries to Nyíregyháza went unanswered).

Oh yes, he was a wily one, this Jaroslav Kam. His conduct was exemplary without being self-promoting. But Radosz had no doubt at all that Kam was a hazard. Kam might be able to govern his actions, but he had no power over his eyes, which were filled with sardonic amusement at the whole charade. Of course it was all a charade, everyone with a brain knew that; but whereas Radosz knew that the charade had a deeply important purpose, he could see that for Kam it was merely a game. It wasn't as though Kam was trying to cover up seditious thoughts or intentions with a show of solidarity – rather, his meticulous performance as a dutiful citizen was in itself the most eloquent expression of contempt. Radosz, in truth, never formulated his feelings with quite this degree of precision. All he knew was that, when one cold April day he had brought Kam into the headquarters of the secret police, the AVH, for questioning, he'd been left afterwards with the sensation of having been shamed and mocked.

There was nothing in principle to prevent the police chief from simply arresting Kam and having him locked away. He didn't need a reason – one could always find a reason. He'd done it plenty of times before with other troublemakers. But with Kam, that would have signalled a kind of defeat. He even wondered whether Kam was daring him to do such a thing. In the end, what this meant was that Radosz still had the notion that he possessed a soul. He could beat a man viciously and go home with his soul intact. But to have done that to Kam, to have reduced him to a bloody, mewling thing on the floor of a cell in the dead hours of the night – that would have brought visions of the black pit looming up before his eyes. That was never going to be the way to deal with Jaroslav Kam.

Physics was a difficult subject to teach at the University of Budapest in the early 1950s. The Communist Party, following the lead of Moscow (but always some distance behind), scrutinized everything for its political implications, and science was no exception. The physics of the nineteenth century had been beautifully, even proudly, materialist. It was all about forces and atoms, clear lines of cause and effect. The new physics of the twentieth century, the physics of Einstein and Bohr, was not like this. Probability and uncertainty had a dangerously metaphysical aspect. Relativity was anti-materialistic, even deistic, and in the 1930s some leading professors at Moscow University had been forced to resign because of their support for it. Yes, this was the science of the bourgeoisie, and 'Bourgeois scientists make sure that their theories are not dangerous to God or to capital,' as the Marxists put it.

So were you allowed to teach relativity and quantum theory? No one was quite sure. No one really knew what to think. They heard rumours that Hungarian physicists from the 1930s who had emigrated to America were now very famous there – Teller, Wigner, von Neumann. These men had embraced the new ideas, and they were hailed as geniuses. That made both academics and officials swell with nationalistic pride, but they were simultaneously ashamed that these men had capitulated to the West. Von Neumann spends his time gambling and whoring, it was said – that's what the capitalist system does to you.

Neder and Kam were taught quantum theory and general relativity, but nervously, diffidently, as if it was being left up to them to decide whether they wanted to believe it. This made Neder anxious. His instincts rebelled against it, but he was disgusted by the suggestion that science should be held hostage to political expediency. He considered the daily rituals of Party obeisance to be stupid and debasing, and he made little attempt to conceal the fact. (That is why he never entered Radosz's ledger of serious suspects.) He was determined to reject Einstein, but could one do so without appearing to kneel before the Party?

Maybe there was a way. Perhaps the old physics – Maxwell's diligent equations, Kelvin's vibrating ether, Newton's web of gravity – could be extended to produce the manifestations of quantum theory and relativity without having to invoke its apparent absurdities. But Neder had no idea how to do such a thing.

Towards the end of his first term, he believed he had found a way forward. At the heart of Einstein's theory of general relativity, he read, was the so-called equivalence principle. He had learnt at school that the weight of an object was proportional to its mass: the weight was equal to the mass multiplied by the strength of the earth's gravitational field. Isaac Newton knew that, and Einstein assumed it too. If it wasn't true, then something had to be wrong with relativity.

Neder knew that weight was a force, and could be measured. You simply attached an object to a spring, and looked at how much the spring extended. But what is mass? If the equivalence principle is right, you can calculate mass from weight, just by dividing by the strength of the gravitational field. That's the gravitational mass. But mass is also a measure of how hard it is to move something: if it is more massive, you have to push it harder to start it moving, or to change its speed. That's the inertial mass. If the equivalence principle is right, the gravitational and the inertial mass of an object are the same.

But are they the same? In 1889, a Hungarian nobleman named Roland Eőtvős decided to find out. (This was another shock for Neder. Here again was a question he had never even considered asking. The very idea that there were two different definitions of mass hadn't occurred to him. It was frightening to find that science did not consist simply of questions to which no one yet knew the answer, and on which one had only to bring to bear a set of tools acquired from books. Instead, you had to find the right questions. Scientists like Eőtvős, Neder discerned, could become renowned not for making great discoveries or devising ingenious equations, but merely for identifying a question worth asking. But how did one learn to do that?)

So Eőtvős, working at the university in Budapest, devised a very sensitive balance to measure mass according to the two definitions, and he reported to the Hungarian Academy of Sciences that they were the same to within a factor of one twenty-millionth. Seeing his report, the Royal Scientific Society of Göttingen decided to offer a prize to anyone capable of making the measurements even more accurately. In Budapest, Eőtvős took up the challenge, and after three years of painstaking work, he announced measurements with an accuracy of one part in a billion.

Eőtvős's measurements had become legendary in the

Hungarian Academy of Sciences as an example of experimental virtuosity. But that did not stop others from trying to do better. In the 1930s, his student János Renner, a tutor in physics at the Lutheran high school in Budapest where von Neumann and Wigner had studied, built a new balance and claimed to have achieved an accuracy five times greater than Eőtvős.

In other words, Eőtvős hadn't proclaimed the final judgement on the equivalence principle. Not by any means.

In 1950 the University of Budapest elected to celebrate Eőtvős's experimental genius by naming the entire institution after him. It was a way of announcing to the world that Hungary had a mighty heritage in science, and was even today a force to be reckoned with, and it convinced Neder that the equivalence principle must be one of the most significant concepts in physics. To celebrate the occasion, the faculty of science put the baron's 'torsion balance' on display in a glass box. It did not look like much: a simple tripod, like the stand for a small telescope, with one arm dangling and another held rigid. It was like a caricature of an imperious official, pointing accusingly at the viewer.

Was this all you needed to put Einstein to the test? Karl Neder realized that what he had to do was to repeat the Eőtvős experiment – to repeat it and perhaps to ferret out the infinitesimal difference between gravitational and inertial mass, which would bring relativity tumbling. But he had no money to make even the most basic of apparatus. He needed a sponsor, and his benefactor turned out to be Jaroslav Kam.

Neder might never have spoken to Kam if it hadn't been for the student riot in the winter of 1951–2. It was a cruel winter which made the people of Budapest turn on one another. Fresh food was almost impossible to find, and the citizens lived on tins of meat and sacks of hoarded flour. But hoarding was a capitalistic crime, and those who had neglected to take such precautions complained to the AVH about their neighbours' secret stocks, in the vain hope that some of those stocks might be redistributed to them. Everyone glowered at everyone else with fear and suspicion.

It wasn't clear what triggered the protests. There was some suggestion that the father of one of the students, a building contractor in the Herminamezã district of Budapest, had been detained because his neighbour had inspected the contents of his dustbin and found chicken bones. How could the man afford a chicken? Or maybe he had painted his flat in too garish a colour – obviously a bourgeois act. Or he had been heard listening to an American jazz record. In any case, a small deputation of students went to the AVH headquarters to argue in the man's defence. Unfortunately for them, it was on this day that General Bielkin was visiting from Svabhegy. Bielkin probably could not care less about a handful of angry students, but the police chief was embarrassed and instructed his men to beat the protestors ruthlessly. When one of them turned up, bruised and tearful, at the university, scores of his furious classmates walked out of their lectures and gathered to demonstrate on the Erzsebét Bridge across the Danube. One of the protesters was Karl Neder.

If it had been Radosz's problem, he would probably have waited until the whole thing blew over and the students got cold and hungry and drifted back to their barracks. But it was not Radosz's problem. Instead, a squadron of policemen was dispatched to the bridge carrying guns and sticks, and they marched up to the students and began to strike them to the ground. The students panicked and ran, pursued by the police. Mostly they ran back towards Pest, but Neder saw an escape route westwards, in the direction of Gellért Hill. He hurtled into the park around the foot of the Citadel, all the while expecting to feel bullets rip between his shoulder blades. But the policemen in pursuit did not want to risk shooting, because even then it was not a simple matter to gun down unarmed citizens in the centre of Budapest.

And there was Jaroslav Kam, holding a heavy coat and wearing a Russian hat with flaps of fur that covered his ears, which he pulled off and thrust roughly onto Neder's head. Then he threw the coat around Neder's shoulders and pulled him over to a bench, where he lit cigarettes for both of them. He flung open a copy of *Szabad Nep*, the official Party newspaper (the title meant 'Free People'), and gave it to Neder. After that, he smoked and said nothing. Two policemen came panting up the path, and one gasped at them: 'A man running... which way?'

'Up the hill,' said Jaroslav. 'But you look like you could do with a smoke.' As he pulled the pack from his inside pocket, the first policeman gazed at it wistfully, but the other shoved him in the back.

'Up,' he said. And they were gone.

'I wonder,' said Kam after a few minutes, 'why we have not spoken?'

'What about?' Neder did not trust any of his emotions in the slightest. He was exhilarated, and told himself it was because of the danger he had just escaped. He was angry, he was pleased, he was turbulent but also calm.

'I think there is probably a great deal we could talk about. Science. Politics. Philosophy. Religion.'

Neder snorted. 'What could we possibly say about religion? Except how nonsensical it all is.'

'Oh, I agree with you entirely. But listen, have you ever read *Paradise Lost* by the English poet John Milton?'

Neder resented this. He knew hardly any English, certainly

not enough to read English poetry. And one wouldn't find a Hungarian translation of Milton, not in those days. So Kam was asking him to admit that he couldn't read English. He didn't respond.

'It made me see,' Kam said, 'that religion isn't about God. It is about man. Man and the devil, perhaps. You and I, of all people, ought to see that.'

'Why you and I, of all people?' Neder did not like the way he was being entirely reactive, while Kam led him where he pleased.

'Because we share a similar heritage, I believe.'

'You mean,' Neder said after some thought, 'that there are Jewish roots to both our families?'

'That's right. The religion of the irreligious. The religion of man and the devil. No, for heaven's sake, let's not talk about God.'

Then they said nothing for a while.

'You don't believe in relativity either, do you?' said Kam.

'What makes you say that?' Here we go again.

'You wear your heart on your sleeve, Karl. Do you mind if I call you Karl?'

'Look,' Neder exclaimed, 'were you sitting here watching us on the bridge? Is that it? Were you preparing for this rescue mission? What's your game?'

'Yes, I was watching. I admire your courage.'

'Then why weren't you with us?'

'That's actually quite a complicated question. Let's say that it would have violated a certain set of rules. In many ways you are more free than I am.'

'I doubt it. Everyone knows that you're rich, even though there are supposed to be no rich people in Hungary.'

'That's it precisely. What could be more constraining than being a kind of person who doesn't exist?'

'I would find it a lot easier to be grateful for your help just now if I didn't have the feeling that you'd set it all up.'

Kam laughed. 'I don't have that much power, you know! It could have been anyone who came up that path. I'm glad it was you, though,' he added.

Neder waited as long as he could before asking, 'Why?'

'I think it's time we teamed up. We're the best students in our class, you know that. You might think that doesn't give us anything in common, but you'd be wrong. I think we might be able to accomplish a lot together, instead of orbiting one another like wary moons.'

Neder was thinking furiously. He refused to believe that Kam could have had the same ideas as him about undermining relativity by disproving the equivalence principle, and he had no wish to reveal his inspiration to someone who might possibly be gifted enough to figure out what to do with it. But everyone knew that Kam was rich.

'What do you have in mind?'

'I'm afraid it will sound rather grand. But why shouldn't we dare to be grand, you and I? Look here, three hundred years ago no one studied science the way we are being forced to. They went to college, yes, the Boyles and the Newtons, they studied books and sat exams and so on. But their real scientific work had very little to do with that. They did it at home, or in their rooms, and it didn't conform to any syllabus or prescription. They did whatever they wanted, they followed their instincts. If they wished, they would experiment for three days without sleep, and then they would shut the curtains and sleep for another three days. They would stick instruments in their own eyes. They'd gaze at the sun, and who cared if it nearly blinded them? I'd like to gaze at the sun too, Karl.'

'They were priests with time on their hands, those men. Or they had private means. But then, you do too, don't you?'

Kam exhaled a jet of smoke. 'In my father's castle – well, damn it, that's what he calls it – I am going to set up a laboratory. I am going to call it the Institute Without Walls, because there will be no limits to the questions I can ask there. I have a thousand and one experiments I want to do. For example, I will study the chemistry of the noble gases –'

'They don't have any chemistry. That's why they're noble.'

'Yes, well, I'm not so sure. I think it might be possible to make them react. I'll cook them up with fluorine… anyway, that's one of my projects. I will make new polymers with strange properties – maybe plastics that behave like metals. I want to figure out what beetle shells are made of.'

'Oh, chemistry, then. Fiddling with materials.'

'Chemistry is that branch of natural philosophy in which the greatest improvements have been and may be made.' He was obviously quoting something.

'According to who?'

'Professor Waldmann of the University of Ingolstadt.' Kam sounded so jocular that Neder was not certain he wasn't just making it up. Neder had no idea who Waldmann was.

'But look,' Kam went on, 'it's not just that. There will be an observatory, and I think I can make a simple particle accelerator like Lawrence's in California. The point is, I thought you could join me.'

Neder was afraid he was going to start shaking. Horrifically, he began to blush.

'I don't know,' he gasped. 'I need to think about it. I have projects of my own. I have to get back.' But he stayed sitting on the bench, his breaths fluttering like the heart of a bird.

12

THAT SUMMER, KARL NEDER DID NOT GO STRAIGHT HOME TO his mother and brother in Győr. He left Budapest travelling east, not west: not towards Austria but the Carpathians. He had been filled with trepidation when he wrote to his family.

'I may go for just a couple of weeks,' he explained. 'Then I will come to see you both. István, I have some rare stories to tell you of the things we get up to here. I think even you will laugh at them. Of course, our studies are generally very dry, and you have done well to spare yourself from all these hours of listening to old men droning words whose meaning they have forgotten. Really, there is nothing special about the university life, it is made up to be much more than it actually is. In any event, the three of us will have a lot to talk about, once I return from the Hortobágy. If I am not baked, I expect to be steamed. And desperate for some good Győr pastry.'

But in truth it was not the heat of the Carpathian basin that worried him, nor the coarse peasant food or the arduous journey by train and truck and perhaps even horseback. The thought of all of this made his spirit leap. In contrast, he saw the house on Kun Béla Street, with István crouching in the lamplight over a glass of vodka, the bottle at his elbow, while the fragile tunes of a weary Schubert came from the sitting room. His brother and his mother were increasingly now like an elderly couple who had exhausted their conversation several times over and co-existed like listless animals caged in a zoo.

A black car powdered with dust collected Kam and Neder at Nyíregyháza. Already summer had sucked the moisture from the oozing springs of the great plain, and it was slowly turning the landscape to sepia, like old parchment. The vehicle must have been built around the 1920s, when suspension had not advanced far beyond the laminated tongues of horse-drawn carriages. The two young men were repeatedly thrown laughing to its wide floor.

'I'm going to need precision-engineered equipment,' Neder grinned. 'How do you propose to transport it then – by balloon?'

'A balloon!' Kam sighed. 'What we could do with that! We'd extract our own helium from liquid air, and we'd map out the foothills, take barometric readings. Do you know about cosmic rays?'

'Fermi thinks they are protons whisked up by magnetic fields in space. There are natural particle accelerators out there – no need to build our own. We could take a cloud chamber up into the atmosphere to look for new particles...'

After Budapest, after the constant presence of AVH agents and the fear of informants, they were intoxicated by the open, empty spaces. At one point Kam asked the driver to stop simply so that he could get out and run across the hard earth, whooping at the distant mountains. Above them, sunlight bleached the air until it gleamed like a pearl, crackling with the unruly radiation of the firmament. Neder watched and laughed, but felt too shy to join his friend, despite Kam's remonstrations.

'Tell me!' yelled Jaroslav from a distance of two hundred yards. 'Tell me one thing we cannot do here!'

'There isn't anything,' said Neder, but quietly, as though he were just trying out the words.

But as they drew through the arched gate and into the courtyard of Lázár Castle, Jaroslav Kam seemed to lose his ease. He was no less charming, but his laugh was thrown back coldly by the walls, like a chorus of crows. His dark eyes flickered around the windows and high gables, searching the stones and shadows. He did not show Neder to his rooms, but left that to a servant.

'Listen,' he said, his voice bright and brittle, 'I have some things to attend to. It will be time for dinner in two hours, and someone will collect you then.'

'Should I give my greetings to your father?'

'He'll be at dinner.'

Ψ

Arkády Kam had simply used what he wanted of the inn's shell, and ignored the rest. There was no plan to it. Mostly, the place was still delapidated; in winter, rain and snow fell to the flagstones, wind rasped around gaping window-holes. But in the parts where people lived, there were wall hangings and divans and thick carpets from Istanbul. No electricity, though: candles and oil lamps and open fires, wood-burning stoves and braziers. How could they run a laboratory without electricity?

All through dinner, Jaroslav seemed to want Neder to join him in some private joke, catching his eye across the table while Arkády sliced his food with the concentration of a surgeon. Neder was baffled, and also embarrassed and even a little angry, when Jaroslav said to his father, 'Karl doesn't believe in the theory of general relativity, you know.'

'Why not?' asked the older man, quick as that.

Neder had not expected Arkády to have even heard of relativity. Perhaps he hadn't.

'It's just a suspicion,' he stuttered. 'I can't prove anything.

That is something Jaroslav and I will – talk about.' He was unsure whether Jaroslav had made any mention of their intention to build a laboratory, which would of course be funded by the Kam fortune.

Neder felt he was adrift in time, or rather, that time surrounded him in concentric layers. There was something absurdly medieval about the great hall, its stones burnished by flames sputtering on a baroque chandelier. The staff maintained the dignified remoteness of old Austro-Hungary, while the tableware was in the Art Deco style. And then in the eye of it all, they were talking about modern physics, while beyond the light the old Magyar paganism surrounded them.

'These are Einstein's ideas, Father,' said Jaroslav, as if feeding him a prompt.

'Einstein was a German Jew,' said his father. It could have been an indictment, or a reproof, or a compliment. 'Is relativity Jewish science?'

'That's what Hitler said,' Jaroslav replied. 'Stalin too.' He seemed to be guiding his father towards a ritualistic conclusion, the nature of which Neder couldn't guess.

'Stalin,' said Arkády Kam, 'will die soon. Then we will see.' It was left for the others to imagine what they would see. But Jaroslav pretended that he wanted to know.

'Will it be a good world, with Stalin gone?'

'What makes a world good?' his father shot back at him. Jaroslav flung a glance at Neder and winked.

No, mealtimes were not comfortable for visitors at Lázár Castle. They were an obscure performance in which there was no role for outsiders, except perhaps as a captive, hapless audience. Kam would gurn and smirk, and then finally rise and bow slightly to his father (whose head remained lowered, still dissecting his meal) before stalking out with glittering eyes, his companion forgotten. But in other respects the time Karl

Neder spent with the Kams left him dizzy and awestruck. He and Jaroslav ordered industrial glassware from Nyíregyháza, which arrived in the black saloon in crates stuffed with straw, suffering miraculously few breakages after all. There were boxes of chemicals in corked jars: silver salts that had to be kept out of the light, deliquescent sodium silicate, powdered metals, a great jar of swirling mercury, implausibly heavy. Sluggish acids that turned paper black. Bright compounds of chromium and cobalt. Canisters of natural gas and Bunsen burners, metal tripods and retort stands. They were all carried into a former stables in the north corner of the grounds, one of the better-preserved outbuildings, where Neder and Kam went to work with hammers and nails to make shelves and gas cupboards for their laboratory.

'It looks more like an alchemist's den than a modern lab,' said Neder, sounding more approving than he'd meant to.

'We'll make gold yet!' Kam called back.

Neder's initial disdain for Kam's chemical enthusiasms quickly waned, once he had seen magnesium powder mixed with silver nitrate in a crucible and ignited into a blinding fire-ball with a single drop of water. A tiny mushroom cloud rose into the rafters like a spirit liberated from the metal. They made their own photographic paper and produced grainy, atmospheric images of the castle walls inside a pinhole camera. They pulled a thick slug of nylon out from between two pungent liquids, then ran with it down the dark hallway to draw it into a fine fibre. They did not even try to find out anything new, dazzled enough by the list of tricks in the textbooks Kam had brought with him. More than once they emerged spluttering from the laboratory pursued by a cloud of acrid gas: sulphur dioxide, chlorine, ammonia. There were explosions and fires, and Neder seemed always to have at least one or two fingers burnt and wrapped in lint.

'What about a bomb?' Kam asked.

They had clambered through a loft onto the roof of the stables and were looking out over the plain, their shadows reaching far across it in the early evening. There were strands of smoke rising from distant villages, but otherwise no sign that this parched land was populated. It had not rained since Neder arrived.

'Well, I was wondering about a rocket, which amounts to the same thing. It would be the start of the Hungarian space programme.'

'I mean a device that could be used as an agent of terror. Even assassination.'

'Oh yes? And who would you assassinate?'

'You mean, where would I start?' There was a flatness in Kam's voice that troubled Neder.

'Bombs are crude stuff. Any fool can create a big bang – we know that well enough!'

'But a fool can't carry out an assassination. Yes, anyone can blow themselves up, but there's an art to making an effective bomb. Do you know the book by Boris Savinkov?'

'I've never even heard of Boris Savinkov.'

'He was a terrorist after the Russian revolution. A counter-revolutionary who helped to plan acts against the Bolsheviks. Actually, you know, he opposed the Imperial regime too – something of a nihilist, I suppose. They called him the King of Terror. It's said that he collaborated with the British secret service, until the Soviets caught up with him and put him in prison. That's where he committed suicide.'

They were two black fingers, stretching slowly across the Hortobágy towards Transylvania.

'He was a master assassin, Boris Savinkov. But you see, the thing was that he was also a literary man. He was even Assistant Minister for War in Kerensky's government for a while. Well, he wrote a book called *Memoirs of a Terrorist*, where he explained his methods. They were dangerous, and bunglers blew themselves up. The counter-revolutionaries made bombs in which small detonations set off larger ones. They would have thin glass tubes filled with sulphuric acid, with lead weights attached. The lead would shatter the tube when the bomb was dropped or thrown, and the acid would spill out onto a mixture of potassium chlorate and sugar, and that would explode. But it would just be the trigger for a secondary detonator, which was mercury fulminate. And when that went off, it ignited the main charge, which was dynamite. So there was this escalation of explosions, one after the other. It's the same idea that the Germans used fifty years ago to detonate TNT – hit it first with mercury fulminate. But Savinkov said that as you packed the explosives into the devices, the glass tubes of acid could easily break in your hand. That's what happened to one of his chums, called Politkov or something – blown to bits in his hotel room one night.'

'It sounds like a crazy business to me.' Neder fixed the mountains with his gaze: they were solid ground.

'Well, that's why you need to be a good chemist.'

'So that you can kill other people rather than yourself?'

'So that you can achieve what you set out to achieve.'

'Jaroslav.' Neder forced himself to turn. 'You're not thinking of blowing anyone up, are you? Because if I thought for a moment –'

Kam laughed. 'This is just chemistry, Karl. Bangs and flashes. That's all we've been doing. We've been playing with chemistry. Well, maybe now it's time for some serious work.'

But there was no time left. Neder had already stayed for eighteen days, and he couldn't delay his departure for home any longer.

As he boarded the train in Nyíregyháza, Kam pressed a

small, leatherbound book into his hand. 'One for the journey. Look, after the autumn term we can start to think about relativity. You're planning something, I know that. You can come again to the Institute Without Walls, and we'll see what we shall see.'

The book was, of course, *Memoirs of a Terrorist*. Savinkov described the assassination of Vyacheslav von Plehve, the Interior Minister of Nicholas II, in 1904. Plehve's coach was blown apart by a bomb, so that 'only the wheels remained', dragged by maddened and blood-spattered horses. But what really seemed to captivate Savinkov was the explosion itself: the noise, the scents and colours of the vapours, the material particularities of this fatal blast:

> *Suddenly a heavy and weighty, unusual sound invaded the monotonous noise of the streets. It was as if someone had hit a cast-iron plate with a cast-iron hammer. At the same moment the shattered window panes clattered pitifully. I saw how a column of grey-yellow smoke, almost black at the edges, rose from the ground like a small whirlwind. The column widened ever further and filled the whole street to the height of the fifth floor. It spread just as fast as it had risen. It appeared to me that I saw some sort of black debris in the smoke.*

It was as bad at home as Karl had feared. István was seldom around, and when he was, he was either drunk and silent, or drunk and mordant. He mocked Karl's studiousness, shaking his head at all these books filled with empty ideas. What came of it all, in the end? Did it feed the people?

'It's a good job I can look out for you,' he said. 'They're arresting the intellectuals, you know.'

'I'm just a student, István. Hardly an intellectual. I know I don't do anything as productive as you, but our country needs technology too.'

'Engineers, sure. But you don't want to be one of them, do you, Karl? Look, I'm only teasing, you go and do what you want. You and your pal.'

Ψ

In 1953 everything changed, because Arkády Kam had been right: Stalin did die soon. He died in March (so Moscow said), and Nikita Khrushchev moved swiftly to claim his place. Word filtered into Budapest that Rakosi was not favoured by the new heads in Moscow. The KGB leader Beria, it was said, mocked him as Hungary's first Jewish king – for Rakosi, like all the leading members of the Hungarian government, had Jewish origins. He was already deeply unpopular in Hungary because of the ailing economy, and now people began openly to refer to him by his nicknames: Old Baldy, Arsehead. In June the Soviets ordered Rakosi to stand down as Prime Minister, and replaced him with the liberal Imre Nagy, who had fought with the Russian Bolsheviks after escaping from a Siberian prison camp in 1917. This was a man who had served under Béla Kun, who had lived in exile in the Soviet Union during the Horthy era, who returned to Hungary with the Red Army, and at once he spoke of a 'new course', denouncing the evils of the former regime and promising to set right the previous miscarriages of justice.

But Old Baldy was not gone. Rakosi remained General Secretary of the Hungarian Workers' Party, and he battled against Nagy's reforms. Towards the end of 1953, Prime Minister Nagy nonetheless secured the release of thousands of political prisoners, and one of them was Gábor Neder.

There was no announcement, no message; he simply turned up one day in October at the house in Kun Béla Street. He walked in and told Dora that he could do with a glass of tea. Dora stared at him for a full minute.

'Well, it's me after all,' Gábor said at last. 'Did you think you'd seen the last of me?'

'I must fetch István.'

'No. The boy is working, yes? No need to interrupt that. Probably not a boy now, I guess.'

'He's not a boy. He will be so glad to see you, Gábor. We all are.' But Dora wasn't so sure, and she knew that Gábor knew that too. She didn't know what she felt, as she sat down and cried.

Gábor said nothing, he just put the kettle on the stove himself. He'd done all his crying long ago.

'Gábor, do you still love your boys?'

'Do they still love me, I wonder.'

Ψ

István took it badly. He seemed convinced that his father disapproved of him, and he began to pick quarrels right away. Even Gábor was perplexed by this, for now he himself drank far less, and he did not fight with Dora any longer, and had no wish to fight with István. Where before there had been ox-like brawn, now he was a lean, wiry figure; he endured his son's anger with lassitude, not even raising his voice.

Dora wrote to Karl to tell him that his father had been released, but it was not until Karl returned to Győr in December that they met again. Karl shook his father's hand, and the grip was exploratory for both of them.

'When I was in prison,' Gábor said, 'they threatened to arrest my family. They demanded that I sign this document and that one, and sometimes I did what they wanted, but other times I lost patience with the charade and told them to go to hell. So they said they would bring you all in.'

'What did you do then?'

Gábor turned away so that Karl could not read his expression.

'You know what? I don't remember.'

13

KARL AND JAROSLAV CELEBRATED THE APPOINTMENT OF IMRE Nagy by launching a rocket in the scorched Hortobágy. Well, they did not exactly launch it. When Kam triggered the electrical detonator, the device a hundred yards away disappeared in a burst of golden light, and pieces of shrapnel sizzled over their heads. They both fell to the ground, pointlessly, seconds too late. The sound of the blast seemed to continue rolling around them for ages, tossed between mountains.

'You're not hurt?'

Kam was laughing quietly.

Ψ

Karl Neder went to Lázár Castle whenever he could, and stayed for as long as he felt able. Arkády Kam began to treat him as one of the domestic retinue, with distant familiarity, which suited Karl just fine.

'I don't understand,' he said to Jaroslav one day, 'how this place has gone unmolested by the officials here. Not even the Hortobágy is so remote that you can escape their hatred for the nobility here. And Jewish nobility, at that.'

'We have never escaped their hatred. In fact, living at Lázár Castle has helped me to understand how much the people in this country dislike rich Jews. I now know precisely how much – to the nearest forint.'

'Oh, I see. I suppose that must make you very cynical about human nature.'

'On the contrary, it makes me rather optimistic. The price is so low, you see.'

Ψ

In early 1954 they finally built an approximation to Eőtvős's balance, although Karl suspected that Jaroslav's heart wasn't really in it. To his dismay, their measurements did not even come close to Count Roland's level of precision. 'Well, it's only a prototype, Karl. We'll make a better one.'

The Institute Without Walls grew to occupy the whole of the north tower, including a modest library of books and journals. Kam was always keen to begin a new project, so that no experiment was ever truly finished.

Ψ

During their final year at university, Rakosi struck back at his old enemy Imre Nagy, accusing the Prime Minister of rightist deviation. In March the Central Committee of the Hungarian Workers' Party echoed his words, and the newspapers lent their pages to Rakosi's agents. The economy was still in a bad way, they said, but now it was surely Nagy who was to blame. Many of those in positions of influence began subtly realigning their friendships and allegiances, sensing a shift in the political power struggle. In April Nagy was dismissed from his post, and Rakosi was once again the leader of Hungary.

And the arrests started. The AVH did not come knocking on the door at Kun Béla Street, but the prisons were filling up with rightists and 'capitalist agents'. This time, however, Rakosi was out of step with Moscow. Khrushchev needed to rid himself of the old Stalinists, and rumours were circulating that the father of the Soviet people was about to get a posthumous bashing. In February 1956, the delegates at the Twentieth Congress of the Soviet Communist Party heard their leader accuse his predecessor of political and military ineptness, false ideology, and mass murder. Worse still for Rakosi, Khrushchev criticized Stalin's followers in Eastern Europe, claiming that they had been responsible for miscarriages of justice. Rakosi did all he could to keep the news from the Kremlin out of Hungary. He banned *Pravda*, and his officials made pronouncements that contradicted the Soviet premier's anti-Stalinism.

Karl Neder and Jaroslav Kam graduated in the summer of 1955, and they both did well enough to secure postgraduate positions at the university. Neder was studying the theory of atmospheric electricity with a professor named Keleman; Kam seemed content to measure the dielectric properties of liquids, a mundane task in which he had minimal interest but which left him plenty of time for his other pursuits. He and Neder were still collaborators, but now they tended to discuss one another's projects rather than working towards common goals. They lived in the austere university accommodation, still with a foot in their former student world. Like almost everyone else in Hungary, they were biding their time.

Nagy's liberal rule had emboldened the discontented factions in Hungary, and under his regime the students had made loud demands for reform. With Rakosi back in power the situation turned ugly. There were demonstrations and declarations, which were met with threats and detainments.

Yet everyone seemed genuinely shocked when a bomb exploded in the exclusive Café Liszt, where the Minister of Defence Mihaly Farkas took his breakfast. Farkas was not there that June morning, having been called to Party headquarters for an urgent meeting (Rakosi sensing the tightening of the Soviet noose). But there was little doubt that the bomb was meant for him. Instead, it killed three citizens of Budapest – all, as it happened, minor Party officials – and injured dozens of others.

Kam and Neder were at work in the university laboratories when the AVH came for them. They were, unfortunately for them, found in conversation while Kam was purifying a toluene derivative, one of the liquids on his supervisor's list. It would not be hard for the prosecutor to present this as the attempted synthesis of trinitrated toluene, or TNT.

The new police chief, Gyorgy Pusztai, was less cautious than old Radosz – or perhaps, in that climate, more worried about his position. Karl and Jaroslav were never told that Pusztai in fact arrested more than twenty people for the bombing of the Café Liszt. He thought he could pin it on them all, and who was going to ask questions?

The goal of the AVH was to make every suspect condemn one of his fellows. They did not use extreme torture, because they did not imagine that was necessary. They kept the students awake for two nights, forcing them to stand in their cells and cuffing them if they closed their eyes. At the end of it, Karl's feet began to swell. 'It gets much worse after two weeks,' the guard told him. Then he was taken to an interrogation cell, where he had to go on standing as Pusztai thrust a sheaf of photographs at him, waving them one by one under his nose. They were pictures of the scene at the café. One man had lost a foot; another had his chest caved in. 'Not nice,' said the police chief.

They asked him about his work at the university, over and over again, in such detail that Karl knew they could not possibly be following a word he was saying. Although he was not too sure what he was saying, in any case.

'Your father was inside for four years. Why was that?'

'I don't know. No one ever told us.'

'You're a fool. What do you think they were going to do – send you a letter about it? He was inside because he was a bad citizen. But we don't think he was ever as bad as you.' And so on.

'How many bombs have you made with Kam?'

'We don't do that. Make bombs.'

'How many?'

'We don't.'

'That's not what he told us.'

Not what he told them? Jaroslav had told them something? Surely this was just a ploy. Except, of course, they *did* make bombs. But not to kill anyone with. At least, Karl had never done so, and he could not believe that Jaroslav – No, they had to be making it up –.

Neder never remembered much about this interview. He remembered little about the entire period of his incarceration in Budapest. What he did come to understand, however, was that it was Khrushchev who saved him.

Back in his cell, he was sure that there was nothing for him now but a succession of increasingly brutal questionings, followed by a cursory trial and then execution. But that didn't happen. Nothing, in fact, happened for weeks, except that he was given a bowl of slop every morning and otherwise left alone. It was as though they had forgotten about his terrible crime, forgotten in fact all about him. He discovered only later that during that time Rakosi's power collapsed. Khrushchev asserted that the Hungarian leader had rigged the trial of Laszlo Rajk, the former Foreign Minister, who had been Rakosi's main rival. Rajk, an impeccable Communist who had fought in Spain and in the wartime underground movement, had been accused of being an agent of rightists everywhere: not only of Horthy, but also of Tito and Trotsky and the Western imperialists. He was said to be guilty, in the

Stalinist phrase, of 'nationalist deviation' – placing his country's interests before Moscow's wishes. Worse still, he had plotted to murder Rakosi and his cohort Erno Gerő. It was all lies, and Rajk refused to make a confession even under torture. But his close friend Janos Kadar, who had previously replaced him as Minister of the Interior, persuaded Rajk that his confession, although admittedly untrue, was needed by the Communist cause. It was imperative, Kadar explained to Rajk, to discredit Tito, who Stalin had denounced for his own nationalist deviation. You will be quite safe, Rajk's friend told him, and so will your wife (who was also under arrest) and baby son, Kadar's godchild. We will say you have been executed, but you will in fact be taken away to a safe place in the Soviet Union where you can live a free life under an assumed identity. So Rajk confessed, and, without being allowed to see his wife, he was hanged.

Rakosi was confident that he could evade Khrushchev's accusation by pinning everything on Kadar. Unknown to Kadar, he had a tape recording of the conversation that had taken place in 1949 between the Minister and Rajk, and now he played it to the Central Committee of the Communist Party.

Who can explain Rakosi's carelessness? Or did he, after all, sense that his time had run out? Whatever the case, the Committee heard not only the incriminating part of Kadar's plea, but also the section right at the beginning, which Rakosi had apparently intended to omit. There, Kadar made it clear that he was speaking to Rajk on Rakosi's behalf.

In July 1956, just before Rakosi was about to order Nagy's arrest, the Central Committee dismissed him on the orders of the Kremlin's representative Anastas Mikoyan, and he was forced to flee to Moscow. Mikoyan installed Rakosi's accomplice Erno Gerő in his place, but the power of the dictatorship was broken.

Now no one knew what to do with the 'political prisoners', which was how Neder was categorized. Many, like him, had not been formally charged with any offence. Pusztai was one of Rakosi's men, and fell victim to his enemies; but after he had been replaced as police chief, it was discovered that his staff had destroyed many of the detainees' case histories. Their supposed crimes were a mystery. One officer made the ill-advised suggestion that the police ask the prisoners themselves what they were accused of. It was a politically dangerous predicament, and throughout August and September the prisoners were kept in their cells, but treated and fed well, and brought reading material when they asked for it. Neder was desperate to find out what had become of Kam, but this was not permitted.

For most of the prisoners, this regime was a blessing. Although they were dismayed that they could not let their families know of their comparative ease and safety, they suspected that things could not go on this way for long, and that they would soon be turned out, to save money if nothing else. But Neder spent these days in torment. Was it possible, he asked himself again and again – was it possible that Jaroslav could indeed have planted, or at least manufactured, the bomb? Repeatedly he told himself that his friend was not capable of such inhumanity, such violence. And every time, he was forced back to the realization that he simply did not know what Jaroslav Kam might or might not do. If only he could ask him to his face... whether Kam answered with the truth or not, Neder would know it.

In late October, Neder and several others were taken from their prison cells to the police station, where they were immediately locked up again, but in an almost amiable manner. The police – these were municipal officers, not the black-booted AVH – gave them cigarettes, they even sat and chatted with them, and that was how Neder discovered that the city was on the brink of revolution. Rajk had been given a reburial, the policemen told him, and over a hundred thousand people turned out for it. The press was openly criticizing Gerő and demanding that Farkas be properly punished for authorizing the deaths of thousands of political prisoners, as the Party now admitted. 'You can say anything now,' they told him.

'Why are we here?'

'Oh, you'll be set free any moment. It's just a matter of paperwork. The chief wants you all off his hands before any trouble starts.'

'Will any trouble start?'

'Was Engels a Communist?' Once this would have been a trick question; now it was just a figure of speech.

Then late one evening, everything seemed to happen at once. Neder heard shouting from the front of the building, and the noise of policemen running back and forth. One of them came and unlocked the cells, shouting, 'You're released, comrades!' They surged in a crowd into the lobby of the police station, where among the turbulent throng were Karl's father and brother.

For an instant he thought that they must be the cause of the confusion; but their presence was incidental. No one noticed them as they grasped one another's arms.

'What is it? Why are you here?'

'They are fighting in the streets... Shooting each other –'

'Who? Why?'

'The students and demonstrators, and the AVH.'

'But they are letting us go...'

'The police, yes. The police are joining the demonstrators – the army too...'

'Wait. I must find Jaroslav.'

'You won't find him here,' said Gábor. 'He was released soon after you were arrested.'

Nothing was making sense.

'Kam signed a confession against you,' István snarled. 'He told them you made the bomb.'

Ψ

It began at the statue of Sándor Petőfi, the poet and hero of the 1848 revolution against the Austrians. The students, workers and intellectuals of Budapest gathered there on 23 October and marched through the city chanting Petőfi's lines from *Arise Hungarians*: 'This we swear – this we swear: slaves we are no more!' As the crowd gathered that evening around the Hungarian Radio building, where Gerő was lambasting the agitators, the AVH made arrests and fired teargas, and when that failed to disperse the protestors, they used bullets.

Gábor and István had been in the city for almost a week by then, but only that morning had they finally discovered where Karl was being held. They made their way through the tense, unfamiliar streets, and with every passing moment their urgency and foreboding increased. When they arrived at the station, police were dashing out with rifles and they knew that the storm had burst. They wondered whether they were about to be shot; but they were simply ignored.

'We've been trying to trace you since August, when you didn't show up,' István shouted as they hurried along. 'At first we thought you must have gone to stay with Kam, but eventually we got in touch with the university and heard the whole story, about the bomb and the arrest and so on.'

'I had nothing to do with the bomb.'

'Of course not. It was Kam.'

'Who told you that?'

'Why else would he have dumped you in the crap, except to save his own skin?'

'How do you know he did that?'

'It's what the university said. We spoke to the prof you work for. He told us that he'd gone to the AVH a few days after your arrest, and they told him what was up. They said you were really in the shit. Kam had vanished by then, of course. Finally last month we managed to contact the prison, and they said they didn't know anything about your case. The files had been lost. We kept going at them for weeks, and in the end we decided to come here ourselves.'

Karl was seized by a sudden urge to hit his brother.

'I don't believe it.'

'Believe what?'

'Even if Jaroslav made the bomb... I don't believe he'd have testified against me. It's not as if they really tortured us.'

Now István grabbed him. 'Listen, idiot. I don't know much about your friend Kam, but I do know that he's a high-born type. You made that clear enough. Well, don't you see? That's what they do. They look out for themselves.' He shook his head. 'When I find that Kam, I'm going to kill him. And if you try to stop me, I'll kill you too.'

Then both of them were struck at once by their father, who hurled himself at them and crushed them against a wall. At once there came the rapid cracks of gunfire and the twang of ricocheting bullets. A group of men in army uniforms rushed out of a building across the road and ran in all directions, and then there was another burst of shots and two of the men crumpled to the ground.

'We came for you, Karl,' Gábor murmured harshly. 'But now that we're in the revolution, we might as well join it.'

Ψ

Budapest was a battlefield, but it was also still a city. No one had prepared for a fight, and they were not sure of the rules. If you were obviously a citizen walking briskly to work, would the AVH or the Russian troops shoot at you? Would the students, for that matter? Were you invisible to the warriors, or fair game? Some people, resolutely refusing to take sides, went about their business while explosions boomed out threats from distant avenues. They did a solid day's work, and if it was labour without purpose or effect, nevertheless they could not think what else they should do.

A kind of normality rose to the surface whenever the fighting moved on to another part of the city, like shoots sprouting in the wake of a forest fire. Shops and cafés opened up again, people queued for bread and meat. In these districts the rebels and the Russians might even reach unspoken pacts because of the sheer ambiguity of the situation – they'd join separate queues or sit in different restaurants and pretend they had not seen each other. Soviet tanks would rumble past with guns averted, smelling out danger in far-off sectors.

But still the Russian flags were publicly burnt, and the Hungarian tricolour hung from countless balconies with a hole in the centre where the Communist symbols had been cut out. And when violence erupted, no one was safe. Even the children joined in, yelling slogans and hurling petrol bombs at the soldiers and the hated security police. Rumours circulated about an old man they called Uncle Szabo, who led hordes of urchins on bare-handed raids against the AVH, a troupe of agile little monkeys who leapt from hidden perches to seize guns and swarm over tanks. Bullets buzzed around the old squares of Budapest like murderous insects.

The revolutionaries knew their position was impossible: their enemy was not Gerő and the AVH, but the entire Soviet Union, with its tank divisions and jet fighters and atomic bombs. The United Nations will intervene, some said, but few believed it. President Eisenhower had voiced his support, others claimed, but that seemed thin encouragement when Budapest was being shattered street by street.

And yet, after just seven days, the Russians announced that they would withdraw their troops from Hungary and enter into discussions with the rebel leaders about the future government of the country. It seemed incredible, but there it was: on 1 November, the Soviet high command began talks with the Central Council of the Revolutionary Armed Forces. The Council insisted that Hungary was now a neutral country, outside the Warsaw Pact, and ready for a democratic socialist government. They had won; peace had come.

Gábor Neder sat with his sons two days later in a café on Szervita tér, and told them that it was time to return to Győr. But István would not go.

'Are the streets free from the AVH?' he rasped. 'Has Moscow kissed Nagy on the cheek?'

There was a Russian semi-automatic rifle lying by each of their chairs. Karl Neder had fired his gun twice, both times at unseen snipers. He had no idea where his bullets had come to rest, and he hoped never to pick up the weapon again. He'd happily leave it there in the café. He didn't even know if it was still loaded.

Karl had felt nauseous for the duration of the fighting. In seven days he'd barely managed to keep down a bit of bread and milk. He ached from head to toe, and his skin felt greasy, like an old and neglected suit.

Everywhere he kept expecting to see Jaroslav Kam – he longed for that, and was terrified of it.

'It's not our job to chaperone the new Hungary,' said Gábor. 'I'm thinking about your mother –'

'You!' István's accusation was virtually spat out onto the table. He was drinking fiery apricot pálinka; the others had tea.

Gábor said nothing, but merely inclined his head as though considering some intransigent puzzle. Karl sensed that he was not even angry.

The three of them had said very little over the past week. They had teamed up with a band of factory workers who carried out raids, with minimal strategic planning, wherever the security police gathered in sufficient numbers to present a tempting target. István threw himself recklessly into these attacks, but for all his relentless energy he had seemed curiously unconcerned about the task at hand, as though the AVH troops were just an irritation obstructing his true goals.

'Well.' Gábor rose. István kept his gaze on the table; he affected not to notice the finality in his father's gesture.

'I –' Karl could look at neither of them. 'I will stay, for a bit, I think. Just see out the… the end game. Then we will join you at home.' Did Gábor see? If they were to separate, it could not be István who was the odd one out.

'We won't be long.' All the same, he could not help feeling like a deserter.

It was a Saturday evening when Gábor caught the train out of Budapest. Things were returning to normal. People left the shelter of their cellars, and began to stroll along the Danube in tentative, excited groups. Throughout the day they queued for bread and potatoes, and in the evening they sat out drinking in the bars, despite the chill. There was a cold wind coming from the north, and with it a low, growling noise.

There was no moon that night. In darkness, Budapest was swallowed up.

Ψ

Gábor's train was the last to leave the city, but it seemed indecisive, unwilling to slip away. It stuttered through faceless villages at little more than walking pace, moaning softly to itself. Finally it stopped, and he fell asleep. When he awoke the carriage was cold and there was an unutterably miserable light oozing out of the sky. They were barely thirty miles out of Budapest, and there was no power. By sheer force of will, it seemed, Moscow had sucked it out of the whole country.

The announcement came on Radio Free Kossuth shortly before it shut down its broadcasts for good. 'This is Imre Nagy speaking, President of the Council of Ministers of the Hungarian People's Republic. In the early hours of dawn Soviet troops launched an attack against our capital with the obvious purpose of overthrowing the legal Hungarian democratic government. Our troops are fighting. The government is in its place. I want to inform the people of our country and of the world of these facts.'

It seemed to Karl Neder that his brother had known precisely what was going to happen. When the dawn was lacerated with the most ghastly screams and roars and detonations, a mad cacophony that made no sense to anyone else, István calmly sat up, put on his boots, picked up his rifle and left their makeshift lodgings. He was gone even before Karl was sure this was not a dream, another horrible replay of the days past.

Karl ran empty-handed into a street that tasted of dust. Only half of it was left: the farthest buildings were smashed to smoking stumps, bits of random rock. About what followed, he was never sure. Sometimes, in the years to come, he saw his brother kneeling with his gun levelled, firing into the billowing clouds. Other times István was just standing there as though transfixed – waiting with patience that was suddenly inexhaustible. But Karl suspected that in the true version of events he saw a form already slumped on the tarmac, kneeling curled up with the crown of its head resting on the solid surface.

What came after was even more confused. He ran forward, yes, but after that the clouds rolled in and blocked his sight; they filled his lungs until he was gasping, drowning among tiny particles. The top of his head seemed to explode, something white-hot was laid across his scalp. Budapest fell apart; apartment blocks slipped away like cliff faces in a storm, uncovering gaping holes that were dark with writhing life. Streets cracked open and people fell into the crevices. Great chunks of masonry rolled around, as flimsy as crumpled paper in the wind. Then the sky caught fire. He was shown these things, one after another, like images flickering on a newsreel. Finally the pictures gave way to a blankness in which voices muttered at the edge of hearing, holding mundane conversations with an inexplicable urgency.

There was a stench of decay, and he was crawling in slime, but he seemed to be blind. Far off, dogs yelled savage threats.

Ψ

When Karl Neder was able to understand where he was, he was in Austria.

They got out, the rebels, they fled right away, before the Soviet cordon had time to tighten. Them, and thousands of others; they were political refugees, herded into great encampments in the swamplands east of Vienna.

He cried out when he understood that his fevered journey west had taken him within a few miles of Győr. At first he was determined to recross the border, risking his life to get back into the prison that his country had become. He would find his mother and father, and they would either take their chances under the new regime or all make the hazardous exodus over the frontier. But he could barely stand: his head wound, still covered by a crude bandage, left him unsteady on his feet. 'Not now,' the others told him. 'Write to them –

eventually something will get through. Something can be arranged later.'

'And my brother? What happened to him?'

No one knew anything about his brother.

Ψ

An organization funded by a Hungarian civil engineer in Atlanta, Georgia, one of the pre-war diaspora and now a magnate responsible for much of that part of Atlanta that rose above six storeys, brought Karl Neder to the United States. After six months, a letter reached him. It was the last time he heard from any member of his family.

> *My dear Karl,*
>
> *So you are safe. I knew it must be so, although I have not dared to think it. So much else has pressed down upon me. I cannot tell from your letter exactly what you know and what you do not. You were thinking perhaps that your father is here with me in Győr? Alas, that isn't so. You must have been separated in Budapest, then. That was where he was killed, as I have discovered from a very brave and honest man who communicated this to me many weeks ago. This man, his name is Denes, he was one of the fighters with you and Gábor and István, he told me that he identified my husband's body three days after the Russians invaded. I am sorry; I don't suppose you knew this until now.*
>
> *What can we say about Gábor, you and I? I do not intend to put him on the balance and see which way it tips. I do not need to excuse him of everything in order that I can grieve for him. You knew him well enough. In any event, he was your father.*

But of István I know nothing. No reports have come back to me, but I fear he will not return now. I cannot quite understand from what you say whether you know more than me. If so, please tell me. I think, however, I can imagine all too well how the fighting will have affected him. Long ago, I lost the ability to protect István.

I cannot pretend that things are anything other than hard here. It is like it was in the old days, when your father was in prison. Of course the regime will always be harsh after a rebellion, and I imagine things will improve. That, at any rate, is what we tell ourselves. Old women have less to fear, although I don't think they are supposed to have an entire house all to themselves. Well, it is too big anyway, and I have no use for it. I am not so well, Karl. I will be honest with you, because I cannot be sure whether my words will reach you or not, and so I cannot risk nuance or gentleness here. When I cough, it is not because of the dampness. But there are friends here who will look after me, and you must not even consider trying to return here. It is not worth it. I will not see you lock yourself away inside the old country, and absolutely not for my sake. Such opportunities you have now, there in America! Seize them, Karl, because everything here is lost.

Your loving mother,
Dora

UNFINISHED BUSINESS

14

'IT'S GOOD IN PLACES,' SAID TIM EVERS. 'VERY GOOD. IN PLACES.'

'No good in others.'

'Well, it's just... it lacks something, Lena. And we both know what that is, don't we?'

She hadn't expected him to take the story, not as it stood. She had continued to toy with the idea of ditching the commission altogether – calling Evers and telling him that she had been wrong, that there was nothing to say after all. Not because there was indeed nothing to say, but because in Vienna she had glimpsed an entire world that confused and disturbed her, and she was not sure she had the stamina to enter it. She felt she had no real idea what was at stake in those fantasies of liberation and disorder. And she kept dreaming of Frank Symons leaping from church steeples like a myopic gargoyle.

But in the end she'd sent it along anyway. Three pages fed through the mangler of her new electronic typewriter, which remembered a full line of text before printing it. That way the pages emerged a little less encrusted with sanitizing scabs of correcting fluid, impatiently overprinted before it was fully dry so that the corrections were embossed rather than inked.

Here was the story of *The Bitter Road*, the disputed territory of the electromagnetic ether, the machines that ran on indefinite entropic credit. Here was the delirious chaos of the

Vienna conference – so far as Lena could reconstruct those baffling days at all. Here was Aitchison with his sardonic satire, Neumann's defiant challenge, here the heated, combative appeals to an imperturbable Roy Battle. But –

'For a start, there's the science. I don't really understand it, Lena.'

'No, Tim, that's the point. You're not meant to.'

Tim was not quite ready for that kind of double bluff. 'I mean, I did physics at school – magnets and motors and stuff. But the theory of relativity – you're asking a lot of our readers.'

'No one really understands Karl Neder, Tim. Even other scientists say they don't. That's part of the question I'm raising. How do you decide if the theory is right, when it's incomprehensible?'

'*Is* it right?'

'Oh God, Tim, what are you asking *me* for?'

'Well, don't you think you have to take a position? We can hardly leave the reader to decide.'

'I'm not sure the story is really about who's right or wrong.'

'Yes... well, maybe.' Tim's focus was draining away. He never could keep something in his field of view for more than a few minutes. Grasping around for a new object on which his attention could alight, he said, 'Why don't we talk about it, Lena?'

'We are talking about it, Tim.'

'This isn't talking. Phones aren't for talking, they're just information machines. Why don't we have lunch?'

'You'd prefer to talk about relativity over lunch?'

'I'll talk about anything you want over lunch. Anything at all.'

With the scales of power so tilted, how to turn down an invitation like that? All the same, she did.

'Could be tricky, Tim. I think I'm going to be heading out there again soon. I want to get what you're after.' It was true, but only once she'd said it.

Ψ

'You could save yourself all this trouble, honey. One night of passion and he'd print anything. He's a pushover, believe me. And look, you don't even have to worry about mishaps. I don't mean to be insensitive, but your condition does have its advantages.'

'Ani, please. We're talking about Tim Evers. I *have* met Tim Evers, you know.'

Ani's silence left Lena suspecting that her flatmate didn't see much reason to worry *who* they were talking about. She'd have no qualms of that nature. Or perhaps Ani knew Tim better than Lena had thought.

'How much are you getting for this, anyway?'

'I may not be getting anything without more reporting. But it'd be the standard *Observer* rate, I suppose – fifty per thousand, something like that? I didn't ask, actually.'

Ani brought wine for the two of them. She handed Lena her glass with a grave expression.

'You can't go on doing business like that, sweetie. I've told you about this. *Cosmo* fleeced you. Ask at the outset, and then demand 50 per cent more than they offer.'

'I'm useless at that. And they'd only say no.'

'They don't say no. Not to me. They expect it from us. They respect us more for it. That's how I got my job – by asking for more than I was offered. *Always* ask for more.'

Ani was half-American; she grew up in Colorado before her parents divorced. She left her mother in Boulder and chose to come to Britain with her father, a consultant in fine chemicals. And to change her name to Ani, because she thought Annabel sounded fey and girly. Annabel was always a size larger than she wanted to be, but Ani turned youthful padding into toned muscle; she went sailing on the Solent and climbed rock faces in Snowdonia. When she laughed, people looked her way. At the journalism training college, Lena had been impressed by Ani's capacity for demanding attention. Yes, that must have been it.

Getting the flat together in Brixton's Shakespeare Road was Ani's idea. Most things were Ani's idea. The other students were frightened of her, and so were several of the tutors. But Ani in dreadlocks had been waiting, impatiently waiting, to become Ani in a powder-grey trouser suit, dictating her terms.

Lena had only one regular job now, which no one else wanted. She took the graveyard shift trimming stories at the last minute for the news pages of *Open Channel*, a current-affairs and media weekly. It meant being confined late into the Saturday night in a cramped print room in Covent Garden, and it was a thankless task. The printers grumbled when the columns still leaked overmatter after the fourth pass; the journalists grumbled (or more often, they raged) the next day when they saw what the clueless subeditor had done to their gracefully structured prose ('That paragraph was the crux of the whole fucking story, couldn't she see that?'); the news editor grumbled about the execrable, overpriced bottles of wine that they bought from the Europa store across the road.

Ani would never have done a job like this, and Lena knew her flatmate disapproved of her doing it too, especially now she'd had a Big Piece published. But it wasn't just a matter of cash; Lena loved this work. Here her journalism training finally came into its own. Here she didn't have to try to antici-pate the capricious, off-the-cuff whims of a commissioning editor, nor endure the self-important droning of an interviewee larding slender facts with bloated opinion. There was poise and purity to this task of paring down a collection of words into a regulated surface area. It was an almost geometric challenge, a question of fitting shapes into other shapes. Here was a lone, flailing word, what printers called a widow, waiting to be sacrificed in the name of efficiency, replaced by a shorter, cheaper alternative so as to reel in a line. Here was a sentence that said the same thing twice. Here was a mealy-mouthed qualifier, invisible to the reader and added only to cover the reporter's back. It was endlessly satisfying and reassuring to Lena to find that everything that anyone ever said could be said in half the length – so long, of course, as the words were someone else's. Herself, she always overwrote, but she made it a point of honour never to complain about the ministrations of the subeditor. She knew the story from both sides, knew that you had to be heartless with other people's words. Very few people could discipline their own literary progeny – someone else had to knock them into shape, strip away the flab and display clarity of thought and intention. Journalism seemed to Lena to involve a necessary act of submission: you laid yourself out and let others set to work with their scalpels.

And where better to perform this butchery than surrounded by the heartless glamour of Covent Garden? Who in the noisy, expensive streets below would care about the terrible, callous things being done to text in this garret, where the floors were littered with the bromide scraps of lexical surgery? Where two lost souls peered at eight-point characters under the unforgiving, yellow-eyed Anglepoise, while in the background there was the hum and clatter of the machinery that gave body to that delicious phrase, hot metal.

But this too was a dying trade, as Lena knew when she bought her electronic typewriter with its digital memory, however pitifully small and short-lived that was. The silicon recall of these devices was growing by the week. Before long, they would hold entire documents, books, libraries; Remingtons with minds of their own. Hot metal was doomed by cold silicon, anyone could see that. Even the strikers at Wapping could see that, and it was why they had fought with the police and the press chiefs that winter with such sad and bitter fury.

Wapping was just another conflagration in a country that had come to seem tinder-dry. And Lena was living in one of the most flammable zones, as she'd discovered one weekend last September. *Open Channel* had called her in to subedit news for the whole of Saturday, which meant a bleary 6.30 start with the moon still hanging overhead. All day in the frantic office she collated the stories as they were filed, gave them a rough edit for grammar and spelling, and dispatched the proofs up the road to be transformed into a crude paste-up, awaiting her attentions in the evening. It was intense, head-down work, and no hint of the uproar in South London reached her desk. So she was mystified and irritated when, at a quarter past midnight, the last tube to Brixton pulled in at Stockwell and refused to advance any further. 'Brixton's closed,' the station guard mumbled as he pulled the grilles across the entrance. 'Some kind of trouble.' The scattering of late-night passengers emerged dazed into the night, and the most alert of them snapped up any taxis that happened to be idling in Stockwell at that unfriendly hour. A short walk home, then, and if South London was not an ideal place for young women to wander alone in the dark, midnight was still early enough in Brixton's shifted time zone to offer some safety in numbers.

But the crowds that night were not revellers, not clubbers drifting in the dissolute orbit of the pills-and-dance dens, not dealers or buyers or pushers or pullers. Brixton had become unhinged. Night creatures ran down the streets, some wearing masks of panic, others laughing or taking loping, loose strides like animals set free. Even the policemen were running, and they wore the armour that was now, in these days of unrest, coming to seem like their standard uniform. Helmeted and shielded like troops at Poitiers, with batons as blunted broadswords. One of them demanded to know where Lena was going. 'Home.' Where had she been? 'At work.' Wasn't that the London equation: Day = Work, Night = Home? The policeman was not convinced. He seemed to have forgotten the formula. But in haste he passed on.

Sirens voiced their mindless alarm, and Lena felt as though she had wandered into London's collective memory, into the trauma of forty years earlier. London at war.

And that's what it was. She saw it when she reached Brixton Road, and found the place in flames.

Shops had been ransacked, their glass fronts now jagged maws ready to consume the consumer. Groups of young men were carrying away the casualties of the raids: television sets, hi-fi stacks, anything that made a noise when it was plugged in. Just beyond the tube station, the road itself was barred: a barricade had been constructed from the hulks of shattered cars, disgorging fluorescent streamers of fire and turbid, toxic smoke. Londoners had forgotten what to do amidst such scenes, and they improvised as best they could. Here and there, gangs hurled missiles, sometimes at knots of policemen but sometimes just into the night, as though warding off demons that prowled beyond the firelight. Pieces of brick and slate rained down, objects tore blazing trails across the sky: an urban meteor shower. The policemen clustered and conferred; they would launch charges, clumsy and encumbered with their see-through rectangular shields, only to find the space emptied as the night absorbed their quarry.

Now Lena, protected only by her improbability, was scared. Here was a place where violence had lost touch with motive. That happened in war zones. Killing could become just another activity, like smoking or breaking windows. A random act, something that occurred merely because it could.

There on Brixton Road, Lena understood that the world was not partitioned into good and bad, safe and dangerous. This city too could become a wasteland, a blasted and savage place, as harsh and alien as the crater-faced moon.

Ψ

'That's the spirit. You see my point, then?'

'There's a gaping hole in the piece.'

You couldn't write an article about a wayward, controversial, vagabond scientist without putting him at the centre of it. Without even having met him. Yes, she knew that. That, she said, was why she was heading back east.

'Ah. Fantastic. I know it can be hard to track down characters like this. Of course I see that, Lena. But we'll pay your expenses – I mean, on the understanding that we do publish this thing in the end, naturally. It's a nice story, I'm quite sure about that.' She thought he sounded a little like he was trying to convince himself. Was she blowing it already?

'OK, Tim. I'll do my best. I may need another few weeks.'

'End of April then, that's perfect. There's no rush. You do see my point, don't you? We've got to hear from him. That's playing to your strengths, Lena. I can see you're good with the personal stuff. That's why we want you to do this for us.' Either he was remembering his manners, or he had not yet given up on that lunch.

Ψ

Lena knew that she had not suddenly decided to head back in search of Neder just to appease Tim Evers and cling onto her assignment. She knew this was a great opportunity, but she didn't kid herself that it was going to be career-changing. No, she suspected that she'd simply been waiting for Tim to prompt her towards something she'd otherwise feel unable to justify to herself.

She had pinned a page from one of Neder's papers on her wall, frowning at the thought that this was a slightly unhinged thing to do. The symbols revealed nothing to her, and now she knew that the equations might not even be correct. But they had begun to represent something quite unconnected to their ostensible function. 'Here I stand,' she whispered. 'Here I stand.' A heretic's defiance: for the sake of this, I will go into the fire.

It took only two days to find a number, via Aitchison, (who sounds almost contrite) and then Neumann. He told her it would connect to somewhere in Linz, Austria. One of those enigmatic European phone numbers where there was no way of telling whether all the digits were present, or how to divide them up. A numerological code, devoid of clues. But the sequence evoked a phone ring at the other end. It rang and rang each time Lena dialled, day after day, until she began to suspect that this was after all the purpose of the number: a code to trigger a distant ringing mechanism.

Then one day in late March the monosyllabic tone was cut short by a voice that, in a brief and incomprehensible mash of syllables, sent down the line a bewildering mixture of brusqueness, suspicion, weariness and nervous energy.

'Karl Neder?'

There was silence.

'I am trying to speak to Karl Neder. I am an English writer, and I would like to talk to him.'

'Why?'

Try answering that one.

'Well. For an interview. I am writing for the *Observer*

newspaper in England, a story about the theories of Dr Neder. My name is Lena Rom–, ah yes, Lena.'

The line went quiet again, but she knew that there was still someone on the end of it, making a careful reckoning.

'I can travel to where you are,' she offered. 'That is, I am speaking to Dr Neder, I take it?'

'Come then. But it must be as soon as you can.' The speaker rasped an address, which she transcribed phonetically, too disconcerted to ask about the spelling. Then he hung up.

15

I asked Sally whether she felt bitter about it. 'I don't think it's bitter, exactly,' she said. 'I feel numb, I suppose. It seems unreal. But in another way, you know, I guess I'm lucky to be alive at all. Some days I sit and watch the sun gleaming on the rocks, and listening to the surf and the sea birds, and I think, "Well, I'm still here, and that's something, isn't it?"'

Ψ

Lena was sixteen when she tried to kill herself. That, at least, was the official story. She argued afterwards that to classify her action as an attempted suicide, as the doctors seemed determined to do, was ridiculous. It was all just a silly mistake. Late at night in her mother's house, she'd started and then mostly finished a bottle of gin before swallowing five benzodiazepines to blot out her nausea. 'You might never have been here now,' the doctors told her after pumping her stomach, 'if you hadn't vomited as you passed out.' But she knew better than that; she knew they had just wanted to scare her. Half a pint of gin and five benzodiazepines don't add up to eternity. She'd obviously misread the instructions or something, though she didn't really have any recollection of the pills at all.

They came from her mother's bathroom cabinet. Barbara Romanowicz never slept well. Her sense of hearing seemed to get more acute at night ('I should have been a bat,' she'd joke inaccurately), and before she and George separated she'd watched many a dawn brighten the walls as he lay muttering beside her. Her husband's dreams were always filled with conversation (but with whom?).

Barbara took it badly that her daughter had apparently tried to end her life in her, Barbara's, bathroom. 'I was barely three yards away,' she cried. 'To think that you would be that close, and not come to me for help.' Barbara, giving the pills a miss that night, had been woken from a fitful doze by the grating sound of her daughter voiding her guts.

'That's the point, Mum,' said Lena. 'Suicides don't do what they do because there's no one nearby to help them. It's drowning people who die that way.'

'Don't talk about dying, please.'

'The doctor said I should. He says it makes it less likely that I *will* die.'

Lena could not bring herself to say that if she had thought her mother could help her, then of course she would have gone to her. She knew that talk of suicide frightened her mother. She imagined that was because Barbara had contemplated it too.

Instead, she alternated in the subsequent weeks between dismaying her mother with bold indifference to the matter, and perplexing her by curling into a ball and weeping.

'Where are all these tears from?' Barbara sighed as she stroked her daughter's pliant, frail bones. 'Why so sad?'

Not sad, Mother. Angry. Helplessly angry. What else did she expect?

Her father was a realist, of course.

'If you wish to kill yourself,' he said, 'there is nothing either I or your mother can do to stop you. I want you to know that I know this.'

It had the intended effect of disconcerting her, but she tried to fight back.

'So you wash your hands of it.' And triumphantly, she saw wrath ignite briefly in his eyes.

But he did not speak until it dimmed. He knew better than that.

'I do not wash my hands of it, Lena. I have no wish to see you kill yourself, and if I can prevent it, I shall. What you did has distressed us both deeply.' Damn him, she thought she might burst out sobbing.

'What's the point of all this drama?' She tried to steady herself with anger. 'Anyone would think you all *want* to believe I'd top myself. Didn't you ever have too much to drink? Or would that damage your precious self-control?'

'I've spoken with the doctor,' he continued. 'We would like you to see a psychiatrist. That is, he would like that, and I have no objection. I should be... glad, I suppose, to consider the opinion of a professional. But I want to tell you something. I hesitate to do so, because I would not like to goad you into any more sensational gestures of this sort. But on balance, I think it's worth saying. The fact is, I agree with you. That's to say, I don't believe you wanted to die. I say this because I think it's important that you hear it. I don't really understand what you were after, but I hope that you can at least be clear about your intentions.'

Yes, of course. George Romanowicz was always championing clarity.

Romanowicz never admitted that he had been given some advice by the 'professional' who talked gently with Lena every week for three months after she collapsed on her mother's bathroom floor. But it must have been this advice that prompted him to try for a second time to tell her about his work.

While she was a child, they had never discussed it – not

properly, not as an exchange of information. At seven Lena was old enough to realize that her father did something when he was not with her, and she asked him what that thing was. He told her he was a physicist, and that that was a person who tried to understand how the world worked. That seemed to suffice for another six years, until she had acquired a vague image of what physics entailed – forces and masses, electricity and gravity, friction and string and stars – and wanted to know what there was still to be understood about the way the world works.

Had she put it that way, it would have been an invitation that few scientists could resist. But instead she said, 'So what do you physicists do, anyway? Sit and think?'

'That's pretty much it,' her father replied. 'If it seems a strange way to earn a living, remember that most of the population does only half as much. The first half.'

'Yeah, they're smart – they get away with only half the work. So what do you think about?'

And then George Romanowicz made a mistake. He fetched his latest paper, imagining that he could show her that behind all the inscrutable algebra and words lay simple ideas about how matter behaves. He put it like that, too: 'how matter behaves'. Lena was not accustomed to the idea that matter 'behaved' in any way whatsoever, nor indeed to the notion that one thought about 'matter' as a generic thing, rather than as people and cars and rain and earth. So although Romanowicz was on this occasion patient and kind and softly spoken, his attempt to explain what he thought about all day was a failure. And they both knew it.

What the thirteen-year-old Lena had really wanted was not for her father to sit her down with a scientific paper and try to reduce it to normal language. What she wanted was to get a letter from him now and again at the school where she boarded.

To have him stroke her hair and tell her she was beautiful, even if she knew she was bony and sallow and had bad posture. But he didn't do this, and she couldn't ask for it, and so it didn't happen.

Romanowicz suspected that it was the conversation he had with Lena after her overdose that set him on the road to a strange kind of semi-celebrity. Was that the right word? It was hardly celebrity. Physicists were never celebrities, semi or otherwise – or rather, they were never celebrities because of their physics, and Romanowicz did not delude himself that he had anything else to offer.

Was an appearance on *Tomorrow's World* the making of a celebrity? Honestly, now: interviews on Radio 4, invitations to the Cheltenham Festival, calls from journalists – it did not add up to much in the end. Enough to make George conscious about his appearance, however, so that he kept his beard neatly trimmed and took to wearing contact lenses, and – he could hear it happening, slightly to his dismay but not enough to make him do anything to prevent it – let his voice drop a little and become more brandy-toned. He was not especially adept at flirting on set with young television producers, but you did not have to be particularly adept to do that; it was sufficient to show willing. The industry ran on a mode of low-level flirtatiousness, where it was understood that anything more overt or, God forbid, more serious was not simply just more of the same but an entirely different matter. Not forbidden, just different. George did not really have the energy or the appetite for that kind of thing. Not any more.

So that was perhaps where it started, with Lena lounging in the conservatory in Whitstable Road, while a muggy summer dragged on. During the school holidays she spent a couple of weeks with him and the rest with her mother, except that now she typically devoted a week or so to camping around Britain with friends, which could be a euphemism for various activities about which George and Barbara preferred to remain ignorant. There was a lethargy about Lena, even before the overdose, that George Romanowicz tried hard to accept as a symptom of youth rather than anything constitutional.

She dressed in black: a gypsy skirt shredded at the hem, like a widow's weeds, black granny boots, two ripped T-shirts that together did a passable job of concealing stray patches of white skin. Black was Lena's colour. She dyed her hair, already deep umber, until it had the shade and lustre of sable. She carried Edgar Allan Poe in her bag, but mostly she read books about Hell's Angels and boot boys.

A few years later Romanowicz would notice this style everywhere, and would feel gratified at his daughter's prescience. In 1975, however, in an age of turquoise blue and flame orange and sparkling gold – the colours of psychedelia faded during the Autumn of Love until only the least natural ones remained – she looked odd, and shopkeepers would watch her through narrowed eyes.

She was drawing, biro in clenched fist, which she often did when she stayed with her father. While she did not exactly hide her pictures, Romanowicz knew that he should not make too much of a show of looking at them, let alone talking about them. He thought of them not so much as pictures, in fact, but as diagrams. She was working something out. It was not clear what the question was, but the solution involved trees, dense and gnarled, hunched into a forest that light could barely penetrate. Her sketchbook was full of dark forests. She bought books of engravings by Dürer and Altdorfer, and sat staring at them for hours. In fierce secrecy she wrote little stories, in which she drowned in swamps or was eaten by rooks or sat and watched the sun go out. Barbara was convinced it wasn't normal.

Of course it wasn't bloody normal, thought Romanowicz. Bugger normal. He despised normal. Normal was everywhere, normal was Double Diamond and *That's Life*. Normal crept up on you when you dropped your guard. He observed Lena as if she were an exotic species, a scrawny marsupial escaped into the orchards of Kent.

He knew she wasn't mediocre, but he wasn't sure that she intended to do anything with her lack of mediocrity. Except to wear it, perhaps. Sometimes he suspected that she felt rather resentful about not being mediocre.

By unspoken agreement, they didn't talk much. That was what her mother was for. Barbara could talk to her. Romanowicz knew that Lena would often get irritated with his former wife, condemn her conventionality, her good taste, the anxious timidity with which she voiced her worries about her daughter. But the two of them were far more intimate than he would ever be with Lena – more, indeed, than he had been with Barbara. When Romanowicz and Lena were under the same roof, he felt as though they were two widowed people who had unexpectedly found themselves living together. Their cohabitation rarely led to explicit hostility, but they both showed a kind of persistent baffled resignation at having to manoeuvre around one another. Sitting in silence, however, they could be comfortable, able to prevent their thoughts from getting in each other's way.

'You must understand,' Lena's psychiatrist had told him, 'that whether we regard this as a genuine suicide attempt or, as I am inclined to do, as self-harm, it is an extremely angry act. Extraordinarily angry and violent.'

Romanowicz did not see how anger could be so passive, so placid. 'Surely,' he said, 'she is depressed. She is in despair. I'm sure she despairs about her mother and me. We really didn't do very well, I know that.'

But the psychiatrist would not have it. 'Despair is not enough to make somebody do this,' he said. 'At least, not in her circumstances, where she is well provided for, she has friends, she is socialized. This is not a case of giving up. This is an attack.'

Ψ

Romanowicz carried his sherry into the conservatory, and was surprised at how nervous he felt. It was contrived, he thought, this act, this measured nonchalance, but it was what the doctor ordered. Talk to her.

'I'm writing a paper,' he said. Don't let this be like the last time. She doesn't care that you're hoping to get it into *Physical Review Letters*. She won't be impressed by the neatness of your argument.

'You know,' he said, 'I love the fact that there are all these gaps. In physics, I mean. Problems that are completely bloody obvious, but no one has studied them. Everyone's digging deeper and deeper, but they haven't even looked carefully on the surface yet. Can I really be satisfied with understanding the structure of subatomic matter if I don't know how a bee gets from flower to flower?'

She was looking at him with an inscrutable sixteen-year-old gaze, neither interested nor bored, not encouraging, not disapproving. He'd surprised himself with that unconversational 'flower to flower', a self-consciously vivid turn of phrase.

'I was talking to a chap about sand, and we both decided we know nothing about it. Not just us, but anyone. You stand on it, and it's a solid. You pour it, and it's a fluid. Which is it? The thing is, nobody knows. Chemical engineers have studied powders for decades, but they don't understand them. They know what to expect, but that's not the same thing. And they're not always right, anyway. Powders. They're the next big thing.' And then he was off. It was a remarkable performance. He talked about salt cellars, the grains tumbling through the holes and sometimes jamming even though each of them was too small to block the gap. The cohesion of wet sand and the whys and wherefores of sandcastles. Breakfast cereal in packets and how the biggest pieces always rise to the top. The statistical quirks of avalanches and landslides. He was lucid, even eloquent, he drew connections between the most unlikely phenomena. He put physics into the garden, the landscape, the seaside, the kitchen table, into baking cakes and mixing cement and timing eggs.

He came to an end. That's what he did: it was an end, a rounding off, a summing up. It completed the structure. They looked at one another, Romanowicz feeling a little shaken. Lena had her mother's eyes, but in that moment Romanowicz found in them *his* mother's eyes. He had to concentrate to remember who she was. She made a small smile, as though she was reading a mildly amusing book; it looked like an involuntary reflex. Then she got up and went inside.

Romanowicz swept up his words and placed them back together in an article that he offered to *New Scientist*, which published it. He got a call from the BBC, discussed 'the physics of sand' on the radio. They loved the bit about sandcastles. 'Tell us more about the sandcastles. What's the trick to making a good sandcastle?' He had no idea, but he gave an answer, and they all beamed. The *Daily Telegraph* ran a short article, and then it was *Tomorrow's World*. Romanowicz's colleagues were entertained.

The publicity stopped soon after that, but Romanowicz wrote some more, a popular piece about the aerodynamics of animal flight. Old stuff, really, but people didn't know about it. Vortices shedding from wing tips, eddies of thick air that the bee could mine for buoyancy. He began to receive calls from journalists, every month or so at first, and then more frequently. Sometimes he could help, sometimes he had to direct them elsewhere. He began to perceive how it worked: he was now a name on a list. Journalists did not want to work too hard. If they needed a quote or advice about the design of nuclear reactors, the implications of space flight or the sighting of a comet, all they wanted was a media-friendly scientist. They had no idea what Romanowicz researched; perhaps they did not even appreciate that physicists *had* research specialities. He spoke well, he was relaxed on camera, he managed to avoid jargon, he sounded confident and persuasive – what more could you want? George Romanowicz became a Public Voice of Science.

Ψ

When her father gave his great oration in the conservatory on Whitstable Road, Lena was silent because she could think of nothing to say. While he was speaking, she had listened. He had a pleasant voice. She watched the changes come into his face as new ideas occurred to him; she followed the gestures of his hands for their coded signals. He began, and he ended – it was a complete story. What do you say after your parents have told you a story? There is nothing to say. They should expect nothing, they may demand nothing. The story ends and you go to sleep.

But Lena knew that her silence disturbed her father. She did not particularly intend it to have that effect; in fact she regretted it. But there was nothing she could do about it. It embarrassed her too, to find that her father could after all explain so elegantly what he did and why it mattered, and that she could find nothing in the way of a response. He was not asking for her approval, or for her comments or criticisms. He was not asking for anything, and so it did not seem unfair that she gave him nothing. But it was embarrassing all the same, and neither of them spoke subsequently about the incident.

ψ

'He was lucky to survive, falling from such a height. Where was his angel when he needed it?'

Lena had to admit that her plan didn't seem to be working. When she'd suggested to her father that they meet, he had at first proposed lunch at the Royal Society: 'Much easier for you than trudging down to Kent.' But she didn't feel like being surrounded by pictures of austere old scientists. They gave George an unfair advantage, egging him on to extremes of level-headed scepticism. Newton and Hobbes, the hard men of the Enlightenment. 'No, I'll come to you,' she told him. 'I thought we could meet at the cathedral for a change.'

'Splendid,' said George, and there was a genuine enthusiasm in his voice that disconcerted her. Far from being thrown off-balance by the heady religiosity of Canterbury's Gothic gloom, here he was expounding on the gorgeous blues of the Thomas Becket window ('There's one just like it at Chartres'), and telling her how the architect William of Sens had fallen from the scaffolding in the late twelfth century. What was he up to?

'I'm beginning to see that I've been underestimating this place. There was less superstition in those days, not more. The cathedral is really a way of expressing a belief in an ordered universe – the kind of place where science is possible. It's just that in the Middle Ages they regarded that order as the work of God, the Great Architect.'

'The First Church of Science. I bet that would have gone down well with the bishops.'

'They were the best-educated men of their age, Lena. It

wasn't just the Bible they were reading, as it is today. They studied Plato, Aristotle, Euclid, Ptolemy. They carried all the advanced knowledge of their culture.'

'I've heard that it's common for people's religious impulses to emerge in their later life. I'm starting to think there's something in that.'

'I'm so glad, Lena, that at least I managed to cultivate your talent for disrespect.' He said it with what seemed almost like happiness. He was invulnerable today.

'I'm off to Austria again for a few days,' she said. 'I just thought I'd let you know.'

'That sounds exciting. So you're still working on this story in Vienna?'

'Yes, except that now it's in Linz.'

They walked around the ambulatory, where multicoloured lozenges danced over their clothes.

'It's a strange thing, you know. While you were in Vienna, something happened there to a member of my department.'

'Have you informed the police of your suspicions?'

'Now, now. It was Frank Symons – you may remember him. Poor chap. Seems he took a very bad turn. And at a scientific conference, of all places. At least, that's what it purported to be. The fact is, it was the kind of event we should really be more strict about, and if I'd known about poor Frank's state of mind before he left, well, I do hope I could have found a way –'

'OK, Dad, I give in,' Lena sighed. 'How is he?'

'Bones can be mended, at least.'

As they strolled down the south aisle, Lena adjusted to the idea that her father clearly had a fair notion of what she'd been up to. And she realized that she was not terribly surprised by this. But among other things, it forced upon her a familiar conflict. She knew her father could provide trustworthy answers to a host of questions, and that they would be clearer coming from him than from Iain Aitchison or Roy Battle or anyone else she knew. But to let him do so would be to capitulate, to take on their old roles, to bury herself even more deeply in her past. It would be to allow him a vehicle for affection, too – but he would only squander the chance.

'I suspect the message of early Gothic unsettled the clergy themselves,' said George. 'Why else would they try to hide it later, to mess it all up, with these dreadful frilly screens and ornaments and fan vaults? They couldn't even do their sabotage tastefully.'

'What do you know about Karl Neder?' Let's get it over with.

'I think,' said George, without hesitation, 'that he is probably another Barry Vender.'

This took her by surprise, which was presumably the intention.

What she'd been hoping, Lena now saw, was that she would be able to force her father to raise the matter of Neder himself. 'And there I was,' she thought, 'behaving as though I wanted to conceal it. But who, honestly, did I think I was fooling?' Who else, after all, could it have been who had ripped Margaret Strong's story from the copy of *Natural Science* sitting on his desk in Canterbury, and then closed the magazine in the lame pretence that it had not been open at that page, with a letter to Roy Battle drafted by the side?

Dear Roy,

I am puzzled by this article. I see in it no news of relevance to the scientific community, and not particularly to any other community either. Surely it will be a sad day when passion and sentiment come to exert a greater command

*over the pages of your journal than reason and sound
science. I hope it will not be considered necessary to tell us
about any more of Dr Neder's shenanigans.*

*With best wishes,
George*

Of course he'd noticed – and then, in typical fashion, affected
ignorance or indifference. You could never accuse George
Romanowicz of firing the first shot. He was a pacifist, after
all.

But how much, then, did he really know about the whole
business?

'Vender? The American?'

'That man is a total charlatan. It's a long-standing tradition,
you know. In the Middle Ages they stood on benches and did
magic tricks. In the Enlightenment they talked about animal
magnetism. The Victorians had their seances. Now we have
the infinite-energy brigade. Isn't Neder one of those?'

'I'm not sure. That is, I suppose he is, if you mean that he's
after perpetual motion. It seems he... gets under your skin.'

'I don't know about that. But I do have certain responsibilities – and they extend to poor Frank, at least.'

'Where does Symons fit in?'

'Oh, I wish I knew. I really do. They worry me, affairs like
that conference. That chap Frank brought over from Italy.
Terribly hard to know where to draw the line. But one has to,
you know. Draw a line. One truly must. So are you going to
write that Karl Neder is a maligned genius?'

'I'm – I'm not sure what I'm going to say. That's why I
need to meet him. I'm a journalist, Dad, and this is the first
break I've had for ages. The first since that *Cosmopolitan* article.' She was annoyed to hear a pleading note in her voice.

'Yes. I thought you did that very well, by the way. I've told you that, haven't I? It's terrible what those people get away with.'

Ψ

Davey and Lena saw each other less often after he moved north, and for the past couple of years even their phone conversations had become sporadic. She felt bad at how life kept getting in the way, though she could never reconstruct in retrospect precisely what her life had contained which had actually been as urgent or distracting as it had seemed at the time. Was this a way of admitting that a phase in her life was passing? Yet what was there to replace it? Lena could not believe there was truly anyone or anything more worthy of her time than Davey, and the thought left her faintly panicked.

But he could be relied on for a Christmas card, always a handmade ironic collage of cut-outs from last year's batch assembled into a scene of Brueghel-like saturnalia. The year before last, his offering was as comically inventive as ever, and gave no hint of the short letter inside.

Been a bit of a rough year. Got cancer. But colorectal, so suitably Rabelaisian. Would send you the photos, but you might be about to tuck in to turkey. Thought I could always cast myself off Whitby cliffs, but decided instead to have a few rounds of chemo, and guess what? – it's in remission. Chemo is very bad (good) for the complexion, and now I've got cheekbones to die for. So, much as I'd like to haunt the abbey, seems I'll be making a noise in Westfold for a little while yet. Otherwise, it's the usual story – making no money by painting, playing music, putting on camp-horror theatre in little pubs around Scarborough. Reckon I've found

the best way of making no money that there's ever been.
Pop by if you're up this way, it would be lovely to see
you again.

As soon as she was free of Christmas obligations, Lena caught a train to Scarborough, from where a bus wound its way over snow-dusted moorland to Davey's pebble-dash council house in Westfold on the Yorkshire coast. When he came to the door, she did not even try to hold back her tears.

'God, am I really that bad? Well, you'd look like this too if you were a vegetarian in Yorkshire.'

'No, Davey, I'm amazed that you look so good.' She sniffed and smiled. 'Ghastly, but in a good way. The world's only veggie vampire. No, the fact is, I'm crying because I realize I'm just so glad to see you.'

She'd expected the remembered chaos, abandoned guitars, nub-ends of mascara, overdue library books and random scraps of sheet music. But it seemed that the congenital suburban tidiness of his parents had finally come through. Either that or he'd now had more than enough disorder among his cells to tolerate it in his habitat too. The kitchen gleamed, a bowl of fresh fruit sat alone on a table of well-oiled oak. They sipped Japanese twig tea from clean cups while she marvelled at the previously undisclosed complexity of his cranium, now barely covered with stubble when he took off his woolly hat.

Then he told her about the incinerator.

'They built it in the early 1970s, and there's been a local campaign ever since. There always is with these things, of course, but this particular operation does seem a bit dodgy. You get this film of ash on the leaves from time to time, so I guess it gets into my veggie beds too. I thought at first the protests were just a reactionary thing – everyone wants someone they can blame for their aches and pains, don't they? But there's been a lot of cancer in this village over the past few years. Stomach, lung, liver. The woman from the post office got ovarian cancer, and now she's got no ovaries. Anyway, I've joined the campaign.'

'And what happens to these people, Davey, in the end?'

Once he had always seemed the younger of the two of them, a boy who knew only breathless happiness and wistful sadness. Now Lena understood that behind the apparently frivolous way he spent his days there was absolute resolve and clarity. 'This is the right thing for me to be doing,' he told her. 'This is what I need. Because in my terms, I'm old already.'

Lena never intended that her research should lead to a story. It didn't occur to her at first that this was a journalist's work – she just wanted some facts. With initiative that surprised herself, she found a paper in the *Lancet* entitled 'Incidence of cancer of the larynx and lung near municipal incinerators in Great Britain, 1975–1984', which claimed to find á slightly enhanced risk for people living within one kilometre of the disposal units. But the study concluded by saying: 'It is not certain that this small increase in primary cancers is due to emissions of pollutants from incinerators, as residual socio-economic confounding factors cannot be excluded.'

The researchers had not included Westfold in their statistics, so Lena contacted one of them, an epidemiologist at University College in London. To her surprise, he took Davey's anecdotal evidence very seriously, but warned that establishing any cause-and-effect argument was always extremely difficult, and would require much more study. 'What we can do,' he told Lena, 'is at least check out whether the Westfold incinerator is meeting the safety regulations for emissions.'

And so he and an analytical chemist had gone up to Yorkshire and done just that. Without notifying DispoTech Ltd, the company that ran the plant, they took samples of air, water, soil and foliage, and found that the releases of dioxins, furans, heavy metals and particulate carbon were all at least three times the legal limits.

From there it became a matter for the courts, and it was August 1985 by the time DispoTech was fined several million pounds and forced to close the incinerator until proper clean-up procedures had been implemented. Lena was busy in the meantime. She interviewed several of the inhabitants of Westfold who had developed cancer, and used their testimonies for an article that broke the story by presenting a circumstantial case for DispoTech's culpability in a cancer cluster.

It was not the kind of material one would normally expect to find in *Cosmopolitan*, slotted between advice on how to make your sex better and your hair glossier. But the central interview of the piece was one that the magazine's editors knew would resonate with its readership. Lena described how the Westfold postmistress, a twenty-eight-year-old woman named Sally Harvey, was still struggling to come to terms with the fact that she would never now carry a child inside her.

Ψ

'You handled it very… movingly,' said George.

'Yes, well, it's made me a people person, hasn't it? That's apparently why I got this job. The story won't be "Karl Neder – right or wrong?" It'll be –'

'A people story. That's the way it is, isn't it? Look, you should do what your job requires. I know you're not going to ask for my blessing, and you know I'm not going to give it. But I would like to give you something else.'

It arrived by mail the day before Lena left for Linz: a cassette tape of *Science Now* on Radio 4 the previous November, on which Barry Vender defended his claim of having invented a 'free energy motor' against Britain's public physicist. Vender had recently become big news on American TV, and the BBC wanted their slice of the pie.

'Do you record everything you do?' Lena had asked, and George knew his reply sounded defensive.

'It's not a question of vanity. Doing interviews and debates is an art, and as is the case with all art, you have to work at it and be critical of what you produce. I listen to learn and to improve.'

It was a strange debate that the two of them had, and the presenter Christine Farr was unable to decide if in the end it was compelling or terrible. Since the programme went out live, it did not make a great deal of difference what she concluded. But she imagined the puzzlement, the genteel furrowed brows from Aberdeen to St Ives. She'd explained Vender's claims and his patent dispute, but then the two men had barely mentioned perpetual motion at all.

'I don't deny that my ideas are unconventional and that current physics can't cope with them,' said Vender, 'but you see, as I watch the scientific community line up to condemn them, a name keeps popping into my head. What was it the papal commission called Galileo's theories? "Foolish and absurd" is what I think they said.'

Vender was at the end of a satellite link to Chicago, so for Romanowicz, clamped into headphones, it felt like having a debate with a madman inside his head.

'Ah yes, good old Galileo,' he said. 'The patron saint of scoundrels. Isn't it remarkable how everyone with a – with an unconventional theory compares himself to Galileo. But why do we remember Galileo? Because he was persecuted as a heretic? Oh no. The Church persecuted thousands of people for having heretical thoughts. But Galileo's name is remembered because he happened to be right. That, and because he had proof, but we can argue about what proof truly is. The Church had proof too – it was the proof of the Scriptures. That is not good enough by today's standards, but quite honestly I'm not sure if in the terms of the seventeenth century they weren't absolutely right that their proof was the more compelling. Well, never mind that. The point is that there were any number of would-be Galileos with all kinds of bizarre and crazy ideas, and they were denounced too, and they were plain wrong. Some, like poor Giordano Bruno, came off much worse than Galileo.'

'The point I am making,' Vender replied, 'is that science is the new Church. It has its own Scriptures. You say that the papal commission relied on Scripture – well then, what are your laws of thermodynamics, if not another inviolable dogma against which a new idea can be judged right or wrong without even checking it out?'

'Do you know,' said Romanowicz, 'if I was paid to check out claimed violations of the thermodynamic laws, I would have a job for life. They are two a penny. They are cheap, to be honest. That's the problem. They ought to be the most expensive items in science. I'm talking here about investment of time and effort and thought, and perhaps even money too. A true scientist, encountering a violation of thermodynamic laws, does not say, "Goodness me, what a fine discovery I have made, now I can sit back and await my Nobel Prize." He says, "What a fool I am, I have fouled up my experiment and I had better work out where it has gone wrong." And sooner or later he finds the error. Or maybe he does not, and so then he thinks, "I had better come up with another experiment to show me what is wrong with this one."'

'And if that gives the same result?' Farr decided to let him run.

'Then he will say, "This is going to be embarrassing, but I

will have to bring in a colleague to point out the flaw." He will think, "There must be some other way of looking at this that doesn't violate thermodynamics." He will persist, despite the evidence, in the belief that he is wrong.'

'This doesn't sound to me,' said Vender, 'very much like the idea of the open-minded scientist.'

'A scientist should not have an open mind. Open minds are like open pits, liable to become filled with junk. The alternative is not necessarily a closed mind. A scientist must have a mind with strict entry requirements. Open to all, but only if they satisfy certain fair and transparent tests.'

'Excuse me for saying so,' Vender interjected, 'but there's something truly British about this. I don't quibble with the importance of falsifiability, but I don't think the history of science owes a great deal to people who have said, "I am wrong! I am wrong!" It's those who say, "I am right! I am right!" who have moved things forward. Those who saw little anomalies and believed in them, believed in the evidence of their senses, did not merely dismiss things that didn't fit with traditional thinking.'

Romanowicz was remembering the CBS images of Vender, a man in dirty dungarees standing outside a rural barn. His antagonist, he began to appreciate, was an acute judge of his audience, ready to play whatever part the occasion demanded.

'In the end,' said Vender, 'what matters is simple. Are you wrong, or are you right? I have carried out experiments which either show the creation of energy or they do not. I have put forward a theory to explain these observations, and either it is right or it is not.'

'That's what matters, certainly, but it isn't simple. Sorry, Chris,' Romanowicz acknowledged the presenter, who was looking more and more demoralized as she imagined the ladies of Cheltenham searching the ether for the afternoon play, 'but we can't really understand science at all unless we recognize what I am going to say. Let me propose a strange idea: suppose that Isaac Newton had come up with quantum theory. I mean all of it: wave functions, the uncertainty principle, quantization and so on. He tries to publish this theory in the *Philosophical Transactions of the Royal Society*, and his colleagues offer nothing but derision. Are they right or wrong to do so? Well, Newton is right, of course, since we know now that quantum mechanics does govern the fundamental behaviour of matter. But his colleagues are right to dismiss his theory, because it explains nothing that is not already explained, and predicts nothing that can be tested. There is no use for it. And there is no motivation for it. Without the blackbody catastrophe and the photoelectric effect, there is no reason to introduce it.'

'Maybe we'd better say what those –'

'There are two ways of being right, you see. There is one that relies on twenty–twenty hindsight, and one that we must apply when judging new ideas in the context of our times.'

'Professor Romanowicz,' said Vender, 'I should like to issue a straightforward challenge to you, and I hope you will not meet it with sophistry. Thousands of people have seen the demonstrations of my Energy Machine, and are persuaded by it. I assume that you haven't seen it yourself, so you still have the luxury of being able to deny it. But the theory that I have presented to explain these effects is much, much more important in the long run, because it will change physics forever. I shall send you my papers, and I challenge you, using the rules of your own dogma, to find fault with them.'

Romanowicz laughed. 'Do you know,' he asked, 'the story of Martin Luther at the Diet of Worms? He was asked by the papal representatives to recant his heresy, but he insisted that he would do so only if he could be shown to be in conflict with Scripture. He refused to recognize the authority of the bishops and princes, and even the Pope – Scripture alone was the arbiter. And to this, one of his accusers replied, "Martin, your plea to be heard from Scripture is the one always made by heretics." Well, perhaps I am simply giving you a new role model to identify with, but you see, I have heard this over and over again: "Unless you can prove my unconventional theory wrong, we must assume it is right." And so I say again: no. You must assume you are wrong until you run out of objections. I do not believe you have spent very long looking for them, Dr Vender.'

IN ORBIT

16

'JOIN ME', SAID BARRY VENDER TO KARL NEDER IN A SAN
Jose diner in 1958. 'Come and work in the American space
program. There's nothing you can't think or say there right
now. No one's inclined to feel dutiful to the so-called laws of
physics. They're not going to tell you that something's impossible because it violates some equation in a textbook. They
just need to get these machines up there, one way or another.'
Then he gave his broad, emphatic laugh. 'Well, maybe there's
one prohibition. You'd better not say that you're a member of
the Communist Party, or else your compatriot Ed Teller will
be on your case.'

Once again, Neder found himself unable to judge how seriously he was meant to take this remark. Was Vender warning
him that he knew of his Communist inclinations and that he
should keep them to himself? Or did he merely consider it
comically implausible that anyone might harbour such sym-
pathies?

In such ways, America exhausted Karl Neder daily. It was
not just a matter of struggling to decipher the language; he
found that the customs, the personal politics, all the unspoken
implications and expectations in every phrase and action, left
him confounded. He liked to imagine he'd become adept at
interpreting hidden meanings after several years of coping with
the ritual codes and duplicities of Budapest, where one wrong

move could land you in a police cell. But he'd thought these to be the enforced rubrics of an oppressed society, and that in a free land you simply said just what you meant. He was astonished to discover that the United States seemed to have accepted a multi-layered and treacherously nuanced form of social intercourse purely by choice, and for reasons that, as far as he could tell, were more or less frivolous. It was like an elaborate game – except when you commited some genuine transgression, which could alter the atmosphere in an instant.

He discovered how easy it was to make such errors the moment he arrived in the United States as a refugee two years earlier. He was asked for his middle name, and explained that he did not have one. The immigration officer insisted brusquely that everyone had a middle name, and Neder, terrified that he would be sent back for this breach of American etiquette, made an obvious choice on the spot. Now he was Karl Laszlo Neder: German, Hungarian, Jewish. A citizen of the world.

It happened again when Vender took him later to the Jet Propulsion Laboratory in Pasadena and introduced him to his new colleagues. They were joking about the disastrous launch of the Vanguard rocket at Cape Canaveral last December, calling it 'Kaputnik' and 'Stayputnik' – it had risen only four feet before keeling over and exploding in a fireball – when he explained that *Sputnik*, or to give it its full Russian name of *sputnik zemli*, meant 'Earth's travelling companion'.

'How did you know that?' they demanded abruptly.

'Guys, he's Hungarian,' Vender explained. 'They all speak Russian over there. The Russkies have been running the place since the end of the war. But he's one of the good Hungarians – jeez, we of all people should know about them.'

The Jet Propulsion Laboratory had been founded by the Hungarian émigré Theodore von Kármán to develop rocket technology in the 1930s. Yet von Kármán did not want to link the laboratory name to rocketry, since that smacked of science fiction. At least, it did until the V2s began to rain down on England.

But by 1958 Wernher von Braun, the architect of the V2, was making rockets in Alabama, and he was a national hero in his new country. In January he softened the horror and disgrace of Sputnik's triumph by launching his Explorer I rocket into orbit. Now there were two new pinpricks in the heavens: one Soviet, one American. At JPL they were determined that there would be more. But that was the least of their ambitions.

When Vender enlisted Karl Neder at JPL in the summer of 1958, outer space had become the boundless receptacle for national anxieties. Some regarded it as a strategic issue, forecasting nothing less than the extinction of America if it didn't catch up with the Soviets. For there was now a new breed of V2s, and their arcs could reach beyond the atmosphere and around the globe, and their tips were loaded not with high explosives but with city-levelling uranium and tritium. The Americans had their own versions, the Corporal missiles that looked sleek and deadly but which, the experts knew, relied on the old wartime radar systems for guidance and hit their target less than half the time. JPL engineers had helped to make these unreliable angels of destruction, and were now working hard on a successor.

But what few of the rocket scientists recognized was that command of space was at root a psychic affair. If you controlled the heavens, you had the power to control people's minds, because that is where they still looked for hope and guidance. That was the real reason why Americans feared and loathed Sputnik. They imagined it passing overhead every night, mocking them and stealing their secrets. Watching them in the bathroom.

Everyone knew what would happen next, if they did not get cracking. It would take more than Explorer I to even the score, for the Soviets had trumped von Braun already. At the end of 1957 they sent Laika into orbit, the first canine cosmonaut. Sooner or later a man would follow, and then he would take a ride to the tarnished silver disk that looked down on the world at night. I do not wish, Lyndon Johnson had thundered at the Eisenhower adminstration, to go to bed by the light of a Communist moon.

All this left Barry Vender gleeful, because it meant that the government would stop at nothing to beat the Russians to the goal. Only weeks before he met Neder, JPL had become a part of the new National Aeronatics and Space Administration. There was no shortage of funds, and just about any idea seemed worth a shot. Even the implosion machine.

Now here was Karl Neder, a physicist Vender had found eking out a living designing circuits for a radar company in the Bay area. He got chatting by chance on a business visit, and Neder told him with a mixture of caution and fervour about the experiments he was conducting with scavenged components in an abandoned garage – an attempt, it seemed, to determine the Earth's absolute rotation. Everyone knew that the Hungarians were geniuses: von Kármán, Teller, von Neumann and Wigner. It would be a coup to have one on his team. Vender saw with elation that Neder was an engineer at heart, and shared his reservations about relativity and the thermodynamic laws. At JPL, he explained as they sipped coffee in San Jose, we don't need those things. What we are after is energy.

'To send rockets to the stars?' asked Neder.

'Partly for that, yes.' Vender smiled. 'What we want is free energy.'

Neder could not work out whether Vender was speaking

technically or colloquially. In a thermodynamic sense, free energy was energy that could be extracted to do useful work. When rocket fuel was burnt, only a part of the energy released could be put to propulsive effect; some (so the textbooks said) was always squandered, an inescapable tax demanded by the second law of thermodynamics. But it wasn't clear if Vender had this in mind, for he seemed to imply that energy could be captured without cost. The universe, he appeared to be saying, had a potentially infinite supply, if only we could tap into it. Energy for free.

'That's how the implosion machine works', he said. 'Von Braun wasn't the only one with scientific secrets in Nazi Germany.'

He explained that during the war the Nazis tried to develop a secret weapon at Castle Schönbrunn, near the Mauthausen concentration camp. Labourers were taken from the camp and instructed to assemble objects that looked rather like turbines enclosed in ovoid shells of steel. They were designed by a man named Viktor Schauberger, an Austrian forest warden.

Schauberger had become obsessed with the notion that water was alive with energy that could be harnessed in implosions: negative explosions, catastrophic collapses that would trigger an immense release of this occult power. The SS had seen his patents for energy generation, and they made him an officer, incongruous in jackboots and Darwinian beard. He was told to use implosions to create weapons of devastating power that would cow the Allies into surrender.

'He is a vitalist,' said Vender, 'almost a Neoplatonist, you might say. We mustn't take his theories too seriously.' Neder did not know these words.

Vender encountered those theories in the bitter winter of Sputnik, when a Bavarian entrepreneur who had moved to America and started up a successful metal fabrication business heard about Schauberger's implosions, and wondered whether they might offer a new means of propulsion. So he tracked down Schauberger in Linz and flew him to Texas, only to find that he could not understand a word the old man said. Schauberger was convinced that everyone wanted to steal his ideas – that's what happened with Heinkel's jet engine, he said, which was based on his own work on water vortices. And so the Bavarian metal magnate sought help from Vender, who he'd met while collaborating on rocket-casing designs with JPL. But Vender had been unable to rescue the project, and Schauberger had flown back to Austria, where he promptly died.

Yet Vender decided that Schauberger's work, for all its theoretical idiosyncrasy, held the seed of a viable technology. He agreed with the Austrian that implosions of water could release free energy. He explained all this to his colleagues at JPL, and they listened eagerly. Most of them had come from the jet aircraft industry, and they were engineers, not physicists. To them, it sounded like wonderful stuff. Sure, they were planning to burn solid fuel in the next generation of ballistic missiles. But an energy source that sucked power from water? That would give the Reds something to think about. So they listened to Vender, and they began to draw up plans for a prototype implosion engine. Vender was given a little workshop and a team of technicians. Implosions were, after all, familiar fare at JPL, for it was von Kármán himself, along with Teller and the other Hungarian émigrés, who had solved the implosion problem at Los Alamos that squeezed the radioactive hearts of Trinity and Little Boy and Fat Man to bursting point.

'You know,' Vender told Neder, 'Schauberger claimed that E equals MC squared wasn't Einstein's doing. He said that a Professor Hasenöhrl of the University of Innsbruck formulated this equation several years before. He said you can look it up at Innsbruck.'

'Is this right?' asked Neder. He was disconcerted to find that he had mixed feelings about Einstein being robbed of his glory.

'Einstein was smart in many ways,' Vender said. 'But he had his limitations. I worked with him, so I know.'

Neder was not sure he had understood correctly.

'You say to me you work one time with Einstein? As scientific comrade?'

'Sure – though "comrade" is an interesting way to put it. This was in the summer of '51.'

Ψ

Vender went to Princeton to study economics, because his father, a Baltimore banker, did not want to see him 'wind up making light bulbs in Schenectady'. That had otherwise seemed a likely trajectory. As a teenager, Vender made his own radio sets and listened in to Hamburg and Helsinki. He read *Astounding Stories* and Jules Verne, and rigged up alarm systems for his bedroom, and sketched designs for lie detectors and monorails. Nowhere in all of Maryland was there a more Edisonian boy, a better recruit for America's technological army.

He might have dared resist his father's demands to 'get into the money world', if his father had not enlisted in the navy in 1943 and left for the Pacific. When Barry Vender Snr returned two years later, conversations in the family got abruptly shorter, and they did not permit much debate. The older Vender seemed to have trouble making his mouth fit the shape of words, so he used them sparingly and forcefully.

Vender's talent for mathematics might have stood him in good stead as an economist, if it wasn't for the fact that he didn't give a damn about what the numbers meant. He came to regard the economic system as a kind of vast experiment whose inner mechanisms were encoded in the spasmodic jerks and cycles of the Wall Street indices. He saw a way to do physics by stealth.

Then he discovered that this was not really what one was supposed to do in economics. He had to learn about employment law, and business strategy, and trade deficits, which sent him fleeing to Princeton jazz clubs where he was tall enough to order drinks, and then afterwards to parties where girls drew slow and long on cigarettes, and bone-white pills or lumps of crumbling resin would pass from hand to hand. His rangy athleticism got him noticed, and he began to exude irresistible charm and confidence.

To make himself feel a little better about flunking his coursework, he sought out the economics textbooks that contained the densest mathematics, like Edgeworth's monumental *Mathematical Psychics*, and would start to play around with the equations – just fooling, looking for connections, trying out different solutions, making approximations and plotting graphs with his table of logarithms to hand. It was a kind of relaxation, but little by little he began to suspect that the Great System that lay beneath all these partial differential equations was actually more elusive than he had suspected. Yet an abstract thinker like Edgeworth, he reassured himself, would be incapable of formulating all this algebra into a concrete form, whereas a physicist like him ought to be able to find a mechanical analogy that would reveal the entire structure in a flash. Keynes had tried hydrodynamics, but that wasn't it. Perhaps something more like an electronic circuit, with oscillators and valves and thermistors.

But nothing came. Gradually it dawned on Vender that the notebooks he had filled with elaborations and variations on

Edgeworth's themes were simply that. They were empty doodles. He might as well have spent his time instead at the poetry bars and music clubs, not to mention the unofficial campus brothel on William Street. So he stacked his books in the little grate in his lodgings and set them alight.

He began to read physics in earnest, going along to the lectures and asking questions afterwards. By the end of his third year, his strangely compelling geniality could no longer sustain the goodwill of his economics tutors – but they would be free of him come fall in any case. So they let him go his own way. He hung around the physics department, and took out books from the library on astronomy and quantum theory and statistical mechanics. He read Einstein's popularization of relativity in *Natural Science*, and then McVittie's *Cosmological Theory*. He bought new notebooks, and scribbled down ideas of his own. And it suddenly struck him that the man behind it all, Albert Einstein, was right there in Princeton, at the Institute of Advanced Studies.

So Barry Vender went to visit Einstein.

He expected to find the most famous physicist in the world housed in a grand suite, attended by doting students and feted by his department. But the Institute of Advanced Study did not work that way.

It was not a part of the university. It kept its own counsel up on Olden Lane, cushioned by dark woodland. No one seemed to know a great deal about what happened there. It was full of people so brilliant as to be already mythical. In monastic tranquillity, under no obligation to excel, or even to work at all, they were free to spin webs of genius and madness. The idea was that such a concentration of great minds would spark off intellectual fireworks, leading to advances that none of them could have achieved alone. The truth was that those great minds were generally the very sort that blossom alone and without heed to their surroundings, and the corridors and coffee rooms of the Institute did not buzz with vitality. They remained mostly empty,while nervous and lonely figures scratched out tortured sums in their offices before slumping home in the dark long after suppertime had passed.

Einstein, sometimes, was one of these.

People at the Institute avoided him. This was not because he was unfriendly, or unpleasant, nor because he was growing deranged or senile. He was as photogenic and alert and affable as ever. But everyone feared him.

He had long ago passed the point where one is regarded as an oracle and is constantly interrupted by callers wishing to know one's opinion on this or that. None of his fellows at the Institute would dare take him any question, for they were sure it would prove far too trivial to warrant distracting Albert Einstein from his work. It was rumoured that this work was to be the pinnacle of his life's achievements, greater even than the theory of relativity. Einstein was searching for a unified field theory, a description of the forces of nature in which they were all revealed as different facets of one great *Ur*-force. The magnetic attraction that turns the compass needle, the gravity that unites the sun and moon with the earth, and the terrible nuclear forces that created a flash over Nagasaki seen by Barry Vender Snr from a US destroyer 170 miles away – all of these, Einstein believed, were variations on the unified field that filled all of space in the first moments of creation.

Compared with the unified field theory, relativity and quantum mechanics were classroom arithmetic. Some days Einstein filled page after page with barely legible scrawl; sometimes he simply sat and stared at the woods outside his window. He suspected that neither activity was any more productive than the other, and he had begun to fear that he was never going to solve this problem before he died.

Einstein had an assistant, a bright young German physicist named Ernst Straus. But Straus could offer little help with the unified field theory. That kind of assistance might once have come from Einstein's sole close friend at the Institute of Advanced Study, but this friend was getting crazier by the day.

He was Kurt Gödel, whose incompleteness theory had run a bulldozer through mathematics in the 1930s. Gödel showed that there are some theorems that can never be proved right or wrong. A mathematical claim might be stated with crisp precision, but you could never know if it was true. It was a piece of absurdist invention to rival Heisenberg's hedging uncertainty, and perhaps Gödel felt that he shouldn't have done it. Another refugee from Vienna, he washed up at Princeton with a sense that someone wanted him dead. He refused to open his office door, receiving messages only when they were pushed under it. He ate with reluctance, suspecting poison, and then finally not at all.

But on the day Barry Vender arrived at the Institute, Gödel took lunch with Einstein and Straus. Had he seen the news of MacArthur's return from the Korean campaign, Straus asked. 'Yes,' Gödel replied, 'it was on the front of the *New York Times*. But that was not MacArthur.'

'I beg your pardon?' said Straus.

'It is not MacArthur in that photograph, riding down Madison Avenue. It is an impostor.'

'Why do you say that, Kurt?' asked Einstein softly.

'His face.'

'It looked like MacArthur to me.'

'His face is the wrong size.'

'You can tell that?'

'Do you know,' said Gödel, suddenly animated, 'how to

spot a disguise? The face has proportions that cannot be changed. The length of the nose and the distance between the tip of the nose and the chin. The ratio of those lengths cannot change, no matter what you stick on your face. I measured that ratio for MacArthur in the *New York Times*. Then I found an old picture of him. I measured the ratio in this picture. The two numbers are different. It is not the same man.'

'That is surprising,' said Einstein, while Straus sipped his water with evident unease. 'I did not know that about faces. I imagined I had changed a great deal since my youth.'

'It is not MacArthur,' said Gödel, but then said no more.

Ψ

When Vender wandered down the corridors of the Institute, there was no one around to apprehend him, and he sauntered straight into the office of Albert Einstein, where he found the old man sucking on a sweet-smelling pipe and gazing at his stockinged feet.

'He said to me – that is, he said to this person who had just entered his office,' Vender explained to Neder, 'he said, "Even physics can be cruel. I do not wish to think it so, but sometimes I do."'

'What do you reply to him then?' asked Neder.

'I told him that I understood he was working on a unified field theory, and that I had been thinking about that too. I showed him my ideas and my calculations.'

Neder was dismayed by what he was experiencing. Ever since his university days he had felt antagonism towards Einstein's ideas, convinced that they were arbitrary and superfluous. They disturbed him in a manner he could not explain. But for the past five years he had been starting to suspect he could find a way to avoid them – it was not yet a theory that he had, but it was already more than a hunch. To Neder, relativity and quantum mechanics had polluted the purity and elegance of nineteenth-century classical physics. And Einstein was the culprit.

Yet when Barry Vender described how he had sat at Einstein's desk and talked about physics, Neder understood two things. First, that he himself would not have had the nerve to do something like that. And second, that he could think of nothing more desirable. He had from time to time imagined himself standing up during a lecture by Einstein and pointing to the blackboard:

'You have made an error, Herr Professor, just here. Your conclusions are wrong.'

But faced now with the reality of Einstein's existence, he felt only shame at such thoughts, as if they were somehow disgraceful. It was not by contradicting Einstein that Neder would have felt pride, but by having collaborated with him. And now Einstein was dead.

'Did he listen?'

'Yes, he listened. He said these were interesting ideas, and that perhaps I would like to come by again so that the two of us might develop them further.'

Ψ

Einstein, delighted that a young physicist had sought him out in his silent office, welcomed Vender the next day, and they spent that morning, and the next, working through the equations that Vender had written down. 'Perhaps we can prepare a paper,' Einstein said over lunch.

The following morning Einstein greeted Vender as warmly as before, and they sat down in his office with mugs of coffee.

'Well, we have made a pretty story,' he said. 'But I discovered last night that it is just that – a pleasant fiction.'

'How do you mean?'

'We cannot find a unified field theory this way. I should have seen it sooner.'

'I don't understand.'

'Look, it is here, you see...' Scribbled notes which Vender could barely decipher. 'Here – a basic definition. You see, we have made two quantities seem equal that were nothing of the kind.'

'But that is easy to fix,' Vender protested tautly, his scalp prickling.

'I thought so too. But what it really means is that we are working in two incompatible metrics. Which means that the whole house comes tumbling down. And so pretty it was.'

Vender could not move his arms. It was not a sensation he had known before. Einstein touched his shoulder lightly, unbearably.

'You are an impressive young man. But the problem we are attacking here is monstrous.' He giggled. 'I think sometimes it is too hard for me. I think a younger man will have to solve it. But not this way.'

'I – can – fix it.' Vender wondered what had happened to his voice, like gravel sliding around in a tin.

'I honestly don't think so.' Einstein looked at him. 'Perhaps we might find a studentship for you here.'

Vender stood up. His arms hung like ballast. If they should reawaken, he did not know what they might do.

He felt that he was drifting over a kind of threshold. A smile had appeared on his face, he realized, uncontrollable as a rictus. It made him afraid. The elderly man was about to speak again, but Vender suddenly could not bear the thought of that voice.

'Give me a moment,' he rasped. The old man put out his hands, palms first – a gentle gesture, placatory perhaps, a little cautious.

Vender did not return to the Institute, but he sent Einstein a letter explaining his new strategy. Einstein wrote back politely, pointing out why it would not work, and reiterating his offer to see whether Vender could be found a junior post at the Institute. 'Really,' he ended his letter, 'you should not trouble yourself that your idea has come unstuck. I have had two hundred ideas about this problem, and they have all come unstuck sooner or later. This is too hard a nut. But there are many other problems you might like to work on. Do not bash yourself against this rock.'

Vender replied: 'Your new objections do not seem to be very fundamental. I am intending to write up this work in a paper, and was hoping that you would co-author it. But you seem to be losing interest in the problem.'

'My interest in the problem,' Einstein wrote back, 'is very deep. But I do not have faith in this approach. I would advise that you do not write a paper, because I do not think this work is publishable. I gather, by the way, that you are not a student of physics, but of economics. That is very remarkable. But I am sure you could transfer to physics for postgraduate research. I would endorse such a move.'

When Einstein received no reply, he called by one day in June 1951 at the street address from which Vender had written previously. The landlady told him that the young man had left two weeks before. No, no forwarding address. Yes, before his final exams. Yes, she thought it odd herself.

Ψ

'I didn't write back,' Vender told Neder, 'because I began to suspect what was happening. He feared that if indeed we together – or I alone – found the unified field theory, there would be nothing further for him to do. He wanted the problem to outlive him. I was very disappointed, because I had until then rather respected him.'

'Did you write the paper?'

'Oh, the paper. Well, of course, the physicists didn't want to know. I sent it to *Physical Review*, and they sent back some trash from a referee. But you know, that was just the beginning. I discovered that my equations showed that there was energy in the vacuum – in empty space, you get me? All this energy, an infinite amount in fact, just waiting to be unlocked. It's like – like we're living beneath the Hoover Dam, and there's just tissue paper between us and all the water.'

Ψ

Vender and Neder worked on Project Implosion for just over a year, until Neder found out that he was not just designing engines for space rockets.

By that time, the bosses at JPL had lost interest in sending up more satellites. In April 1959 they selected the first team of astronauts, optimistically scheduled to fly into space in the Mercury Program by 1961. When Neder occasionally glimpsed these men in the canteen, he came away convinced that the Soviet astronauts must very different. To these crew-cut Americans, space was an adventure: they contemplated the journey into those airless wastes with the cheerful stoicism of the frontiersman. They would set forth from the bustling coast of Florida, every bit as dazzling and daring as the Spaniards who first landed there. Yet they could never, ever experience the joy and liberation that awaited the men who, one day soon, would buckle themselves into a metal pod in the arid plains of Kazakhstan. It was all a question of what they were leaving behind.

Neder soon appreciated that Project Implosion was not a NASA priority. In fact, he suspected that hardly anyone at JPL knew of it except him, Vender and their three colleagues.

Vender pulled in the money from somewhere, but its source was never clear, and it never went quite far enough. In any case, it seemed most unlikely that the laboratory chiefs were ever going to abandon chemical fuels for a speculative new propulsion system that seemed to get its energy from nowhere. Neder was able to understand very little of Schauberger's theory, which seemed to be expressed pictorially rather than mathematically. Neither did he really understand how it was supposed to fit with Vender's notion of 'vacuum energy'. He was happy enough assembling the steel casings of their implosion chambers, but he did not yet grasp exactly how an implosion was to be orchestrated within them, less still what it might yield.

In September, they all heard the news that the Russians had sent an unmanned spacecraft crashing into the moon. So they had won that race too. Yet Vender seemed, as ever, to extract only encouragement from the Soviet victory.

'The further we fall behind, the less likely they are to shut the book on implosions. Do you know who is most distressed by this Russian crash landing? Not the Mercury guys, but the military. You see, a guidance system accurate enough to hit the moon from here could certainly make sure a missile comes down on New York.'

'But how is that helping us?' Neder wanted to know.

'Because, my friend, we have more than one string to our bow.'

'I do not know the meaning of this.'

'When we get this implosion machine working, it'll do more than send men to the moon. The generals will want it too.'

'To fire their missiles.' Neder had always feared that this was so. He had told himself that it was a noble thing to be trying to send men into space, but he knew that JPL existed for other reasons too. Vender kept one of the new British die-cast toy models of the Concorde missile on his desk, straining against its coiled spring. ('It's probably more accurate than the real thing,' he laughed.) The lack of the remotest prospect of an implosion machine materializing in the near future had allowed him to evade until now the thought that he might be designing a way of sending nuclear warheads to Moscow, and perhaps to Budapest too. But Barry Vender had something else in mind.

'Karl, we are at war. I know it doesn't seem that way, because no one is being shot at. But you have heard what Khrushchev says. He is ready to rain missiles down on Europe. Now, you and I, we are looking for free energy. We believe that it can liberate mankind, isn't that right? But we can't hope to do that without the kind of support we get here, and so we have entered into a kind of social contract. That's the way things happen now. Fermi, Oppenheimer, von Kármán, all those guys did the same. We're now reaping the harvest they sowed at Los Alamos with these atomic power plants they're building – what is it they say? Too cheap to meter. That's what it gave us.'

'And the price is Hiroshima.'

'There's always a price. Even free energy has its price. You know what von Kármán used to say? "A scientist should be neither a Teller nor an Einstein insofar as public affairs are concerned." We shouldn't meddle in those matters. What do we know about them? Maybe that was Einstein's mistake, thinking he could be a physicist and a statesman at the same time. We're here to advance the science, Karl, and we must take the money where we find it. This world has got itself so het up right now that the cash is all in the hands of the brass.'

'Los Alamos did not exist to make nuclear reactors. It was a bomb factory.'

Barry Vender sighed. 'Yes, Karl.'

And then Neder understood.

'Our implosion machine... it is not to send men to the moon!'

'It may do that, Karl. It may.'

'But you want also to create a bomb! Like the Nazis! And I am just like concentration camp labourer!'

'That's not how it is. Boy, are you being dramatic! We are doing science here, Karl, we are testing my theory of the vacuum energy, and out of that will come a new technology. That's our job. Calm down, there's nothing squalid in this.'

But Barry Vender had misjudged Neder. Within three days he had spent most of his savings on a ticket for a flight from New York to Paris. The moment he contemplated leaving America, he realized that he missed the Old World desperately. And it was not just that: in America, he admitted, he was just hiding away, shirking his responsibilities. For what? There were things needing to be put right in the world that no one here even knew were wrong. Here there was nothing to struggle against except complacency and an absence of conscience. He was outraged by what Vender had drawn him into, but more than that, he saw that he would achieve nothing in America.

All the way back to Europe, he brooded on the mocking words that Vender had flung at him on their rancorous parting. It was another piece of supposed wisdom from his compatriot von Kármán, and it stung:

'Nothing is so pathetic as an idealistic man talking of situations which he doesn't have the strength to control.'

17

Dear Dr Battle,

I should like to comment on certain aspects of the article written by Margaret Strong in your issue of the 23rd May 1982. Mrs Strong writes that 'The Soviet Academy of Sciences has agreed to launch a fresh investigation into the causes of the death of cosmonaut Yuri Gagarin, who died in an air crash in March 1968. The findings of the official inquiry conducted shortly after the incident were never published, and over the ensuing years many rumours have circulated. According to one, Gagarin was drunk at the controls of his aircraft. Others charge that the crash was a staged 'accident' designed to eliminate Gagarin after he had fallen from political favour.'

Do you then in all seriousness assert that this 'fresh investigation' will be any less of a 'cover-up' than the official inquiry? If Mrs Strong believes this, she is far more the dupe of the Soviet regime than I had credited her after our meeting in Brno. Do you imagine for one moment that Brezhnev will admit to the truth of this 'accident' that he himself arranged (or one should rather say, his KGB stooge Yuri Andropov)? I have written many times to Brezhnev that he should confess to this crime, and of course I receive no answer. The silence of

*the powerful is their most potent weapon (do I need,
dear Dr Battle, to be telling this to YOU!?). I implore
you: do not be taken in by this latest ploy. The Academy
will tell us nothing new about this despicable act. Mrs
Strong will know the smiling faces of the Moscow
Academicians. Do not forget what this smile means! Just
because in former days there were no smiles from Stalin's
apparatchiks, but only coarse laughter and brutal leers,
does not mean that the Soviet masters have learnt
gentler ways. They have only put on a cleaner suit.*

Sincerely yours,
Karl Neder

'I have told you before,' Margaret Strong gasped, 'that I am
not married.'

'Why do you wish me to know this?'

'Good God, man, why do you think? Slow down, I'm all
done in. It's not a blasted proposal, you know. I dislike being
addressed as *Mrs* Strong.'

She might have known that Neder would insist on going
by foot to the old town of Várhegy in Buda, spurning the
funicular as a 'bourgeois conveyance'. Good on the blinking
bourgeoisie, she thought. It could not have been much below
a hundred degrees in the Hungarian summer, and even if she
looked like a Carpathian peasant (she knew it was so), she did
not have a peasant's constitution. *They* didn't seem to suffer
from rheumatism that had to be smothered in ointments reeking of menthol. The miasma that surrounded her may have
turned heads in the street, but it worked wonders against bit-
ing insects in the sticky evenings.

Neder, with the stocky frame of a hammer-thrower, took
the steps two at a time, and was obliged repeatedly to wait,

poised on one foot, while Strong heaved herself along in his wake.

'Your breathing betrays your indulgences,' he admonished her.

'Oysters? Don't be personal.'

'No, no, I mean your cigarettes. These local brands, you might as well be sipping oil from the, ah, sump.'

'Oysters and cigarettes have got me this far,' said Strong, neglecting to mention single malt whisky, German sausage and custard tarts. 'And they'll get me a lot further, I shouldn't be surprised. My mother is eighty-seven.'

'Ha! Your mother will outlive us both.'

'That's because she doesn't climb mountains in the middle of the blinking Continental summer.'

'Then she will not have such a view as this. Look at it! This is the scene I loved. This water takes you to the Orient. It traces the history of the Magyars from Vienna to the Black Sea.'

They came at length to the castle walls. There was hardly a soul around, and no wonder. It was the time of day for sleeping, Margaret Strong thought. Damn the man! Why couldn't he have left her drowsily sipping black tea in her blockhouse of a hotel? She decided suddenly that she must go on the offensive.

'Now look,' she began, 'you are not to call me Mrs. That is the form of address for married ladies only. I have no desire to be one of those. I have never had such a desire, and I do not expect it to come upon me. I am not telling you this as some kind of intimacy, and you are not to receive it as such. It is merely a fact.'

'Ah, but then, you see, I do not know what I must call you. I don't ask for us to take the good-friends habit of using our given names, so I need to have some title to give you. And you are not a doctor, yes?'

'I have never pretended to be a trained scientist, although I believe I am far from ignorant about scientific principles. There is really no difficulty about this. The proper form of address for a woman in my situation is Ms.'

'Muzz?'

'Ms. There are no vowels.'

'An English word with no vowels? Do you make a jest with me? So it is like Miss?'

'Not like Miss at all. Not at all. Miss is for young girls and schoolteachers, which is often the same thing. Do not pretend to find this mystifying, Neder. It is a simple courtesy.'

'Of course. But why, ah, Miz Strong, have you not married? Perhaps that is an impertinent question?'

'It borders on being such, but I will overlook that. I can tell you very simply. I have no wish for the impediment of a husband. I have seen a great many women so impeded, under the illusion that they will fade and wither otherwise. Taking a husband was the worst thing Virginia Woolf ever did.'

'I do not know this lady, but I share your point of view. It can be an, ah, impediment to have a marriage companion. I speak as one who has never married, but who has rarely been without a, ah, close woman friend. Sometimes I think it is utter foolishness to take a companion in a life like mine that needs dedication and concentration. I spend many nights in my laboratories, and sometimes I cannot converse at all except about gravitation and electrodynamics. I do not pretend that those things are pleasant to hear for a, um, a companion of the heart. No doubt that is why so often these relations do not work out as I might like. That reason, and also as I have to move so often from place to place. And I am not good with money – this I know. I have never borrowed without intention of repaying, but it is difficult sometimes.'

Strong had her lips pressed together as though to crush

something held between them. She felt this talk was all a little *close*. She did not much like the way that Neder would often converse as though they knew one another better than they did. She had the unwelcome suspicion that it amused him to do so, and that her disapproval sharpened his amusement.

'We have come here,' she reminded him, 'to speak about Gagarin.'

That was true, in a sense. She did not expect to learn anything of great significance from Karl Neder on the topic of the cosmonaut, despite his excited letter to her at *Natural Science*: 'I MUST tell you what I know about this. You are risking your reputation if you swallow the line of the Soviet jackals,' and so forth. She'd received letters from Neder before; she had the measure of their tone and their value. Frankly, she was forced with some reluctance to admit to herself, it was Neder in person who interested her more. She could not suppress her admiration for his dynamism, the way he got around and the people he managed to see despite the many bans and restrictions that were supposed to inhibit those things. When she had been denied access to the dissident Soviet physicist Andrei Sakharov, she was glad of what Neder had been able to relate to her of the man's circumstances and state of health. In Innsbruck he had even succeeded (by plying her with tea at one of the city's finest restaurants – for which, however, she had found herself in the end feeling obliged to pay, perceiving with a sense of defeat that she would not be able to bring herself to claim it on her expense account) in persuading her to translate some of the poems of the imprisoned Russian writer Sergei Radzinsky, which had been smuggled out of Siberia. As a matter of fact, she was going to have to bring up *that* unfinished business, as he had promised that she would receive a small fee from the Austrian publisher, since when the matter had been dropped.

The fact was, he had a hold over her. Whenever they met – and this was a disconcertingly common occurrence, whether in Leipzig, Trieste, Prague or Tblisi – it would not be long before she was suppressing the urge to wring his neck. Bull-like though it was, her big red hands were possibly equal to the task. But still he would go on proposing some rendezvous, and she would acquiesce. She tried to rationalize this on the grounds that he was an informant, one of the many links in the network she had established throughout the Communist countries and on which she relied at least as much as on the official channels such as the Soviet Academy of Sciences. But he rarely had much in the way of hard information, except in so far as it concerned his own harebrained schemes for making perpetual motion machines and plotting the downfall of relativistic physics. The blasted man was wretchedly hard to refuse, and it troubled her that she could not quite understand why.

They had come to blows only once. Not blows, exactly. More of a tussle. Bodily contact, in any event. It was in Venice in 1980, and Neder had seemed to be unusually agitated. He kept darting down foul-smelling alleys, casting glances about him into the throngs of fish-eyed tourists. He flinched at the flash and click of cameras. He was convinced that 'the Relativists' had someone trailing him. 'Who are the relativists?' Strong had asked. 'Do not make the fool,' he shot back. 'Do not make the fool, Mrs Strong.' And indeed Margaret Strong had some intimation of what he meant, for she had seen his diatribes, his Anti-Relativists' Manifesto. But she could not abide conspiracy theorists. There were too many real conspiracies on both sides of the Iron Curtain for her to feel any sympathy for the paranoid ravings of those who turned frustration and disappointment into grandiose fantasies. She resented this invitation to collude. 'Whatever I am,' she had replied, 'and that may be many things, and not all of them are what I would choose to be, but whatever I am, I am not a fool.' 'Then do not hide behind this pretence of ignorance, like your good Dr Battle,' he said. 'Do not say to me that the Relativists, who you know very well, are benign idiots. They have their Special Services too, their SS. They are always behind my back, following severely my every pace.' And to Strong's immense alarm and discomfort, Neder had seized her arm and tried to pull her around. 'See there,' he exclaimed, 'that fellow who watches us intently, why do you think he does this?' She had emitted a small shriek, an animal sound strange even to her own ears, and had pulled herself loose – for although Neder had a wiry strength, he had never really meant to lay hands on her, and was hardly conscious of doing so. But in the struggle they toppled, suddenly aware of how close they were to the canal, and it was more because of this disorienting realization than because of any fierceness of engagement that Margaret Strong fell to her knees while Neder stumbled backwards. Tourists looked at them with the same stare that they directed at the Piazza San Marco and the Bridge of Sighs, as if wondering whether this scene deserved a photograph. A few of them did raise their cameras, framing the image: Margaret Strong, momentarily winded and unable to move, nevertheless recovering herself sufficiently to gasp huskily that Neder was a wretched idiot and had better not come a step nearer. But he had no intention of doing so. He looked at her with horror before turning and dashing away down the alley.

Whatever sharp words passed between them subsequently, neither made any mention of the Venice incident.

'You must know he was murdered by Brezhnev.'

'I know that rumour, but it doesn't seem at all likely.'

'Perhaps you think that Brezhnev does not murder people?

That because he condemns the mistakes of Stalinism, he is a civil man. The fact is, there is more Stalinism under Brezhnev than ever there was under Khrushchev. I did not like Nikita; they are not one of them much better than the other, but at least he dug up the old tyrant and filled his grave with concrete.'

'Please,' said Strong, 'don't lecture me on Soviet history.'

'Well, if you know all this then you will know that Yuri Gagarin's death cannot have been an accident. He was Khrushchev's state hero. To Khrushchev he was something like a son. I do believe he loved Gagarin. Brezhnev knew he could not kill Khrushchev, that he had to leave him tending his tomatoes and wait for him to die. But there were other ways of showing now who was in charge.'

'I've heard all of this before. It's standard stuff. No one believes in accidents any more, not in the Soviet Union. That's the harvest a totalitarian regime reaps – it is assumed to have power over everything, good and bad. All the better for the leaders, when random deaths become examples of what you get if you don't obey the Party line.'

'Exactly! That is why the rumours are tolerated – maybe they even are encouraged. I would not be surprised if it was the KGB who started them. But I do not talk about rumours. Look at the facts.'

Actually, there really had been a cover-up, and it was common knowledge. Yuri Gagarin crashed in a MiG jet fighter in March 1968, close to Zvyozdny Gorodok – Star City, where the cosmonauts were trained. Forty kilometres north-east of Moscow, a region guarded by dense, impenetrable forests of pine and birch. Scarcely more than a bleak concrete barrack when Gagarin began his training there in 1960, Star City grew quickly into a town with bars, hotels, sports clubs: a place for men and women to lead comfortable, comradely lives while they learnt how to leave the planet. Close at hand to the south, the air force base at Chkalovsky provided the jets and landing strips that allowed would-be spacemen to develop their flying skills – for rockets were still the ungainly progeny of jet technology, and the space age a mere offshoot of the struggle for military dominance of the air.

When Gagarin and Vladimir Serugin left the runway at Chkalovsky one morning in March, Muscovy was still in its dark phase. Low cloud cover, pricked by the spear-tops of pines, leaked a cruel condensate midway between rain and sleet. Soggy grey flakes were torn apart by the jet's approach. Gagarin, sidelined, grounded and out of practice, was Deputy Chief of Cosmonaut Training at Star City, and perhaps in line for promotion to division head, which would give him the rank of general – but this was nothing more than routine advancement, a bland reward that could be purchased with good behaviour. Gagarin knew that he was unlikely ever again to see the sky turn from blue to black as the stars surrounded him with a gaze that no longer blinked through the flickering atmosphere.

Ψ

'You know about Ivan Ivanovich?' Neder asked. They sat now drinking sweet black coffee in the Ruszwurm patisserie off Szentháromság tér, watched by a stony Pallas Athene bearing the Buda coat of arms on the corner of the old town hall. Margaret Strong munched contentedly at her *szilvás papucs*. Let him talk. This was more like it. Mouth full of plum pastry, she made a noise that could have seemed discouraging to anyone but Karl Neder. Ivan Ivanovich, she thought lazily. Never heard of the blasted man. Was he a Karamazov brother?

'He was the first Russian cosmonaut,' said Neder. 'He died.' And gave a guttural laugh. 'Ivan Ivanovich piloted the

Vostok spacecraft in March 1961. He ejected after re-entry and came by parachute to Russian soil. Peasants saw him land. He fell over, and they ran to help him, but soldiers appeared and surrounded him. They let him die.'

Neder sat back, pleased with himself, and sipped his coffee. Irritated at having to interrupt the business of tearing pastry apart with her teeth, Strong spluttered, 'Talk sense, man. What is this drivel?'

'Ah, ah, look it up,' Neder taunted. 'There are all sorts of legends about Ivan Ivanovich. Some people say he is another man, not an Ivan at all. Your own Interplanetary Society in London says that Gagarin was preceded by Sergei Ilyushin, a young pilot who went into space weeks earlier, came back and collapsed, and is even now lying in a coma in a Moscow hospital.'

Strong was re-engaged with the contents of her plate, and could do nothing but growl. She was already feeling the stirrings of desire for a second *szilvás papucs*. There was, after all, still the descent from Castle Hill to accomplish, and she did not wish to attempt that until the sun was much lower.

'During his flight, Ivan broadcast radio messages to the launch base at Baikonur. What did Yuri say, once he was in Ivan's boots? "I can see seas, mountains, big cities, rivers and forests. I can see the clouds. I can see everything. It's beautiful."'

In an instant, Neder's bantering tone was gone. He had undone himself. His jaw trembled, he set down his cup with a clatter. He took a sharp intake of breath as he gazed across at the warrior goddess, and his eyes had a liquid glitter. Margaret Strong saw none of this – the sudden silence was kneaded by the steady motion of her nicotine-yellow teeth. She suspected that she might shortly begin to enjoy herself.

Ψ

'I can see everything.' Was that it, Neder wondered? Was that the fatal phrase?

Moving ever towards the sunrise at a speed of 28,000 kilometres per hour, Yuri Gagarin was for 108 minutes able to see everything. He caught up with the sun and outpaced it. Over the Pacific, he journeyed into the night and was left alone with the stars.

Someone was the first to see Everest. Someone else Niagara. Even the Danube had to have a discoverer. A being only just beginning to be human, perhaps, with a primitive mind waiting to be filled with God. With gods. Did they fear these sights, run screaming from them? Did they weep, half in animal reflex, half with the awakening of their humanity? Well, humanity makes sacred places from such sights.

But Gagarin was the first to see everything. The world in eighty minutes, more or less. After that, there is nowhere left to go. Except down.

ψ

'Have you been to Kazakhstan?' Neder asked.

'No.' Strong signalled to the waiter, and shortly another plum pastry was placed before her. The traces of her refreshment were accumulating: a smear of red jelly darkened her chin, while tiny flakes of pastry adhered to the corners of her mouth like the marks of a disease.

'I have,' Neder said. 'I could not get to Baikonur, of course. There are not often space rockets there now. Instead, other sorts. Rockets that do not have men in their tips, but warheads. Rockets that come back down with a very big bang.'

Baikonur, they both knew, was not really Baikonur at all. The Soviet leaders could even rearrange the landscape, compressing or expanding it, cutting and pasting space to fit their arbitrary designs. Stalin had been dead two years when the engineers arrived to construct concrete barracks in the middle of nowhere: a nightmare zone in Kazakhstan where blizzards raged until April arrived and sandstorms took over. The place was once called Tyura'tam by the nomad Kazakhs. Somewhere under this hard, cold earth lay the bones of the son of Genghis Khan. But to confuse capitalist spies, the Soviets stole a new name from a town 370 kilometres away. The Baikonur base does not appear on Soviet maps. It must be found instead from the air, as the Americans did. Seen from high-altitude spy planes, it was a modern Nazca, a pattern of hieroglyphics carved into the desert. Experts pored for hours over these photographs, trying to decode the signs.

'But,' Neder went on, 'I saw where Yuri landed. It is just outside the village of Smelkovka, in the Saratov region. For what that is worth, ha ha. Names have no meaning out there. It is comical, don't you think, to take a patch of icy desert and call it Saratov or some such? Maps make sense in Europe, but in Siberia and Kazakhstan and Mongolia they are not the right way to draw the earth. The Aboriginals of Australia have so much the better idea.'

Let him talk, Margaret Strong decided. There is always cake.

'So there is a marking stone there, a – what do you call it? – obelisk. His parachute was seen by a peasant driving a tractor. Do you know the peasant's name? You will like this. You know his name? It was Lysenko. Ha ha ha!' Lysenko, namesake for Stalin's biologist, who denounced genetics as bourgeois science and thereby destroyed Soviet agriculture.

'This obelisk, all it says is, "Y. A. Gagarin Landed Here." Landed! What does that mean? It is as though almost he came from nowhere. They say the re-entry capsule was picked apart by locals. The KGB never recovered it all. Some of the school-children ate space food from tubes.'

'What,' said Strong impatiently, 'about this man Ivan?'

'Yes, yes, Ivan Ivanovich, the first man in space. Well, what was I saying, about his radio broadcasts? You know what he said? He spent his time in space telling the Soviets how to make cabbage soup and borscht.'

'For goodness sake,' Strong exclaimed. 'Have I climbed a mountain to hear a madman rave?'

'Good, yes, you see the madness. Oh, Mrs Strong – that is, ah, Miz Strong – you must surely appreciate the madness of it all. It is important that you see the madness. There is nothing more crazy than the Communist Soviet Union. And I say this, as you know, I have told you about myself, I say this as a member of the Italian Communist Party.'

'I am a socialist too,' said Strong irritably. 'My father was from the Ukraine.'

'Yes, now I remember that. This unites us, Miz Strong, because we are both world citizens and Europeans with our roots behind the Iron Curtain.' He could not mention this colloquialism without making it sound like a real object, a ferrous Berlin Wall. 'But, you see, it is true. Ivan broadcast borscht recipes from space. Oh, Miz Strong, I should not be so mystical with you, but I cannot help it. I hope you will forgive me, but I have this playful spirit inside me sometimes. And I do not like to deny myself the laughter. There is not so much of it. The fact is, Ivan was not a man. Ivan was a, ah, a mannikin, a thing as is clothed in the windows of shops. He was the next stage in the programme, after all the dogs, after poor Laika and Chaika, after Strelka and Belka and the others that were incinerated or sometimes made it back home and given a bone, I suppose. Ivan was put on board the Vostok with a tape recorder, and the officials did not want to broadcast anything that would alert the Americans. You know what? They thought at first of broadcasting songs, you know, good old Russian folk songs. But then they decided that the Americans will hear this and think that a Soviet cosmonaut has lost his mind in space. So what then do they do instead? They broadcast recipes for cabbage soup, as though that is the sign of a cosmonaut with sounder mind! Ha ha. Well, it is even crazier than this, because also on the tape they put recordings of a full choir. Ivan is sitting in his spacecraft and it is sending out a choir of celestial voices, as though space has suddenly become filled with angels. And this from a regime of rigid atheism! Ha ha ha!'

Ψ

Yuri Gagarin was desperate to fly again. The authorities were not keen, for Gagarin was a national symbol to be preserved for display, but he argued that he could not command the respect of those he was instructing unless he remained a good pilot himself. So on that gloomy March morning he climbed into the MiG cockpit in front of his instructor Serugin. At half past ten, the Chkalovsky controllers lost radio contact with their aircraft. Alexei Leonov, the first man to walk in space, was piloting a helicopter that morning on a training mission. He heard two bangs in close succession. One was like a supersonic shockwave; but the other? A search helicopter was sent out to survey the area where Gagarin's jet was last seen on the radar screen, and through the sleet and the mist the pilot saw a bare black hole in the woods and steam rising from it. He landed and tramped through snow until he came to a great crater, strewn with charred and twisted metal.

Later, a patrol found bodies. The parts were scattered – there were bones up in the trees, which had to be felled to recover them. They scoured the woods for every scrap. Sometimes searchers would see a hole in the snow, they would dig inside and pull out a finger. Leonov thought he recognized a birthmark on a part of a neck, which he'd noticed once when accompanying Gagarin to the barber's. But not everyone was so sure.

There was an official investigation. The plane was old, it said. The altimeter was faulty – Gagarin could not know how close he was to the ground. The weather was atrocious. Serugin was no longer a young man, not so alert any more. The weather reconnaissance planes had been delayed that day, so the pilots had been given wrong information about the cloud height before they took off. Imagine, the engineers said, Serugin coming down below the clouds at 450 metres, thinking he was still a kilometre above the ground. He sees the danger and tells Gagarin to eject. But the MiG-15UTI is not built that way – the rear seat, where the instructor sits, is meant to eject first. If the front seat does so instead, the person in the rear seat is trapped. So Gagarin will not do it. They argue, and the trees have come too near.

But the official line was simpler. The cockpit canopy was shattered before the crash, it said, perhaps because the aircraft struck a weather balloon. Then they lost control. That was all.

Ψ

'Now, no one believes this,' said Neder.

'I know that. It's why I wrote my blinking story. And before you start on the theories, I know all about the "other plane" too. Frankly, I consider it a rather likely tale.'

'Likely, yes. But the reasons, Miz Strong, the reasons. What do you think of them?'

'I know what you think. It was all a state plot. I can't honestly say that I see the argument.'

'Item one –'

Oh dear, this might take some time. A third *szilvás papucs* would be pushing her luck. But another coffee, surely?

'Leonov's testimony in the 1968 inquiry was forged, along with his signature. And some parts were changed.'

'Forged documents are the bread and butter of the Soviet state. Commissions like this are judged on how well they tell a story, not on whether it is true.'

'Oh Miz Strong, your cynicism shows you have lived in London for a long time.'

'You will find its equal in Moscow.'

'But here in the Communist world we – that is, the people – we throw our cynicism at corruption. We are cynical because we expect the worst from our leaders, but at least we know that they have been corrupted. In the West you think this is just human nature. It is not that. Human nature is generous, you know, Miz Strong. It is what I saw in this country when I was young, among the peasant people which you no longer have in the West. Our cynicism is not complacent. We still fight back. You have nothing to fight against.'

'Look, Neder, I hear this all the time. I have heard it since I was a child. *I* am not one of your Western cynics. I am here because I think there is still such a thing as decency.'

'Decency. A lovely English word. We talk about honour and respect and even, yes, integrity, but none of these things is the same as decency. I sometimes believe that is to be found only in England. I do not make a joke here. It is what I like about your country. I do think Roy Battle is a decent man, although he tries me very sorely. That is to say, he has a fundamentally decent character that fights against his baser motives.'

'I'm sure he would be overjoyed to hear you say so. Now, listen. You apparently have a list of items to go through. I am going to have another coffee, and if you wish, I shall get one for you, since I am apparently a decent sort too, or half-decent, since half-English. But you must understand that I am fully aware of the rumours, and for what it's worth, I'm inclined to accept the "second plane" theory. I think it will be vindicated if this new inquiry ever gets to happen, which with Brezhnev almost catatonic and Andropov at the reins is anyone's guess.'

Ψ

Leonov believed there was a second aircraft involved in the crash, and so did Sergei Belotserkovsky, the man in charge of the cosmonauts' academic training at Star City, who was now calling for a fresh investigation. The air traffic controller asserted that on the morning of the crash he had seen another blip on his radar screen. Eyewitnesses who had been in the area and had claimed to have seen an aircraft identified it from charts not as Gagarin's MiG-15 but as a Sukhoi SU-11 supersonic jet, a new model in the late 1960s that was supposed to fly at altitudes of above 10,000 metres. And then there was the supersonic boom that Leonov's trained ears had registered. That could not come from a MiG.

Gagarin's plane, said Leonov and Belotserkovsky, had been caught in the supersonic backwash from a low-flying SU-11 and had been flipped over. It was not a freak accident, but a mistake. And mistakes always had to have a culprit.

Ψ

'But,' Neder insisted, 'this is very naïve. If there was a brand-new, top-secret supersonic jet flying in this area, would there have been truly no record of the flight? And who would have authorized such a dangerous low manoeuvre? Leonov cannot be right, unless the SU-11 was sent out to do something it should not have been doing, a mission that people were not supposed to know about. And what could that be? It could be only one thing. The jet was sent to kill Gagarin.'

'He was a state hero,' said Strong. 'An icon. You can't just bump them off. He was world famous. He met the Queen, you know – the Queen of England, I mean.'

'He was also a – a – what is the word when someone becomes awkward, a danger and an embarrassment to you?'

'Liability?'

'He was a liability. You know how he jumped out of a window at Foros on the Black Sea, when he was drunk and surprised in a love affair by his wife. You know how close he was to Khrushchev, and how Brezhnev resented all the attentions he was given when the two of them were seen together. Yuri's brother is certain that Brezhnev ordered his death.'

Margaret Strong was silent. She considered Karl Neder to be somewhat unhinged, but she had not really heard the case pieced together like this before. She knew that fame and power were indeed thin armour in Russia. Beria, Stalin's loutish head of the KGB, had plotted his ruler's demise, only to be executed himself when Khrushchev seized power. Khrushchev would surely have disappeared in turn, if Brezhnev had felt he could get away with it.

She should have known better, she decided. This is what Karl Neder always did. He ranted and raved, and you thought him a fool and a lunatic, and then all of a sudden he had you trapped in the web of his words, and you found yourself wondering: what if there is something in this? What if his madness has cleared his vision? She could feel the soft pulse of an approaching headache. Too much heat, too much coffee.

Ψ

Later, Karl Neder walked alone along the west bank of the Danube, heading for the shady respite of Margit Island. It was early evening, but the air was hot and close, and the slanting sun was relentless when it found you. He remembered tanks in these wide roads.

This city is regaining its swagger, he thought. Old Europe is in the very stones; you'd have to level the place to destroy that. He thought of Yuri Andropov, the architect of the suppression in 1956, who was now poised to replace an ailing Brezhnev in the Kremlin. Andropov, who engineered the exile of Andrei Sakharov to a faceless, rubbish-strewn corner of Gorky. Could it really be coincidence that the KGB put Sakharov in an apartment on Gagarin Boulevard? To Neder, it was obvious what they were saying: 'We can do anything. No one is too tall that we cannot cut them down, not the first man in space and not a Nobel Prize winner.'

Well, well. Karl Neder had plans for Sakharov.

Before Gagarin, he thought, no one had really flown. Oh, they had grown wings and glided through the air in a relative kind of way, making futile little hops from city to city, but Yuri's flight was absolute. He went out into absolute time and space. The only breeze he felt was the wind of the luminiferous ether.

Was that it? In any event, something, surely, had happened to Yuri in those 108 minutes – something that had scared the Soviet state. Something he had seen, Neder guessed. He felt that men like Khrushchev and Brezhnev, these crude but wily products of the Politburo, men with ambition but no imagination, did not appreciate what travelling in space would actually mean. Only after Gagarin's flight did they truly understand that he had been *up there*, looking down on all of them. There was nothing you can hide from the heavens. You can go to remote regions and put security gates on the roads, and evacuate hundreds of thousands of poor and ignorant people from their bleak homeland, and build high walls, and block radio transmission; but from space, your plans are laid bare.

*

The politicians did not want to do anything in space except *be* there. To Kennedy and Khrushchev, the moon and the stars and the sun were all one and the same. It was all heaven, and they wanted to rule it.

Neder suspected several possibilities, not necessarily exclusive. It was of course conceivable that Brezhnev's plot against Gagarin was motivated by nothing more than blind jealousy of his charisma and popularity at home and abroad, and suspicion of the friends of his predecessor's regime. But perhaps he also thought it unwise to harbour, and even to celebrate, within the Soviet Union someone who had seen the world at a glance, the finiteness of mankind's estates. People exposed to such things would become ungovernable. Neder strongly suspected still more than this, however. He felt sure that Gagarin had seen something over the Kazakh wastes that he was not meant to see. Not a military or research establishment, for anyone in his position would have taken it for granted that there were more of those. No, Neder sensed that there were more cryptic, more powerful insignia carved into the barren plains. It was an ancient land.

And there were still deeper levels. For those who fall from heaven to the earth are not men. They are angels. There is no greater threat to a godless nation than that posed by an angel among its people.

18

O Galileo, will thy trial desist?
As ages pass, still are thy words denied;
Not only priest but learned sage insists
Thou were the fool to reason with thine eyes.

But thou, e'en thou would put thy truths aside,
A coward yet, to save thy mortal frame.
A fraud, thy piercing wisdom thou deride,
And sacrifice the honour of thy name.

Yet now I see the wisdom of thy path,
A bitter road, that men will make us tread
For they hear not, they curse us both and laugh
And mock to see the tears we each have shed.

So shall I too recant and hide my face,
The price you set: renounce absolute space?

Karl Neder, 'Eppur si Muove'

Vladimir Novikov pulled his cap down harder as a gust shot along the wind tunnel of Chkalov Street, kicking up white flakes and firing them like serrated bullets at the two huddled men. 'In a few weeks,' he said, 'these people will be baking to death in their concrete oven.'

'There are places on earth where man was never meant to live,' said Neder.

'Yes, but not here,' Novikov laughed. 'Those are reserved for political prisoners. He's lucky he got the Peace Prize, or else he'd probably be out east now. *Then* you'd need more than a hat and scarf to go visiting!

'Personally,' he added more soberly, 'I think they have something else in store for Andrei Dmitrievich. It can't go on like this.'

'But that is terrible! We must do something.'

'He has chosen this himself. I know –' registering Neder's frown '– that this sounds harsh. I do not mean it in quite the way you think. Andrei knows what he is doing. And we – not all of us, but most – we support him in that. We can make his life a lot easier; we bring him scientific papers and journals, make him feel that he is still part of our community. By citing his papers we keep his name alive internationally, and it all adds to his armour. Brezhnev's hands are tied – he knows he cannot do to Sakharov what they did to Sergei Kovalyov. Seven years in a labour camp, not easy for a theoretical physicist.'

Novikov worked at the Physics Institute of the Soviet Academy of Sciences, where Andrei Sakharov had once been a colleague. Sakharov was no longer officially connected to the Institute, but it treated him as an honorary member, helping him to attend scientific conferences from time to time.

Andrei Sakharov was no longer officially connected to anything in Soviet society. The head of the KGB, Yuri Andropov, had declared him public enemy number one, and the father of the Russian hydrogen bomb was generally shunned by anyone who cared about their reputation. So the company he kept in his cramped Moscow flat on Chkalov Street was, in one way or another, disreputable. His wife, the activist Elena Bonner, was considered by the KGB to be a harridan with an explosive temper who had turned Sakharov from state critic into anti-Soviet delinquent. He consorted with dangerous types like Alexander Solzhenitsyn, and all manner of desperate and despicable characters congregated in his kitchen to brew up seditious schemes.

When Karl Neder and Vladimir Novikov arrived at the apartment where Sakharov and Bonner lived, the kitchen was already crowded. All the visitors had the hollow-eyed stare of people under surveillance, some with the coarse black hair of peasant stock, others delicate, bespectacled intellectuals. Some were scribbling furiously at the table, in the spaces between a battalion of glasses half-emptied of dark, sweet tea. Others were debating too heatedly and too fast for Neder to follow, though his Russian was good. Bonner, hair drawn back in an iron knot, was talking earnestly to a compact, powerfully built man by the stove. Sakharov, listening at the table, looked tired. But his eyes, with their slanting lids of Tatar ancestry, brightened at the sight of Novikov.

The physicist handed him a bundle of papers – 'No treason here,' he joked, 'unless your creed denies quantum chromodynamics.' Sakharov scanned them hungrily, and it was clear that he would have preferred to take them into a corner and escape from the disarray of the kitchen. But Andrei Dmitrievich did not neglect his guests.

'This is Karl Neder,' said Novikov. 'He has come from Austria to speak with you.'

'That will not have been easy!'

'I have obtained an affidavit from the University of Linz,' Neder explained, 'which says that I am a scientist attending the conference on quantum gravity in Tblisi.'

'Which he was!' grinned Novikov. 'But then we got him back up here with me.'

'So you are still beyond suspicion, Vladimir? No one watching over you, even though you consort with felons like me?'

'I must lead a blessed existence.'

'That's the kind of talk that will get you into trouble.'

Sakharov fetched them tea. 'Look, it is a very bad situation,' he said gravely. 'First there were these deaths – murders, we must say – on the subway. I cannot prove that the bombs had anything to do with the KGB, but I suspect it very strongly. They want to discredit activists for human rights by associating them with violence. That not only turns the people against them, it withdraws their moral authority in the eyes of the world. It is just like the Reichstag fire in '33.'

He cast his eyes downwards. 'Elena thinks I was wrong to voice these opinions to Krimsky – he's the reporter from Associated Press, you know. Maybe she is right. Krimsky has been expelled from the country. And I was summoned to the Attorney General and told to sign a statement warning me against my "criminal acts". The press have called me a slanderer, of course.'

Then he cheered up a little, and Neder had the impression of watching a man lost and alone in a vast forest at night who stokes a small fire and sees a few embers kindle.

'You know what happened when Krimsky was leaving? On his exit visa, they wrote his name as "Krinsky". So the border guard was going to stop him from passing. He said, "Fine – but you might want to check that if you wish to remain in the army."'

'Before he left,' Sakharov went on, 'I wanted to give Krimsky this. But he decided it would be best not to take it.'

It was a typed essay called 'Alarm and Hope'. Neder read the inscription at the top: an epigraph from Martin Luther King. 'Injustice anywhere is a threat to justice everywhere.'

'But now then,' he said, turning to Neder, 'do you come to me to talk about physics, or politics, or perhaps about poetry?'

'I would enjoy discussing all three with you, Andrei Dmitrievich,' Neder replied. 'You see, I too am a dissident, an exile from Hungary, where we know your man Andropov very well. Wasn't he the very same who orchestrated the tank divisions that rolled through Budapest in '56?'

'Yes, I believe so. One day, I think, Yuri Andropov will be the president of this country. Then we shall truly have a battle on our hands. I swear he means to outlive me.'

'Yes, yes. Well, the fact is that I am a Marxist too. You know, I am a member of the Italian Communist Party. Why the Italians, you might think? They are the only ones that will have me. Communist countries are very distrustful of Marxists.'

They both laughed.

'But first of all, comrade Sakharov, forgive me, but I have to ask you this. When you developed the hydrogen bomb, how much did you know about Stalin's regime?'

Sakharov sighed. 'This is of course for me the central question. It is what must determine my innocence or guilt.'

Ψ

Sakharov was standing in a world without end. A bowl of dirty, dusty rock and coarse grass capped by a steel-blue sky: this was Kazakhstan, seared by a merciless sun. There were twenty miles of nothing between him and a flimsy tower, where a fat metal bulb squatted, waiting to ripen.

Once these parched steppes had been home to tens of thousands of people, surviving at the edge of the world where no one ever saw them or thought about them. Then they were ordered to leave, just a few weeks ago, with no reason given. Just clear out. It was not until the last moments before the test that scientists at the Installation realized these people would be downwind when the first Soviet thermonuclear weapon exploded on 12 August 1953, missing the eighth anniversary of Little Boy by six days. So they had to go.

Evacuations on that scale take their toll. Several dozen people, it was estimated, would die in the process. And they did. As Sakharov, looking out towards their former homeland, knew.

He wanted to see the bright birth of his creation. It was foolish – his eyesight could have suffered permanent damage. But he welcomed the violence of it. After the first flash, which would have burnt out his retinae, he pulled off his smoked-glass goggles and felt the fierce heat on his face, he watched the cloud turn purple and orange and finally the blue-black of a bruise in heaven. He was punched by the blast, almost knocked over, the air wrenched out of him. The rumble was the sound of a mountain falling.

Later – mere hours later – he walked over black glass to a twisted monument of concrete and steel. The glass was fused rock, and it crunched like burnt treacle toffee beneath his feet. This stroll in the steppe gave him fevers and nosebleeds by the end of the year.

Ψ

'That would all have happened,' said Sakharov, 'whether Stalin had died or not.' The Georgian ox had collapsed in his own piss five months before the test. His death, like that of an Egyptian pharaoh, demanded the deaths of scores of his subjects, trampled in the rush to see his embalmed corpse. 'By the time I was working at the Installation, we knew what Stalin was. Landau, one of our greatest physicists, was thrown in prison for accusing Stalin of hijacking the revolution. They'd have done the same with Kapitsa if they could have spared him. That was what saved most of us – they considered us unruly and untrustworthy, but no one else could do the jobs we did.' He sighed. 'Yes, we would have delivered the bomb to Stalin.'

'But our hand was forced,' Novikov interjected. 'America had a bomb, and Britain had a bomb, so what else could we do? Besides, Andrei wanted a ban from the beginning, isn't that right?'

'We calculated that the fallout from the testing would kill ten thousand people for every megaton. If another nation had inflicted casualties like that on us, we'd have waged war without restraint. And yet these were just tests. These weapons were slaughtering our own people, not protecting them.'

Neder looked agitated by all this talk. 'Andrei Dmitrievich, I need your help!' he burst out.

'If I can give it…'

'You are a courageous man. I believe we share the same causes in this life – to oppose dogma and dictatorship, to fight for political and intellectual freedoms, to exercise free thought and speech. And we both know that one must sometimes be bold. Two years ago, I tried to contact you, but I do not think you ever received my message. If you received it, you would have found a way to reply, I can see that now. You see, I – I have shown that relativity is a fraud.' He plunged his hands into his briefcase, pulling out papers.

'Please don't think that I am a Stalinist or a fascist who denounces this as bourgeois or Jewish science – I won't have any of that nonsense. Everything I say is supported by detailed argument, here in these documents. If you will read them, you will be convinced. Two years ago, I held the first International Conference on Space-Time Absoluteness. We wanted you to be our patron, because your name is respected throughout the international community. I wrote to you, many letters, asking for this favour, but we heard nothing and, well, then it was too late. But it will soon be time for another conference, because now there are more experiments and more evidence that relativity is nothing but a phantom! Please, read these papers, and then write to me, tell me your views. Even if you do not agree with everything, though I think you will agree with it all, but even if you do not, please write and let me know. And we can correspond. I do not have many freedoms myself, because I am doubly a heretic, in my science as well as in my politics, and heretics are poorly treated now, as they were in the Middle Ages, and of course you know this. But if I can obtain things for you, send you other papers, I will do this with pleasure. Please, read my papers.'

Sakharov was silent for a moment. 'I have always found,' he said quietly, 'that relativity works very well for me. Of course, one might convince me that it is flawed, but not, I think, without difficulty. Yes, I will read your papers, and I am grateful that you have made such efforts to bring them to me.'

'And the conference? You will endorse it?'

'I think I should read your papers first.'

'Good, good. But look, there is something else I want to give you. This is my book, a satirical book, I give it to you!'

It was more of a pamphlet than a book, printed in Russian, called *Devils are Here Too*.

'Thank you,' said Sakharov. 'But why do you give me this?'

'To make you laugh a little bit, Andrei Dmitrievich.'

'Then that is kind. I need to find reasons to laugh, but there seem to be so many more reasons to weep.'

And it appeared to Karl Neder that Sakharov said these last words with such deep sorrow that he could barely refrain from weeping himself.

19

But Neder did not hear from Sakharov, for a little over a year later, on 22 January 1980, Sakharov was on his way to the Institute when his car was pulled over by police on the Krasnokholmsky Bridge. He was ordered to get inside their vehicle and was driven to the Attorney General's office. From there he was taken in a KGB van to Moscow airport, from where he was flown to the old city of Nizhny Novgorod, renamed in 1932 after the great Russian writer whose name meant 'bitter': Gorky. There Sakharov and Bonner lived under house arrest, with a policeman standing outside the front door twenty-four hours a day.

Karl Neder continued to make preparations for the Second International Conference on Space-Time Absoluteness, and he felt sure that Academician Sakharov would approve of his name being included in the announcements. If Sakharov had found serious flaws in Neder's papers, he would surely have written before his arrest.

The de facto organizing committee consisted of Karl Neder, Georgiu Constantin and Tomas Neumann. Neumann had the funds, Neder had the tenacity, and Constantin had the office.

It was not much of an office, however. The room in the physics department of Sofia University on Shipka ulitsa was ten feet square, and if Neder and Constantin were to rise from their desks simultaneously there would be a clangourous clash of chairs. Neder was not really supposed to be there at all, but Constantin had persuaded the head of department that he was an assistant. In reality it was rather the reverse: Neder directed much of the activity in Constantin's laboratory, and Constantin badgered the technicians into making the components his colleague required – those, at least, that could not be salvaged from Sofia's scrapyards.

'We don't need much,' Neder reassured him. 'With a car battery, wire and thread, we can show that the Lorentz equation is wrong and the Ampère formula is wrong. And then relativity starts to unravel, and energy starts to flow.'

By Christmas 1981 both of their desks had lost all equilibrium. Correspondence about the conference (fifty-six attendees so far) mingled with papers in progress, tables of data and sketches of new devices. And here too, on the top of Neder's heap, was an important letter to the intransigent Dr Battle:

Dear Dr Battle,

Once more you did not stay behind your word and you do not send to me my article for introducing the corrections which you intend to suggest. I MUST see this article before it is to be published. I am telling myself I must not doubt that you will publish in Natural Science, *as you have said, despite that I hear nothing from you after this promise for many months. I said you the last time on the phone that if also this time you will not write me, then I have to cut my relations with you. It is senseless to lose my time and money for contacts with you. I think, however, that I have not deserved such an attitude from your part. We are not for a single day on this Earth! Think a while on these words.*

I published this autumn the third part of my book The Bitter Road to Truth. *I send you the book which I grant to* Natural Science. *Read it attentively! You are the principal protagonist in this book. The problem is important. I HAVE INVENTED A PERPETUUM MOBILE! All is explained how and why and the results of my last experiments here in Sofia are presented in detail. I think you are obliged to give your opinion on this book in the press. Better earlier than later. I give you a friendly advice – review this book until it will be not too late for you. If this is not reason enough, I make this offer to you: review this book, and I shall pay one thousand dollars to* Natural Science. *You may say that I have not this money, but it will soon be in my pocket because of the rewards that must come from my PERPETUUM MOBILE. That and more. The review may be good or bad. Better even to be bad. Indeed, if you will even dare to write one scientifically motivated objection to the arguments in my book, I promise to pay the $1,000. The objection must be of the kind: 'Neder asserts that… According to me this is not true because…' Nothing more.*

Still I do not see the advertisement for the Second International Conference on Space-Time Absoluteness in the pages of Natural Science. *Please do not tell me, as last time, that the funds have not been forthcoming. I have given you my word, that when I see the advertisement appear, then the money will reach you. I cannot give you before. I have been too many times tricked from my money by false promises, some of them from you Dr Battle. Do not deceive me this time. But as for now, even with this device in my hands, I live as a vagabond at the kind discretion of Dr Georgiu*

Constantin of Sofia University. Now I must insist on another thing from you. Understand that I do not make demands lightly. This is a matter of extreme urgency. I send you my open letter to Leonid Brezhnev. PLEASE PUBLISH IT. The text will take no more than half a page. You may add any comments which you, probably should like to add. I do not need to see the proofs of the letter, so that it can appear as soon as possible. Introduce any linguistic corrections, but please, do not change the sense of the letter. As we are in good gentleman-ish relations (you see, Dr Battle, even now I still believe it is so), I have no reasons for preoccupations. It will be good if, too, you can print the letter with a photograph of Sakharov.

I can free Sakharov, but I need your help. The appearance of my letter in Natural Science is a very important pace to the liberation of this man. His freedom is in your hands. If you do not accept these materials, I shall be forced to come to London to plead for them.

Thank you, Dr Battle, thank you for the support which the 'Western scientific world' has given me. The policemen here do not know who I am or what I have done. But you know, and you did not before now allow that the world can hear what I have done. Anyway, Dr Battle, without money, without documents, living as a vagabond, I shall run the perpetuum mobile. Very soon! Read my book, to see WHERE I AM!

It is too late. Good night.

Yours sincerely,
Karl Neder

LETTER OF NEDER TO BREZHNEV

Dear comrade Brezhnev,

As I announced recently, I do not intend to patent the electromagnetic perpetuum mobile, discovered by me, and I grant them to humanity. I wish, however, that this big discovery, which will drastically change the whole planetary energetic structure, would also lead to substantial changes in the world's political and moral structures. As an energetic source, the electrodynamic perpetuum mobile (P.M.) is cheap, clean, decentralized, and unlimited, i.e. all its 'parameters' are diametrically opposite to those of all the present sources of energy, first of all the atomic one. Thus the P.M. will introduce economic and political changes simply because of its own substance. (Let me cite our teacher: 'Neue Produktionsverfahren fördern immer neue Produktionsbeziehungen.') We have, however, to do our best, so that the new 'production relations' should bring humanity quicker and easier to the world Communist society (Christians call it 'paradise on the earth'), where man will be no more a serve of the Mammon.

One of the important paces on this way is the quick and profound democratization and liberalization of the Soviet Union and the other countries of 'real socialism', so that the latter simply becomes 'socialism'. With the present letter I beg you to do any efforts in the frames of your limited possibilities (I recognize this limitation) and to give freedom to my Russian colleague Dr Sakharov. In the case that Sakharov will not be liberated for Easter, I declare with the present letter that I, as a discoverer of the P.M., do not permit that this source of energy should be used in the countries of real socialism.

I have already declared in 1979 that I do not permit my cosmic speedometer (apparatus functioning because of the light velocity's direction dependence) to be used for military purposes. Nevertheless NASA uses this apparatus without asking for my permission. I have not the power to impose my will on NASA. In the same way I shall not have the power to impose my will on the Eastern countries if my plea will be ignored. Thus my 'ultimatum' has only a moral background. I think, however, that in the present world, where the physical power has reached an unlimited effectivity, the unique effective power will become the moral power. Otherwise our civilization is doomed to perish.

I beg you, dear comrade Brezhnev, to do your best and to try to persuade your colleagues in the Soviet leadership that people like Sakharov, with his high morality, are of an immense importance for the salvation of the freedom and the prosperity of world Communism.

With the profound hope that my plea for mercy will be satisfied,

Sincerely yours,
Karl Neder
Citizen of the world, born Hungarian,
Member of the Italian Communist Party

On the evening of 4 April 1982, Karl Neder and Georgiu Constantin were approached by two men as they left Constantin's apartment on Veslets ulitsa, overlooking the Vladaiska River. They had packed corned-beef rolls and bottles of beer, planning an evening's work that was likely to stretch well into the night. The great bells of the Aleksander Nevski church were chiming seven as the figures drew alongside.

'You must come with us, please.'

'So this is where the special forces intervene,' said Neder. 'But we are very busy tonight. We are staging an international scientific conference in twenty days.'

'This will not take long. Just a talk.'

They were not thugs, these men. They smiled, they kept a respectful distance, they neither avoided nor held eye contact. Not that any of this mattered.

Neder and Constantin were driven to the police headquarters and delivered into the office of a man who wore the weary, harassed expression of a market trader. He looked and acted like an unremarkable fellow, but Ilian Dolev played that part with consummate skill. As a teenager, he had fought in the Fatherland Front against the Nazis. His credentials as a loyal Communist were impeccable, and it was a sheer fluke or oversight (Dolev was never sure which) that had allowed him to stay floating around the middle reaches of the hierarchy, rather than being promoted to high office, or shot. Or first one, then the other. Perhaps, he flattered himself, his few, small, finely judged errors had succeeded in their aim of anchoring him to the echelons of mediocrity. Those errors needed exquisite planning; Dolev considered them his finest achievements.

'We are interested in your conference,' Dolev told his two visitors. 'Please tell us about it.'

With a sinking heart, Constantin saw that Neder interpreted the question at face value. 'It is an international event.' They were speaking Russian. 'Many famous scientists will be there. We shall debate the structure of space-time. You surely know, comrade, that there is an absurd conspiracy today to conduct all of physics within the frameworks of general relativity and quantum mechanics. The second of these has serious flaws, which I can explain if you wish, or I can provide you with papers. But the real monstrosity is general relativity, which has been foisted on the scientific community for essentially political reasons. The scientists at this conference are those noble few who have penetrated this conspiracy, and have noticed the contradictions and nonsenses at the heart of Einstein's theory. So we shall –'

'Are there American scientists coming to this conference?'

'Yes, and some from Britain and West Germany –'

'Let me be frank with you, Dr Neder. We know the names of everyone who is supposed to be attending this event. We have been watching you and Dr Constantin for some time. You are conducting experiments, are you not?'

'These are very important experiments, comrade. We have found a way to extract infinite amounts of energy from the electromagnetic ether. This discovery will revolutionize the generation of energy.'

'We are not keen to have any more revolutions. What do you intend to do with this discovery?'

'Well, that is… that is delicate. I wish to make it available to all the world, so that there will be no more wars to be fought over primitive sources of energy like oil and gas. There will be no longer the fear of accidents and leakages from nuclear power and so forth.'

'You would get rid of these things? And what do you suppose would happen to the economies that rely on them?'

'I am not really an economist, comrade. All I can say is that this energy would be cheaper, cleaner, safer –'

'What do you say, Dr Constantin?'

Constantin was looking thoroughly dejected. He understood what Dolev was implying by switching to Bulgarian.

'These are just preliminary experiments, comrade,' he said

at length. 'We are just physicists, tinkering to see what we can make. There is still much more to be done.'

'And when it is done, what then?'

Constantin could not frame a reply; all he could do was to open his hands, palms outwards.

'There is a name on your international advisory board,' said Dolev to both of them, 'that is very well known. What are your links with Andrei Sakharov?'

'He is a scientific colleague,' Neder replied. 'We know that Moscow rejects him and calls him a dissident and a madman. But he is not a madman. He is a great scientist.'

'I ask again. What are your links with Andrei Sakharov?'

'I have spoken with him in Moscow. Two years ago. He supports what we are doing.'

'You mean this conference? Just what *are* you doing in Sofia, Dr Neder?'

But it was Constantin who replied. His words were slow and studied, as though he had memorized them years ago.

'I am a Bulgarian and a Communist,' he said. 'Dr Neder is also a Communist. We believe that we have discovered something useful. We would both wish to place a useful discovery at the disposal of the state. But we, like Dr Sakharov, believe it is the scientist's responsibility to ensure that his discoveries are delivered into responsible hands. While scientists like Dr Sakharov are detained and imprisoned by the Soviet Politburo, we cannot be assured of the responsibility of the authorities in this country. The perpetuum mobile could be an instrument of great power. We would be failing in our duty as human beings if we did not respect that power.'

Dolev's eyes seemed to be at the other end of a microscope: that of the observer, not the observed. It looked as though he was trying to remember something.

'Your duty as human beings? I am amazed, Dr Constantin,

to find that I have lived all these years in Sofia alongside people like you. We may have brushed shoulders in Aleksander Nevski Square, who knows? And yet that seems impossible. Do you know what my duty is right now? It is my duty to become angry and scream at you. But I am choosing to ignore my duty. Why is that? It is because I have learnt that duty is not a set of rules saying this or that, telling you how you should behave in this or that situation. That is how you see your duty, isn't it? It is a list of moral strictures, and when in doubt you look them up and they tell you what you should do. Rules, rules. Any fool can make rules, and any idiot can follow them. You know what they say in Moscow: "On the whole everything is forbidden, but anything permitted is obligatory." That is their duty, to avoid what is forbidden and to say what is obligatory. But who does this duty? Only the idiots. We need rules, everybody needs rules; they need to be publicly stated and rigidly imposed. But that is not to say that we – I mean the chiefs of police, the special police, the government, your superiors – it is not to say that we expect everyone to be following these rules. Everyone breaks the rules whenever they have the chance, including me. All the same, I acknowledge that the rules are iron rules, and it is right to punish transgressions seriously.'

He stopped and ordered some tea for them all. He was not angry, he was not genial. Neither are hagglers in the market-place, if they know how to conduct business.

'If you think,' he continued, 'that I am now telling you that I am about to punish you seriously, then you still don't understand. You say you are a Communist, Dr Constantin, but what on earth do you mean by that? You want to imply that you are like me, but we are not alike at all, and we can both see that. Or perhaps you wish to prick my conscience by saying, "Look, I have remained faithful to the ideology that you have abandoned." But have I abandoned Communism? You are scientists, you will understand this analogy. Let us say a man walks in here, he is stooped and hairy, he has a jutting jaw, he looks like an ape. He says, "Look here, you fellows, I am still *Homo erectus*, I am the real human, I have remained true to the human form this past four million years." He has failed to grasp that his form is not a thing in itself, not an end, it is a process. Is it meaningful to say that St Peter was more Christian than the Borgia popes? No, you are not a good Communist, Dr Constantin, for the simple reason that I am an authority in a Communist state and I say that you have committed a crime.'

'But what crime?' Constantin blurted.

'What crime? What crime? Please, this is ridiculous. Conspiring with a Soviet subversive. Conspiring to conceal secrets from the state. We know all about Dr Neder's seditious literature. Which crime would you like? Stop invoking the rules, Dr Constantin – this has nothing to do with any rulebook.'

The tea arrived. Neder said, 'But if you arrest us, this big conference will be jeopardized, and there will be an international outcry.'

'That may be true,' said Dolev, 'although I do not take it for granted. I am not sure you are so big a fish, Dr Neder. But the point is, I am not arresting you.'

Astonishment from both detainees. 'Then we can go?'

'No, you cannot go. You have committed crimes, so you cannot go. But it is not your fault, so you cannot be arrested. You are both mentally unstable, and will have to be sent to hospital.'

Constantin groaned, and his shoulders slumped.

'Oh, it is not so hard,' said Dolev. 'A matter of a few weeks, I should think. That should put your minds straight.'

'Why,' Neder grated, 'are we not sane?'

'Because you believe in perpetual motion.'

It was not the answer he'd expected.

'It is well known,' Dolev explained. 'Perpetual motion is thermodynamically impossible. That is why the American Patent Office refuses to grant patents on devices such as yours.'

'The *American* government?'

'Yes, I have checked with the embassy. It seems like a very good policy to me.'

'But wait,' Constantin broke in. 'If perpetual motion is impossible, how can we be guilty for proposing to withhold it from you?'

'Really, doctor, that is a simple matter. If you plot to kill President Zhivkov by buying him a bottle of fine Bulgarian wine, you are no less guilty of plotting to kill him; you merely have no idea how to go about it. Now then, gentleman,' as the police chief rose from his seat, 'you will be taken first to your apartment, where you may collect some basic items. Then you will be taken to the Pavlov State Asylum, where they will begin your rehabilitation.'

He called for their escorts. 'Personally,' he said to them as they were leaving, 'I wish you very good luck with your future research. It seems to me to be potentially of great interest.'

Their minders were now far less amenable than before, and forbade any attempts at talk during the journey. But Neder and Constantin snatched a few words as they picked up some meagre belongings on Veslets ulitsa. Neder was agitated, but Constantin went about his business with quiet conviction.

'What about our experiments?'

'They will be confiscated.'

'And the conference? We must get out a press release.'

'I don't think we can do that, Karl. They will take care of that too. They can be very efficient when they want to be.'

'You mean they will cancel it? Just like that?'

'Karl, it will not surprise anyone who has ever visited Bulgaria, or Romania, or the Soviet Union. This is what happens here, you know that.'

Neder looked out at the river. Their guards (no point in pretending now that they were anything else) were loitering in the hallway, smoking.

'There is no other way out of here, Karl. We will be put away for a month, and then we will be free again.'

'But you know what those places are like.'

'Yes, I do. I have been inside one before. A lot depends on which doctors they assign to us – but we are not so very important.' He stole a glance towards the door, then grasped Neder's forearm. 'Remember that, Karl, because I know you do not always think this way. *We are not so very important.*'

Ψ

Breakfast at six in the morning: a mush of white substance, flour mixed with a little fat and warm water. No heating, cold showers. Then the medicine.

They gave Neder five white pills, and would not tell him what they were. 'Just swallow.' He swallowed, and they checked inside his mouth.

They did not taste of anything, those pills, and they did not seem to do anything either. He slept a lot at first, because fear sucked up all his energy. Then he began to believe that it would not get worse than this, and he relaxed a little, and that was when he found himself several times each day on the verge of tears. He was permitted to take exercise in a small yard overlooked by high, dull panes. Figures stood there, as indistinct as angels, and watched him sprint furiously in circles until his eyes stopped burning.

Some patients did not get the white pills. They got injections which made them howl like beasts.

'What is it?' he asked his friend Miroslav.

'Insulin.'

Miroslav was a chemical engineer who designed heat-management systems for power stations. He agreed with Dolev that perpetual motion would put him out of business, but he regarded the idea cheerfully. 'I would be a baker instead,' he concluded.

'Why do they give them insulin?'

'Because it messes you up. Those are the hard guys. You're like me, Karl, they just want somewhere to keep us for a bit. They don't really expect us to change, but neither do they have much to fear if we don't. We'll just be back inside again in a year or so. I organized a workers' strike at the Yambol plant – big bloody deal. But some of these blokes have been in here for years, and getting insulin every few days.'

'Do you know what it does to them?'

'It gobbles up all your blood sugar, and then you go into shock, and start to convulse. They tie you to the bedstead while that happens. You become incontinent. Then you get a big dose of glucose, and you come out of it.'

Neder had not seen Constantin since the day they were admitted. But he is not important to them either, Neder told himself.

Ψ

He escaped from Pavlov. It was quite easy, really. They were kept dressed in pyjamas all through the day, but he went to work in the laundry room and stole some trousers, and then he took a pair of gardening boots and one of the rough jackets they were given for labouring in bad weather, and he climbed out of the window one night. There were no guards, no barbed wire – this was not a prison, after all.

'Of course we could get out,' Miroslav had told him. 'So

what? I've nowhere to go but home, and they would just bring me back and start my term again. I might as well sit it out.'

Neder was so tired he did not trust his indifferent grasp of the Bulgarian tongue, knowing it was sure to draw suspicion. He had no money. He thought first of breaking into Constantin's lab and seeing what he could salvage, but it was probably too late, and in any case he did not have the strength.

Instead he walked all the way to Cherni Vrâh, opposite the South Park in the city centre, and entered the US embassy at five in the morning. An armed guard escorted him to a waiting room. 'The ambassador is not here,' he was told by a red-haired American woman with a bandsaw voice. And the ambassador did not come. Instead, it was two Bulgarian policemen who entered forty-five minutes later.

'I am claiming political asylum!' Neder yelled in English. The first policeman hit him in the stomach, just hard enough to knock the wind out of him. The second clubbed him smartly on the back of the head. He did not pass out, but the pain was dazzling.

Ψ

They gave him different pills, with a faintly soapy taste, and he began to get headaches. His eyes itched, and he could not help rubbing them raw. Other than this, little was different in his hospital regime.

'How are you getting along?' his doctor asked in considerate Russian.

'I don't know,' he replied, and it was true. 'I don't know what was supposed to be wrong with me, so how can I know if I'm any better? I feel worse.'

'Well, we're keeping an eye on you.'

After seven weeks they released him, a stone and a half

lighter. They gave him an exit visa and an escort to the Greek border. 'My papers?' he asked. There was no record of any papers. 'Dr Constantin?' There was no record of any Dr Constantin. That was when he lost control, there in Dolev's office, with his bags packed and the car waiting for him outside. He called Dolev some filthy things, and beat his hands against his head, and then he wept impotently.

In fact, Constantin was released three weeks later, but Neder did not discover that for over a year. Dolev waited solemnly for Neder to exhaust himself, and then the guards helped him into the car.

20

'IT'S THE WAY THE WORLD HAS ALWAYS BEEN. CREATIVE PEOPLE die poor,' said Barry Vender.

Dan Rather looked stoical at this prospect. 'There you have it,' he told the nation. 'A brilliant, self-educated inventor against the US Patent Office. If he's wrong, I guess we're stuck with the gas pump. But if he's right, it'll herald a revolution to rival the discoveries of Albert Einstein.'

CBS viewers knew all about Einstein, because the trusted, smiling anchorman had told them he had 'changed the face of physics'. Revolutions were in the air that day.

Ψ

There was a tumble of flaking shacks clinging to the road out of Bogalusa, and the smell of baked mud in the air. The dogs looked ready to fight with anyone, for the slightest of reasons. They glowered at a lone crow on a pole. It was that kind of place: lone crows on poles.

And here was a dirt track, guarded by signs saying KEEP OUT, NO TRESPASSING and PRIVATE LAND. But who were they discouraging? Who would take this turning, except to break a law? Tom Holz, CBS reporter, in a suit that was sticking to every crevice, knew the place. Not Bogalusa as such, but the whole damned state, and he figured you might as well put a KEEP OUT sign on the Mississippi border. He'd grown up in Jackson; he could take care of himself down here. Every mile along the flight path from Chicago, his heart had sunk a little lower.

Ψ

'What's the answer to the energy crisis? Suppose a fellow told you the answer was a machine he has invented which makes energy from nothing? Before you scoff, take a look with Tom Holz.'

Ψ

Actually, Barry Vender wasn't poor. Not *Mississippi*-poor. Vender had benefactors, faceless men in Houston and Fort Worth and Reno. 'It's a fine thing you're doing,' they told him, and, 'This country would never have been great if we'd listened to the experts.' 'I never listened to no experts,' said Jack Brophy, who was worth thirty billion and lived on a ship in Puget Sound. 'And look at me.'

No, Vender wasn't poor. But he had been. He knew what poor was. He had lived with five other fellows in a condemned corpse of a building in chilly Minneapolis, and they had gradually burnt all the floorboards in the winter, stripping the decaying carcass to a skeleton whose ribs they learnt to cross in the dark. Those were the Nixon years. As the Apollo program gathered pace and America began to enjoy supremacy in space, Vender found himself shut out of aerospace, and he was forced to take whatever work he could find. He had done stints along the west coast as a street magician: San Diego to Seattle. He was, for one long and acrid summer, a hospital janitor in New York City. But there were a few fat times too, contracts from Westinghouse and Boeing, a stint as a technician at NASA Langley. His address book never stopped growing; he knew the value of contacts.

'It's possible his theory could be correct and that this could revolutionize society,' said a man identified in the strapline as Link Harting, engineer with the Mississippi Department of Transportation. 'This stuff goes way beyond what you read in the textbooks.'

Ψ

Vender was standing with folded arms in front of his garage when Holz's Dodge drew up. It was as though Vender lived on this precise spot of dry earth. He wore oily overalls, pebble glasses; his hair was shoulder-length and tobacco-yellow. He looked kind of familiar. Here, thought Holz, was a guy who could fix a broken car on a lonely road at night.

The cameras were not allowed inside the garage – 'Boy, are there some people who would like to get a glimpse in there!' – but Vender had an Energy Machine set up on the trestle table outside. He hauled a twelve-pack from his fridge and distributed it among the crew. 'Hot work.' 'Oh, you bet.'

The Energy Machine seemed to be a motor from a power drill, propped up on wooden blocks and fed by wires to a car battery. 'Doesn't look like much,' he confessed – now was that a Mississippi accent, or what? Where had they said this guy came from? 'But you put one in your home, and you'll never have to pay another electricity bill.'

CBS wasn't the first to come knocking. CBS was never the first with these local-colour stories. Seymour Pouliquet had been running it for eight weeks on WWN-TV, a CBS affiliate in New Orleans. For Pouliquet it had become something of a personal crusade. 'I was sceptical at first, sure I was,' he told Holz. 'It was just a show-closer, you know, something kind of quirky. But you know what? It became a monster that I couldn't let go of.' Utility rates in Mississippi were about to soar, and viewers from all over the state called in demanding to know more about Vender's Energy Machine. Where can I buy one? What's the problem here? This guy got an answer, so who's blocking it? Whose interests are at risk here?

'That's what I figured too,' said Pouliquet. 'Who's out to sink this, and why? You know what, I speak to the college professors about this, they say it's all bull, but the moment I ask them to come on the program and say so, they back out. I guess they figure, maybe if this guy really has discovered something, you know, something really big that we've all missed, we're gonna look pretty dumb. OK, then get this. There are a couple of engineers on this show, guys who know about mechanics and electrics, the sort who build their own hogs and wire up their houses. So I get them to come with me up to Bogalusa, and they bring along their oscilloscopes and meters and whatever it is they use, and guess what? It all checks out.'

Ψ

'This is what I saw,' said Jim Crowther.

'Look at me if you can, Jim,' said Holz. 'Not into the camera.'

'I took along some little batteries, the sort you use in a pen-light. We hooked them up to a motor in Vender's backyard, and we ran that thing till there was no more juice left in the batteries. Then I wired them to this Energy Machine and set it spinning. We left it that way for maybe an hour, then I took out the batteries and connected 'em to the motor again. And it ran for twice as long as before.'

'You charged them up.'

'Ah, but y'see, you add up the power gone into the machine, and the power put out by the batteries, and you find you got extra energy from somewhere. Vender let me look inside his machine – I had to sign this affidavit first, saying I wasn't gonna reveal nothing – and there was no hidden source. This gadget works.'

And then there was Link Harting, who had a degree in physics and had done a teaching stint at the Grace and Perry Sperry Mississippi College. He heard about Vender from his brother Dick, who tested toys for Tonka. Vender had sent Tonka Toys a description of his invention: 'No more batteries.'

'Yup, I think he's done it,' said Harting to the CBS team. 'Barry's an original thinker.'

'Here's the catch,' Dan Rather told his viewers. 'In 1911 the Patent Office got tired of looking at energy-creating devices that never worked, so it ruled that no patent application for a machine that puts out more energy than it uses up would be considered until an actual operating model had been filed and demonstrated to run for a whole year. That's what is letting the Patent Office refuse to accept Barry Vender's Energy Machine.'

'I'll keep fighting,' said Vender, staring right into Tom Holz's lens. 'I'll keep fighting till hell freezes over. The Patent Office may not want this, and the energy industry may not want it, but you know who does want it, who needs it desperately? The human race, that's who.'

Ψ

They did. They wanted it *bad*. Bad enough that, after the Dan Rather slot, CBS had to delegate to a junior staff member the almost full-time job of forwarding mail to Bogalusa, Miss., where it overflowed the mailbox at the end of the dirt track and was carried off for private consumption by scavenging dogs. Some intrepid souls managed – maybe it was Pouliquet who tipped them off – to locate the dirt track itself, and paid no heed to the instructions to KEEP OUT. Vender decided that it wouldn't take a criminal genius to break into his garage and cart off the Energy Machines, for which he'd already received five-figure offers. He packed up and moved to Hattiesburg, leaving a confidential forwarding address with Tom Holz.

That was the least of it. Within a month, Vender was on the *Johnny Carson Show*. The *New York Times* ran an article, and so did *Science* magazine, quoting Link Harting and Jim Crowther. (A photocopy of the first page arrived on Roy Battle's desk, and scrawled along the bottom margin: 'The second page is as stupidly written as this one, and there is no need to see it, so that I do not send it to you. Why all this nonsense gets so much excitement??? Yours as ever, Karl Neder.') Then Vender decided to follow the advice of Seymour Pouliquet, and he rented out the New Orleans Superdome for a week. Thousands of people, alerted by advertisements in the *Mississippi Daily News* and the *Louisiana Herald* and even the *Washington Post*, not to mention daily announcements on WWN-TV, filled the stadium to see Barry Vender demonstrate his energy-creating machine. He had scaled up the design witnessed by Crowther, making a three-hundred-pound armature out of copper wire that he wound by hand in his kitchen. It was an ungainly construction, but the crowd wouldn't see it in any case. Vender installed it in a gleaming red Sterling sports car, eviscerated beneath its bloody hood. As the lights dimmed in the Superdome, the car purred out into the arena at four miles per hour, and the audience leapt to their feet.

Out of the automobile climbed Vender, and cheers and wild cries pierced the fragile air like firecrackers. There were no denim overalls now: he was dressed in all in black, his jacket skimming his knees. His hair was scraped back into a ponytail.

'Are you here,' he cried into the microphone, 'to see the world change?' He patted the Sterling. 'There's no engine in this baby. There's no gas tank, there's no fumes. You know what it's running on?' The crowd fell silent as Vender held up something so small, no one could see it. 'Here it is. This is the battery from a transistor radio. The Energy Machine takes the juice out of this and doubles it, trebles it, multiplies it a hundred times, and goes on doing that. On and on and on. I tell you, folks, I could drive this car around the New Orleans Superdome forever, and this little feller would never run dry.' Whoops and whistles. All over the dome the Dixie flag was waving.

'This machine,' Vender declared, 'is going to save the world. You know how I can say that? Simple. I say it because it's the truth. Truth is like a laser beam, and it will burn away the garbage. Now, let me put that to the test. You know what physicists say when I tell them this? They say it's impossible. It breaks the laws of physics. You feel like breaking some laws?' Oh yes, they sure did. 'So here's my challenge. If there are any physicists here today, let them come down, and let them debate my theory with me.' The auditorium fell silent. Spotlights roamed the crowd. People looked at their neighbours; they tittered. Vender sent his gaze roving over the stands. 'No? No one home?' he snickered. 'I guess the experts all stayed away.'

Ψ

'Well, the pace of technological change is breathtaking these days, isn't it? Now a backyard tinkerer in Mississippi says he's built a machine, a kind of perpetual motion machine, that defies the laws of physics – and you know, some people think that just maybe he has. Today Barry Vender used his Energy Machine to power a car. He says it's based on theories that go *beyond Albert Einstein and will one day provide the world with inexhaustible energy. ABC's Jed Pilkner was in New Orleans to see it.'*

'And where the hell were you?' demanded George Romanowicz.

'Where the hell are we ever?' said Ted Doyle. 'Who do you think wants to hear from the American Physical Society? Dan Rather?'

'You just let him do all this?'

'No, George.' Doyle's shrug zipped audibly down the line from Washington, as fast as light. 'We issue statements. Powerful stuff, eh? We send out press releases that say, "The American Physical Society denies the possibility of perpetual motion." Gee, you bet that sent shivers down the spines of the network chiefs.'

'But you're the authorities, surely.'

'Oh, that's cute. That's what I love about you Europeans: you still have authorities. You have debates. We have celebrities, George. Barry Vender is a celebrity.

'Now look,' he went on, 'don't think I've been on my derrière all the while. It's not strictly in my contract, but I've been calling up these TV people. I spoke to Tom Holz. I asked him why he didn't interview any real physicists. You know what he said? "Come on," he said, "this was a story about Barry Vender, about the little man against the establishment. It's a human interest story." That's what we're up against, George. How do you compete with human interest? We do the same ourselves at the APS, you know that. When we put out a press release, we have to ask, where's the human interest?' Doyle was in charge of APS's public relations. 'What's the Beeb's line on this, anyhow? How come they're onto it too? We thought you had standards over there.'

'Not their fault, Ted. If you chaps insist on splashing this over the *New York Times* and *Time* magazine, who are they to look away? What can you tell me about the hearings?'

'Well, I'm worried, frankly. This is Congress we're talking about here. There's this Republican from Lousiana, Bob Torrip, who's filed a special report called "The Patent Office and Barry Vender: An Abuse of Power". He claims that the Patent Office has been arbitrary and unfair. He's got six other members of Congress to submit something they call "private relief" bills to try to force the Patent Office to issue the patent. The state of Mississippi is behind him – just imagine the kudos for the governor if the energy problem is solved in his backyard. I've been asked to sit in on the hearing, and the Patent Office is bringing its own experts, and so is the National Bureau of Standards. Vender is being supported by these dupes Harting and Crowther. The mere fact that it's come to a congressional hearing is giving the story legs. I hear there are going to be executives from Ford and GE there – they want to find out what all the noise is about. Vender will play to them, you can bet on that.'

'I see. Now, what about the theory? The BBC is bound to ask me about that, it's a science show after all.'

'Oh, don't let them do that, George, not if you can help it. The theory isn't even wrong, you know what I mean? There's some stuff about a new kind of gyroscopic particle that orbits in a magnetic field like electrons in an atom, and slowly loses mass with an $E = mc^2$ term. These guys don't like Einstein, but he has his uses. The point is, the machine is slowly eating itself, that's Vender's story.'

'So no perpetual motion after all?'

'Who knows? It's all gibberish, of course, but he'll make it sound good on the radio.'

Ψ

Barry Vender's hearing before Congress started well. In his legal suit against the Patent Office, the judge had called for a special report to be prepared by an expert, an electrical engineer and former patent commissioner named Joseph Natt. Natt concluded that the Energy Machine was indeed producing more energy than it was consuming. The judge overruled the report, but now Vender produced it before the congressional panel. And he produced Natt too, who told the committee with an angry tremor in his voice that 'When I see injustice, it makes me boil like a damned tornado.' But then Vender was examined by the Senator from Ohio. And Vender realized that he was facing John Glenn, one of the original Mercury astronauts from his JPL days in the fifties, and the first American to orbit the earth.

Glenn challenged Vender to turn over his machine to the National Bureau of Standards for testing. Vender, visibly disconcerted, explained that the device had already been through thorough checks, and that to conduct more would be to impugn the scientists who had conducted them. Finally, Glenn pointed out that Natt, far from being an impartial expert, had represented Vender in a previous patent application, which Vender could not deny. After that, people seemed to lose interest, and the hearing limped on without conviction to a dismissive conclusion. The men from Ford and GE snapped their briefcases shut and left. The committee chewed their pens and the room was suddenly airless and sour.

'Well,' said Vender to no one in particular, 'it seems I'm back on my own again.'

LIVING FIRE

21

AFTER TWO DAYS IN LINZ, LENA FELT SURE THAT KARL NEDER
had left there for good. To judge from the way his apartment
looked, he had just dashed out to buy a loaf; but it was the
town itself that somehow persuaded her he would not be
returning to Bismarckstrasse. She spent irresolute hours sitting in cafés on the Hauptplatz, clutching a poor photocopy
of a bad photograph bleached of its half-tones, and she stared
at anyone in the passing crowds who wore a close-cropped
beard. Sooner or later, she hoped, everyone in the city will file
through the Hauptplatz in an unwitting identity parade. But
she did not even know the colour of his hair, and the photo
was maybe ten years old. She tried to focus on the region
above the nose, the third-eye forehead that passport inspectors were said to examine. Wondering what was the purpose of
this futile exercise. Soon her eyes strayed from the Austrian
faces, and she began to seek Neder's blanched, vulpine profile
in the stones of the buildings, the graven contours of the Altes
Rathaus, the shadows of the balcony from where Hitler once
greeted adoring crowds. She was trying to coax Neder out
of the city itself, out of the sad department stores and the
dour churches and the sickly skin of the grey Danube. But he
wasn't there.

She went to back to Bismarckstrasse every hour in the rain,
passing through empty streets under the shallow custody of

an umbrella she had bought at the station, compact enough to fit in her pocket at the cost of a collapsible canopy that barely covered her shoulders. Up and down Landstrasse which led to the square, until she knew the stores by rote. The push-button bell marked Apartment 4 said 'Neder' in black type, but it asked you to take an awful lot on trust, for it made no sound on the street, and, for all she knew, might have been disconnected for years. After darkness fell (and it seemed that since her arrival in the early morning it had never fully lifted), no lights came on at No. 8 Bismarckstrasse.

The next morning she simply pushed at the door, and it swung open. The stone staircase was lit with the damp grey radiance of monasteries. The steps were in a cold sweat, or maybe their sheen was just the shoe-grease of old, dead residents. Apartment 4 was two storeys up, and she rapped on its front door. The rain was still pouring down, and its noise leaked into the stairwell – somewhere there must have been an open window. Beneath the sound of the deluge came the steady patter of a small cataract falling onto paving from a great height. She pressed her ear to the door.

You hear a lot that way, but it is unintelligible. It's like putting your ear to the membrane of another world. Lena realized this as soon as she did it – the act would tell her nothing. The wood was full of rustling and murmurs, sighs and grunts. If they were not merely the sounds of metal and stone, of a building communing with itself, then they might as well be noises from one of those parallel universes that supposedly sprout out of the quantum tree. She felt as if they had nothing to do with whatever was going on beyond the door, but could have been resonating in the grain for a hundred years. No, fool, what she was hearing was the rush of her own blood, the white noise of her life.

She knocked again, and stood for a couple of minutes. That

seemed a respectable length of time to wait before grasping the door handle, which made no resistance. The place wasn't locked.

It was only when she knew she would have to speak that she became nervous. The dimness and the rain-rasped silence were troubling enough, and now her quavering 'Hello?' threatened to wake slumbering spirits. It made her an intruder here. All at once she needed to find a light switch before nightmare visions reared up. If it didn't work, she was done for.

But the queasy tungsten glow affirmed that there was nothing amiss here, after all. It was hardly a cosy place, but it was just a piece of Linz. The wallpapers were embossed and heavily glossed, the doors had patterned-glass inlays. She was in a little entrance hall with a mosaic floor, and it offered her three doors to choose from. The closed one, she guessed from the full frosting of the glass, was probably a bathroom, and there was also a bedroom and a kind of study. She switched on every light she could find, and then without glancing at what was in the room, she crossed the study to the window and, from behind the curtain, looked down onto the street. It was the colour of a rock pool, and a couple hurried by without an upward glance. Once she had thus plugged the apartment into the coursing channels of the city, she was ready to look round.

He wasn't here, of course, but at first it was a shock to find that he didn't seem to have fully left either. There was a desk of almost black wood that looked as though it belonged in the grim city Schloss – Lena began to feel that the riddle of Linz was how its dwellings had come to be fitted out with furniture that looked heavier than ironware, and of such dimensions that neither doorways nor windows could have accommodated its girth. It was as though these rooms were designed to imprison their furnishings. This desk was strewn with loose sheets and notebooks, and there was a small travelling type-writer with a half-written page in German still wound on the platen. By its side, a cup of black coffee. And also, bafflingly, half a dozen stones scattered about. That's to say, rocks: fist-sized chunks of the earth. Proterozoic paperweights.

Lena resisted the urge to sit down and start reading through the papers. She stayed at the window, aware that she needed to assess everything here, to assemble the situation from its constituents. The shelves were planks on brackets, and discouraging scientific-looking books rested there. There was an electric heater, and a sofa given up to the slackness of late middle age with, shockingly, a blue-grey pullover draped over one arm. It might as well have been a sign saying, 'Gone for lunch – back in fifteen minutes.' In one corner, a small porcelain sink and a mirror, and a little gas ring. A carton of milk, a few packets of desiccated foods, an electric kettle.

Lena returned to the hall and passed at once into the bed-room, conscious that at any moment the image liable to congeal in her head was that of a body lying splayed on the bed, lifeless and already in the early stages of putrefaction... But the bed was empty, although crumpled and, she felt sure, still exhaling microscopically from its human imprint. No doubt there would be hairs stiffening on the pillow, but she did not check for that. In any case, the bed was just a distrac-tion, because most of the room was a workshop of trestle tables and wire, tools and bits of cast metal, and various instruments with dials that Lena did not recognize.

Then she had to get out. The desire to escape was abrupt and absolute. It was not that she wanted to flee exactly, there was no panic involved. It was as though her senses had reached their capacity, so that she would be unable to process anything further until she had digested the present input. She left the lights on, closed the door, returned to the street and wandered at random until she found a café, where she ordered tea with lemon. Then she did something she had not done for five years: she bought a pack of cigarettes. She let herself be guided by body memory, not trusting her conscious mind to do this correctly any more. Almost at once she knew that she had no real appetite for tobacco, but she allowed herself to continue puffing, giving her body something to play with while her mind set to work.

Not that this called for careful thought. The likely scenario was clear enough. Neder had gone on a temporary errand, something out of town perhaps, but not too far away. He might at this very instant be making his way up Landstrasse. There was no mystery. In which case, what she ought to do was go back, turn off the lights, and resume her schedule of hourly visits. No, much better simply to slip a note under his door, giving the address and telephone number of her hotel, and wait. But she was not going to do that. When she went back to his apartment, she realized, she would stay there and look through everything. She was going to pry like a tabloid journalist. That didn't trouble her morally, or at least hardly so, because she was not looking for anything one could call scandalous, and would ignore it if she found it. She was about to do these things because she had been set a puzzle – it was not really so different from looking through the letters between Neder and Battle, or reading *The Bitter Road to Truth* in the British Library. That was why she had needed to come away and drink tea and smoke a cigarette: because she'd sensed all at once that she was now in a maze, and could do nothing but see where her path would take her.

Am I really so passive, she wondered? That's probably what Dad has been saying all this time – or rather, failing to find ways of not saying. I've been kidding myself that it took resolve to come back here, and not to simply abandon the story and go back to my tepid existence as a word-serf. But what, really, has brought me here? What choice did I make? When my father summons me, I oblige – and now I'm letting Karl Neder do the same thing.

Wait a minute. Neder summoned me? Where did that come from? He'd never have known I existed if I hadn't called him – assuming that was indeed his voice on the phone. All you have, Lena said to herself, is an idea of Neder built from his words. Only your idea of him is in any position to issue a summons. She was suddenly sickened by the thought that she might be chasing an elaborate fantasy, a mystery of her own making, a man bodying forth from her own desperate need for – what? For what?

Damn miserable bloody Linz, and damn all these stupid, incomprehensible notes and these pointlessly enigmatic vanishing acts. Furious tears threatened, but she pushed them away as she shoved her cup clattering across the table. She needed to see what was in that apartment, and never mind where Karl bloody Neder had run off to now.

She left the cigarettes on the table. Even at eighteen she'd had the wit to know that she was never destined to be a smoker.

Ψ

By mid-afternoon, she decided it was time to wash out Neder's cup and make herself some coffee. She'd long given up any pretence of making her visit invisible. The milk was a good clue that the apartment had not been occupied for about three days, although it meant that she had to take her coffee black.

At first her muscles kept twitching in readiness to spin round as Neder walked through the door. But it did not take long before that idea began to dwindle, and she started to relax into the place. There was never any sound from the stairwell –

the bells on the street indicated that there were twelve apartments in the block, but so far it appeared that they were all
uninhabited. Lena wondered briefly about bolting the front
door, which would at least enable her to compose herself if
Neder returned. But the whole street was silent too, and she
began to feel that this was a deserted district, hermetically
sealed out of time from the murmurous life of Linz.

First of all, there was the incomplete typescript. But it was
in German (why not Hungarian, then?), and most of what
Lena understood of it was based on guesswork and English
homology. It was highly technical, and apparently concerned
with chemistry. Recurring throughout was the abbreviation
'Hg', and Lena wracked her brains for long minutes trying to
figure out which German word that might represent, before
remembering that it was the chemical symbol for mercury.

That was when she glanced at the books and papers surrounding the portable Remington, and found one in English:
Inorganic Chemistry, by T. Martin Lowry. It wasn't promising – the book looked at least fifty years old, and indeed on
the mottled inside cover someone had written 'For Robin,
Oct. 1922' in ink that was now the colour of a coffee stain.
The book was open at a page which read:

(d) Amalgams – *Mercury dissolves many metals,
forming AMALGAMS. It does not dissolve the metals of
the iron group, and is therefore commonly packed in
iron bottles or flasks, each holding 76½ lb. of the metal.
From some amalgams crystalline compounds have been
obtained.*
(e) Uses – *The largest quantities of mercury are used in
the extraction of silver and gold; other uses are the
manufacture of mercury fulminate for detonators, of
mercurial drugs, and in the construction of physical*

apparatus (barometers, thermometers, vacuum pumps, etc.), where a liquid of high density, good thermal conductivity, or low vapour-pressure is required.

Now this, Lena thought, is very odd. She'd seen no sign that Neder was interested in chemistry. His mission, surely, was to reform physics: electrodynamics, relativity, that kind of thing. She rummaged among the papers until her eyes fell on equations, and she greeted these inscrutable symbols with a sort of relief, reassured that she had not after all passed through a quantum portal to a parallel universe containing a different Karl Neder. Here were the familiar B vectors and r vectors, integrals and partial differentials, labels Lena had learnt as if they were the Latin names of flowers. More searching produced a harvest of letters.

Dear Dr Battle,

I send you my CORRESPONDENCE to which you may give the title COMMENTS ON THE KAM EFFECT. I should be enormously thankful to you if you will publish this letter as soon as possible. I wish to mention that the publication of your article on my book THE BITTER ROAD VOL. V brought me about 250 orders. The publication of this note will bring me other orders on my books and with the accumulated money I will be able to carry out the differential 'coupled shutters' experiment and to demonstrate the effect of absolute motion to every one who wishes to see it. Thus the simple publication of this note will be decisive in my fight for a scientific truth. If you would like to introduce certain changes in the text, please, do what you think is relevant, even without asking for my approval.

I beg that you do this. I am not so proud that I will not use that word. You know that I have no other means to defend myself against the East and West machines of repression outside this publicity. My unique arm is the public opinion and the help of personal friends.

Looking forward to your speedy answer,

Sincerely yours,
Karl Neder

Ψ

Dear Dr Neder,

It was good to hear from you. I'm glad that our note has helped you to sell some copies of your book. But I can't, I'm afraid, publish your letter, so I am returning it to you.

Yours sincerely,
Roy Battle

So life went on. Heartened, Lena got up from the monolithic desk. She did not like the rocks – they seemed to possess an ominous, totemic presence, an anachronistic crudeness. She wandered through to the bedroom and looked at the machines.

If you ripped out the guts from a car – the organs made of steel, with wide flanges and rotating spindles and splayed legs with bolt holes – and if you then screwed to them disks perforated with a ring of holes, and if you attached insulated cable with thick globs of soft solder, and screwed them onto wooden blocks, then you would have machines like the ones Karl Neder made. They were the devices of the scavenger, the mechanisms of the breaker's yard. They were evolving according to their own peculiar, inorganic laws. Some were obviously fossils, failed species stacked like skulls. Some were disembowelled in a ghastly tangle of burnt copper wire. One was apparently the current model, with a squat black body and a gleaming silver moon of a disk, and its wires trailed away to a wall socket, ready to suck nourishment from the building. And the wires threaded in and then out of a control box – almost a caricature of a control box, a simple aluminium square with a plastic-finned switch.

This was obviously another child of EDEN, the perpetuum mobile that Lena had seen photographed in Neder's papers. She looked at the switch. Plugged in, she thought. This machine is plugged in. What kind of perpetual motion machines runs off the mains? She flicked the switch.

Nothing happened. The machine's inactivity had a sullen aspect. But what did she expect? Who was to say if the disk was meant to rotate or not? Perhaps even now the device was drawing energy out of the earth's rotation, preying on the cycle of day and night. She imagined leaving it on and finding tomorrow that the world was spinning more slowly, that dawn came at nine o'clock and dusk did not arrive until past midnight. Or maybe the machine would gather so much energy that it would explode, triggering nuclear fission and turning Linz to ash. She pushed the switch back to its original position and pulled the plug from its wall socket.

Well, that was a neat test. Do I believe any of this? Apparently I'm not fully prepared to disbelieve it. Professor George Romanowicz FRS would happily have left the device plugged in, and would have slept soundly. If nothing else, Neder was inventing new technological superstitions.

Lena ate in the café and returned to her research. By eight o'clock she could tell that there was no longer a sense of anticipation in Neder's apartment. It did not expect him back. The bed was fully relaxed, devoid of any lingering imprint of a human form. The pullover, forsaken and deprived of the hope of body warmth, died quietly on the sofa. Lena closed the curtains and switched on the electric fire, sensing the approach of the deep chill of disuse. She peered under the bed and found more files and books, thrown into old suitcases. Combing all this for clues to where Neder had gone could take days.

Then the doorbell rang.

There was the moment of stasis, the body suspending all its automatic functions. Then the jabber of voices, all contradicting, all demanding attention. Hide on the upper floor. Turn off the lights. Admit to everything. Climb out of a window. (They don't necessarily make any sense, these voices.) But gradually, one voice bellowed its way to the front, and it said: That is not Karl Neder. He would not ring his own bell.

It rang again. Lena made her way to the window and pinched the side of the curtain to create the tiniest aperture. The street now had the texture of sealskin, and was poorly lit, but she could make out a figure below, and it was a woman's face that looked up at her. Lena pulled her head back, then understood the absurdity of doing that, since it was evident to the woman in the street that someone had peeked down at her. So she yanked the curtain back, gave a feeble smile that probably made her look like a halfwit, and signalled that she was coming down to let her in.

Descending the stairs gave her enough time to imagine that the caller was collecting for charity, or was another tenant who'd lost her keys – in any event, nothing at all to do with Karl Neder. But when she opened the door, Lena could see it was not going to be that simple. The woman appraised her meticulously.

In bad streetlight, everyone has hair the colour of dead leaves and eyes like clay pits. She was a good ten years older than Lena, and dressed rather too stylishly for a wet March night. She said something in German too fast for Lena to have even a faint chance of deciphering – except that it included the name on the bell of Apartment 4. Lena did not know the cadences of Austrian German – as far as she could make out, the woman might have been speaking angrily, or wryly, or officiously, or even politely. All she could do was to make a weak attempt at replying with '*Karl Neder ist nicht hier.*'

'American?'

'English.'

'I do not speak English, but I think you do not speak German more.'

'I think you're right.'

'I know Karl Neder is not here.'

'Oh.'

'Karl Neder is not here since three days.'

'No, I see. But I have come to Linz to meet him.'

'So now you stay in his apartment.'

'No, I am just – I am staying at the Hotel Mühlviertlerhof.' Which did not sound much like anything on Lena's lips, but she wanted to provide some kind of alibi, however mangled. Not that her visitor seemed to care.

'You can move into his apartment and it take less of your money. Neder is gone.'

'Where has he gone?'

The woman laughed. 'I don't know where he goes. Why you think I will know this?'

'I don't know what you know. I don't know who you are.'

'My name is Maria.'

'Hello, Maria. I'm Lena.'

'Yes,' said Maria, and for an instant Lena was disconcerted by the impression that this implied foreknowledge. But she decided it was just Maria's way.

'I am Karl Neder's girlfriend until four weeks,' she declared.

Which immediately seemed to invite the question of why Lena was meeting Karl Neder in Linz, so she said, 'Oh, I have only come to interview him,' which was, of course, tantamount to saying, 'and not to make love to him'. But there wasn't much nuance going on in this conversation.

'You are journalist?'

'Yes, that's it. From London.'

'Well, now you have nothing to write about, Lena.' It was a simple statement of fact.

'Maria, perhaps you had better come in.'

'There is no need. I only ring the bell because I see light behind the *Vorhänge*, and I think that maybe Karl Neder has come back and he can give me the money he owe me.'

'Oh. I'm sorry.'

Maria looked at Lena as if wondering what she was talking about.

'Does he owe you much money, then?'

'If he owe me much money, I will not come here for hoping he has perhaps returned, because I will never be pay anyway. He owe me only a little, but I have not much money myself. I work as a, ah, *Serviererin*, I take food to people, *ja*?'

'Why does he owe you money?'

'Since I am his girlfriend, he stay in my apartment. For five months he stay with me – him and all his, ah, *Maschinen*. All evening he is taking a hammer and burning bits of metal, and then he start to, to work his *Maschinen*, and it sound like... like *der Fliegeralarm*, you know, like the aeroplanes come with bombs. And all my *Nachbarn*, the people who live near me, they hit on my door and they shout. It is very bad.'

'So what did you do?'

'What? I throw him from my apartment, of course. I tell him to go and he must take all his *Maschinen* and big sounds. And he say, "Maria," he say, "this is the biggest *Entdeckung*... the finding out..."'

'Discovery?'

'*Ja*. "This is the biggest discovery in the last *hundert* years," and I say I do not care because I must get the sleep and I do not want people to think I am bad person.'

'His machines are all here. Maybe you could sell some of them, if he owes you money.'

Maria gave a throaty laugh. 'Who will give me money for this? Will you? For bits of old *Auto*? No one will pay for them.'

'And you have no idea where he is now?'

'*Ach*, who can know what Karl Neder do? Read his *Journale*, Lena, maybe you will find out.'

'You can take what you want from his apartment. The doors are not locked.'

'I think I do not want to see what is in his apartment.'

Ψ

That phrase kept coming back to Lena. At first it had seemed merely dismissive, as though Maria did not care to set eyes on Neder's *Maschinen* ever again. But afterwards Lena thought there was another flavour to Maria's words: sadness, perhaps, or even – fear. Clearly she felt only contempt for Neder's machines. But what about this strange business with mercury?

Lena began to appreciate that the volume of material in Karl Neder's apartment was truly overwhelming. There were pieces here of many jigsaws, all intermingled. Old rail tickets to places throughout Eastern Europe. Textbooks on hydraulics and the calculus of Green's functions, maps of Istanbul, stacks of faint Xeroxes in Russian. She couldn't face it all tonight; tomorrow she'd make a fresh start. It crossed her mind to sleep here, for she was no longer worried about

Neder showing up. But she had no wish to sleep in his bed, least of all with a perpetuum mobile (unplugged thought it was) waiting to drain away her energy as she lay there.

No harm, though, in taking some material back to the hotel with her, and she picked up a couple of notebooks at random from the desk. Then her gaze fell on the rocks.

They were black, but not coal-black. It was a metallic pitch-colour, redolent of graphite's oily grime. This, she thought, was the colour of black bile, the humour of Saturn. A strange image, and it made her smile, thinking of the occult books she'd read on dull days, in bed with Davey. She picked up a stone.

And dropped it at once. And heard a ringing sound that seemed to issue from the walls of the room, until she realized that this was the after-hum of the scream she'd let loose. The stone was warm. Not room temperature, but body heat. It was like picking up something living.

Now revulsion twisted her features, as the stone seemed to crouch like a malevolent thing. It wasn't just the heat of it. The other discovery that had shocked and disgusted her was its immense weight. It wasn't heavy as a piece of iron is heavy – it did not have that reassuring solidity. It was much heavier than that, so that as she'd lifted it, her arms seemed to be pulled downwards. There was something unnatural in that density – it defied all her intuitive judgements about the relation of mass to volume. It did not seem possible that so great a weight could fit into an object that size.

She gave a shudder that wrung a sob from her throat, grabbed the notebooks and ran from the building.

Ψ

Lena was aware that she never knew when to stop. A balanced person, she understood, would have brought a good book with them, some page-turning novel about sex or war (OK, then, *not* a good book), and spent the evening with it at the Hotel Mühlviertlerhof, dining on veal and Prädikat. But she'd never been able to make the kind of distinctions that separate labour from a healthy enjoyment of its fruits. That, she suspected, was the characteristic failing of the academic, which was probably all very well if you were one. Her father's nights in the laboratory were now rare events, but there were always lights on somewhere in the Rutherford Building at Canterbury, some solitary researcher choosing to wrest the secrets from innocent matter rather than spend a quiet night at home. But for someone whose working life had as little structure, as little focus, as Lena's, this habit of never clocking off was deeply corrosive. It meant that she ate badly for days on end and didn't notice; she woke up early, confused by dreams; she forgot to return calls, and was always having to iron laundry dry so that she'd have something to wear. She could justify this behaviour as over-enthusiasm, even passion, but in the end she suspected it was really a form of laziness.

And so she sat with sausage and beer and the notebooks of Karl Neder, and the first thing she told herself was that she was terribly slow on the uptake. What had she been reading about in Neder's apartment that morning? Mercury. And what was one of mercury's most striking properties? Its density. So what were those rocks, in all probability? Mercury ore, of some sort. Lena had no idea what manner of minerals contained mercury, but maybe T. Martin Lowry could tell her tomorrow.

And the warmth? That was harder. But nothing to scream about. Maybe the density had simply confused her senses. At any rate, she had become a little more composed by the time she opened the notebooks, and that was just as well, for they were not in themselves terribly reassuring.

For one thing, they seemed to be smeared with blood. Here and there, a page would be disfigured with a bright red streak, although not always, it seemed, by accident. Some of these marks were blended, like diagrams, into the text, which was truncated a few lines in advance of them, and resumed a few lines later.

It couldn't be blood, Lena decided. For one thing, the marks appeared to be made by a dry substance – there was no warping of the page, such as a liquid would induce. When she peered close, there looked to be a graininess to the red smudges, as though they were made by something like chalk. And they were too red to be blood, which would have darkened to brown when it dried. Nonetheless, it was unnerving to come across these sanguinary pages, which took on the aspect of some pact sealed in the most ancient and binding manner.

Is Neder's mind like these notes, Lena wondered? A mixture of several different languages, clippings copied from books, marginal formulae, a cacophony of disorganized data and supposition? There were passages in Hungarian, German, English and Russian – and occasionally, and most perplexingly, in Latin. Moreover, even Lena could see that the German was not always quite as it should be – the words were oddly changed, as though in a vernacular form.

The further she read on, the more Lena was thankful for German sausage and beer. The salty meat had a plain honesty that was, it was – she fished for the word, and came up with: hale. It was a hale substance. The cool beer fended off a feverish heat that seemed to emanate from the strange words Neder had copied, often now in English.

Many who seek this Science without the Light of Nature
are precipitated into very great Errors; because they

> *know not the true Subject of this Art, but busie*
> *themselves about other things altogether unfit for*
> *the Work.*

This passage was apparently from some book called *Sanguis Naturae*. Blood of Nature.

> *Now I will speak but a very little of the fixed living*
> *Fire, which is hidden in the Earth or the Centre of the*
> *World, and there hath taken up its most fixed*
> *Habitation; and by many Philosophers is called the*
> *Corporeal Water; but it may be better called the Fire of*
> *Bodies. To know this is the most secret Mystery in all our*
> *Philosophy. The Operation of this fixed Fire is invisible*
> *and very secret, and yet very powerful, which also few*
> *know; for it operates by its heat in all things which lie in*
> *the Earth.*

Lena could recognize what this 'Philosophy' was – this was from an old text about alchemy. But that made no sense. Whatever Neder was, he was not some mystic who believed in medieval magic. Maxwell's equations and Lorentz's transformations might look to the non-initiate like cryptograms, but of course they were nothing of the kind. Even if Neder was a crank, he was not this kind of crank. What could he be expecting to find in alchemy?

> *This living Fire, with which the Heavens and all things*
> *that are filled by the Creator, descends through the*
> *Elements into the Subject, which is called the Balsam of*
> *Nature, Electrum immaturum, Magnesia, the Green*
> *Dragon, Azoth Vitreus, the Fire of Nature. For the*
> *Power and Virtue of this living Fire is so great, that if*

that were absent, the Elements would be dead,
especially the ethereal Heaven, an Element which most
of all stands in need of this Light.

The elemental ether. Were we back with Frank Symons's quintessence? Or with Michelson and Morley's phantom bearer of light?

Then she read a passage that, even through the bad translation, set her neck prickling so that she had to rub it, though there was no reason she could discern for this physiological alarm signal. The text was attributed to someone called Paracelsus, who sounded vaguely familiar – a wizard's name, if ever there was one:

*That coruscation, or scintillation is a certain sign of
metals that are unripe, and yet in prime ente, and
according as sparkling or fire is carried, so the Veins lie.
And that this coruscation, or sparkling of fire, is to be
seen in the night, as if Gun-powder were sprinkled in a
long time, and then fired; so it goes along; and shines,
and does glitter and glimmer even as Gold or Silver
upon the Test of Cupel, when the Lead is separated from
it. For this reason the Sages use none but this natural
fire, not because it is made by the Sages, but because it is
made by Nature.*

*The distilled water is the Moon; the Sun or Fire is
hidden in it, and it is the father of all things. It is also
called Living Water, for the life of the dead body is
hidden in the water.*

*Know, ye Scrutators of Nature, that fire is the soul of
everything, and that God Himself is fire and soul. And
the body cannot live without fire.*

Then Nicolas Flamel (a distant memory of bookshops on the Seine: didn't he live in Paris?), quoting from something called the Emerald Tablet:

The Sun is its father, the Moon is its mother.

Lena began to feel she was reading all the wild theories of Symons, Kam and the Vienna crowd as though reinterpreted by some thirteenth-century apocalyptic seer. She closed her eyes. She was very tired, and it was foolish to be reading this stuff tonight. It was not, in any event, going to tell her where Neder had gone. She was stiff and aching from head to toe. But she could not stop herself from opening the next notebook, and saw at once that there was science in it, not occult gibberish.

$$^{196}Hg + {}^{1}n \rightarrow {}^{197}Hg^* \rightarrow {}^{197}Au + \beta^+$$

More mercury. But was this chemistry? What was n, and what β? She read on:

Three to four hundred grams of mercury were bombarded with fast neutrons from the Li + D reaction. The deuterons used were produced by the Harvard cyclotron with an energy of 11 MeV and currents of 5-15 μA. After irradiation the mercury was placed in a vacuum distilling flask with the addition of 50 mg of gold. The latter readily formed an amalgam with the mercury and served as a carrier for the radioactive gold and platinum. The residue of the distillation was then treated chemically to separate the gold and platinum activities.

These were not Neder's words – she could see that they were too fluent, although they were written in his hand. And since when would he have had access to the 'Harvard cyclotron', whatever that was?

> *The mercury had been subjected to a number of distillations before use and gave results in complete quantitative agreement with samples of C.P. analysed mercury, indicating a high state of purity. Furthermore, the same mercury was used repeatedly with concordant results, indicating that the distilling process carried out at the rate of approximately 50 cc per hour was indeed removing at least 99 per cent of the added gold. Control tests made by bombarding Pt and Au simultaneously with the mercury showed that the amounts of Pt and Au which would have to be present in the mercury as impurities were of the order of 10 mg of Au and 250 mg of Pt. Impurities of this magnitude are impossible, as shown by the fact that a second distillation yielded an activity of less than 0.1 div./min., while the first distillation gave 30 div./min. for the platinum fractions.*

She yawned. This really was enough for today. OK. Pt was platinum, Au was gold...

> *The residue (gold of the mercury distillation) was dissolved in aqua regia –*

Lena blinked and looked again. 'Aqua regia' didn't sound like modern chemistry, but more like alchemy again. King of Waters. But that was what it said.

*– in aqua regia and platinum carrier added. The
solution was adjusted to 1.2 N in hydrochloric acid after
complete removal of nitric acid. Gold was precipitated
with hydroquinone and removed by filtration. Platinum
was reduced by hydrazine...*

She skipped a discussion of 'potassium chlorplatinate' and the
like, and read:

*Three radioactive gold isotopes were found to be formed
by the n-p reactions: 65-hour ^{198}Au, 78-hour ^{199}Au,
and a new unassigned electron emitter with a period of
48 min.*

Gold isotopes. Reactions. She dimly sensed that the Hg equation was describing a 'reaction' of some kind, a reaction
involving n (those 'fast neutrons', maybe?), and that this reaction was producing Au: gold. That threatened to set off her
neck again, what with the aqua regia doing its hermetic business, but she closed the book, collapsed into bed, and dreamt
of fire and earth.

Ψ

The next day the rocks were gone. It took some time for Lena
to admit this to herself, but there was no escaping the fact.
Everything else looked the same in the apartment at No. 8
Bismarckstrasse, but there were no rocks. The doors had been
closed, and no one had opened the curtains. Nor did Lena. She
rushed into the bedroom: the pile of *Maschinen* was undisturbed. Then she looked more closely at the desk, and was
fairly certain that the notes and papers had been rearranged.
And she thought there were fewer of them, although it was
hard to be sure.

Had Maria come to reclaim her debts after all? But why should the rocks be of any value? Might they have been not mercury ore, but gold ore, a fact Maria had concealed from Lena? Yet why would Maria have come back in secret, when Lena had invited her to help herself? Lena looked up 'sources of gold' in T. Martin Lowry, who said:

> *Native gold is distributed widely, as in the case of the Transvaal mines, in veins or reefs of quartz intersecting other rocks, the particles of gold being usually so small as to be invisible to the eye... The proportion of gold in the ore is usually very small, varying from 1 part in 50,000 in gold quartz to 1 part in 1 to 15 millions in alluvium, but nuggets of gold, formed by the segregation and welding together of gold-particles in the river-beds, have been found, especially in Australia, weighing from a few ounces to 184 lb.*

In other words, you didn't get gold from any ore; you found it pure, as nuggets. And in any case, she was sure that quartz wasn't black.

Then she remembered the typewriter, and found that the half-written page had been removed. Had she done that herself, or had she read it on the reel? She couldn't recall taking it out. But there was no sign of it anywhere.

Neder's flat had not been looted for easy profit. Someone, she decided, knew what they were looking for, and had come here to take it.

'I shouldn't be here,' she thought. She peeped around the edge of the curtain, but the street was as silent as ever. No rain this morning, though the sky was stressed with clouds and wind. Lena pulled out the suitcases from under the bed, select-ed one that seemed a good compromise between capacity and weight, and added to it any of the notes and books from the desk that looked vaguely promising. Then it was too heavy, and she had to do a quick and crude pruning before arriving at something she felt she could drag back to the Mühlviertlerhof.

What was the likelihood that the coincidence of her arrival here and the subtle ransacking of the apartment was a matter of chance? Not great, she figured. In which case, what was the likelihood that this place was not now under observation? Don't ask. It was time to get out of Linz.

It became now a city of spies. At the hotel, Lena threw her things together and jumped in a cab for the railway station. There was a day to go before her flight home, but she was not thinking about that. What she needed was to escape somewhere and think. She bought a ticket for the first train out, which was headed for Salzburg, and on the platform she eyed her fellow travellers with suspicion. But they were all far too clever to return her glances.

She sat clutching Neder's suitcase for the entire journey, and only when they pulled into Salzburg did she begin to relax a little. At the information office she found a cheap guest house on Linzergasse, opposite the ornate Sebastianskirche, and after some deliberation, decided that she would have to trust to leaving the suitcase there. The worst that could happen was that it might vanish, but after all, she barely knew what was in it.

March was bright in Salzburg, and the castle glowed like a chalk cliff on its high perch. Lena wandered along the right bank of the Salzach and found herself in the manicured geometry of the Mirabell gardens. How men dreamed of an ordered nature with the world gone mad around them! Elsewhere the Thirty Years' War was eviscerating Germany; here reason and sobriety reigned. At least, that is, until some joker had added the stone dwarfs that leered at the conceit. Fabulous Alice-creatures like unicorned goats watched Lena's meanderings in this world beyond the looking glass.

> *It is true that Sulphur is the true and chief substance of the Stone. Yet you curse it unjustly. For it lies heavily chained in a dark prison and cannot do as it would.*
>
> *And the Sun and the Moon shall make it Red, and this is the end of the Great Work.*

Neder's notebooks were full of this stuff, and it oppressed her. She felt that she was reading illicit things.

> *Do not think that Salt is unimportant because it is omitted by the Ancients; they could not do without it, even if they did not name it, seeing that it is the key which opens the infernal prison house, where Sulphur lies in bonds.*
>
> *Nature cannot work till it has been supplied with a material, the first matter is furnished by God, the second matter by the Sage. But in the philosophical work Nature must excite the fire which God has enclosed in the centre of each thing. The excitation of this fire is performed by the will of Nature, and sometimes also by the will of a skilful Artist who can dispose Nature, for fire naturally purifies every species of impurity.*

'What do you want now, Karl Neder?' she murmured to herself. Here and there were pages stained with that same vivid red. She touched her finger to it, and felt as though she were letting go of some part of herself. Her fingertip came away dusted with the slightest hint of a red powder, as though she had brushed the depths of a flower and smeared its pollen. Her skin seemed to tingle with it.

Alchemist: Yet the Sages say that their substance is found on the dung hill.

Mercury: What they say is true, but you understand only the letter, and not the spirit of their injunctions.

Men have it before their eyes, handle it with their hands, yet know it not, though they constantly tread it under their feet.

And then underlined and boxed in with bold, reckless strokes:

This is how we make the Sun and Moon Corrupted.

Ψ

It was time to speak to someone who knew Neder. And how thankful she was now for her journalistic habits, which prompted her not only to take people's contact details but to keep her address book with her. It took three attempts, and then five minutes of waiting after a voice had said something incomprehensible and vanished, and then he was on the line.

'Hello?'

'Is that Georgiu Constantin?'

'Who is this, please?'

'My name is Lena Romanowicz. I need to speak with Dr Constantin.'

'This is Constantin. I know your name, I think.'

She reminded him of the Vienna conference.

'Lena! Of course. This is a nice surprise.'

'Well, Georgiu, it's a long shot, but I wonder whether you might be able to help me. I'm calling from Salzburg. I've just come from Linz, where I was supposed to meet Karl Neder.'

'Ah, yes, yes. And he was not there.'

'That's right. You know?'

'Yes, I know, because Karl is here with me.'

'He is?'

'Yes, he arrived three days ago. But Lena, something is not good.'

'That's what I'm thinking.'

'He – I cannot say much now Lena, there are difficulties, you understand?'

'Of course. But he is staying with you?'

'Yes, but for how long I do not know. There is something happening.'

'Can I come to you?'

'Well – certainly, if you are able. But I think you must do it quickly.'

'As fast as I can. Georgiu, thank you. I'll be with you soon. I have your address here – are you still on, er, Veslets?'

'Veslets Street, yes.'

'I'll be there very soon.'

But no sooner had Lena hung up than she realized it was an absurd thing to have said. She couldn't simply jump on a train and cross the Balkans to Sofia, and she had no idea how long it might take to arrange a visa for Bulgaria.

22

'WHAT ABOUT A BOMB?'

'Well, of course. A bomb is always possible. I would say a bomb is probable.'

'It's easy?'

'Making a nuclear bomb is never easy, but it can be... done crudely. I'm really not an expert on this –'

But that didn't tend to matter to George Romanowicz. It was his stock disclaimer, a matter of form. If his colleagues were dismayed about his readiness to talk on subjects far from his own, that was no more than how felt about it himself. He'd frequently be horrified at what he heard himself saying on the basis of a dimly remembered conversation, or a discourse he'd drowsed through at the Royal Society. The shakier he felt his ground to be, the more authoritative he sounded. It was becoming a compulsion, he knew, fed by the easy awe of his questioners, these eager young men and women who seemed determined to award him unwarranted omniscience. Last week it was epidemiology: a meandering chat on *Science Now* about chaos and the logistic equation, and suddenly there he was, sounding off gravely on the modern plague, the San Franciscan pox, the wasting disease – the scourge, some fashionable new moralists said, falling on Sodom (it reassured them to imagine that this was a virus that made biblical distinctions). A rogue scrap of RNA, eating its way into the next generation of dictionaries.

Nuclear bombs, though – they were home territory. They involved some of the most impressive hydrodynamics of the twentieth century: the beautiful symmetry of the implosion that created a critical mass.

'Look at how many countries are running nuclear reactors. Not just the superpowers, you know – there's Argentina, Mexico, Pakistan. Iran is developing a nuclear industry. North Korea. They all use uranium, there is an immense world market in it. They're digging up uranium all over the planet – in Australia, Namibia, South Africa, Kazakhstan. There's more of it than we know what to do with. Too much to keep track of it all.'

'You mean uranium goes missing?'

'All the time. A study at Bristol made an estimate of how much. I forget the figures, but we can say that there is plenty of slack in the system. Enough for a few bombs, without a doubt.'

This time it is fright night on the BBC: deep into the watershed, late enough to alarm only insomniac liberals. The topic is supposedly *The Turner Diaries*, a white supremacist fantasy about a terrorist war against the 'Zionist Occupation Government', a paranoid version of the United States government. In this 'crude anarcho-fascist rant', as Romanowicz put it, Earl Turner, survivalist leader of an organization ominously called the Order, detonates fertilizer by the vanload in his war against the Feds. But he has bigger plans: to capture America's nuclear weapons and turn them on Israel. Why does the BBC have a physics professor to talk about this stuff? Because *The Turner Diaries* is written not by Andrew Macdonald, as it says on the flimsy, self-published cover, but by Dr William Pierce, ex-professor of physics at Oregon State University. Someone at the Corporation had a vague notion that the book took a scientific slant, and this late-night current-affairs show is steered by vague notions. It has to be, with only half a day's notice of its subject. But never mind the Zionist Occupation Government; terrorism is in the air these days. Literally, as often as not, although the hijacks of the 1970s are less the fashion now. No one has been much inclined to look beyond suicide bombers in transit vans, let alone a DC-10, but at 12.15 on Tuesday night we are allowed (this is BBC2) to imagine the worst.

The fact is, the BBC's researchers did not know in advance that George Romanowicz was a vehemently nuclear-free zone. You don't expect that in a physics professor. Didn't these blokes *invent* nuclear? Now he wasn't going to miss a chance to freeze the blood of late-night pub returnees who have hit the wrong button in a hops-reeking stupor.

'Look at it this way: there's no doubt that you can flatten a city with 1940s technology. Oppenheimer did it. Just like their televisions and computers, their atomic bombs were cobbled together – jerry-built, to use a singularly inapt expression. Of course, you can't do much with raw uranium, you need to enrich it to military-grade stuff. But what does that require? Just a set of tubing to spin up a volatile uranium gas, to whisk out the heavy uranium-238 and collect the component you want, the 235. I simplify, but you get the point. From about two hundred kilos of natural uranium you can get one kilo of bomb-quality stuff. A dozen times that, and you have enough for a bomb.'

'But how do you get uranium in the first place, Professor? You can't exactly buy it at the pharmacist's, surely.'

'Oh no?' He'd been laying the trap for this little set-piece. 'If I say it's a piece of cake, I'd not be far wrong. They call it "yellow cake" – or on the black market, simply "cake". That's uranium oxide – it looks a little like sulphur, and it'll cost you, pound for pound, about the same as a slab of Battenberg. Now, the thing is –'

He was warming up. Indignation fought with showmanship as he took command of the camera. He could say whatever he liked now, the lens would indulge him.

'– you have to get just a bit clever when you're working on a tight budget. I'm exaggerating, naturally – not about the cheapness of uranium, but about its accessibility. You have to go to a pretty specialized baker, an illegal one, to get your hands on this kind of cake. My point is that raw cost is not the limiting factor. But the baker will slap a surcharge on it. A very big surcharge. So you can afford only a few kilograms of enriched uranium, and you need over fifty kilos to reach critical mass, which is what will produce a runaway chain reaction and trigger a nuclear blast. But you make the stuff more potent with a neutron reflector.'

The BBC didn't need this, not even after midnight. Current affairs did not need neutrons. But that is what happens when you invite physics professors on the show: they go and talk about physics. So the presenter let him run, and Romanowicz explained that neutrons were the key to a chain reaction. They are the dissidents, he said, that infiltrate an atomic nucleus and tear it apart, if it is big enough (a florid metaphor that was wasted after the witching hour). To propagate that fission from one nucleus to another, the neutrons should be confined, since every one that escapes beyond the surface of the uranium ball reduces the heat of the ferment. The solution, then, is a neutron reflector: a material that encases the fissile core in a skin, a shell that acts as a mirror for the hot little particles. Beryllium is the standard item – a featherweight as metals go, but a daunting deterrent to a flighty neutron, which is sent buzzing back into the maelstrom. It takes just a few milliseconds for the chain reaction to bloom, and then the whole game is over. Whiteout.

'That way,' said Romanowicz, 'the critical mass falls from

fifty to about a dozen kilos. Grapefruit size.' Strange fruit, bought by the kilo.

To a somnolescent nation, the unfathomable distinction between fifty and a dozen kilos. It was unlikely that anyone started thinking bags of sugar. But there it was –

'It reduces the critical mass.' A phrase murmured involuntarily by Lena Romanowicz, who was unsure what it meant. She *was* the archetypal pub returnee that night, mildly confused by vodka and lime – a high-school drink: it was absurd, verging on scandalous, to be ordering it at her age. A reflex choice in extreme circumstances. And she always swears there is a split second, as she turns on the box, in which she knows that her father is about to appear, in full Delphic flow. She always knows. 'Oh, you again.' She feels an obligation to sit it out; she has never – *never?* – been able to switch him off. Once started, he must be allowed to finish. She figures she is his most devoted viewer, doesn't miss a show. Now she watches with the suspicion – strong at this late hour, with these foreign chemicals combusting in her metabolism – that he is about to diverge into some personal theme, to speak to her, direct to camera. 'Nescafé is *not* bloody coffee, Lena.' 'Not in the fridge, for God's sake, it's red.' But because it is his voice, her father's voice, it keeps her attentive, because there is always a chance that it might find other words to say to her.

Ψ

Lena nearly jumped out of her skin when Margaret Strong accosted her in Sofia's central station. With her headscarf and tent-shaped black dress, her bundles of knotted cloth and her ruddy complexion, she was indistinguishable from the Bulgarian peasant women milling about the concourse. Perhaps that was the point, although Strong's presence here was perfectly legitimate.

'No need to guess who you are,' Strong proclaimed. 'Got London written all over you.'

The bundles, it turned out, were filled with baked cheese pastries, half a dozen of which Strong insisted Lena should take. 'I've had the food on that blinking Belgrade train, and it's a load of rubbish. You look as if you could do with some grub.'

It was true that Lena hadn't eaten since she left Zagreb, but not for lack of hawkers trying to thrust items upon her. She had been reading more of Neder's notebooks, and they left her faintly nauseous.

It had taken four days to get here from Salzburg, but Lena knew that if Margaret Strong had not been in Bulgaria she'd still be sitting in her room on Linzergasse.

At first she had wondered about calling her father – he had contacts all over the place, perhaps there would be one at Sofia University. But she could not face that prospect. It was while she was riffling forlornly through her notes that she thought of Strong. 'She could be anywhere between Poland and Armenia,' the news editor of *Natural Science* had said. Well, this time he turned out to be a little better informed: Margaret Strong, he told Lena when she called, was reporting on the opening of Bulgaria's new computer centre in Plovdiv. Lena had no idea where Plovdiv was, but she gave a yelp of joy that heightened the timidity with which the news editor proffered a hotel phone number. 'We've been in regular contact with her while we get the story straightened out. But you'll need to be a trifle persistent –'

So Lena stocked up on schillings and fed them into the pay phone until she got through to a receptionist who understood that the noises she was making corresponded to the name of a guest.

'You're after who!?' The line from Plovdiv could barely contain Strong's bellow, and for a moment Lena feared that it

343

really had severed the feeble link. 'Is there no escaping that wretched man?'

But she relented. 'Ms Romanowicz, it so happens that I am flying back from Sofia, so I'll be there in a few days. I don't mind helping you out, and I think I know how to fix it up. What was the name of your Bulgarian again? And may I take it that you are the daughter of the physicist chappy who's always on the box?'

'Will that help?' Lena sighed.

'I daresay it would make our story a tad more plausible. But look, who gives a stuff whether you are or aren't, the point is that that is the name on your passport. So yes, I can make some use of that. But listen. I'll sort this out for you on the strict condition that you promise you will not let Neder know that I'm in Sofia. I'm in no hurry whatsoever to renew my acquaintance with that man.'

Now in Sofia station Margaret Strong looked her up and down, and Lena could see she was evaluating whether this girl had either the physical or the mental wherewithal to be let loose in Bulgaria.

'You say you've never met Neder before?'

'Never. But I know Constantin.'

'Yes, well, I've not really come across that one, but I gather he's one of their crowd. Look, Neder isn't exactly what I would call a dangerous man, but one has to take great care with him. Difficult, is what I would say. Blasted awkward. You never know quite where you are with him.'

'I've had some practice with difficult physicists. You were right about my father.'

'Well, at least I've warned you. Now, remember that you are for the present purposes a physicist yourself, and that you will cease to be such in four days, by which time I trust you will no longer be in Bulgaria.'

'Dr Strong, I can't tell you how grateful –'

'It's *Ms* Strong, Ms Romanowicz.'

Ψ

She was shivering as she climbed the stairs to Constantin's apartment on Veslets ulitsa, although the weather was turning mild even in this high city. He gave her sweet tea and some clear liquor that crept up the sides of its small glass under its own superfluid potency. It was intended to calm her, but Georgiu's own agitation was plain.

For Karl Neder was no longer with him.

'I know Karl since ten years, more than. But never before I see him like this.'

'Like what?'

'Lena, if I do not know Karl Neder better, I have to say he is frightened. He does not say it, he is a proud man for one thing, he makes like he is angry at me, but I see that it is not anger in him. When we work together, we have very hard things put onto us, enough to frighten me, for sure. But Karl is always calling the fool to our enemies and oppressors, he is like a strong tree. But when he is here it is just one week ago, there is something changed.'

'Why did he leave?'

'Why did he come? He does not tell me these things. You know, many times it is not easy for me to understand him. I ask him, of course, I say, "Karl, what is it you want?" One time he just looks at me when I say this, as if – as if I must give him the answer myself. But another time he says it is not a good thing that he says any answer to a friend. Well, at least then he calls me friend. You see, other times he looks at me as if he does not know who I am, or as if he… as if he thinks I mean to do some bad to him.'

'Why would he think that?'

Constantin sighed.

'Well, it can happen that we come to see things this way. Every day there is someone watching, from the street outside, from across the park, in the library. Different faces each time, so even if you learn how to know them, you are never sure who you can trust. If that happens, their job is done. They can leave you alone, because you have started to – to invent your own watchers. That is all that matters – that you believe they are watching.'

'Surely Neder does not suspect you of, of what, of collusion?'

'Of helping the watchers, you mean? I want to say not, but – he will not show me his work, which before he always shares. When I ask, he shouts at me, "This is not for you!" He rushes away, and shows me no esteem. And that makes me very sad.'

Constantin insisted that Lena take his bed; the narrow, mean sofa would be perfectly good for him.

'Why have you never married?' she thought to ask him, surprised by her own directness. Such intimacies came easily in conversation with Constantin, who seemed to have built no walls around his own life. How did he avoid doing that in a place like this, she wondered? Perhaps it was simply another way of coping – an antidote to ward off state-prescribed paranoia.

'Perhaps I marry soon.'

'Oh! Then you have someone in mind.'

'No one. But that does not matter. Many others think the same. First we see the end of President Zhivkov, then we marry. Into – I believe you say, happier days.'

'Then Zhivkov is coming to an end?'

'You would not think it, would you? The DS, his special police, they are busy as ever. But there is change coming. Now, as we all know, the talk in Moscow is of *glasnost*, openness, and old Zhivkov is becoming an embarrass to them. Then also, Bulgarian economy is bad and people have little money, and they grumble. We have droughts, bad harvests, power stops. The regime is becoming like – like the end of a string…'

'Frayed.'

'Yes, afraid. I believe that is so.'

As if on cue, the lights went out.

'Well, that is it,' said Constantin in absolute darkness. 'Lights out in cells, is what we say here.'

Laura dreamed she was buying eggs in a crowded market-place. Eggs by the kilo, with bright yellow yolks. The fear of dropping them petrified her.

And there they were, at breakfast: hard boiled, with sweet bread and thick coffee. She wondered if her dreams were starting to leak out.

'I'm going to have to find him, Georgiu,' she said. It sounded like the admission of a guilty secret. Constantin looked fretful.

'This I expect you to say. But you see –' He pushed his glass of coffee dejectedly around the table '– I cannot come with you.'

Lena could not suppress a laugh. 'Well, I never thought you would!'

That did nothing to alleviate the physicist's wretchedness.

'I cannot leave this place without someone will notice. And will follow. I do not think I can get further than the Sofia ring-way. No way to go across the border.'

'You know where he has gone, don't you?'

'Oh, Lena, I do not see how you can go there.'

'You make it sound like Hades.'

'Not so bad as that, though you must cross a great river, it is true. He is going to Kiev.'

347

'I was afraid you'd say Siberia. Or Kazakhstan. Kiev – well, at least I know where that is. More or less.'

'But – is Romania in between, and most of the Ukraine…'

'It sounds as though he isn't on the run, then. He's looking for something.'

'Maybe it is both. Listen, the day after he is gone from here, this apartment is searched when I am at the university.' As if propelled there by habit, he moved to the window, where sunlight was filtering out of a frosted-glass sky. 'Of course, my home is searched from time to time. It is standard routine for a suspected dissident. It does not happen often, because I am not important. The DS do not think to find anything here – they are just saying to me that they are out there. So I know that this time is a different sort of search, as one that really does hope to find something. They do not mind to make a mess, to empty my cupboards, to move my tables and chairs. This was not the DS.' Then his wan smile, and a quavering giggle. 'They do not find it, however, because it is not here.'

'So you know what they were looking for?'

'Maybe I do. Karl left something behind. Let me show you my laboratory, as you are visiting academic, no?'

They took the Bulevard Levski, skirting the golden globes of the great church. 'The gold,' Constantin observed, 'comes from Moscow. A gift.'

'A devotional offering from the godless state.'

'Moscow is never thinking too little the value of a – what is it? – an opiumate.'

Men in hats and women in dark headscarves were hurrying into the church, drawn by the smell of incense, the promise of old Byzantine solace.

Ψ

Solenoids, liquid helium cylinders, blocks of polystyrene insulation: these were all items she'd seen before.

'Gravitational shielding,' Constantin grinned. 'You remember Deepak Pindar and Novikov effect? We cannot let the Americans make it first, ha ha! I have funding from the Ministry of Energy. I am almost respectable now, you see.'

The tiny office was so full of papers and books that they were the furniture. Why do scientists seem to need all this paper, she wondered. It's as though it is there to mop up everything spilling from their brains. But couldn't they ever throw any of their thoughts away?

'Let them try to search this,' Constantin said, sotto voce. Then, without hesitation, he reached into the midpoint of a precarious pile and withdrew a sheaf of documents.

'He stays in my apartment, he will not go outside. When I come here, he locks himself in. Then one morning the phone rings here, and when I pick it up there is no one, a dead line. But I feel what this is about, and I hurry home, and Karl is gone. The door is still locked, but he is not inside. He is leaving a few clothes, razors, his packing is not careful. There is not even letter from him, no explanation. But that evening I find, inside my refrigerator, this bundle. I do not know if he leaves them for me or just makes to hide them quickly.' Constantin shut the door. 'This is a safe place, no microphones. So we can read and talk.'

There were plans and diagrams – blueprints. A building, labelled in Russian, threaded with lines that might denote plumbing or electrics. Constantin thought this was some kind of power plant. There were sketches of concentric circles, like slices of the world, the outer layers divided into segments, a geometric sunburst. It was labelled in Hungarian. 'I am not sure how this is translated,' said Constantin. 'It is something like "egg of the cosmos".' One of these circular structures was mounted on a vase-shaped plinth:

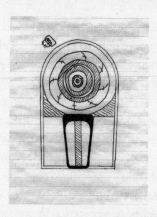

Then, jarringly, some newspaper clippings in English – no dates, but faintly browned at the edges.

They were fragments of a story that made Lena shudder.

'MOSSAD KILLING' INQUIRY MOVES TO UK

The South African police chief who claimed last month that the Israeli secret service Mossad murdered a British businessman in Johannesburg nearly three years ago has visited England to interview his relatives and business associates.

Lieutenant Colonel John Varghese caused a row between South Africa and Israel with his claims that Mossad killed Peter Walling because he was involved in international arms smuggling to the Middle East.

Mr Walling, who emigrated to South Africa 16 years before, was sales manager of Odin Chemicals, a British multinational based in Maidenhead, Kent.

In Natal it operated the largest mercury reprocessing facility in the world, while other of its chemical products were sold to the South African defence forces.

Lt Col Varghese believes that Mr Walling was

involved in smuggling red mercury, which is said by some to have applications in nuclear weapon technology.

Lt Col Varghese was accompanied to London by three colleagues, including Warrant Officer Paul Hertzog of the Peninsula murder and robbery squad in Cape Town, who is investigating connections between Mr Walling's death and that of another chemical expert, Christiaan Blaaiberg. He was bludgeoned to death in a hotel room last April.

On a Thursday evening in November 1982, Mr Walling, who was 51, received a phone call at his home in Johannesburg. He told his wife, Cairo, that he was slipping out for a short while. He had many international contacts, having travelled extensively in the Far East and Latin America.

The next morning two youths found his unlocked BMW parked downtown and drove it to Soweto where they began to dismantle the radio and sound system.

Then they opened the boot. Inside was a jumble of flesh and guts. A torso was covered with a black substance. The arms and legs had been surgically severed. There was hardly any blood.

The body was found by police on the Saturday. Within days they were suggesting that Mr Walling had been involved in a red mercury smuggling ring and was killed as a warning to others.

But it was not until last month that Lt Col Varghese told the Johannesburg Star that Mossad killed him. 'Peter Walling was involved in supplying hi-tech chemicals to Middle Eastern countries. The chemicals are used in the production of nuclear weapons. There is one thing for sure: this guy was dumped for a reason – it was something only a government would be involved in.'

Lt Col Varghese has so far produced no hard evidence for such a weighty claim, although it is understood that he has based his assertion on an Israeli informant.

After his death, Mr Walling's family looked for other reasons. At first they thought he might have been killed by white extremists. The couple had recently moved into a small Afrikaner suburb: Cairo was Brazilian, and could have been mistaken for a Coloured. Was the black substance a macabre racist message?

Then South African friends suggested that the manner of his death might point to a Zulu ritual, according to which the legs of an enemy are cut off so that he cannot pursue you.

Odin Chemicals had made many bitter enemies in South Africa. After being threatened by the Health and Safety Executive with legal action in Britain, it moved all its mercury reprocessing operations to its factory in the Valley of a Thousand Hills in Natal in 1978. By South African standards the company was a generous employer of its Zulu labourers.

A year later the Umgeni Water Board found mercury pollution in the Umgeni river and traced it to the Odin plant. The results, 1,000 times higher than World Health Organization recommended levels, were leaked to the Natal Witness newspaper in 1980.

For the next two years Odin was at the centre of an increasingly acrimonious row with environmentalists. In April 1982 a local group called Earthlife Africa began to receive the first reports of 'mercury madness' among the company's workers. The symptoms were all consistent with mercury poisoning.

Finally a government inquiry found gross negligence at the plant, leading to the poisoning of at least 29 workers.

Mr Graham Darent, the Odin chairman, suggested
that the pollution and Mr Walling's death may have
been the work of 'environmental terrorists'. Mr
Walling's brother Mark, who runs a training company in
Sunderland, has enlisted the help of his MP Bob Clay to
try to get some answers.

'We know Peter wasn't a dishonest person,' said Mr
Walling. 'I wouldn't like to think it was Mossad. A
civilized country should not do these sort of things. But
if it was one of those people, they should be brought to
justice.'

A photo of Peter Walling accompanied the story: the blurred contingency of an over-magnified snapshot. He wore a light V-neck sweater over a checked shirt with the top two buttons open. A nervous, lopsided smile. A family man, no airs or graces, who played golf in Kent.

A jumble of flesh and guts. There was hardly any blood.

A civilized country should not do these sort of things.

Red mercury. Red Hg. 'They were suggesting that Mr Walling had been involved in a red mercury smuggling ring and was killed as a warning to others.'

'What,' said Lena at last, 'is red mercury?'

'You better read more,' Constantin replied.

DOOMSDAY GEL, FAKE OR FACT?
From Alan Henderson in Kiev

Oleg Ishchenko teeters so close to the edge of the Soviet
Union's 'new physics' – a spooky realm of nuclear
voodoo, mafia intrigue and, just possibly, dazzling
science – that he hates having his picture taken. 'You can

353

kill any living creature from 1,000 km with a photo,' he says. 'We've done the research to prove it.'

A 42-year-old scientist backed by Mikhail Gorbachev, Mr Ishchenko is the master alchemist of 'red mercury', a substance one British nuclear expert believes can produce a nuclear bomb no heavier – and smaller – than a watermelon. Others consider it a hoax, a cover for money laundering or plutonium contraband.

'Red Mercury makes it possible to do things only charlatans could pretend to do before,' boasts Mr Ishchenko, whose private firm, Prometea, was given exclusive rights last year by Mr Gorbachev to produce, buy and sell stuff his security ministry calls a phantom.

Reported applications of the cherry-red gel range from nuclear bombs to bewitching perfumes. It is also sold as an ingredient in anti-radar coating, self-targeting warheads and oilwell anti-coagulants.

With a nuclear archipelago comprising 189 separate facilities, the Soviet Union spawns countless scams and scares – e.g., the 'elipton', the secret and, the military says, non-existent weapon that Edward Shevardnadze allegedly wants to sell to China.

Red mercury keeps better company. 'I'm pretty well convinced it exists,' says Dr Mike Avery, a former scientist at Aldermaston, Britain's nuclear weapons laboratory. 'It's an enormous conspiracy if all the people I have spoken to are lying.' Most bomb-makers are more sceptical. 'This is the unicorn of modern science,' says Ted Vaughan, analyst at Los Alamos National Laboratory, America's nuclear research centre, where the first atom bombs were devised. 'You can put your hands on a Kalashnikov, you can touch plutonium. With red mercury there just doesn't seem to be anything there.'

But there is enough smoke, and at least one body – a Briton left smeared with a black slime containing mercury – to suggest some sort of fire.

How or where Mr Ishchenko found red mercury he won't say. All the same, he convinced a Californian company, KPI International, to sign a contract for $24 bn (£16 bn) for 84 tons of the miracle gel. He claims a string of other deals, too. 'I'm already a millionaire. In 10 years I'll be a zillionaire.'

There is little sign of any such prosperity at Prometea's headquarters, a row of spartan offices off a dingy ninth-floor hallway. They are modest premises for the premier trader of a product priced at $250 a gram – 22 times more than gold.

Many rooms are empty. Alex Vlasyuk, a chemical engineer, sits at a rickety wooden table and explains why few people have seen red mercury: ' As we say in the Soviet Union, the less you know the better.' The entrance to Prometea has a heavy steel door; other doors are welded shut; gruff security guards impersonate James Bond villains.

Mr Ishchenko, who also has a scruffy office in Moscow, declines to provide samples of his product: 'We tell everyone, "You want to see it? Then buy it."'

Numerous sightings of the substance have been reported. Self-proclaimed dealers have been arrested in Sweden, Finland, Italy, Germany, Austria and Bulgaria. A Czech journalist says he bought some in Vladivostok. Soviet police say they arrested Kazakh smugglers in Omsk with a five-kilo consignment.

The most gruesome episode occurred in South Africa, where the sales director for Odin Chemicals was found stuffed into the boot of a BMW, his dismembered body *daubed with a thick, black substance.*

'The legend goes back a long way,' says Dr Vaughan. 'Run each story to ground and you end up with the same thing – nothing. Call it red mercury, call it a Big Mac, whatever you want. I call it a scam.' A security ministry report to the Soviet government said red mercury was underworld jargon, 'like the word cabbage for money'.

But Mr Ishchenko's deal with KPI in California is real, as is the order signed by Mr Gorbachev. Mr Ishchenko shows off a signed contract and a photocopy of the Kremlin decree; and he has a letter from the San Fernando Valley Chamber of Commerce that speaks highly of KPI and its boss, M. R. Ramirez. Here, however, the trail goes cold. The hunt for KPI's headquarters leads to a garage. The letter of recommendation is disowned by the man who signed it, Chamber of Commerce Vice-President Tony Peroia, who has since retired to a houseboat in the Philippines. He says that he was tricked.

Dr Avery says he used to be a sceptic, too. He first heard of red mercury in 1981, after the arrest of a South African smuggler in Greece. What changed his mind was a recent trip to the Soviet Union for a television documentary. 'Even if 95 reports out of 100 are fraudulent, there is a residue that is not.'

In red mercury's more lethal form as a trigger for nuclear reactions, it is said to be antimony mercury oxide. It starts out as a powder and is synthesized under intense radiation and pressure into a malleable gel. Legend credits the technique to Soviet military researchers in the 1960s, and says it was perfected at the laboratories of the secret research base called Zvyozdny Gorodok, or Star City , north-east of Moscow. It was rumoured also to be a potent medicine, even an antidote for radiation sickness. According to some sources it was tested on early Soviet cosmonauts as a possible protection against space radiation.

Scientists at the Soviet Academy of Sciences in Moscow have a collection of so-called 'red mercury' potions. Fakes from around the world range from the worrying (depleted reactor fuel and low-grade uranium) to the laughable (mercury tinged with brick dust and an empty bottle painted with nail polish).

But Prometea presses on: 'This is a revolution, a triumph. This will be the salvation of the Soviet Union,' says Mr Ishchenko.

Clipped together with these cuttings was a third, short item.

NUCLEAR EXPERTS BLAME RUSSIAN MAFIA FOR RED MERCURY DEMAND

On 10 May 1984 the police in Tengen, near Konstanz, Germany, searched the home of known criminal Horst Körper. By chance they found a vial with a reddish, radioactive powder in a shielded lead container. This was found by nuclear experts to consist of six grams of weapons-grade plutonium in so-called red mercury.

The nuclear establishments of the Soviet Union, the United States and Britain have dismissed the notion that red mercury actually exists, although general mercury technology does have limited military applications in explosives, guided missiles and nuclear research.

All the authorities take the view that the Soviet mafia, using common mercury compounds, has created an artificial and highly lucrative market in Third World states with nuclear pretensions.

*Inspectors from the International Atomic Energy
Authority say that they have uncovered dozens of offers
for red mercury from states such as Libya, North Korea
and Iraq, which are suspected to have clandestine
nuclear programmes.*

*The Tengen raid uncovered one red mercury
operation quite by chance. Indeed, the scientists who
analysed the material seized were said to be initially
quite puzzled by what it was they had found.*

Too many images collided in Lena's head. An egg: yellow centre, red shell. A vermilion smear on a blank page. And a limbless torso daubed in black.

Rocks warm with life.

'I look in the journals,' said Constantin softly. 'And in textbooks. I ask my colleagues in the chemistry department. But I find nothing about red mercury – not one word. No one knows of it. My friend Petâr, who is a chemist with very much knowledge, all he can say is, it sounds like alchemy.'

'Oh, Georgiu. I wish you hadn't said that.'

Constantin looked perplexed. 'It seems here,' he persisted, 'that red mercury is to be used in fission bombs, as what they call a neutron reflector.'

'I know what that is, oddly enough. I saw it on TV once. It reduces the critical mass.'

'The critical mass. Yes, I think so. You know how to make a bomb, then!'

'I don't even know what it means, Georgiu. I'm not a scientist, I'm a parrot.'

'You are halfway to there, then!'

He took another sheet from the pile, a grainy Xerox. 'This is all I find myself.' A paper from the British journal *Chemical Forensics*. It was about the German forensics case, written by researchers at the Institute for Transuranic Elements in Karlsruhe.

In the case of the seizure of weapons-grade plutonium (Pu) at Tengen, analysis first confirmed the presence of Pu by α- and γ-spectrometry. Because the material was a heterogeneous powder we used an electron microscope to determine qualitatively the chemical composition of the constituents. This led to the discovery that the Pu particles are always associated with gallium. We also learned from glow discharge mass spectrometry that the composition of the material was originally $Hg_2Sb_2O_7$ and Hg_2O_2, which had subsequently reacted with the surface of the Pu-Ga metal particles. The ratio of Pu to Ga (1.046:1 by atoms) indicated a military origin. Moreover, electron diffraction showed that the Pu was at a stage of production ready for melting and casting as the product weapon. Why the sample also contained the mercury compounds is unclear, but in our opinion this was probably used as a camouflage for the clandestine export of Pu.

We were surprised to discover high enrichment of Pu-239 to 98 per cent. Although earlier reports had pointed to Pu isotope enrichment in Russia, our analysis is the first known proof of Pu enrichment for weapons applications.

However, most illicit trafficking of nuclear materials involves natural uranium or low enriched U-235 fuel used in power stations. Figure 1 shows one example of a uranium oxide ('yellow cake') pellet from the numerous U-235 seizures that we have analysed at ITU. By comparing the U-235 enrichment and main impurities against data in the ITU database we were able to

determine that the material was produced in a plant in
Kazakhstan. This plant in turn provides fuel for several
known nuclear power stations in Russia and the
Ukraine, any of which might also have been the source
of our pellet.

So this was it: a name, Prometea, and a city, Kiev. That was all she was going to get. A pretty fuzzy target to hit when you are travelling illegally.

'Was there some newspaper article I was supposed to be writing?' she thought to herself with a weary smile. 'I could have sworn it was something like that.'

'I am ashamed.' Constantin like a sad marionette, a fundamentally comic figure. Chaplin with an East European accent, bouncing back after every blow. 'It is only for selfishness that I want you to go. Because Lena, I have a thought that if you will find him, if you find my friend Karl, he will need to be… to be saved. If you can, please do it.'

'I'm not sure I know how to save myself.' Let's be honest, she thought. At this stage, we might as well.

He gave her a letter and an address: a city called Ruse, on the northern edge of Bulgaria, where the Danube drew a blue border with Romania. There was a direct train.

'This person can help you. He is one of the Cambodians – well, you will see.'

She sensed that Constantin might soon get mawkish, so she shook his hand. 'Good luck with anti-gravity. Maybe it will keep you out of trouble.'

Ψ

The train meandered through the Balkan Range and plunged into the Iskâr Gorge, an axe-stroke into the massif where boulders waited in formation on the skyline to drop and crush trucks on the narrow road. Sickeningly far below, an olive-coloured river denied any responsibility for this over-emphatic chasm. Then the gorge squeezed them out like paste from a nozzle into the hills that studded the great Danubian plain, the product of a river so swollen that it smoothed the furrows for thirty miles to either side. The Danube, exhausted and viscous, could now smell the iodine tang of the Black Sea. Between Pleven and Levski you could see the river far off in the afternoon sun, a golden skein in the north, heavy with the sediments of Europe. Then the train swung towards it, as though remembering the old route to the East, the way to the pleasure gardens of Constantinople.

Ruse could have been the Empire's last gasp – a fading memory of Austro-Hungary left behind on some *fin-du-siècle* crusade. Art nouveau contours in sinuous defiance of rectilin-ear Stalinist technocracy. Its elegance had been laid out on the Soviet dissecting table, and bourgeois residences were now carved up into cramped apartments. Party-approved concrete worked only on its own terms; confronted with artistry, it looked thuggish, crude and improbable. Ruse might have been a city touched by greatness, yet now it smelt of bleach, the residue from the Romanian chemical plant across the mighty river.

This close to the border, you could swim to Romania if it were not for the eddies that boiled like serpents in the syrupy river, promising fatal embraces. Close enough for everyone to look shifty, as though they were all pursuing ulterior missions.

Lena had two items that might take her some unspecified distance towards Kiev. Without them, she'd be wandering forlornly in central Europe like a refugee from the future. The first was a map scribbled in ballpoint by Constantin, a sparse network of improbably straight roads and the barest scattering of landmarks: Liberation Monument, train station, athletics stadium. The second was an envelope with a name and address. The name was Zahari Dimitâr, and the address, as the map disclosed, was dismayingly far from the city centre.

Tramping a mile from the blasted barn of the train station, her spirits rose as she passed though the middle of Ruse, then sank as the Aleksandrovska carried her out to the north-east, a place of long shadows and dreary high rises.

Then there were the dogs. A tar-black mongrel padded alongside her as she left the station, barely a smudge in the gathering dusk. Neither friendly nor not, but ready to offer its silent services if the price was amenable. The lanes and alleys disgorged their own candidates for the post, joining the pack in ones and twos on the strength of a whined password or a ritual circle dance. They began to lose interest in Lena, or rather, to lose interest in her good opinion: tense and restive, they became a volatile, increasingly ominous cloud. The smell they made was of bitter leaf-rot and old meat. The streets were empty – it was as though dogs had come to live in these brutalist Party buildings, these colonnaded cardboard cut-outs of bird-blanched concrete.

The beasts were vying with each other, growling in boredom as they awaited a signal – which never came – to tear this young woman to shreds.

The darker it got, the worse. The town now let itself go in a welter of dingy bars where blank-eyed men clustered around brown bottles under the mosquito buzz of unforgiving striplights. As they watched Lena go by, they whispered comments to one another with the attitude of grim, sardonic pavement-prophets. The bars became corrugated shacks, iron-clad limpets stuck to the sides of concrete cliffs.

Here was a woman with a roadside stall; you could only describe her wares as charred lumps of matter on wooden skewers. As Lena approached and held out the envelope, the woman fixed her with a steady gaze. Impassively, she looked at what was written, and Lena wondered whether she might be illiterate. Then she uttered a guttural cry, nothing like the language Lena had heard all day. Was it a curse, or a benediction? Nothing happened for twenty heartbeats, and then a rangy youth stepped squinting out of the night, smoke curling from his nostrils.

These people, she could see even in the gloom, were darker than the others. Perhaps they were Turks, part of the country's large Muslim population. Or Tatars, ancient nomads, sons and daughters of the Golden Horde. An insight came to Lena with the intensity of a bell tolling, and it made the street sway: you are about to leave behind the things you know.

Events had unfolded here, out on the plain that emptied into the Black Sea, that she could never imagine. Here the past leaked into the present.

The material was produced in Kazakhstan. But this was already the land of the *kazaks*, the Cossacks: the word meant 'outlaw', or you might say, 'adventurer'.

Kazak. Tatar. Circassian. The untouchables, the fallout of the Soviet peoples. In the dark places of the earth.

But Zahari Dimitâr was none of these. A deceptively Bulgarian name, because he'd made it so. Seemingly submitting to the nationalistic campaign that encouraged minorities to 'Bulgarianize' their names, he had in fact taken advantage of the *Vâzroditelniyat protses* – the Regeneration Process – to turn invisible, to wipe away the suspicions that dogged his origins and become a regular citizen. And then to go on doing what he had always done. While the Muslim Turks rebelled against this infringement of their ethnic rights, against the closure of mosques, the suppression of their language and their identities – and were duly reviled, beaten, imprisoned and shot – Zahari Dimitâr carried on his business without police harassment, without the security forces of the DS on his tail. And so he became the spectral hub of a dissident network that reached from Siberia to Prague.

The lad who guided Lena to Dimitâr took so many back routes and shortcuts, sliding through gaps between tumble-down hovels, that she knew she could never escape from this district alone, even in daylight. She tucked the map away, marvelling at Constantin's optimism in drawing it at all. It was a wonder that these streets even had names. This, Lena discovered, was Cambodia. The Cambodia of Ruse. Every major city in Bulgaria had a Cambodia, or else an Abyssinia. That was what they called the gypsy ghettos, the encampments of the *Tsigani*, who referred to themselves as Roma.

Zahari Dimitâr was a Roma, and he had a taste for honey cake. He was fleshy, with long, lifeless hair that seemed itself to be steeped in nectar. He did not look at all bright, and that too was enormously useful to him. He read Georgiu's letter, and he looked at Lena, and he said, 'Not speak English.' Which, evidently, was not strictly true; but the words came only one or two at a time, formed on his heavy lips with difficulty.

'We go tonight. Cross bridge. To Bucharest.' Lena, on the verge of collapse, did not know how to object.

'I'm very tired,' she confessed at last. He nodded.

'Cross bridge tonight.'

Dimitâr was no shack-dweller; he had an apartment in a block that Lena thought at first must be abandoned, since no lights showed. But as the boy led her up the stairs it turned out to be filled with tenants, most of whom left open their doors as they entertained by candlelight. There was apparently no electricity. Dimitâr's apartment was already crowded when they arrived, but it was unclear how many of the shrieking children, the rasping women and the sombre men called it home. He spoke rapidly to one of them, who dashed out into the corridor and reappeared shortly with two bicycles. Lena felt a pricking in the corners of her eyes.

'We're going to cycle to Bucharest?' When she said that, Dimitâr allowed some of his intelligence to flit across his face: irony, humour, humanity.

'To the docks. Cycle to docks. Truck to Bucharest.'

The Danube had expended its charms far upstream; Ruse was not interested in it. No grand waterfront here, just a greasy railway and the inky slabs of warehouses. And indifferent street lighting, so that Lena's bicycle, itself lacking any illumination, shuddered in surprise at every rut and pothole. Cars hooted as they rattled past – a warning or a reprimand. The dim bulk of Zahari Dimitâr, faintly ludicrous on a bike, pulled off the road ahead, onto a track leading into a scrubland of oily sleepers. His wheels grated on gravel. They came into a concrete yard where trucks waited in line.

'I drive trucks to Bucharest,' he said. 'All places. Maybe one day Sofia, one day Budapest. Not can go to Kiev. You go there other way.'

So after Bucharest I'm on my own, Lena thought. It's a start, but not by much – Bucharest was barely fifty miles away, but the Ukrainian border was on the other side of the country. Dimitâr climbed up into one of the lorries, and the noise of the engine coming to life was unnervingly conspicuous on the deserted waterfront. Leaving the motor running but the lights off, he descended and slung the two bicycles in the back.

There was another sound in the night air: a rising hum, then a mournful wail in the distance. A train was rushing down the track. It was all aglow, the carriage lights throwing yellow streaks onto the sooty ground. For an instant, the skeletal forms of cranes and pylons flashed up all around the dock-yard. The train passed between them and the river; faces stared out from the windows, frozen or entranced by the coming of night. And from the corner of the yard, two shadows were running towards them.

'They're coming!' Lena cried, not knowing what she meant by it. Dimitâr seemed to mount the cab as if climbing up the air, and he hauled Lena after him, throwing her across the seat. The headlamps flared, and the approaching figures scampered to either side of the beams. Roaring in defiance, the lorry leapt out onto the street. Still curled on the seat, Lena glanced at the wing mirror and thought she saw another set of lights cut open the night behind them. But it was hard to tell.

'Who –' was all she could manage. But he just kept driving.

It all became indistinct. Time depends on your reference frame. It might have been five minutes, an hour, the duration of a long black night, and then there were no buildings around them, but ahead in the dark some monstrous form loomed, something vast and prehistoric.

'Take off this,' Dimitâr told her, prodding her pack. She stowed it under her feet.

'Are we safe?' she whispered. He looked at her with an expression she could not read in the half-light.

'In Bulgaria?'

The ground was suddenly less substantial: hard and brittle. They were roaring down a long cage suspended in the sky.

'*Dunav most,*' he said. Dunav… that must be the Danube. Below them was the river, haemorrhaging into the void. They were on the Danube Bridge, and on the other side was Romania.

She had no visa, no authority to travel. But such things could be purchased at the checkpost, after a fashion.

The guard peered in, letting his torch wander over her. He

said something to Dimitâr, and they both laughed. Quick as bats, their hands met and parted. The deal was done, and Lena could imagine how it went. Easy pickings for both men, that was supposed to be the idea.

From the Danube to Bucharest, in the pitchy stillness of the night – nothing at all to be seen or said. The land would hide itself until morning.

She could not look at the road in case figures lurched out of the ditches. A surge of heat came up from beneath her feet, a warm engine-breath, but she could not sleep. So, with eloquent use of a minimal vocabulary, Dimitâr told her about the Roma. Lena suspected there was a lot she was not getting.

'My people. Work with beer.'

'Beer? Brewers? You make drink?'

'No, not drink. Beer.' And he gave a low snarl.

She puzzled over this. Another growl, and clawing of the air.

'You mean – bear? The animal?'

'Bear, yes. We are *ursari*.'

Ursus. His tribe were once bear tamers.

This, it turned out, was the plan, this was how Constantin's contacts would ferry her to the Ukraine: there were Roma all over Romania, especially in the mountains, the Transylvanian Alps and the Carpathians. Lena would be passed between them like a parcel. (More like contraband, she thought.) Dimitâr wrote her a note, and told her that it said in the Roma tongue: 'I am a friend of the *ursari*. I do not speak your language. I must reach Vadul Siret.' That was where the road from Bucharest to the Ukrainian city of Chernivtsi crossed the border.

They were in Bucharest before daylight, and by then Lena could scarcely register anything that was happening. The Roma ghetto looked just like the one in Ruse – all over central Europe, there were these forsaken concrete bunkers, these shanties of corrugated iron and scavenged timber. She slept on a wounded mattress, and almost at once it was dawn. Dimitâr had left, and another truck was taking her towards Transylvania.

23

WE WERE WRONG, DAVEY. VAMPIRES DON'T LIVE IN Transylvania after all. They don't want these high lands, these pungent forests and craggy castles. They gravitate towards the places of power, they cart their caskets of damp earth to Piccadilly, where they can look out onto the palaces of monarchs and ministers. The more remote the village, the less it has to fear. The Count, the blood-leech, he's in Bucharest right now; he leaves folk huddled and shivering in dank city blocks, starved and bloodless. From Brasov to Bermondsey, it's the same story for the small people of the cities, while in the wild country, up near the snowline, they sit around the stove and drink *tuica* and eat roundels of ground beef and don't fear the night. We make the old mistake, thinking we can push our demons out into the remotest darkness, until we can no longer recognize those walking among us.

Lena was close to collapse, but never had she felt or looked better. Moving now in a place beyond fatigue, she could sleep and wake in an instant. A week of travelling on dirt roads and sheep paths, in wooden carts and ancient, scratch-built cars, sometimes on horseback. Dressed like a peasant in wide black trousers and embroidered skirt, a stained and rust-coloured cardigan, padded jerkin, a headscarf that once perhaps was white. It was getting to be a warm spring even at one thousand metres, and her skin, where exposed, was brown and red and chapped. It seemed she had shed a soft pulp and found hard husk beneath – or that she had aged twenty years. Rising at dawn for a bowl of yoghurt and a hunk of black bread, moving along until the sky was purple and the dogs were howling. Her shell was thickening, her core diminishing, and a part of her welcomed it. She was cooling, solidifying. Eventually there would be nothing left but tough crust, giving off a ripe smell.

The notebooks and papers in her pack were dead weight; more than once she'd considered dumping them. Karl Neder scarcely entered her mind – he was not now the object of this journey. As she passed from one set of Roma minders to another, as the rows of white peaks marched by, she imagined she might be circling in these mountains forever.

It did not take long for the myth of the noble gypsy to be shattered. It was clear what some of her escorts hoped to gain for their services. A tirade of South London abuse usually did the trick, although there was one evening where things might have got difficult if the alcoholic stupor of her guide had not overwhelmed his alcoholic ardour. On the whole, however, there was something almost ritualistic about these clumsy advances, as if the men were doing no more than their duty demanded. They were just the way people are, she decided: some leery, some cheery, some mournful and dour. They lived in mountains.

That is how Lena crossed Romania and descended into the valley of the Siret in Bucovina, where the road passed into the Ukraine at Vadul Siret. But this was no good; it was an official border. When she managed to impress on her two escorts – Aurel and Emil, father and son – that she needed, without papers, to board the train to Kiev, they laughed, and she feared that this was because it was a ridiculous thing to hope for. They took her, however, back up into the foothills, where they picked their way among giant boulders until young Emil flashed his golden teeth and said, 'Ucraine.' They walked northwards, crossed the Siret at night over the railway bridge, and followed the tracks to Chernivtsi, where they arrived at dawn while the city was still dazed and bleary and easily fooled.

Aurel rubbed his forefinger and thumb together. 'Dollar.' She understood; was twenty enough? He kept rubbing until she reached fifty, and then he vanished, leaving the grinning Emil perched on the arm of a bench in the shabby little park, humming tunelessly. An hour passed, and another, and she began to imagine Aurel enjoying a royal breakfast in some grand café – though it was improbable, frankly, in his herds-man's boots.

But Aurel was taking care of business. The piece of paper he gave Lena did not, she suspected, come from the ticket office at the train station. Nor was it likely to have cost $50, but if Aurel had simply added on the fee for his son and himself, she realized suddenly that it was a pitiful return for their efforts. As they bundled her onto the train, she tried to fumble in her money belt for more of the green notes, but Aurel admonished her angrily – it was neither the time nor the place for a gypsy girl to start throwing US dollars around. They showed her to her carriage, and then they were gone.

If there was a cheaper ticket than this, she decided, it would have to be for a place on the roof. The seats were of bare wood, and people squeezed onto them remorselessly, with grunts and sighs, buttocks jammed together tighter than a tin of plums. That was good, though; she became invisible, sub-merged beneath the poor people of the Ukraine, of no conceivable interest to anyone.

They left Chernivtsi in the early afternoon, and the train travelled all night. Wedged upright, Lena dozed on a shoulder that was gone when she woke in Kiev.

She was glad of the universal rule that all main railway stations are the repositories of the outcasts, the drugged, the crazy people – the *kazaks*. No one here would question how a peasant girl came to possess a Karrimor rucksack, why she asked for a coffee and *bliny* in a strange, grunting accent, or why she sat alone tracing lines with her finger on a map of the city.

Finally she found Yервоноармийска: vulitsya Chervonoarmiyska. Not far at all, then, a ten-minute walk away. And along this unremarkable street she began a slow and highly conspicuous decoding of every Cyrillic brass plate on every building that looked capable of housing offices. Which was most of them – and it was a long road. But she was strangely encouraged by the task; it was a systematic course of action, and it resembled a plan, which meant that she didn't need to actually formulate one.

When she found what she was looking for, it was with a sense of inevitability. Прометеа: Prometea. Just as the newspaper had said, there was little sign of prosperity at Prometea's headquarters. There was little sign of anything. The meshed-glass door was unlocked, and beyond it Lena was met by mouldy half-light and silence. There were shabby inscriptions on some of the doors; faded posters on the walls showed sunny beaches and rocky shores, perhaps Croatia or the Crimea. Was this a travel agent? Or were the images a promise of paradise to motivate the workers? But there were no workers here any more.

Nothing would persuade her to step into the rusty cage, imprison herself behind a collapsible steel lattice and press buttons in the expectation of upward acceleration. No, she took the stairs, which left you with options. Once or twice she thought she heard murmurs on the stairwell, but it could have been some old machinery rumbling in the depths that the last man out forgot to turn off.

On the ninth floor, Prometea had evolved a logo, a mixture of Cold War and cabbalism: the teardrop flame of a candle, and superimposed on it, like a blunted Star of David, the archetypal atom, thrice orbited.

Now I will speak but a very little of the fixed living Fire, which is hidden in the Earth or Centre of the World.

She passed through: seeker of fire.

Ψ

Many rooms are empty. Well, now all rooms were empty, it seemed. Not just unpeopled, but cleared out – they were hollow shells. It appeared that Prometea was no longer in business. Whatever that business had been.

But as she advanced down the hallway between these naked cells, a sound began to leak into her head. It was like a persistent drip. No, more like a clock. Yet surely not that either: as she stood there straining to identify proximity and direction, she discerned that the little ticking noises were erratic – time disjointed, a juddering Morse pulse. As she moved slowly up the corridor, Lena thought the sound was becoming louder.

The last door was closed, and when she saw it she could not suppress a little cry. Like a gigantic claw mark, three streaks of a black, bituminous substance disfigured the white gloss. The ticking came from inside the room.

What was the alternative? This was a one-way street now; closed doors had to be opened. Better done quickly.

So she entered Prometea's final chamber, and found it a place where nothing made any sense. There was too much information here, and the cacophony was like a force both physical and psychic. Prometea had imploded into this room, mutated, tried new evolutionary forms, died and been reborn.

The walls told stories of biblical proportions. Revelation. The Book of Daniel. Comets and signs. Astrological projections. Angels. Maps, geological strata, solar systems, suns and moons. Timetables, Polaroids of concrete buildings and slate-sheened lakes. $E=mc^2$, $R_{ab} - \frac{1}{2}Rg_{ab} = -8\pi GT_{ab}$, speculative new geometries. Woodcuts of a king burning on a funeral pyre. Rockets standing on the steppe. Missile silos. The length of the sky. Every mad theory in the multiverse.

Patterns of crazy energy rippled through these wild propaganda sheets nailed to the walls like a hoard of heretical theses. It was a jabber of too many voices, too many tongues, like the outpouring of a mind crammed beyond endurance. Heaving a sob, Lena lashed out and ripped a handful of papers from the wall, throwing them to the floor.

It was a futile act, because (as she had subconsciously expected) there were more beneath. Oscilloscope traces. Mappae mundi. Maxwell's equations. She kept flailing, tearing the sheets away, layer after layer. Defeated, she sat down among the crumpled pages, hands pressed to her temples, and cried tears of fear and despair.

The stuttering clock kept ticking. Lena fixed her thoughts on it, allowing the sounds to irritate her. Irritation: what a wonderful, prosaic, pragmatic emotion. What a foil to the grandiloquent, the baroque, the overblown declamations all around her. She embraced her irritation at the whole bloody narcissistic nonsense of it all, the grand guignol conspiracies and the egotistical theories of everything. What was that irritating noise?

The lunatic walls were not all there was to see in the room. A window, like that in an oven, was grimed with soot and grease, dispensing sickly yellow light. There was a grey metal desk. And one corner of the room was piled high with bulging black plastic bags.

A jumble of flesh and guts.

'Cut it out,' she snapped. She sniffed the air: there was no smell of corruption – unless, perhaps, the faintest whiff of sulphur. A jumble sale, more likely, she told herself. A jumble sale of a failed and wayward business.

The ticking was coming from within the desk, which seemed to amplify rather than to muffle it.

There were drawers in the sides. Each of them had a little silver lock, and every lock had been attacked, defaced and smashed with hacksaws and blunt instruments. Not the work of a proper thief, yet betraying rather too much effort for the casual pillager, who would have been likely (his mind not filled, as hers was, with images of surgically dissected bodies) to search through the bin-liners too. So, agent Romanowicz, we conclude that whoever broke open these drawers was looking for something specific.

But not, presumably, this ticker. It was a gun-metal cylinder, the size and shape of a microphone. Lena was pretty sure she knew what it was: a Geiger counter. Making its frenetic, forgetful tally of ionizing radiation, a tick each time it scored a hit. And along they came, in ragged procession: invisible flies meeting their fizzing, popping death on the electrified grid, sacrificing themselves in a tiny spark. Plenty of sacrifices.

What did that mean? Lena recalled the mesh-guarded little button they were given at school, to be handled with long tweezers, a snare for a grain of radium which set the counter crackling. The boys all scattered, clasping their groins, half play-acting and half genuine in their fears for their procreative potency. 'You'll go sterile!' they called at Lena, who laughed at them and waved her radioactive wand like a witch turning the milk sour. And then she leaned out of the window and pointed the stubby Geiger counter at the sun, and the crackling surged to become a continuous surf of white noise. The sun will get you first, boys. Put on your lead codpieces if you want to have babies. Space is alive with deadly, child-stealing spirits, streaming down on the planet. These angels of death are all around us.

So now, what is this latest riddle telling us? What's the pace of the rhythm here? Is this incessant clacking an indication that Kiev has become spook-infested, filled with unseen baby-snatchers? Or is this just life as normal, the typical bounty of a strong April sun?

She considered probing the black bags, or waving the counter over the tarry smears on the door. But there are some things it is best not to know.

What else was in here? Anything useful had probably been taken – but look, there were documents in one of the drawers. She spread them on the desktop.

Most were totally useless to her, a scatter of impenetrable Russian. Yet she could see that they had been riffled through, and there were some empty envelopes and the stubs of pages torn from stapled sheafs. The diagrams were scarcely any more informative, but they drew her attention simply because they gave relief from the incomprehensible text. Yet suddenly she came to a page on which she knew immediately what she was looking at.

It was the building plan, the one with the anatomy of pipes or wires in Neder's abandoned file. The main caption gave nothing away: 'РБМК 1000'. RBMK, a technical abbreviation that could mean anything. This was enough, however, to encourage her to scan the rest of this document closely. Mostly it was just more cryptic text, studded with numbers and symbols. But one image, hemmed in with Cyrillic, appeared at last to yield a vital clue: a map. In the lower right-hand corner there was what appeared to be a lake, and a word she now recognized: 'Киев'. Kiev. It was paired with another word she did not know: 'Озеро'. Lake Kiev, maybe? Was there such a thing? Two meandering black lines fed into it. From the north-east, 'Днипро' – OK, she could decipher that, it was the Dnipro, the Dneiper. And from the north-west, 'Припять', which Lena unravelled letter by letter: Pripyat. This river was crossed, just above the lake, by a railway line: the universal stitching was unmistakable. At that point there was a town, or a city, named after the river.

Pripyat.

Lena stowed the map in her rucksack and, after a moment's hesitation, left the Geiger counter where it was, its chaotic heart still beating. Averting her eyes from the walls, she slipped back into the corridor. That was when there came the jolt of gears engaging, a mechanism coming to life somewhere below, followed by the groan of things in motion. She knew at once that it was the elevator.

She sped along the hall and took the steps two at a time, her pack lurching and threatening to tip her over. The stairwell hummed, taking up the tune of the lift shaft. She had reached the third floor when she heard the wheels and pulleys grind to a halt higher up, followed by the guillotine swish and clatter of the grille opening. She did not even pause to consider that there might be someone else waiting outside the entrance, and realized only as she ran up Chervonoarmiyska, with cars gliding by, that she could not be sure there had not been.

She headed back to the railway station – not because she would take a train (out of the question without documentation), but because the throng, the polyglot crowd, would enable her to disappear. And because here they would sell maps. She bought several at random, hoping to find one that would cover a region big enough to encompass Lake Kiev, or whatever that body of water was called. Then she forced herself to sit down calmly with a drink and trace the course of the

Dneiper – first downstream, where it broadened into a broad loch, presumably a reservoir created by dams, then upstream, where the same thing happened as the river wriggled north into Belarus. And there it was, almost at the border, 110 kilometres away: Pripyat.

A hundred and ten kilometres. A train was ruled out already, but what about a taxi? Weren't the taxis here state-operated? She wasn't sure, and didn't know how she might find out. 'Excuse me, are your taxis run by the government, because if so, I'd rather not take one.' She was sure she had enough dollars to persuade just about anyone in the city to drive her seventy miles, but how could she be sure they would not take her money and then drive her to the nearest police station – or worse? She saw that she had become distrustful of everyone. 'That's how it works', she said to herself: don't ask for help, and don't offer it.

But Lena baked brown from a passage through the Carpathians was ready to contemplate things that would never have entered the mind of Lena pale and listless in Brixton. Seventy miles? That couldn't be so much more than the pilgrim route from London to Canterbury. She would cross it on foot.

Lena walked out of Kiev in the evening – that was 28 April. It was unseasonably hot; all day the golden domes of the city had shone like little suns, and now the night was balmy. She gambled that it would stay that way: a light pack was her first concern, and besides her documents she took only a blanket and the several layers of Roma clothes. The moon gave all the light she needed. According to the map, for the first fifty kilometres the road skirted a reservoir and carved a path through conifer forests on the western flank of the water. The few vehicles on the road ignored her. Only once a car slowed after she appeared wraithlike in its lights, and then she plunged among the trees until the driver lost interest. Later, deep into the night, she slept on a soft bed of needles, and if the sky was too clear to retain the day's heat, nonetheless she dozed until the stars were washed away.

It was chilly before sunrise, but the beauty of the place distracted her from the air's bite. She estimated that she was twenty-five kilometres out of the city, and now there were spring flowers on the roadside. Streams dampened the mossy rocks as they tripped into the river. A lone stork watched Lena from a hump-backed rock as she bathed for the first time in days. Her jaw quaked as she rubbed her numb skin with the headscarf. Parts of her body were now entirely different colours; she was patterned like an animal. While she munched, naked, on a coarse, sweetened roll and a block of hard cheese, her every hair and pore tingled from the cold water. The sensation was like a soft rain, making her look up reflexively at the dawn sky; but there was not a blemish in the yellow canopy. A shower of morning quanta on her skin.

By the afternoon the road began to veer west, away from the water's edge, and Lena saw from her map that a choice was imminent: follow the highway to Ivankiv, or keep heading north, a more direct but unknown and unmarked route. That would eventually bring her to the inlet where the Teteriv River met the Dneiper, which could make for an impossible crossing. For the sake of saving twenty kilometres or so, the uncertainty was not worth it; she stayed on the road, keeping far enough into the forest that even in daylight she would be no more than a dim sylvan spook half-seen from a speeding vehicle. This also gave her shelter from the sun, which by midday was hot enough to soften the tarmac, so that the wheels of passing trucks made a sticky, ripping noise.

Some time in the afternoon, just before she reached the bridge over one of the Teteriv's major tributaries, Lena watched through the trees as a long line of slow-moving black Volgas drove past, heading out from Kiev. It looked like a state funeral – these were evidently Party officials. But whose death would warrant this procession into the wilderness?

Now the scene was not so pretty. The fir trees thinned, the ground became harsher, colonized by tough grasses and shrubs. The leaves did not return here before May: it was a winter landscape that Lena plodded through, in spite of the heat. Flocks of squawking geese flew far above.

People lived here. Along the road there were low houses of brick and timber, some roofed and patched with sheets of red iron. The countryfolk shuffled by the roadside, stooped and defeated, the women in white scarves shaking their heads. Grandmothers stood at their wooden gates and watched the walkers without expression.

The sunlight brought no joy to these regions. Lena wondered whether the inhabitants did not trust the sun, did not believe that the remorseless winter was over. Perhaps they were just dully amazed that they had survived it. Yet all this activity meant that she could relax, for apart from her pack – which was now in any case far from the condition in which it had left London – she looked much like everyone else. She was a wanderer too, her destination of no interest to anyone. An army lorry passed by, the young men calling and whistling from the open back, but only because they did not know what else to do.

In the early evening she crossed the bridge that led into Ivankiv, a town so enervating that she continued on her way as soon as she had a cup of tea and a bowl of soup inside her. The streets were full of people, entire families, but they were not there to take in the air. They stumbled about as though the hot day had confused them. In the town square a brass band was putting away its instruments. All this humankind – the town did not seem big enough to contain it. How would it pack all these people away?

A curious thing: the road leading north-east had become an unofficial bus station. Dozens of lemon-yellow vehicles waited in line for passengers who showed no sign of turning up.

Ψ

Lena awoke to the sound of immense wings beating in the air above her, and with a shout she raised her hands to shield her face. But it was not a bird; way over the treetops a helicopter ratcheted past, heading north.

She had walked too far yesterday, and sensed that now it would be better not to remove her boots and check the state of her feet. Whatever was happening down there was best left alone.

To delay starting out, she took Neder's notebook from her pack and opened it at random. A madman's *I Ching*.

> *Many who seek this science without the Light of Nature*
> *are precipitated into very great Errors, because they*
> *know not the true Subject of this Art, but busie them-*
> *selves about other things altogether unfit for the Work.*

'"Unfit for the work",' she muttered. 'Tell me something I don't know.'

> *The distilled water is the Moon; the Sun or Fire, is*
> *hidden in it, and it is the father of all things. It is also*
> *called living water, for the life of the dead body is*
> *hidden in the water.*

Here was something she hadn't noticed before: a diagram.

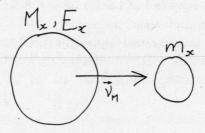

What now? A big orb and a little orb. Sun and moon? But the moon doesn't orbit the sun, nor are they on a collision course, with velocity v_M or otherwise. It was hopeless.

$$\Psi$$

Throughout the morning, the phantom rain returned to brush her face.

More army trucks rumbled by, but now the troops were subdued. Once a driver shouted to her in a tone that was not lewd, but instead eager to be understood. And she began to discern a very simple pattern: all official or military vehicles were going north, while all civilian traffic, from family cars to bucolic carts to groups on foot, was headed south. That, she imagined, was the way it must look in a war zone. The travellers had the scarecrow disarray of refugees. Old men drooping on the backs of wagons. Women dabbing at tears. Sullen, dismal children.

Something was going on.

$$\Psi$$

The pine forest returned, but now it was sodden, crawling its way out of a marsh. In the middle of the afternoon Lena left the road to follow a path through the trees, searching for a place to squat discreetly, and discovered that the track led to a slatted wooden house where an old woman stood in black weeds, as though she had been waiting for her. '*Baba*,' the woman called out. '*Baba*'. She was toothless and barely four feet tall, a fairy-tale creature equally likely to grant a wish or put you in the cooking pot. She started to tell her side of the story.

Lena shook her head. 'I'm sorry, I'm sorry' – English was all she had. The old woman nodded, and Lena became aware of someone else moving in the doorway. An identical creature, but even smaller and even older. '*Mama*,' said the first woman. And Lena had the uneasy impression that this process might continue: behind each woman, a tinier and more ancient version, each called into being by that incantation: '*Mama*'. A nesting that shrunk beyond history. The figure in the door spoke in a sandpaper crackle; it seemed like a negation – '*Nye, nye*' – as her hands spread open in the motion of scattering grain. Then she shut the door.

Ψ

The sun was falling with defiant brilliance. Two army lorries had stopped at the side of the road, and the soldiers milled around as people drifted past. It was perfectly obvious that Lena was going in the wrong direction, and equally clear that, as she walked towards the troops, this was what they were shouting at her. The way was blocked.

While there was no need to think beyond the confines of her crumpled map, she'd been able to keep going. It had taken all her energy to keep her legs moving, nine hours a day for the past two days, and she had no resources left to manage this obstacle. She had become an automaton, quite unable to cope when her sole impulse was denied. She began to shake with weariness and frustration, increasingly fearful at what she might find herself doing now.

A frail man appeared before her, and she realized that she'd glimpsed him watching her as the soldiers sent her back. He carried a heavy suitcase and there was desperation in his face and his voice. He was speaking rapidly, asking a question, and at last she made out the repeated, insistent word: 'Pripyat'. She nodded blankly, and stuttered *'Da. Pripyat'*. With a glance at the bored young men with rifles, the man pulled her into the trees. He fumbled in the pocket of his jacket, where he found a pen and an old ticket to scrawl on. First a number, then an inscription in Cyrillic, but this much she could understand by now: *vulitsya*. Street. It was an address, then. There was more – detailed directions, presumably – and then he drew her deeper into the squelching forest. She could tell from the emphatic bars of shadow that soon they were moving north again.

The further they went, the more uneasy the man became. Lena thought at first that this was a simple fear of discovery, a nervousness at their transgression. It was not expressed in the manner she would have expected, however – no frightened glances through the trees, no attempt to move quietly. There was a kind of existential discomfort in the man, as though he had become disturbed by his own skin. He pawed at his face and rubbed his palms on his shirt. Finally, in great distress, he stopped, waved towards the north, and gabbled out a phrase like a chant or a blessing. To her alarm, he crossed himself. Then he fled back down the track.

When she found the road again, there was such an air of dereliction about it that Lena could not believe concealment was any longer necessary. The forest still bordered the tarmac on each side; and as the firs received the last rays of the sun, Lena gasped.

The trees had turned red.

At first her senses rebelled, insisting that the hue of the branches – the rust of drying blood – was a trick of the light, an apparition enforced by the evening red shift. Yet no sun, no dusty skies, could effect this transformation: an evergreen forest in decay, as if autumn had come at the end of time.

> *And the Sun and the Moon shall make it Red, and this is the end of the Great Work.*

So that's it, Lena thought. I'm now in the Red Zone, beyond all the cordons, past all the boundaries. I'm in the Zone, where new rules apply.

The road showed her the way to Pripyat.

Ψ

The forest ceased, and the plants that remained were like fossils, Triassic fauna, stunted and bare, the sour fruit of this inhospitable soil. There was an avenue into the city, lined not with trees but with short, ugly street lamps, silhouetted in the dusk like awkward, stylized birds. None of them was lit. Nothing in the city, in the hulking gangs of tower blocks, was lit. Pripyat accepted darkness like a destiny.

There is nothing that can prepare a person for walking into a city and finding no one at home. City as geological structure: the mind can't figure it out. You can't interpret the surfaces, the intersections and compass points. Hardest of all is the silence, because no city is ever silent, not even in the hours when sleep pulls us to the fringes of death. It is like the chilling absence of being that a corpse displays, and we know that we have no words to describe this object laid out before us. It isn't any longer a part of our world.

Now, at last, she was afraid. This was worse than anything. She did not feel as if she were in actual danger; rather, she had become irrelevant. The terror was eschatological – a fear of the apocalypse. This, she thought, was what it must have been like to stand in the ruins of Hiroshima, under that skeletal brain-dome, after the twentieth century had been ripped in two.

The apartments she investigated by torchlight were not reeking and rat-infested, sprouting moss and fungus. They were clean and orderly. Pictures hung on the walls, family portraits stood propped on mantelpieces over coarse electric fires. The beds were made up; here was a meal half-eaten, congealed but not rancid, the knives and forks resting on the plates. The people had been sucked up, vacuumed out of their homes. Vaporized.

She could not bring herself to sleep in a bed, but curled up on a floor. She would not fit herself into the hollow of another person's absence. She found blankets, but could not get warm.

24

TWO MONTHS BEFORE LENA WOKE TO FIND HERSELF IN A hospital bed at sixteen years of age, her nose and throat raw from the tube that had voided her stomach of alcohol and sedatives, her friend Rachel had a baby. It was a fatherless baby, they decided, because it seemed too absurd to regard immature, chaotic Alan Nash as a father. Rachel's parents and Alan's parents had almost come to blows, but Rachel and Lena liked Alan. They had no doubt that he would fall off the edge of the world the moment he left home. The world was waiting to swallow him, and soon enough it did.

'We'll bring it up together,' said Rachel to Lena. Her baby lay naked and mewling, its black eyes looked blind. It was called Morgan, but for Rachel it was as yet ungendered, as though that might prevent it from changing into a person.

Lena wondered whether Rachel loved her. Was this a sort of proposal? They had kissed once, but had not known what to make of it. And now Lena was with Davey, so the question could be conveniently put aside.

Lena had wanted to be present at the birth, but the doctors were most discouraging of the idea, so Rachel's mother had been there instead, while Lena sat outside with Rachel's father. That sweating and disconsolate man had developed a suspicion of all of his daughter's schoolfriends, as though any of them, male or female, might be plotting to impregnate her again, so Lena went wandering through the hospital on her own. It was three in the morning. She watched a young man being rolled swiftly past on a trolley, his face masked like a diver's, the sheets marked with blood. Bright red, she thought. Arterial. It looked like a brutal wound. An old man in pyjamas sat in the harsh corridor light, taking in breaths as if he was learning a new skill that took immense concentration. It seemed to Lena as though every ward had designated someone to sit up in their bed and keep watch. Warding vampires away from the blood bags, she told herself.

She slept for a bit on random benches, she drank a hot liquid that dribbled from a machine, and as the windows began to lighten she went in to see Rachel with her baby. She never mentioned it afterwards, but that was the first time she fully understood the implications of her own infertility.

In the flushed, drowsy, bedraggled teenager on the hospital bed, she saw at once a mother, and all other mothers too. Motherness. She knew that this would separate them, and within a year she was proved right. That hairless, purple creature had staked its claim, but Lena could not really resent it for that. Oh, she *did* resent it, but tolerably, proportionately, only as much as was warranted. She'd anticipated the changes in their friendship, she could tell that she was about to be displaced. She'd known that Rachel would want to do all she could to make Lena feel involved, and not just for the sake of having another pair of hands to help. Rachel knew that Lena could never have a child, and her efforts to be sensitive were magnificent and touching.

But Lena understood from the instant she saw her friend in the maternity ward that not being a mother would set her apart, and not just from Rachel. She was contemptuous of the sad whispers which she was sure passed around her mother's cabals, of not being a 'complete woman', the shaking heads, the complicit glances. Was Virginia Woolf incomplete? Elizabeth the First? Charlotte Brontë? (She was collecting childless women in her notebook.) No, she dismissed with scorn the notion that wholeness required parturition. She didn't even know if she liked children – or disliked them, come to that. She was not ready to have an opinion on children.

Yet she could see that the dishevelled girl with her twitching baby was secure, no matter how little thought or preparation had brought her to this point. There was a place for her. People knew what to do with a mother and child. They put them on posters, and on altars, and on television. Mothers had already explained themselves. Lena felt that what was going to be different for her was that she would not easily be able to explain herself. What she was doing there, in the world.

While Rachel seemed to regard Morgan as something still embryonic, Lena spoke to him as though to a tiny adult. She did not believe in baby talk. He might as well get to know how things are. Even Rachel, though she did not say a word, was unnerved by this.

Ψ

Lena's periods never started. By the time her mother realized that something was wrong, Lena knew it too. At fifteen she had a name for it: amenorrhea. Not a disease but a description. There were dozens of possible causes, but after three months of being poked and prodded both physically and mentally (she was a thin girl; was she eating properly?), the hospital made its pronouncement: Mullerian aplasia.

'You have barely anything resembling a uterus,' they told her, 'and incomplete fallopian tubes. The upper vagina is largely absent.'

She'd seen the diagrams countless times at school, the

anatomy of the female sexual organs. But now, it seemed, these visceral maps did not apply to her. Her insides did not look that way. They were not fully formed.

Her mother wept copiously in the doctor's surgery.

'Why?' she cried. 'What went wrong this time?'

'It's a congenital condition, Mrs Romanowicz. A growth defect during the formation of the foetus. It has sometimes been linked with paternally inherited genes, but that's not clear. In all other respects your daughter is developing normally.'

'What can you do about it?'

'Do? That's very difficult, I'm afraid. You see, we can't simply build Lena a new set of internal sex organs – not yet, at any rate. One day it may be a different matter. Right now, there really is not much that can be done.' Barbara's tears flowed afresh.

'Mum, it's not that bad. It's not going to kill me.'

'But – but… you won't have babies.'

'I don't even know if I wanted them. Maybe I wouldn't have bothered anyway.'

'Oh, my darling, I gave this to you. *We* gave it to you.'

Ψ

This time. She'd said, 'What went wrong this time?' And Lena had noted it, which is how she finally came to know why she never got the sibling she craved as a child.

Oh, she tried not to feel rancour about the fact that her mother's weeping, as she explained it all in a torrent of bitter anguish, was as much to do with Barbara as with herself. It's not surprising, Lena told herself, that my situation should reawaken the suffering my mother had borne for so long in silence. (A palpable silence – she realized now that she'd always known there was something being hidden from her on the subject of *family*.) Yet now her mother's grief seemed to lay claim to all that her own situation had produced.

'We tried for years,' Barbara said, 'and we got no help from the doctors. There was still so much shame and embarrassment about those matters in the sixties, even in the medical profession.' At last the problem was diagnosed: Barbara had sustained damage to her fallopian tubes, the result of an inflammatory infection which the doctors thought might have been contracted while she was using an intrauterine device for a short time after Lena's birth.

'We didn't want another child so soon, you see. But those things were new then, there wasn't much experience of them in Europe. The Pill didn't come out until a year or two later.'

'So you did it for my sake.'

'Yes. No! Oh, I don't know what you mean by that, darling. I can't think straight any more.'

But Lena was not in the mood to be merciful.

'So then in the end Dad decided he had to prove himself some other way. With someone young and fertile.'

'It was the cruellest thing he could have done. I tried to forgive him, but I couldn't. How could I?'

Ψ

Counselling was recommended; Lena saw a woman called Suzi, who wore ornate earrings with many moving parts. Suzi was big on chunky jewellery, and wrapped herself in intense silks. She exuded the odours of tropical hardwoods.

'Don't let anyone tell you you're not part of the sisterhood, Lena. You're a woman like any other.'

Lena wasn't so sure about that. She thought she might like a few more years of being a girl first.

Her mother became a woman who has survived a tragedy – wounded, but bearing up. Her father was uncomfortable and uncharacteristically hesitant, but he managed to tell her that it was all right to be upset about it. Around her parents, however, she was more irritated than anything else. When she cried alone, it felt like a shallow, perfunctory kind of sadness, not the desperate grief of her mother.

If she had indeed experimented with death a year later, why should anyone have been surprised? She'd denied it, even to herself, but surely that was the obvious course: if not life, then death. She'd been right, though, to insist that drunkenly munching on a handful of benzodiazepines wasn't a matter of *trying to die*. Killing herself was not the point, as her father, without understanding, had discerned. It was the possibility of *making death happen* that had fascinated her stupefied mind. Of taking an affective action, one that might have some impact.

For the first couple of years, her mother combed the *Lancet* and the *British Medical Journal* for articles on Mullerian aplasia.

'There will be surgical procedures in a few years, I'm sure of it. In America.'

'I don't want to go to America to be cut open and have a uterus built.'

'No, darling, of course not. I understand. But we'd find the money. If you did.'

Lena feigned complete lack of interest, and finally Barbara stopped scouring the journals. Lena allowed her mother to begin hugging her again, although the hugs were a little awkward, as though Barbara was not sure how their bodies fitted together, now that she and her daughter were the same size.

Ψ

The morning streets were fringed with foam, as though the sea had washed the city. At the end of a concrete canyon, Lena could see a grey vehicle spraying the asphalt. If Pripyat was deserted, it was not empty.

Into the silence that settled behind the passing truck, storks flew down. They landed on a field of cement, a great feature-less slab flanked by cliffs with windows, and wandered over the level surface checking for flaws.

'Confusing, isn't it?' Lena murmured to them.

There was tea and coffee, but no gas to warm it. The refrig-erators had let themselves go, standing guiltily in incontinent puddles. The menu in the ruins, then, was tinned fruit: prunes, cherries, plums.

Lena opened a window to let in the morning, but the air tasted metallic.

She found a bicycle and pedalled about Pripyat. The army and the fire brigade – the usual emergency forces of the apoca-lypse – were patrolling the streets, but they were a skeleton crew, noisy enough to anticipate from half a mile away. From time to time helicopters chattered over the rooftops, mostly moving southwards. If that was anything to go by, it appeared that Pripyat was not, after all, Ground Zero.

The more she saw of the city, the more she appreciated that it had been a bleak and blasted place even before everyone left. It was like a child's approximation of a real city, a gargantuan model carved from rough stone. Like a foundation layer alone, a project abandoned before all this dry gypsum was clad in the materials of civilization and given the ornamenta-tion and accoutrements that dwelling places were entitled to. A schematic idea of a city, laid out in clumsy blocks. This coarse shell could one day have become a library; that empty square might eventually have grown a fountain and benches and flower beds. But she doubted there had ever been a future in store for those uncouth tower blocks – why would anyone have bothered trying to improve them? If they cared about such matters, the tenants would have had to do it themselves. And some of them had. Bare walls bloomed with the bright lichen of murals: state-approved cartoons, rosy-faced workers applauding the production targets met successfully by Polyisoprene Plant Number 7.

On the edge of town there was an amusement park, a place designed for circular motion. Roundabouts for gyrating the kids in horizontal planes, while mothers and fathers rotated vertically on a big wheel built to an industrial format with industrial components – an outsized Meccano model with its batteries run down. The seats were enclosed in scalloped bowls and canopies: yellow clams, waiting to bite.

Pripyat had no history. It had not grown around a natural harbour or on the riverside like the great cities of the world, it was no progeny of a castle or fiefdom or church. Pripyat had been ordained, then poured into the mould and dumped in the marshes. It was a place to keep people. Cities like this had a job to do.

Ψ

The evacuation had been genteel and orderly, by and large: children's toys were cleared away, shops closed with their can-nonball racks of fruit left to ripen and rot in strict array. But something had gone wrong in the library, as though the ranks of studious autodidacts had snapped when their note-taking was interrupted. Shelf-loads of books were tipped out, the pages bent on impact at ugly angles, like broken limbs. Journals and newspapers crazy-paved the floor. The place was beyond any alphabetical redemption.

She plucked up a volume at random – the fact was that she was beginning to think about fuel for the night – and strode with it down the aisle, thumbing through the Cyrillic codes. And almost collided with an old man.

Like well-rehearsed clowns, they both leapt back and dropped their books, aghast. The old man recovered first. He straightened up and nodded.

'*Dobry dyen.*'

Which she knew by now, more or less, and echoed. That was a daft thing to have done, of course, because it set him off confidently into eager discourse, so that she had to stutter, '*Ya nye ponimaio.*' The only other phrase worth getting your mouth around if you have no intention of learning the language: I don't understand.

'*Ach. Sprechen Sie Deutsches?*'

'*Nein, ich spreche Deutsches sehr,* er, *schlecht.*'

This elicited a muttered remark that Lena guessed to be along the lines of 'You can say that again.' What came next was no tongue she recognized at all; it sounded vaguely Turkish.

'Sorry, that's no good.'

Jackpot. 'Ha! English! You are English!'

'Yes – but I didn't expect you –'

'We did not expect each other, did we? What are you doing here?'

'In the library?'

'In Pripyat!'

'I'm… looking for someone.'

'But there is nobody here.'

'There is somebody here.'

'So then, you must be looking for me!'

Not until then did she see it. The jaw-line beard. The high forehead. The heavy crossbar of the fused eyebrows. It was a version of the bad photocopy she had studied intensely, trying to divine a person behind it:

I publish this picture, so that my cousins can see that I

have also a Kovacsy nose. All Kovacsy have a very
characteristic nose (see my mother's nose on p.9).

There was only one thing wrong. Karl Neder was not an old man.

'You told me to come and meet you. Only that was a long time ago. And you weren't here then.'

'Lena.'

'You remember?' She was genuinely surprised.

'I remember your name.' And as if explaining: 'Gagarin had a daughter called Lena.'

'Who? Gagarin? The astronaut?'

'Cosmonaut. Well, you're not Russian. No, but the age is close.'

'Twenty-seven.'

'Exactly the same.'

She had no idea why they were talking about this.

'Yuri was murdered,' said Neder, as though that would make everything clear.

'Oh...?'

'He was the first one. He – you see...' Karl Neder deflated suddenly, and she saw now why she had not recognized him at first. He was balding, his flesh sagging under the eyes. His hair – in the photocopies a rigid block of carbon black – was now bleached and ashen. Yellow eyes, like old ivory, the eyes of a sick dog.

'You do not need to know about Yuri.'

This was not the paranoid, hyperactive man that Georgiu Constantin had described. Despite his circumlocution, Neder looked at home here, as if it were the public library in Linz, and he had just dropped by to scoff at the latest idiocies in *Natural Science* or to sketch out another plaintive appeal to Roy Battle. Yet there was an ethereal quality to him; Lena felt that if she were to try to shake his hand, hers would pass straight through it.

'You look like a ghost.'

'Of course. Only ghosts live now in Pripyat.'

'Yes. Tell me about that.'

On warm summer evenings, couples would stroll in the square here – one might almost call it a plaza, with its central patch of manicured grass, a cushion for the monument to an old war hero, mounted on a rearing horse in unlikely homage to David's Napoleon. The cafés around the perimeter had awnings unfurled, and some were fronted by tables and chairs. In Pripyat, this had once been as good as it got.

'Forty-five thousand people lived here,' Neder said. 'They were mostly workers and technicians, and the families of them, and those who made services for the workers. There is a name for such cities in the Soviet Union: *Atomgrad*.'

'Atom City?'

'The very thing.'

'They worked with atoms here?'

'Yes!' He seemed to like that idea, and was for a moment distracted by it, mumbling in Hungarian. His eyes flicked over the empty chairs, as though searching for someone with whom to share his thoughts. 'Yes. They worked with atoms. Very large atoms. Uranium.'

'They made nuclear bombs here?'

'No, no, ha ha, not *that* kind of atomgrad! Those are *much* harder to find. They are much less pretty than this, and not on any map. This one is, um, a peaceful atomgrad. Nuclear power. May we sit for a moment?'

The kind of thing an old man says. He was sweating, although the sun had now set and the evening heat was leaking fast into the vacuum.

'I think I see. There has been an accident at the nuclear

power plant, and they've had to evacuate the city. And the countryside around, I suppose.'

'For ten-kilometre radius. Which is not enough. I have spoken to some of the people who live here. They are told they will return in maybe three days. That was four days ago already. Three days! Ha ha huh –' His laughter turned into a hacking cough, and when the spasm was over Neder's eyes were watery. 'They will not come back for three thousand years.'

They heard the sound of a helicopter. 'Maybe this bar is open, and I can get you a drink. The vodka will not be chilled, I am sorry.' Lena asked for a mineral water, and after Neder had poured it, he took out a little brown bottle and let some drops fall into the glass. Now the water was purple.

'If you're making me a cocktail, I'd better know what's in it.'

'Good for your health, this one. It is iodine cocktail. For radiation, you see.'

'How much radiation is there?'

'In this place it is not hard to find a radiometer. I have not measured since this morning, when it was three hundred milliroentgens per hour. This means that in fifteen hours you have more than maximum dose permitted for a nuclear work- er. While you are here, eat nothing fresh that has been exposed to dust. Only from tins. Take water always from bottles. Keep this iodine, add a few drops when you have water. I have some more, although from most of the druggists here it has been taken. Some Pripyat people, they do not understand what iodine is, they think it is just like a medicine and they panic and drink it straight from the bottle. Very bad burns in the throat. Lena –' He seized her hand, and she saw that his own, though substantial enough, was thinly papered with liver-spotted skin. The gesture reminded her of the melodrama, the exuberant passions of his letters. 'I do not know what it is you want from me. But be quick. Be quick and then leave this city.'

'One thing at a time. You could start by telling me about the accident.'

'Accident!' He threw himself back in his chair. 'Yes, that is what it will be called one day, when Moscow decides to call it anything at all. An accident. It was no accident.'

'All right, then. Suppose you tell me where, at least.'

'The plant is one kilometre east of here. It is called Chernobyl.' It sounded like 'cornbill', some species of marsh bird.

Ψ

Begin again. Five nights ago. Begin then.

On 26 April at 1.30 in the morning, Lena was sleeping in a stable eight hundred metres up on the northern fringe of the Carpathian mountains. The hand of her guide, a man whose moustache hung lower than his chin like the whiskers of a walrus, had repeatedly crept up from her foot, and repeatedly been kicked back down again, a wordless game that had drifted into a series of weary, flaccid reflexes. Now the hand lay sprawled across her shin, forgotten, a lifeless form that the moustache had cast off.

At the same time, Karl Neder was sleeping in a shed in the docks of Odessa. When he woke, he would catch the train to Kiev.

And that was when the fire engines of Pripyat sped softly out of town; no need for sirens, which would have woken the workers.

There was an emergency at Reactor Building Number 4 of the Chernobyl plant. Already the firemen could see a pillar of white smoke shimmering above the flames from the burning bitumen roofs.

But the lumps of red-hot material scattered all around the

reactor building were not bitumen. No one knew what they were. This did not look like the scene of a fire, nor even of an explosion; it was as though something volcanic had risen from the depths of the earth and thrust its way through Reactor 4. Some new and flaming element from Pluto's underworld.

By six o'clock, nearly all the fires were extinguished. Everything was under control – except that the firemen had become dizzy, bewildered, possessed by a raging thirst and an impulse to vomit. For these men, the world was growing dim.

The white cloud had vanished. There was a gentle breeze blowing by that time.

Ψ

'The question is,' Karl Neder said, 'how do you plug an active volcano? Well, this they are trying to do. Maybe it will work, who knows. It is like a military campaign. But you would be safer sent to Afghanistan. The soldiers and the firemen, they storm the reactor in waves. They do not have special clothing, but just a stopwatch to protect them. There is a constant bombardment from the air – they are dropping sacks of sand and lead. It is a relentless attack, but the reactor will not easily surrender. It is like a giant crucible, you see, a great alchemical experiment. Transmuting all that lead.'

'How do you know this?'

'I have… I have been there. I had to go, you see. I had to check – what was left…'

'You went to the reactor?'

Neder would not look at her.

'I went – *into* the reactor,' he said softly.

Her eyes were burning in the raw dusk.

'Show me,' she said thickly.

'Lena, there is nothing to be gained now –'

'There is nothing to be lost, Neder. Show it to me.'

25

A FOREST HEMMED IN THE RAILWAY TRACK. BUT HERE THE trees were mutated beyond all recognition, bulbous globes gleaming in the moonlight from every branch like drops of viscous oil. Creepers hung from them, weaving the forest into a vast web.

They were power pylons, receding out of sight in the dark. Electromagnetism seemed to tighten the air, creating a hum of virtual cicadas that snapped in and out of existence on the high-tension wires.

'Chernobyl is still operating, naturally,' Neder explained. 'Still there are three good reactors at the plant, staffed by volunteers. Like Reactor 4 they are of the model RBMK-1000, but it will not do to forget the demands of the state.'

Surely no land could be more unloved than this. Building materials, the slack in an order artificially inflated to satisfy some paper quota, were slung around in shapeless dunes. Dead machinery festered. Bits of railway veered off into the scrub, where they lost momentum and fell apart. There was a lake of pearlescent cement, its reed beds barley-sugar bars of iron licked by rust.

The Chernobyl plant, however, was another matter. This was what, it seemed, you were meant to look at. Floodlights flared at the base of the cubist installation, giving it the character of a medieval castle on display for the tourists. Arc lights swivelled from trucks and fire engines; helicopter spotlights swept over the scene, a gaudy light-show in which Reactor 4 was the main attraction. But the most dramatic special effect was unintentional.

'What's happening to the air?' Lena asked.

Over the damaged reactor hall the night was coming to life: ghostly pale, icy blue, an aurora flickered there.

'Ionization,' said Neder. 'Radiation does that. The inner fire is not stilled, then.'

Now Lena could see that there was a landslide of debris reaching halfway up the sheer face of the hall. The roof had disappeared; what was left looked like an exit wound, ragged, fibrous and messy, torn open with shocking force. The floodlights illuminated a slogan painted on the wall, which Neder translated: 'МЫ ПРИДЕМ КПОБЕДЕ КОММЧНИЗМА!' Communism will triumph!

There were chunks of black debris all over the ground.

'It is graphite,' Neder said, 'and pieces of the reactor core. It is very bad to go near, but there is no choice for the workers. First they tried to use robotic engines – see! – but quickly these broke down. Too much radiation and the electronics dies.' These feckless remote-controlled bulldozers stood sickly yellow in the arc light, like a 1950s vision of what the construction machinery of the future would look like.

'I never imagined how it would be to see right into the reactor.' Neder sat down on a wood pile, out of breath. His face was slick and blue, as though smeared with an excrescence from the moon. 'I feel we are perhaps not meant to see such things. There is something... not right about it. I cannot name such a colour as that. Your eyes cannot focus on the redness, but it is not like flames. I could not have dreamed such a thing as this...' He looked out over the battleground. 'It is what I thought, however. It is living fire, hidden in the centre of the world. Coruscation. Now I see.'

> *And that this coruscation, or sparkling of fire, is to be seen in the night, as if Gun-powder were sprinkled in a long time, and then fired; so it goes along, and shines.*

'It's time we talked about red mercury.'

'Tomorrow, please. Now I am very tired.'

Ψ

The sun, when it came, was weaker, less potent. Less real. As thought Pripyat was farther from it than before. Yes, Lena thought, it seemed smaller, whiter, older.

She could not avoid the fact that Karl Neder was dying. Of course he was. What else could you do in this city, slowly sterilizing itself with an invisible rain of hot dust, but shrivel, grow old, and die? Everything was dying here. This was the barren zone.

'It's the elixir, you know.'

'The what?'

'The elixir. The great purifying force. Except that they were wrong. It smells like heaven, yes, this smell is like a sort of musk, or fine old wine. And what else, I don't know. It is intoxicant. But red mercury is not a purifier – it is a corrupter.'

'I guess you found it, then. Isn't that why you came here?'

'I found it a long time ago, but only a little. I think this substance bewitches a person. That is why, hundreds of year ago, people dedicated their life to make it. They could not stop. And so with me too, maybe. But I have understood some things that others do not see. I have looked in different places.'

'I know – I've seen your notes.'

'Then maybe you remember. "Men have it before their eyes, handle it with their hands, yet know it not, though they constantly tread it under their feet."'

'I still don't see what this has to do with Chernobyl.'

'You have my book? Bring it, then.'

They climbed to the roof of the tower block, high enough to show them the power plant squatting in the dirty wilderness. Pripyat was all light and shadows: de Chirico illuminated by gamma rays.

'You know,' Neder said casually, 'that we are not alone here.'

'I've seen the crews washing the roads.'

'Washing, yes. They think you can wash this corruption away. But I am not speaking about them.'

'You mean – someone else… like us?'

'Who knows if they are like us.'

This was not welcome news.

'I've had this feeling,' Lena said, involuntarily lowering her voice, 'that I've been followed since Linz.'

'That is a familiar condition in this part of the world. I have had the feeling I have been followed since 1956.'

'But it was different for you, too, wasn't it, this time? In Sofia you fled from something.'

'Yes…' He sighed. 'Well, now they are too late, no? What can I fear now? What do you know about the red mercury trade?'

'Not much, really. That it is illicit. They sell it for making nuclear weapons – um, neutron reflectors. That it is a commodity in a violent business, I suppose.'

'Worse than that, I am sorry to say. This is not just about Soviet mafia. This is occult. There are, ah, ritualistic elements.'

'I think I've seen that now.'

'The reason is that this is not only about bombs. Do you know about the philosopher's stone?'

'I was wondering when we would get to that.'

'What do you know?'

'Just the usual – turning base metal into gold. Alchemy as early chemistry. A wild goose chase that ended up helping us after all to understand what things are made from.'

'We have so little idea what they found. Look.'

For if the hidden central fire, during which life was in a state of passivity, obtain the mastery, it attaches to itself all the pure elements, which are thus separated from the impure and form the nucleus of a far purer form of life. It is thus that our Sages are able to produce immortal things, partly by decomposition of minerals; and you see that the whole process from beginning to end, is the work of fire.

'Now I have looked into that fire,' Neder said.

For the Power and Virtue of this living Fire is so great, that if it were absent, the Elements would be dead, especially the Heaven, an Element which most of all stands in need of this Light.

'There is so much to this', Neder mumbled. 'I still do not understand it all. A Spanish man, his name is John of Rupescissa, he wrote a book about quintessences. This is in the fourteenth century. You know of Aristotle's fifth element?'

'Also known as the ether.'

'Yes, and it is the only element that cannot be corrupted. But there are many quintessences, said this John, and they can be, ah, pulled out of earthly matter, as in distillation. Some are great medicines, they do not change or decay. Now, this is all old nonsense, you are thinking, and not at all our modern physics. Am I right?'

'I've a feeling you're going to tell me otherwise.'

'No, of course there is much nonsense. But not all. These men were beginning to understand things, but only such a little. John has instructions for making an ether from hot gold, he calls it "fixing the sun in the sky". Now do you see that? Fixing the sun in the sky. This is what we can say of an absolute space-time, we place the stars on a coordinate grid, then they are fixed in space. And this is what is done by your Newton, who is an alchemist and reads the books of John of Rupescissa.'

If she'd been hearing this in London or even Linz, thought Lena, she'd have found it merely tiresome. But in Pripyat there were no longer any points of reference. Nothing could seem as crazy as what was happening around them.

'I have a feeling', she said, 'that what matters most in all of this is living fire. Tell me about that.'

'Now you have seen it, Lena.'

'You think that "living fire" means radioactivity?'

Neder said nothing.

'But the alchemists didn't know about radioactivity – that's ridiculous! Marie Curie discovered it!'

'Matter of fact, it was Henri Becquerel you are thinking of, playing with minerals of uranium. Curie came after, and suffered the more. But listen, you have seen this passage? Which speaks of "coruscation" and "scintillation", this "sparkling of fire" and what not? Yes? What is that? What do you think we saw last night, glowing over Reactor 4? And if you pick up a piece of uranium ore, and its emissions make this a warm thing in your hand, how can you not be the vitalist who thinks that the rock is alive, that it has an inner fire?'

'So that's what it was. But you don't know that the alchemists could lay their hands on uranium ore.'

'It was plentiful to them. It is not so hard to find. The old name for it is "pitchblende" in English. "Blende", you know, is really German – it means a mineral that is good for nothing; they throw it on the refuse heap. "Pitch" is black, of course. This was a useless black rock, incredibly heavy, more than lead. Lot of it was dug from the gold and silver mines at Joachimsthal in Bohemia. Ha, that is where they made the first dollars, you know, and called them thalers.'

He was flipping pages intently.

*The Sages say that their substance is found on the
dung hill.*

'And look here, this is Hermes Trismegistus, the most ancient father of alchemy –'

'Hermes? That's the god Mercury.'

'Yes, yes, precisely so. Mercury. See!'

The Stone of the Sages is heavier than lead.

'So you're saying that pitchblende was the philosopher's stone…'

'No, not that, it all gets mixed up. It was just the means, not the end. The Stone was called the Red King. Hermes says: "The Sun is its father, the Moon is its mother." That is an easy bit. The Sun is sulphur, the Moon is mercury. These are the two elements of all the metals – so the alchemists of Arabia say. You turn one to another by changing the proportions. When these proportions are perfect, that is the Stone.'

'Sulphur and mercury. But chemists must have mixed them together hundreds of times."

'Ah, yes. It is even done by nature. Cinnabar it is called, that is natural mercury sulphide. Or if made artificially, which to say, by alchemy, then it is called vermilion.'

'Red paint!'

'Red, yes.'

'Red – mercury.'

'Not yet, not yet. Cinnabar can be dug straight from the ground, all the alchemists know of this, it cannot be so easy to obtain the Stone. That was something else. Something more. They needed to – ha, why not say it? – to breathe fire into the equation. Living fire.'

'Radioactivity. I see. From pitchblende.'

'Right!' He was gurgling with delight; deep within this dying old man, the youthful Karl Neder was stirring into life.

'This is what is said about red mercury – I mean by those in the trade, not by the old alchemists. It is an amalgam of mercury metal mixed with mercury antimony oxide – well, let us simply say, a compound salt of mercury and antimony. Now, all the alchemists used antimony compounds. The followers of Paracelsus thought antimony was a marvellous medicine. But they did not always know when it was antimony they were using, and when not. Antimony comes from the mineral stibnite, which is a sulphide. It looks like sulphur itself – yellow, you see, it was called the king's gold, orpiment. If you heat it, you make it into antimony oxide. So then, you have this mercury, that is the moon, and this yellow stuff, it is the sun, or so you think, sulphur – but really, sometimes it is antimony sulphide. And you heat them and they become this red powder, which in fact is mercury antimony oxide, and it looks to you just like cinnabar, like indeed the progeny of mercury and sulphur. But you have too much mercury, always the recipes for vermilion say to add too much mercury, and so you get an amalgam. But how then to turn it into true red mercury? This is the trade secret, as you say – a secret then and now both. The red mercury you can buy on the black market is made by showing, ah, exposing this mixture, this amalgam, to intense radioactivity for up of twenty days – in a nuclear reactor.'

'And you're saying that in place of the reactor, the alchemists used pitchblende.'

'That's it! Oh, what a dangerous business. No wonder they all went mad in the end! If not the mercury got them, then the uranium. Hundreds of Middle Ages Marie Curies, wasting away, though none of them are ladies, I think! And why? They thought this living fire was purifying the red mixture; that was what the Great Work of alchemy was suppose to be all about. Purifying the sulphur and the mercury until they were perfect. Maybe they do even make a little gold this way, in a nuclear reaction, like in Fermi's reactor. Ah, but for the human body, this living fire is not a purifier. It corrupts. As you see. Some of them too, the alchemists, in the end they understand this. Although not always they are worried by it, because some of them believe corruption is the beginning of rebirth. Well, I can tell you, that is not the way it feels. So this is what is the Philosopher's Stone, really: the Red King, red mercury. The sun and moon – corrupted.'

Lena felt weak and dizzy, high up here with the geese and the storks. Maybe the corruption was starting inside her, too. Surely it couldn't be long. In spite of her vertigo she walked over to the parapet. Everywhere she looked, she sensed that figures had just darted around the corners, disappearing into the razor-edge shadows of the high sun. The spooks had the place surrounded. Come out with your hands up.

And yet, as far as she could see out among the tower blocks, everything was as desolate as the desert. This was a city moulded from the tundra. A place fit for testing bombs.

Looking back, she saw that the effort of explanation had exhausted Neder, who seemed now to be dozing. Well, she didn't feel inclined to let him sleep.

It was no accident, he had said. The explosion of the nuclear plant was no accident.

'And just what – according to you – were they up to at Chernobyl?' At first she thought he was too sunk in slumber to hear her. Then he blinked into the midday glare.

'Perhaps all *this* was not quite intended. Maybe the reactor was just meant to have a surge, not a meltdown. Whatever is the fact, all was staged by key workers in the pay of the red-mercury profiteers – I suspect Prometea arranged this. They wanted to make the largest batch of red mercury ever produced. Normally it takes twenty days, like I say, and to find that much time is hard in a nuclear facility, even in the Soviet Union. But with a core operating close to its critical threshold, with the moderator rods taken out farther, then the transformation probably is done much more quick.'

'You know all this?'

'I think that is what the evidence reveals.'

'Oh, you *think*. You think so. You think a lot of things, Karl Neder. You think, if I remember this rightly, that Einstein was wrong and perpetual motion is possible.'

Nothing, it seemed, could have delighted him more. 'You have read my books!' The excitement pulled him from his seat as though he was on strings, a sack of derelict old bones which began to jerk and flail around the roof. 'It is more than think. I have proved these things, even if the grand priests have not caught up. That seems a long time ago now, I must say. In Linz – in Linz, did you find my machine?'

'It didn't move.'

'*Eppur si muove.*' Still it moves. As the scientist said to the bishop.

'Oh, Galileo now!' Lena snorted. 'If you are ever accused of modesty, Karl Neder, I shall defend you in court.'

This too pleased him immensely, and he held out his hands

in a show of innocence. 'No, I am just a poor dissident scientist. You have seen how I live in Austria – I think you would say, a shoveller of shit, yes?'

But Lena was determined not to play the game. 'Do you know what my – what someone once said? Galileo is the patron saint of scoundrels. But at least he was wise enough not to get himself burned.'

'What's this?' Surprise, not all of it feigned. 'Do I detect you are angry at me? For coming to Pripyat?'

'If you knew this was going to happen – and look, don't think for a moment that I believe this fantasy – but if you knew... what could you gain by it?'

Now he became subdued, reflective. 'At first, when I understood what is going to happen, when I followed the rumours and made careful enquiries, not careful enough, it seems, but – well, I thought I must prevent it. Do you know what so much red mercury will do to the trade in nuclear armaments? Of which I have all my life opposed and fought, even though I have been put in prison and beaten for it. Because, you know, I am a citizen of the world. So that was my plan – to sabotage the sabotagers, you could say. But if I ask myself, truly, why did I come here, even when I see that I am too late to prevent anything – then I have to admit it to you. I just wanted to see this substance again. And if I could do so, to obtain some of it. To buy it.'

'Don't be so –'

'I was, yes, I was going to buy some,' he insisted. 'Then, when I see I am too late – I arrive three days after the explosion, the red mercury has long been shipped out to who knows where, to Libya or Iraq or South Africa – all the same, I think maybe they left a little, maybe they left it in there because it is so dangerous. So I go to the reactor hall.'

'Oh, Karl Neder,' Lena sighed. 'Were you so tired of life?'

The helicopters pursued their impossible task, slicing up sunbeams. Every breath in this place was a shallow one, shallower than the last.

'You were thinking of going into Sakharov's trade, then?' That stung, as she'd intended.

'Making bombs is no longer Andrei Dmitrievich's business. It never really was. But in any case, I intended to do not anything of that sort. I only – this material is so much more precious than any cheap-bargain arms trafficker ever knows. All they care is that it can be sold for $200,000 the kilogram. But the true power of this red mercury is – is a thing as cannot be compared.'

Lena shook her head. 'This beats everything. Perpetual motion is nothing next to this. You know what I think? I think that all this – it's what you were hoping for, this... this corruption.' How bitter her words tasted. 'The sun and moon? No, it's the earth that's corrupted now.'

Ψ

She walked the wide boulevards. Let them find her – the army, the nuclear bandits, whoever. Spray her down, slice her up, paint her black and toss her into the furnace, raw matter for the putrid Great Work. She remembered the address the frightened man had given her in the forest – the ticket was still in her pocket, but it was a hopeless errand in this land of nameless monuments. What did he want, anyway, that poor bloke scared out of his wits by an invisible, deadly rain? A paltry fortune stashed in a biscuit barrel? A photo of his parents holidaying on the Baltic coast? A bundle of love letters hoarded from his impetuous youth? Pripyat was full of such things, accumulating dust at the rate of two hundred roentgens per hour. Now they were inside the event horizon, sealed up from the world. Never mind this life, she said

to the refugee with his suitcase. Forget it. Find yourself
another.

Ψ

In the next room Neder sat coughing and shivering, while
Lena read one of the letters she had carried, at great cost to her
shoulders, across most of central Europe. She knew that she
was searching for a way to fit its author into the shape of this
poisoned wreck of a man.

> *Dear Dr Battle,*
>
> *Thank you very much for your letter of the 15th Oct. I
> think that any person decides for himself the problem of
> sacrifice, suicide, assassination, etc. I can, of course, dis-
> cuss with you this problem, however, I think here one
> has to dedicate too much time, which neither you nor I
> have at our disposal. I am 50 years of age, and in my life
> I have many times taken decisions which with a great
> probability had to lead to death, mutilation, or long
> years imprisonment. However, as you see, I am safe,
> sane and 'free'.*

And on it went, as Neder's letters always did – with threats,
imprecations, appeals to Battle's honour and humanity, as he
hastily mortared his wall of assertion with capitalized exclamations:

> *I submit now to you my new article*
>
> *MATHEMATICAL NONSENSES SLIPPED INTO
> THE FUNDAMENTALS OF CONVENTIONAL
> ELECTROMAGNETISM MUST FINALLY BE
> CORRECTED*

It is obvious for ANY STUDENT that this article
CANNOT BE REJECTED. No referee in no country of
*the world can find a **single objection** to this lucid paper.*
If you will reject it, dear Dr Battle, excuse me, but,
I think, there is no more sense to submit papers to NAT-
URAL SCIENCE.

And finally, a declaration of the optimism that now, here in the sun-blanched, hermetic lands, seemed to have deserted him:

Hoping to receive your answer soon,

Sincerely yours,
Karl Neder

He was humming softly to himself, a melody by Schubert. Lena spoke from the doorway.

'I went to Linz to interview you. About your theories.'

His voice had barely the strength to reach her.

'Read my books. Read the papers I have published.'

'Well, not your theories exactly. No one will understand them. Your motivations. That's what interested me. We look for the human angle, you see.'

'I wanted to tell the truth, of course.'

He waited, so she said, 'I won't be your Pilate. Tell me this – why do you hate Einstein?'

He tried to focus on her, tried to take umbrage. Neither came easily to him any more. 'I do not hate him at all. What for should I hate him? I dislike how the Relativists promote his ideas without cease.'

Lena shook her head. 'I think the reason you despise Einstein is that his ideas were even more outrageous than yours. And they believed him, though he was no more than a patent clerk.'

'You think that is all there is to it?' he barked hoarsely. 'He had a stupid idea, and other stupid people believed him? You think an idea so ridiculous can become the sacred scripture by sheer stupidity? Don't you see that relativity, and quantum theory too, had its path brushed clear by larger forces? What do these things undermine, in the end? Let me tell you. They destroy absolute truth and certainty. They say that such things are not just obscure or hidden from us, but they are impossible, they do not exist. In such a world, you can say anything! You can be a Stalin, or a Hitler, or a Chairman Mao, and no one will stand up against you because it has been taken away from them their core being, the gravity centre around which they can build a world. You think this is just an argument about *science*?'

This was more like it. Stoke the embers, why not? Keep the living fire going a little longer. Show me what I came to see.

It had been easy to tell herself she was honouring Georgiu Constantin's plea, trying to save his friend. But she knew all along that her journey was not for Georgiu's sake. It was Neder's defiant vitality, his irrepressible, absurd conviction, that had drawn her here. That, she supposed, was her own red mercury, her unicorn. That, and something else.

'There was a moment,' Lena said, 'when I wondered: what if there is something in all of this? What if Neder is right, even a little bit? Because I think there were times when they were genuinely unsure, you know, even Roy Battle. But you're not right, are you? And what's worse is that you know it. You don't believe your theories yourself. You'll never say it, no, you couldn't bear to do that, but you know. You're enough of a physicist to realize that. You've created an elaborate game, and now it's trapped you. And this was the only way you could think of to end it.'

'Belief, you talk about?' Neder protested. 'What is there to believe in books of idle knowledge? What does it cost anyone to believe in these things they read, their wave equations and Ricci tensors? It is only worth the while to believe when it is a struggle. Yes, I believe in these things I write, with all my heart I do, and why? *Because they might not be true.* Because they are hard to prove –'

'You said a child could prove them.'

'At least a child might try! At least a child believes what it does with passion, not smugly, not with complacency.'

'So it's better to be passionately wrong than complacently right?'

But his fuel was expended. He sagged into the gloom.

'What do you think?' he gasped.

They did not speak for a moment.

'Well,' Lena said quietly, 'this is where your passion has brought you.'

'Yes. And what brought you? You have not told me that.'

'The observer. I'm the impartial observer.'

'Oh, I see. And what do you observe? Impartially?'

'Nothing. A wasteland. A haunted city.'

'Do you think I will haunt it too?'

$$\Psi$$

Night came while they sat there. It could not last long, they both knew that.

'Is the interview cancelled, then?' asked Neder. This was not, after all, said with irony. Or so it seemed – she was finding it hard to tell. There was too much darkness in the way. 'I can give you a few details. People will want to know where I came from.'

Far away, a siren wailed briefly, a banshee in the marshes. 'I have been imprisoned by or expelled from every Communist state west of Istanbul, and yet still I call myself a Communist. Do you want to know why?'

'No, I don't.'

'I am not –' Then he registered her response. It confused him. 'Yes... it is my work on the perpetuum mobile that has brought you here. You want to know how I can believe such a thing, when everyone else does not.'

'No, I'm not interested in that. I don't think I was ever interested in that.'

'You are – not interested...?' He was lost.

She did not mean to sound as harsh as she did – or at least, she had not expected to.

'These are games you've played all your life. They don't have much point now.' Suddenly she was seized by fury. 'There's no point now!' she shouted, and stormed to the window. As though, despite the dark, he might have seen her face.

A small voice behind her, searching for purchase: 'Einstein was wrong, you know. About light. And about space. The conservation laws are postulates, they have never been proved... I am still waiting to be shown my errors.'

Silence. 'I am still waiting.'

At last, wearily, she said, 'What about you, then?'

'My mother's name was Dora,' he announced. 'She sang and had perfect teeth –'

'No,' said Lena firmly. 'No more stories. Enough.'

How much time had passed? She could not bear to think of another sunrise.

'There is one thing more,' he said, his voice now barely audible. 'They say the Stone could – could prolongate life. If you imbibe it, you live for a hundred years or more.'

Now at last, her cheeks were wet. 'I know.'

'Gagarin,' he breathed in a cracked whisper, 'was given

red mercury. This was a test. He was not supposed to know. But he did. That was his crime. Before he flew, Yuri urinates on the wheel of his bus, on the way to the launch pad. This becomes then a cosmonaut tradition. But they do not understand. Yuri is leaving a sample of… of corruption in his body. He is leaving a clue. Now I know it is not what he sees that makes him a condemned man, but what is within him.'

Lena was no longer listening to Karl Neder spinning his webs in the dark. She was ready to let his voice fade out. But there was a toll of tears to be paid for relinquishing the final part of her delusion. Yes, she'd read Neder's notes in Linz, and had seen the passage about a universal medicine, a legendary panacea made from mercury and living fire. She'd known she must dismiss it along with everything else, but her need was too great.

I know someone, she'd thought with brittle excitement, who could use some of that.

Ψ

Lena had no idea how she came to be lying down, covered by her blanket; but there it was. Her eyes were puffy. She knew at once that she was alone in the apartment.

She checked the other rooms, then raced into the corridor. It would not have surprised her to find him tumbled at the bottom of the stairs – but that was not where Karl Neder was. She even risked calling out his name; it simply came back to her, diminished and hollow.

She ran into the street, taking turns at random. That was how she almost collided at full tilt with a cluster of astronauts. Or so they seemed to her befuddled brain. Enclosed in silver-grey plastic, their faces were covered by what looked like gas masks, tapering to a bestial snout which was capped with a cumbersome metal cylinder, forcing their heads to droop like a band of surly dogs. Each of them had a pack strapped to his back, linked via a plastic tube to a funnel-tipped gun. They were squirting jets of foaming liquid onto the road.

The effect of half a dozen masks turning in synchrony is, as any dramaturge knows, most striking. A Greek chorus on the moon.

It would probably not have been hard for Lena to elude the clean-up crew if she had not run into the underpass. For it proved not to be an underpass at all, but the underground section of a car park that had apparently only a single way in. There was nothing for it but to take to the upper levels, in the hope that they might connect to an adjacent building – a pedestrian walkway would do the trick. There were many cars still parked neatly between the white lines, and she paused to try a few doors – it would be a place to hide, if nothing else. But the people of Pripyat were more cautious than that. She found the stairwell, in which the stomping of heavy boots echoed up from below, and the higher she went, the slighter she knew were her chances of escape. When she reached the roof level, she'd had enough. What's the worst they might do – cover her in detergent?

As they arrived up there, flagging from the climb, Lena could not decide if it was comical or ominous that they were still wearing their masks. Goggle-eyed and snub-nosed, they became bizarre beasts that shuffled towards her, capable of anything. But as soon as the first of them pulled off his mask, she knew who he was.

Ψ

He handed her an iodine tablet, and spoke in his treacle-toned English. 'It seems I'm too late, then.'

Lena nodded. 'We were always too late. Even before we set out.' They stood side by side now, the other plastic suits dispatched on errands elsewhere, and looked together down the empty highway that led out of Pripyat, north towards Belarus.

'We could search in this wilderness for months,' said Jaroslav Kam. 'Maybe he hasn't even left the city. The fact is, we have lost him. I would very much like to have seen him, Lena.'

'Would he have wanted to see you?'

'I'm sure he wouldn't. But at least he'd have known the whole story.'

Kam was a corporal in the Soviet army. 'Just for a week or so. You can be whatever you like out here – there are no laws, no one knows what is happening. If you seem sure of what you're about, people are grateful. There's no one from Moscow on the ground – they just ride around up there. Anyone who's been told of the situation, they're so scared that all they care about is when their shift ends. Those who haven't been told are so low-ranking that they mill about waiting for instructions from those who have. I just got into this jeep and drove it away, no questions asked. I think I shall drive it to Poland. Would you like to come?'

Ψ

Jaroslav Kam's confession implicating Karl Neder in Budapest had, before being burned by the stooges of chief commissioner Pusztai, been stamped and authenticated – but Kam never even saw it. It was signed by his father Arkády. That was the price of his release from an imminent sentence of death.

'I'd never realized it,' said Kam, 'but he had one of his servants in Budapest all along, keeping an eye on me. I was his heir, you see, and that mattered to my father, no matter what he thought of me. So when we were arrested, he heard straight away, and he was on a train at once. You could still get pretty much whatever you wanted in Rakosi's Hungary, if you had enough money.'

'And the bomb?'

'Who knows about the bomb? You would quickly lose count of the number of people determined to bomb our leaders in those days.'

'But you never told Neder's family what had happened?'

'I didn't know. My father told me the AVH had decided they had no evidence against us. He didn't want me stirring up more trouble. But I tried all summer to get in touch with Karl. I sent letter after letter to Győr, but never had anything in reply. Finally I got in touch with old Keleman at the university, and he called me a snake and hung up on me. I had to call him several times before I got the truth out of him. That was just before the revolution, and I told my father he wouldn't see me again. I left him among his mouldy stones and returned to Budapest.'

'But you never spoke to Karl again, either.'

'No. I lost him for some years in the States, and after that... Well – pride and vanity, those were the problems for both of us. And something else, I suppose. Something that can happen only as your childhood ends.'

'Yet you came here.'

'Constantin called me when Karl turned up in such disarray, and I suspected that this time he'd really... lost his way. I had a feeling I wouldn't get another chance. So I followed the trail, like you did.'

'Then was it you in Linz? And in Kiev?'

'I've really no idea. Was it me you saw? Was it you I followed? Who has been chasing who? These are the questions people ask in this part of the world.'

'We're all poisoned, Kam, aren't we?'

'Oh, inevitably, Lena. Inevitably.'

Ψ

This place is bright and hot. It is very dry, like a desert. Perhaps it is a desert. Nothing grows. Stones crunch underfoot, brittle like glass. How long has he been wandering here? A very long time, so it seems. Days? Weeks? An old woman found him once. Was that right? An old woman dressed in black, waiting out here to give him tea. Or had he, rather, found her? He isn't sure. There is something else he is looking for. A standing stone, an obelisk. But he isn't certain that this is the right place. A city, yes. Stars and atoms. A kind of fire. Something in the sky, a tiny, shining point of light, moving in a straight line forever. A new star. Or a new atom. He is bathed in fire. He can hear a rumble, a whistling, an ever-growing din. The noise is something like a jet plane, but it has a great range of musical tones and timbres. It is a roar across the plains, it is deafening. Yet he knows it is not around him; it is inside him. Something rising, coming up through him. Leaving him and rising skyward. This place is bright, and it is getting brighter.

ACKNOWLEDGEMENTS

Nothing I have written before has been as dependent on support and encouragement as this book was. My first and most constant supporter is my wife, who has relished watching me leave the comfort zone of non-fiction. My agent Clare Alexander far exceeded any professional obligation by agreeing to plough through the first draft, and thereafter offering invaluable advice. It was a delight and relief to find an editor as receptive, sensitive and perceptive as Philip Gwyn Jones. I have also benefited from the comments and suggestions of many friends and readers, but in particular from the immense generosity of Balazs Gyorffy and István Hargittai, who cast a critical eye over the Hungarian material. Any errors or distortions that remain are, of course, my own.

The image of Canterbury cathedral on page 197 was taken by Hideyuki Kamon, and is available at

http://www.flickr.com/photos/hyougushi/1246874838/.

The image of a Hungarian street on page 126 was taken by Magnus Franklin, and is available at

http://www.flickr.com/photos/adjourned/12348374/in/set-302391.

For news about current and forthcoming titles
from Portobello Books and for a sense of purpose
visit the website **www.portobellobooks.com**

encouraging voices,
supporting writers,
challenging readers

Portobello
BOOKS